SALAMANDERS OF THE SILK ROAD

Christopher Smith

LANTERNFISH PRESS
Philadelphia, PA

SALAMANDERS OF THE SILK ROAD

Lanternfish Press
22 N 3rd Street
Philadelphia, PA 19106

lanternfishpress.com

Cover design by Michael Norcross.

Printed in the United States of America.
Library of Congress Control Number: 2016943503
ISBN: 978-1-941360-08-8

In memory of my fathers,
Carl Smith and Brian Hewitt

Contents

SALAMANDERS
OF THE
SILK ROAD

SON OF ALL MEN,
C. 200 A.D.

THE DAY PRESTER JOHN WAS born, the house salamander died. His people considered this a blessing: an omen of a legendary future. It was only logical. The house salamander was the mortal form of the Great Salamander, from which all creation flowed and through which the created were sustained. The Great Salamander's Milk carved the beds of rivers and nursed the fields into bloom, washing down mountains and cascading over marshes, never curdling, never ending. Her Silk formed the canopy of the sky, woven into nights and days and twilights by the north wind, spanning the Kyrgyz Alatau and reaching the sun; and the sun could not burn it. Her eyes were reflected as starlight against that silken sky, and just as the sun was her heatingcoal, the moon was her nightingcoal, comforting her against darkness and emptycold.

So the death of a house salamander was not a crushing blow to a Salamandric family, akin to the destruction of a Buddha or the desecration of a Quran, but was instead the opposite. The protection of the family salamander was so deeply ingrained in Prester John's people that when a salamander actually died, it was understood that the death could be no accident of nature nor neglect, let alone malice. It could only be because the Great Salamander herself had called home one of her own, and any encounter with the Great Salamander was a blessing on all those it touched.

This was a good thing for Prester John's mother, Tana-ja, who had, nine months earlier, gone on a binge of fornication that involved every man and boy in the tribe, plus more than a few of the women. Tana-ja's longtime mate, Pharasa, had been killed in a battle with mercenary Cyclopes serving the Khitay. In a rush to fulfill their duties as the closest friends of the deceased husband of the most beautiful woman in the camp, all the soldiers in the war party volunteered (before the dead man's blood had even seeped into the mountainside) to take Tana-ja as mate. She was young, with shining black hair and breasts like fresh manti dumplings, and she was also the only woman with green eyes that any of them had ever seen. It wasn't a green you noticed most of the time, in casual glances or first impressions. Only when she truly looked at you would you see how green they were—green like new ivy sparkling with dew, or like the brilliant ribbons that swirled through the sky during the rebirth of a phoenix. The brilliance of this green rewarded any man she bedded—assuming they did so face-to-face, which wasn't as common as one might think. Tana rutted through a half-dozen suitors before deciding to try them all, and after that, well, habits form. (There were lasting rumors that Prester John had no father, that he was born of nature itself, or that perhaps the Great Salamander had taken male form and lain with the grieving widow. In a moment of boredom, Tana-ja had indeed engaged in some unsound behavior with a house salamander, but nothing that would have led to the salamander's demise.)

By the time she was too heavy with child to maintain her interest in the men, she no longer had any idea which one of them had planted the seed. And when she no longer had interest in the men, the men lost interest in protecting her from their jealous women. And that was the reason no one was there to midwife for

Tana-ja on the day of Prester John's birth. That might have made all the difference.

Prester John was born during the 39th Salamandric Effusion in Karatau, a region on the southern edge of the Kyrgyz Steppe long traversed by nomadic peoples, just northwest of the Talas River valley. In those days, the Silk Road was more of a Linen Trail, with frayed dead ends and burlap bridges; Prester later reckoned the year was around 200 A.D. At the time, of course, he wasn't Prester John, Prete Giam, or even Presbiter Ionis, though "Prester John" did derive in part from his birth name, which if put to paper would look most like "Gjona-ja." Prester did not recall ever putting it to paper, having taken the title Presbiter Ionis many years before learning his letters.

The Effusion—a time for the production of sacred milk, which would be poured on virgin ground to re-enact the creation—meant the men were back home with the harvest. The river was now too high and irritable for further reaping. Its currents were known to swallow slow fishermen, and more than a few waves had tripped up a fool who complained of barren waters. Now, it was time for the women to work, to take on the sorting, drying, jarring, and burying. "No use having a harvest if it lasts only as long as a brown-pitch coal." (It was a saying that long outlasted the actual availability or usage of brown-pitch coal, whatever that was.)

The women had spent the summer days in their applewood yurts, sometimes together, sometime alone, spinning salamander silk into cool thread and thread into long blankets of near-liquid fabric, and sealing the fabric with the flames of tiny fires. These women now emerged, pale and creaking, to work the lines of the harvest: massive heaps of fish and fennis, eyeball caviar and river apple. The piles stretched between the camp and the river, and from the river the women could look back at their lives, nestled in

3

a thicket of wood, with desert hills on all sides in the distance—though it was never wise to turn one's back to the river.

Tana-ja by rights should have been exempt from women's work, being enormous with child, but no one asked her to stop. None of the women asked her anything, in fact, or even spoke to her enough to coordinate her work with that of the others. But she didn't need their direction, and she could do without their sympathy, she told herself. She knew what to do.

The women were jarring fennis. They dried the fruit by soaking it in brine, then sliced it open and let it bake in the sun. Once it was crisp, they stored it in clay jars that they buried just below the frost line until they were needed. This served the dual purpose of preserving the fennis and keeping it safe from worms, sentient waters, and tribal raids.

Tana passed the group of women who were sealing the jars with cork and fat. They looked up with contempt as she waddled down the line to the hardest job that seemed to need doing: the slicing. Fennis hulls were tough. An unskilled hand could get a cut that would quickly be salted with slimy brine. Tana had, since her childhood, seen women run screaming to the river to wash the salt from their slit palms.

She steadied her back with one hand and reached down to the pile of slick fennis. Its orange-yellow rind glistened under the dripping-away of grainy water. Tana flipped her knife from her smock—too quickly for the comfort of the women standing nearest—and sliced open the fruit with one jab and two slits. She ripped its flesh wide and tossed it to the cut pile. The other women who had been slicing moved away, some to continue the shunning and some in quiet fear of Tana's knife. This left Tana holding up the progress for those behind her, who took the slower pace without complaint and now found room in their day for longer rests and whispered chats.

Normally, Tana and some of these women would have swapped shifts, but hours into the work, none stepped forward to relieve her. Tana didn't care, not at first. She found the slicing easy. But bending over to pick up some fennis, and standing because she was in no condition to kneel, grew increasingly difficult, particularly as dawn gave way to midday and midday to real heat (heat being a matter of perspective along the Kyrgyz Steppe, where even the most violent of rivers were more icy slush than water).

It wasn't working. Tana-ja's efforts at self-mortification went unnoticed, or worse they were a welcome sight. She'd have to go further. Maybe if she hurt herself, someone would take pity on her. Maybe they'd see what a hard worker she was and how much she was willing to sacrifice for them. Tana was too tired and her hands too sore to register the difference between blade and stiff rind, so when she cut herself, she did so more deeply than she meant to. Brine seeped into the wound, stinging. One of the women passing by—Purna, the wife of the very first suitor to put his seed into Tana-ja—stopped as well, surprised by the sudden stillness of a figure that had been in steady motion all day. Purna was a hard woman whose beauty had been used up in years of long nights tending children and salamander coals. Her body now resembled a tall heap of fennis. Tana opened her bloodied hand, hoping Purna would feel guilty for being so cruel. Maybe she'd even bring her a cool pail of water to wash off the brine.

Purna looked but refused to see. She turned away in disgust, grabbed some fennis, and went back to her work. Tana positioned her hand so the other women could see the wound, waving it slightly to draw their glances. If they noticed, they didn't care. Tana desperately wanted the relief of the river. She closed her hand into a fist, and the brine found new nerve endings to wash over. The pain ripped through her arm like a needle pulling coarse thread. If she rushed for the river, she might fall. And if she made it there and slipped, no one would help her up. She could drown; she could lose the baby. And if she sought relief, they would have won.

That night, after making her way to the hut and washing out the dirt- and brine-caked gash in a basin of stale, sleeping water, she avoided her salamander. He was a jet-black salamasire, almost as black as Tana's hair, and large for his breed, about three and a half feet. He seemed more of a still shadow than a god, draped among the glowing orange and cool gray coals of his brazier, which was suspended by light copper chain from the uuks that formed the beams of a yurt roof. The coals were hot enough, but he wanted feeding, and feeding him would mean opening her mind to him, and Tana was done with that now. After glancing in on the salamander's portion of the yurt—the area containing his brazier took up a quarter of the available space—after pretending not to meet his sullen eyes but feeling the edges of his chiding thoughts, she let the gray curtain fall between them as she half-eased, half-tumbled onto her bed of wolf's fur and silk sheets. Sleep came quickly.

Sometime in the night, Tana-ja dreamed. In the dream, an applewood uuk beam shook in a woman's upstretched fist, a wounded fist. As the yurt's roof shook, bits of dry, white felt fell into the woman's hair, the hair flowing down and covering her face as she wailed in labor. Then the dream wasn't a dream, and Tana's mind ripped open to the sound of her own screaming. It was time. It was time, and she was alone.

She looked up through the tunduk at the stars, and in the constellations she read a grin, whether malevolent or proud she couldn't say. The uuk trembled in her shaking hand and rattled closer to the edge of the kerege that held it up. It slipped a notch. Tana felt it, but she looked up too late to see that most of the roof was crashing down around her as the kerege gave way. She wailed louder. The falling roof had separated, and there was nothing now between Tana-ja and the open air to allow her neighbors to pretend they could not hear. Even those who stuffed their ears with dry rolls of grease could do nothing to stop the sickly red clubs of sound that pulsed out of the collapsed yurt, smacking against neighbors' barred doors and dripping to the ground with low moans. Men pretended not to hear out of fear of their own women, who grew angrier with each passing moment of silence, a silence broken only by the wails of a whore writhing under the debris of her home.

Tana-ja's salamasire, who had been the envy of the tribe when his owner was a fighter of fiercingthirst, had been quiet to this point. He had said enough, many months before, in his daily warnings to the woman to fill her grievingspace with talk or work, not with the cocks of otherwomen's men, for this would draw jealousyhate. The salamasire had offered her sympathywarm and healingthoughts, even, once, his own body, but they were cast aside like damp coal. Now this. He crawled from under the fallen copper chain and settled atop his pile of smoking coals, which lay scattered across the floor. He opened his mind to her needs.

Help me, she felt.

I will not. Not without willingkind from inside you, he responded.

Help me.

I should not. Only your pain is needingwant.

Help me.

I cannot. Not without giving you everything.

Help me.

The black salamasire considered for a moment his options, his purpose, his function. What was his function if not to serve his keepertend? What function was left to him in this coldriver of anger and shame? There was another choice, another function he could fulfill, and in fulfilling, save the woman. This was not what he wanted. This was not what she would want, were she properly the woman. But she was not now properly the woman, and this was his function.

The salamasire lowered his head into the remaining ashes of his toppled brazier and died.

Salamanders from miles away felt the death in cold wind that flushed ashes from their coals, and they jumped to their squat legs, darting their heads toward the collapsed yurt of Tana-ja. This could not be ignored. The neighbors ran from their homes to see what the whore had done now. What they found was Tana lying amid the uuk beams, dappled in bits of long-neglected dry felt, not wholly conscious, clutching against her the still-attached and unwashed baby Gjona-ja. He gripped in his right fist a large clot of black blood. No one knew what the black clot meant, for good or ill, for such a thing had never been seen before and would not be seen again. He sucked madly at his mother's breast, taking each gulp as if it might be his last. And truly, it might have been. But beside the mother and child, tangled in a chain now unattached to anything, was the still-orange hot brazier. And amid the coals was the salamasire, peacefully dead. Many in the mob dropped to the ground in shame, muttering pleas for forgiveness and mercy. Only one woman stepped forward. Purna, with no less anger in her expression than that with which she'd met Tana at the fennis heaps, took from her tunic a knife, short and designed for paring bone. She walked to the brazier, bowed, and rubbed each side of the blade against the dead salamasire. The blade sizzled in purification. She hadn't cared about Tana's wound, but before the death of a salamander she trembled. In the grand scheme of things, she told herself, borrowing a phrase from Kyrgyz figures of speech, even a whore like Tana could be sanctified by a salamander's blessing.

So she knelt to Tana and Gjona, turned the boy over, tied off his cord with a bit of thread from her pouch, and cut it. Other women took the cue. They stepped up to clear the debris and carry Tana on a litter to a place of safety. Tana was told of the events days later, when she woke from a delirium. In that delirium were visions sharper than actual memory, of things she could not possibly have witnessed. In these waking dreams, interrupted only by Gjona's suckling, Tana saw a man in a dark fur cloak whose face she didn't recognize. He had long brown hair and a full beard, and eyes so wide and so richly brown that they pulled her in and made her loins ache. The man walked out into the night alone, when the moon was in full coal, and approached the fallen brazier. No one had yet dared to touch it or the dead salamasire, which was still cooling and not yet ready to turn to ash. The man picked up the salamasire and turned it over. He pushed at its belly and worked away a pouch of skin, pulled it back, and dug into it with one thin finger. The man winced at the heat as he pulled out a tiny thing, a white thing, wriggling in agony at the surrounding cold. He popped the white thing into his mouth, under his tongue, and jogged back to his yurt. The heat of the infant salamander was already strong enough to sear his tongue, but he did not cry out.

FRIDAY AFTERNOON:
THE SENTIENCE OF
WAVES

T HE PROBLEM WITH WAVES IS they get into everything—fishing gear, bathing suits, the keel of the boat—leaving droplets of impatience flipping around in the bottoms of tackle boxes or clinging to your groin like unwanted compulsive thoughts. Then the sentience seems to spread from water to water, until next thing you know the stream flowing from your bathroom tap pulls away in disgust at the idea of being gargled. This was always the problem with St. Brianna Island. It protected the mouth of the Apalachicola River, which flooded the resulting bay with the fossilized nightmares of Virginia hillfolk, exiled Cherokees, and angry Atlanta commuters trying to ride the crest of the sprawling city's survival past 2016. In the confluence where these unsettled fresh waters crashed against the more laconic Gulf of Tenochtitlan, they created an estuary of neuroses hungry for interaction with other sentient forms.

For Prester and Mina John, it was the perfect vacation spot.

The traffic on their six-hour trip south had been worst in the last leg: along the bridge and causeway that led to the island. On the mainland, in Little Hope—a squalid Florida town with broken-down shrimpers popping up at odd angles from rotting piers—the bridge was of ancient cut stone, whitened and pocked by time, decorated with mythological beasts like manatees and pelicans: manatees, the stuff of children's fairy tales, great lumbering underwater cows that fed on grasses and nursed their young; pelicans, the daydreams of sailors, who imagined seeing them scoop fish from the water in mouths like bait buckets. Farther out, better sense prevailed, and the bridge was simpler, stronger, rising higher over the waves in an arc of rebar and poured concrete until it reached a steel apex tall enough for Little Hope's rusted shrimpers to twaddle underneath.

As the Johns' silver Nissan Pathfinder reached the apex of the bridge, the line of cars ahead came into view, stretching along a spindle of causeway where earth, rock, and sand had been piled upon themselves again and again to create a century-old road into St. Brianna. Prester noted this with admiration for the construction crews' persistence as he eased up behind the car in front of him, settling in for the long wait. He didn't mind waiting. On either side the waves playfully threatened to wash a car off the road. They would swell into a great bulge an SUV high (seeming to smile in a cruel, soft foam that spoke of Poseidon's revenge and Caligula's foresight, but Prester knew that was only legend, legend and a coincidence of shifting water) then lunge in a 500-pound splash of salty foam. Prester heard screams from some cars up ahead, drowned out by the peals of the waters' laughter. No one seemed to be hurt, but the salt did considerable damage to their paint jobs.

The line of cars created a perfect opportunity for the waves to carry out their function, which seemed to center on the annoyance of humans. Only rarely did they kill anyone, though with such great bursts of power they certainly could have washed the causeway clean of vehicles, perhaps the entire island. But they stopped short—somehow that wasn't part of their function. For Prester, that raised the question of purpose. Function is one thing, but can one have function without purpose? And if not, what is the purpose of the sentience of waves? The bullying of humans couldn't be an end in itself. Maybe it wasn't their true function but only an afterthought, as they worked under lightless skies across vast deserts of ocean to communicate with the stars, or to birth molecular chains of hydrogen-oxygen couplings, or to prepare themselves for some watery apocalypse so far into the future that humans would then be only a vague memory to scattered surges of the Mediterranean Sea.

Prester hadn't felt purpose in a long time. Well, in several months, anyway. Maybe not in a few hundred years, if he stopped to evaluate it properly. On his way to the Holy Land 875 years earlier with his army of Quaabites and sciapods, Prester John had felt purpose. Rebuilding his empire in Abyssinia, he'd felt purpose. At NSpaces, the extradimensional locations company where until recently he'd handled shipping and receiving of product, he'd felt purpose. Or maybe he only imagined it. But since his sudden dismissal from NSpaces, and with the growing gulf of silence between himself and Mina, "purpose" now seemed like a lost comfort blanket or a failed hobby. Or like the coals that we warm to stay warm, and they go cold and we go cold, and we scramble for yet more coals, and more coals, and more. So much easier to embrace the cold.

Prester took a sip of lukewarm coffee. Not yet.

"How're you feeling?" he asked.

"Fine," Mina said, her voice cracking from disuse. She cleared her throat.

"Looks like this will last a while."

"Yeah."

Checkpoint crabs, orange-red and about two feet wider than they were in height, scuttled in and out of movable wooden shacks at the head of the line of cars along the island's shore. The crabs had caused the traffic backup, though if you asked them they'd only glare and snap at you. Crabs ran the island now. There was a time, many years ago, when they had been kept in check by colonizing Floridians; but that led in part to the Redshell Revolts, and revolts have consequences.

Nearby, a Cyclops child not yet taller than the shacks sat idly rolling a dead porpoise in the sand. His eye (the size of a cantaloupe, Prester decided) shunted out from flaps of skin still pink with youth. Fuzzy tufts of hair popped from moles and unseemly shadows, where the Cyclops's father hadn't quite managed to dress him in a manner suitable for interaction with humans (who were inclined, to a Cyclops's dismay, to giggle when organs flopped loose and crashed into rooftops). The porpoise wasn't yet decayed—it must've been killed that morning, and Prester wondered if it might be intended as lunch for the checkpoint crew. Every fifteen minutes or so, a crab popped up in front of the Cyclops boy (who blinked dumbly as if every supervisor were some fantastic new creature reborn before his eye) and chattered a string of orders. The Cyclops would rise, walk to the roadside, and pick up a shack, spilling angry crabs out the door and onto the beach. Then he would move the shack away from the tide and closer to the constantly shifting head of the line. Forecrabs screamed orders of *left*, *right*, and *stop!* just before being crushed into the sand by a few Cyclops toes or a shack foundation.

The crabs appeared to be taking turns with contraband inspections, searching every car for explosives and imported milk, each crab taking one car, then retreating for the day, union regulations being what they were. They were busy—always busy—and couldn't abide having anyone try to skip past them or get out of their car to argue. But as the causeway widened from a thin line of bricked sand into a shouldered road, the occasional Hittite, seething in frustration, would jump out, slam his door, and walk forward only to be chased back by crabs swinging foot-long billy clubs.

Hittites were like this. Prester found them too quick to anger. He watched from a few cars back as a Hittite couple ahead of them tossed their heads and hands in argument with one another, their shouts muffled by the waves and idling cars.

"That poor thing," Mina said.

Prester looked more closely. The man was waving his arms around but certainly hadn't hit the woman, and she was turned in profile as she berated him with fury steaming from her face. Prester wasn't sure which one merited his compassion—he wasn't good at these things.

"Which one?" he asked.

"The salamander—just look at him," Mina said.

On the shelf of the rear window rested the Hittites' salamander. He was a salamasire, mottled orange and about two feet in length. Just as female salamanders had to be milked, males had to fulminate—belch fire from their furnace-hot bellies—and they had to do it several times a day. This one was smoldering in pain.

"That's just cruel," Mina said. "He must be miserable holding back like that. They ought to have him in a pyrorium."

Good training, Prester thought.

The man in the car pointed back to the salamander, and Prester saw that the salamander must be what they were arguing about. Prester and Mina hadn't argued that way in a long time. Almost a year, actually. It was easier this way.

"Someone ought to take that poor thing away from them, or at least from him anyway." Prester glanced over. Mina was beautiful. So beautiful. Almost more so when she was angry like this—her brow furrowed and eyes burning—though she was holding back, trying not to get herself upset. She kept her long, reddened hair pulled back in a ponytail, which was now adrift over her shoulder, leading Prester's eyes down toward her left breast. (Prester stopped his thoughts. Now wasn't the time, even if his shadow was elongating and lurching in the space behind him. He leaned forward to douse the shadow with a blast of sunlight.) Mina's hair had been brown when they met, but she'd taken to dyeing it with a tinge of red. Prester didn't mind; it reminded him of the concubines along the Tigris River those many years ago. But Mina wasn't from the Middle East. She was a descendant of the Great Presbyterian Mission Crusade to Madagascar, and you could see in her eyes the pearl blue of northern Europe mingled with the deep brown of the native peoples. The passion of those who strove to bring True Religion to the islanders, and the passion of the islanders who resisted it just as ardently. So beautiful, in function and form. And solid now. Prester couldn't see through her arm at all.

"You seem better," he said.

Mina held her arm up to the window. "Not even a glimmer of light showing through," she said.

In moments like this, Prester sometimes considered telling Mina how much she meant to him, how she was perhaps the most passionate, dynamic woman he'd ever known, how he had become closer to her than to any of his previous wives, how he truly and deeply loved her. As the air pulled into Prester's lungs to be transformed into these words, the Hittite ahead of them in line got out of his car and slammed the door.

The man edged along the narrow clearance between his car and the shoreline and opened the back door, while his wife shouted warnings barely audible in the distance. He put on a pair of oven mitts, reached to the rear window, and pulled the salamasire down from his perch (the salamander quivered and nodded in anticipation), then held him out, pointing him toward the open bay. The salamander took a deep breath of wet, salty air and fulminated a cloud of heat and flame that the harsh wind caught up and dispersed. Feeling much better, the salamander turned and purred at his master, but just then a rogue wave reached up, grabbed the salamander by one leg, and flung him several-score yards into the bay, where he performed a spastic five-skip plunge.

"Oh my God!" Mina shouted, and from the back of the Pathfinder they both felt a sickening wave of shocksadness from their own salamanders, safe in their pyrorium but sympathetically hurt.

"OhmyGod, ohmyGod, ohmyGod," Mina muttered, her hands over her mouth. "I can't believe that just happened."

"Hunh," Prester said, unsure how to respond to what seemed to him a perfectly natural turn of events. The man should have known better—waves don't abide salamander flame—but Prester John had long observed that knowing better has little impact on the actions of a Hittite. The man, shouting and crying but also shaking with fear, got back in his car, slammed the door, tore off his oven mitts, and pounded on the steering wheel. His wife reached out a consoling hand, which he shoved aside.

Prester decided that the moment had passed, but he resolved to have that conversation with Mina later, maybe as a good segue into their "decision," as they'd come to call it. That would be nice.

"Are you okay?" he asked Mina, who had begun breathing hard, trying to calm herself, trying to avert what he then realized could come next.

"I will be," she said and began her meditative breathing exercises, closing her eyes and her mind to the scene ahead. "I just need to not think about it."

He glanced over a few times to make sure she was right, and she was. He'd learned long ago to leave her alone when this happened. She'd be fine.

There had been many Hittites among the army that Prester organized for his crusade to the Holy Land almost nine centuries earlier. They were among the first to muster, having had long grievances with the Saracens on their western border. The Hittites were also among the first to abandon Prester when his crusade stopped at the Tigris River, when his supplies rotted away on the banks of a river that would not freeze: despite the promises of Jesus, despite Prester's long months of prayer, despite his supposed commission to save the Holy Land from the grip of the infidel. He didn't blame the Hittites. He muttered no silent curses under his breath at the mention of their name. Jesus, though. Jesus was another matter.

As soon as the causeway was wide enough to allow it, the Hittite got out of his car again and stormed to the crab shack, his wife pleading with him to stop. The Cyclops boy glanced over and put down his porpoise to watch. Prester glanced over at Mina, to make sure she still had her eyes closed in meditation. The crabs, of course, had little to do with the ebb and flow of the waves (that, by exception, was not their doing), but the man blamed them nonetheless for the traffic, for the long delay, for the narrowness of the causeway, and he shouted as much shortly before a red carpet of crabs poured out of the shack, each holding a black billy club in the short claw and snapping eagerly with the large one. They beat him there by the side of the road, in a cascading flurry of black wood and flailing limbs.

Prester slowly turned up the radio—"Don't Stop" by Fleetwood Mac—to drown out the screams.

Had the crab shells not been red to begin with, the sight of the Hittite's blood would have been more striking. The beating and its audience delayed traffic even longer, and lunging fingers of salt water buffeted even more cars. But now the drivers kept their doors shut and windows tight, regardless of the needs of their own salamanders. The crabs soon directed the Cyclops to lift the offending tourist, unconscious and tenderized, and carry him to his own trunk.

Mina looked up just as the trunk slammed shut.

"What just happened?" she said.

"I don't think you want to know."

Before the 9/11 attacks, access to the island had been easy. One simply drove over the causeway, stopped at the local Hell for groceries and enjoyed a week or more of quiet vacationing on the Gulf of Tenochtitlan. But now, a decade later, there were security checkpoints. Inspections. Their own little war on terror waged with billy clubs and traffic backups. Prester wasn't sure what the crabs were afraid of. St. Brianna Island had no buildings taller than three stories. There were a couple of private airplane runways, but nothing accessible to terrorists. Besides, anyone who really wanted to could simply buy extradimensional passage and they'd be able to plant an army in the center of downtown, decked out with AK-47s and grenade launchers.

That had been Prester's specialty. Not organizing armies (he'd certainly done that: during his crusade, during his time in Abyssinia, and even, to an extent, during the Redshell Revolts), but booking extradimensional passage. At NSpaces, his job was to ensure that extradimensional portals, usually fist-sized spheres that could expand to fill a doorway, were safely shipped to the correct locations and then returned upon lease expiration. The process would have been much easier if the portals could themselves be shipped by extradimensional portal, but the last time someone had tried that, the portal-inside-a-portal opened into a separate reality in which extradimensional portals did not exist. While the experiment was a failure, it did allow the emergence of the second Ambrose Bierce, who had come upon the portal while traveling. The incident gave the management of NSpaces the basis for new protocols banning the portal of portals, and it resulted in the collaborative twenty-four-part sequel *The Devil's Encyclopedia* by the Ambroses Bierce.

Prester had no collaborator, and he never wanted one. He barely had colleagues. They had a way of making things too complicated, with too many loose strings left behind. Leave no trace—that was Prester's motto. He kept things clean, orderly. While some of his coworkers invested in transient decor—paintings and posters that could appear and disappear with the doors and windows—Prester found this an obnoxious luxury and much preferred the calming effect of NSpaces' default "Supernatural Taupe" color scheme. His pressboard laminated desk was more machine than work space. He kept projects to be done on one side and projects completed on the other. Sometimes, when the project side ran low, he'd slow down and relax in the calm of it as he waited for more paperwork to arrive. In between these trays of ingress and egress was his milk mug, a gift from his boss that came with an inspirational slogan: "Vision. Creating a new path into the future." Prester had a habit of turning the words away. He preferred his own "Leave no trace" slogan. If a job is done well—if the product is ordered, arrives, works according to specifications, can be easily returned and paid for—then no one should have any memory of who helped accomplish the job, no record that the job was ever done. In fact, the sure sign of a job done poorly is that it requires that one extra phone call, that one extra question, that briefest of exasperated sighs that leads one to wonder who is responsible. It is in failure that we draw attention to ourselves, Prester had concluded. Success is in absence, never in presence.

Once, while cleaning his desk, which was his ten-minute ritual at the end of every workday, Prester came across a document he had neglected to file. It was for Species Control, one of his top clients, which had ordered a "Keeper's Trick"—a vertical portal the size of a soccer goal, used for transporting large objects or animals. Prester went to file the document but realized it was an NS-24, not an NS-42. Someone had transposed the digits, calling for a horizontal product the size of a trashcan. Prester laughed, imagining Species Control agents trying to stuff the bloodied carcass of a black rhino into a trashcan-sized portal. Knowing them, they'd likely carve it up and port it a piece at a time before calling to admit the problem. Prester refiled the order on an NS-42. It's much easier to laugh when there are no consequences. And avoiding consequences is easy: observation, patience, control.

"I'd like us to go the Crab Festival this year," Mina said, breaking the long silence. "It would be fun."

"I suppose," Prester said. "When is that?"

"Monday, I think."

"Oh. I thought we'd be done by Saturday night."

Mina was quiet for a moment.

"But we could put things off," Prester suggested. "Reschedule."

"Maybe," Mina said. "It would be good to go, one last time."

Prester and Mina had started coming to the island on their first anniversary, back when they enjoyed the beach and the warmth of sand rising through their bodies. They'd lie for an hour or more on the fine, white shore, listening to the gulls, to the ease of one another's breathing, to the waves' distant mutterings and chatter. Prester would watch tiny drops of sweat rise atop Mina's thighs, coalesce, and glide down, making one final dart against the curve under her leg before giving up in helpless pleasure and falling to the towel. A few years later, as the melt condition grew worse, they'd had to take precautions. He'd rub handfuls of crushed ice against her back, enjoying the cold trickle dripping between his fingers and down his arms into the sand. But lately, for the Johns, the beach had become more scenery than destination, and a trip to St. Brianna more habit than getaway. This time, it would finally be a getaway again.

They passed inspection—the crabs instinctively gave Prester a wide berth—and made their way along the familiar route to the beach house they had purchased many years earlier, a one-story, pastel-yellow clapboard on stilts with crushed oyster shell and pebbles for a driveway. Opening the beach house door was easy enough. The door was swollen with the sweet stick of slate mildew, a problem that seemed to grow worse each year, but it hadn't completely sealed.

"Do you need me?" Mina yelled from the carport.

Hauling in eight stairloads of luggage was simple, as was transferring their salamanders, one white and one gray, into the pyrorium in the hallway.

"No, I'm fine," Prester yelled back.

But then there was the gun, a Colt 1911 with wood grips. Casually opening the suitcase, removing the gun and the magazine, and stowing them away—that wasn't so easy. Prester didn't want to leave the gun out, but he didn't want to hide it either, like it was something to be ashamed of. He put the gun in the white wicker dresser that they never used except maybe to stash some spare towels, all ratty now with fuzz and holes. He shut the drawer. He turned from the dresser to Mina.

"You okay?" he said.

"Yeah," she answered. "Just tired, you know?"

"I know."

A SCAR FOR GJONA-JA,
C. 210 A.D.

T HE FIRST PERSON GJONA-JA KILLED deserved it. Most of the people Gjona would kill over the centuries no more deserved death than any given football team eighteen hundred years later deserved to lose a game. But that first one, he had it coming.

His name was Rayka, a boy who'd been a knot in Gjona's leather since they were toddlers. Rayka was aggressive, which was common enough, but unlike other boys he seemed to have no limits. Take ordo. It's a simple game of the Steppe where a crowd of boys divide into two groups. Then someone draws a big circle in the dirt, and one group tries to drive the other out by throwing the rounded knucklebones of a horse.

During one game, Rayka threw a sharpened rock.

The rock embedded itself in the eye of another boy, who fell to the ground astride the boundary line, and while some of the boys were arguing about whether the moaning victim was in or out of bounds, a boy named Khali-ro noticed the rock stuck in his eye.

"Hey," Khali-ro yelled at Rayka. "You threw a rock!"

"What?" Rayka shot back, storming into the circle to confront Khali. "Did not."

Gjona intercepted Rayka and stood between them. Khali was a friend—his only friend, actually. Many of the other boys had been warned to stay away from the bastard offspring of forty men and a whore, but either Khali's parents didn't mind or Khali didn't listen, and that was enough to earn him Gjona's protection.

"Look at it, then," Khali said, more to the crowd than to Rayka. "It's sticking out of his head. That's not a knuckle bone."

The rock was half-submerged in the boy's eye socket, with blood seeping out now around the edges as the boy writhed and moaned in the dirt.

"That happened when he fell," Rayka said to Khali. Then to Gjona, pushing past him, "Get out of my way, whoreson."

Gjona grabbed Rayka by the shoulder, spun him around, and, just as Rayka was facing him, connected his fist with the side of Rayka's head, knocking him unconscious with one blow.

Rayka fell to the ground amid shouts and peals of laughter. After that the game broke up. A few of the boys helped the rock-eyed one stand up and ushered him off to the shaman for healing. The rest left to go share the story—or lingered nearby, so they could be there to watch when Rayka woke up in a fury.

That wasn't the day Gjona killed Rayka, but it should have been. It might have prevented what happened later. And what happened later should never have happened to a salamander.

Killing Rayka would have brought Gjona no shame. In their tribe, when a man made a kill, his arm was cut and the wound rubbed with the blood-soaked dirt where his victim fell. This created a series of scars that spoke to manhood more than any beard or boast. Gjona himself was without a beard at the time—about thirteen years old, Prester later reckoned—and as tan as leather, like the other boys, with wiry brown hair that stuck out straight no matter how much his mother pushed it down. Also like most of the boys, he was solid muscle—there was no room in that life for anyone who could stay still long enough to grow fat.

His grey eyes were off-putting for some, but for others they were a reminder that he was the son of the green-eyed blessed whore, as his mother had come to be known. Tana-ja had done everything possible to redeem herself, except become a truly penitent and kind person. Her actions, at least, did no one any harm. But a good story has a way of hanging around, and there was something about a salamander blessing a whore that had staying power. She didn't mind—it kept the more annoying women of the tribe out of her yurt.

The day Gjona killed Rayka was a milking day. Gjona and the other boys were walking, cradling their salamanders in one arm to prove they were strong enough to do so, to the priest's yurt, where they were to be taught the arts of fire and supplication.

On the southern Steppe, when a boy reached maturity, he was entrusted with a salamander, and part of that trust involved learning to care for it. In the first month, they learned husbandry. Salamameres (females) laid the eggs, usually two to five at a time, then passed them along to the salamasires (males), who fertilized them and incubated them in a pouch until they sizzled enough to hatch. During this time, the salamasires would withhold fulmination, keeping their flames inside to bring the fertilized eggs to exactly 178 degrees. After hatching, the salamander young would crawl back to the mother's care, nestling in among the hot coals of her brazier and feeding on her milk. When there wasn't a molten lava stream at hand, for example in Gjona-ja's village, the salamameres would cough up a hairball of sorts for the young to live in while still suckling. It was this hairball, superheated in the gut of a salamander, that was cooled and threaded out to create salamander silk, a fabric so fine it made worm silk feel like burlap. This silk, incidentally fireproof, took on the vibrant color of the salamander that coughed it up.

In the second month, the boys learned about braziers. These were suspended by chains from the roof of the yurt, or sometimes, in non-nomadic cultures, stood upon heavy table stands. The brazier had to be kept filled with a good mix of soft ash and fresh coals. The salamanders, whose skin under ideal conditions was hot enough to cause third-degree burns, kindled the braziers on their own, but a coal heated in a cooking fire was always a purr-inducing addition. The salamanders had to be handled with thick felt gloves. The best pairs had an outer layer made of salamander silk, but horse leather would do. Twice a day, the salamasires had to be carried outside to fulminate, releasing a burst of flame that could extend a full yard.

In the third month, the boys learned to milk the salamameres. This had to be done once a week, except during the two-week season of Effusion, when it had to be done daily. Milking was a careful process that involved heating the salamamere's teats while still conforming to the subtle rituals of respect that salamanders required, in order to draw down good fortune upon the tribe. To disrespect, or worse, to harm a salamander was an unforgivable offense.

Gjona, Khali, and some of the other boys converged toward the priest's yurt, Gjona holding a white salamander in his battered horse-leather gloves and Khali a deep purple one in gloves of bright green silk.

"Who's that?" asked Khali.

Ahead of them, just at the edge of the woods, was a thin man wearing a black fur cloak and sandals too spare for the cold earth below them. He stood watching them, smiling.

"That's the Coaler," Gjona said. "You didn't meet him when you got your salamander?"

"No," Khali said. "I woke up one morning and my father had put her in the brazier." Khali's salamander was often irritable and didn't seem to like being used for training. She was prone to biting Khali's fingers, never hard enough to break the skin but enough to dissuade him from foolish overhandling. "Father never said where she came from."

"You didn't ask?"

Khali pretended not to hear the question.

"The Coaler is where they come from," Gjona said, absently pointing with his salamander toward the man. As the Coaler came toward them, Gjona ran out of time to explain what he'd figured—that the Coaler either raised the salamanders himself or stole them from someone who did, then brought them to the camp in exchange for something he needed. Everyone needed something.

"Blessings to you," the Coaler said, with a bow just slightly deeper than what was appropriate for a grown man addressing beardless boys. As Gjona rose, he found himself locked by the Coaler's dark brown eyes, which were hard to look into but impossible to look away from.

"How's your white?" the Coaler asked, reaching down to stroke the invisible psychic line between the salamander's eyes.

"Good. She's good," Gjona said, watching the skin on the Coaler's fingers begin to redden and sizzle.

"I'm still learning to milk her, and she hasn't yet had any young. Just like you said, I give her fresh coals every night, and I feed her locusts every morning."

The Coaler didn't appear to be listening, at least not to Gjona. He smiled at the salamander, who stared back almost mournfully, and in response Gjona felt an unexplained, resigned sadness wash up his arms and into his chest and heart. He felt an urge to huff into tears, but he tamped it down.

"All will be well," the Coaler said (whether to Gjona or the salamander wasn't clear).

"Thank you," Gjona said, unsure whether it was the right thing to say.

The Coaler pulled his hand away, the fingers black now and smoking.

"Well, we better go."

They turned and continued along the path to the priest's hut.

"Weird guy," Khali said.

"Yeah." Gjona was looking at his salamander, wondering what caused the waves of sadness rising from her body, her downcast head and limping tail.

Most of the boys were ahead of them now, which meant Gjona and Khali, as the last boys in, would be tapped to stay after and clean up the spilt milk.

There was only one boy who wasn't ahead of them.

Rayka, who had no salamander because he hadn't yet demonstrated that he was capable of caring for one, snuck up behind them. Before anyone could process what had happened, waves of spearpain ripped through Gjona's heart and into the hearts of those standing closest, making them shudder and moan like they'd been flayed, all of them hurting with the white salamander. Rayka had smacked Gjona's salamander on the head with a mud-caked hand.

Even Rayka, who might have expected the chain reaction, staggered to a post, holding his gut. But Gjona did not drop the salamander. He held her to him, struggling not to pass out. Khali was on his knees, vomiting in the dirt. His purple salamander had its glassy eyes fixed on the white. Babies were crying and doors were opening onto the path, and the boys, as they recovered, ran back to see what had happened. When the sympathetic pain subsided, Gjona brushed the dirt off the white and coaxed her with a shaken coo. Her head, pink now where it wasn't stained with mud, rested against Gjona's gloved arm.

Gjona-ja cared about the white salamander much more than he'd let on to the Coaler, much more than he'd let on to his mother or perhaps to himself. Gjona had looked to the white many times for guidance: on whether to pursue a girl, whether to tell his mother of a stolen trinket. The white often directed him to slow down, to wait, to do nothing, even if it meant he might then be shamed. More often than not, Gjona respectfully ignored her advice and rushed to do just what he wanted anyway. But she looked to him now, and he knew only one course of action, in her mind and in his own: revenge.

"What'd you do to your salamander?" Rayka shouted, staggering to his feet in front of Gjona. "Can't you protect her better than that?"

He knew he should take her home, back to the brazier where she'd be safe, but instead he entrusted the white and his crude gloves to Khali's younger brother, who had rushed toward the growing throng of children and youth to watch the fight they knew was coming. Khali's brother vowed on his father's knife to see the white home safe should anything go wrong.

Rayka waited, but only long enough for Gjona to turn around. When he did, Rayka returned the punch Gjona had delivered a moon or so earlier.

This one, though, didn't knock Gjona out. He rose from the dirt, watching the horizon and Rayka's body tilting in strange angles, and he thought, This is just.

Rayka's next blow was across Gjona's shoulder, and it wasn't with a fist. Rayka had a small blade in one hand, which sliced through Gjona's shirt about a pebble's depth into his arm. No one had mentioned the blade, if anyone saw it. But there was no law among their people against bringing a blade to a fistfight. That's only being smart.

This too, Gjona thought, is just.

Gjona surprised Rayka by using that same sliced arm to punch him hard under the jaw. Something was cut inside Rayka's mouth. He spat blood. With his other arm, Gjona swung at Rayka's head and missed, catching a jab to the gut from Rayka's knife. Luckily, the knife was small, but Gjona stepped back, clutching the wound to gauge how badly he was hurt.

Everyone in the camp had circled the boys. Tana-ja walked up, wiping her hands on a crude rag, showing only the faintest expression of fear, and Rayka's large brood of older brothers screamed at him, urging him on to make his first kill. Khali's father, Khurta-ra, stood with his arms across his chest and thumb on his chin as if deciding between two young horses for trade. All of them were watching now, after ignoring him for so long. Gjona-ja had their attention, and he liked it. And just as quickly, he was terrified that he would fail.

He edged closer to Rayka, swung hard, and missed. Rayka punched him twice, once with his blade leading the way.

"You like that, whoreson? You like getting poked too?" Rayka said it loud, and the crowd laughed, many of them even daring to glance at Tana-ja. Rayka bounced closer, careless and cocky.

"That was not . . ."

Rayka jabbed, teasing. The knife barely missed Gjona's throat. "Not what, whoreson?" he said, laughing harder.

Small twisters of dust spun up as they circled one another, Gjona with one bloody hand still clutching his stomach. Gjona wasn't sure if he had only heard the words or had said them out loud. And as they came out again, he was surprised that they came from his mouth.

"That was not just," he muttered, grabbing Rayka's knife arm as the boy lunged forward. Gjona pulled Rayka's arm straight, then slammed the weight of his body against it, breaking it backward at the elbow.

Rayka screamed like an old woman. At the center of the wide silence that Rayka's scream draped across the camp, something in Gjona's mind came alive. Once, while on a hunt, Gjona had seen a pack of dogs running across a hillside. One of them tripped over a rock and cried out in pain. The other dogs stopped, as if making a decision with one mind, then ripped into the injured animal. Whatever mission they'd been on in their run across the hillside had transformed into the single purpose of joyfully tearing their brother apart.

Gjona didn't understand it then, but he did now, tingling with pleasure as he punched Rayka's screaming mouth shut. That mouth could no longer speak, but Gjona felt it taunting "whoreson, whoreson, whoreson," and he smashed his fists against it harder each time until little was left of Rayka's lower jaw or of the knuckles on Gjona's fists.

The crowd of onlookers broke their silence with shouted cheers. There was little love for Rayka among the boys, and not much more for his brothers and family among the tribe.

Rayka's unbroken arm was still moving as he staggered. Gjona broke it to match the other, then threw Rayka on the ground. He caught a flash of Rayka's gurgling face. He straddled the body, took the bloody head in his hands and twisted it hard to one side, snapping Rayka's neck.

Gjona stood over the body, his heart beating strong, in time with the heart of the white salamander, taking in and taking out in satisfactionyes and thankingnod. Yes, the salamander feltingsent, yes: Now he was a man.

The sun had risen over the tops of the yurts and cast Gjona's shadow wide and long over Rayka's body. The shadow was starkly defined at the edges, darker and far larger than the other shadows across the clearing. It seemed to pulse and grow, as though feeding on the steaming blood of Gjona's victim.

Cheering onlookers soon turned their attention to Rayka's family. The people had long sought a reason to exile or kill the family, and raising a child who would abuse a salamander was reason enough. Gjona watched from where he stood as Rayka's grandparents, parents, brothers, and sisters were dragged toward the shadow around his body and clubbed to death.

Khali-ro's father Khurta-ra, who more than any other of the men had been a tolerant (if sometimes reluctant) mentor to Gjona, now stepped toward him with the ritual knife. Growing up without a father had been hard on Gjona, and few of the men—any of whom might actually have been his father—had done anything to make his growing up easier. Gjona's only real avenue to Khurta was that the man had to tolerate Gjona as his son's best friend. Perhaps that gave Khurta some excuse for offering compassion. In any case, he'd never done anything to prevent Gjona romping around with Khali, and he didn't completely ignore Gjona when showing Khali how to satiate hostile creeks. In this moment, some man had to make the ritual cut, and Khurta was the only man who now had any right to do so. He took Gjona's left hand in one strong, thick-fingered fist. It felt strange, like an iron clasp, and Gjona was at once scared and overwhelmed by the joy of acceptance as Khurta sliced a red line across the outside of Gjona's forearm. Gjona looked up in admiration. Khurta-ra then reached into the blood-drenched dust near Rayka's body and briskly rubbed the mud of it into the cut. Gjona, too excited to feel the pain, held up his arm for all to see. He didn't allow himself to think that it might not work. The punctures to his gut and the cuts from Rayka's blade would heal—he could already feel the process beginning—but this cut would scar. It would have to scar. And maybe, if it did, Khurta's pride would last, and though Gjona had long said that he didn't need a father, he didn't object to the idea that Khurta might come close.

A girl came forward, a girl who'd been following Gjona for several weeks and whose name he'd forgotten if he ever knew it. That night, Gjona was allowed to take her into the now-vacant yurt of Rayka's family. When he woke the next morning, he thought it must have been a glorious dream: manhood gained and rewarded, from Khurta-ra, from the clan. He looked at his arm in pride, knowing it would scar, in complete faith that it would scar. But the mark was gone. The line had healed, exactly as so many other of his wounds had healed. This time, he had thought, this time it was ritual, it was a mark. Surely it would remain with him.

It did not.

If the girl woke to hear Gjona crying, she never said a word.

FRIDAY EVENING:
SUNSET

T HE RAINBOW SKY FADED TO a river of blue, purple, and indigo, showing off a decaying moon roiling in on itself in bitterness over the waning of its cycle. The waves leaped toward it, spiking into towers twenty and fifty feet high that glistened like steely obelisks. The Johns sat together on Adirondack chairs on the front balcony of the beach house, serious, silent. In that silence, both felt the longing to talk. And both felt the fear.

"So have you thought any more about the festival?" Prester asked.

"Not really," she said.

Talk wasn't about to make things easier. Talk wouldn't change the past or what was left of the future.

Neither of them wanted to revisit the long talks they'd had over the last year—not so much talks as yells, mostly from Mina, with Prester sitting in his chair staring out the window into the horizon while she unleashed everything she needed to unleash, while he patiently, methodically, repeatedly, apologetically explained everything she needed to understand. For most of these talks every light in the house would be on, with Prester's shadow barely visible at the edges of his body, and with blood seeping from fresh staples on the pads of Prester's feet.

Prester should have known something was wrong. He'd had uneasy dreams all weekend, and on the Monday after the incident the shadow had dragged behind him, pulling at his heels and wrapping around door jambs as if it dreaded going to work. Otherwise it was a standard-issue morning: Prester dressed for work, finished a quick breakfast, and yanked his shadow into the hallway closet with him. He turned to face the door he'd just closed, partly twining himself in a staticky old wool coat, and took three steps backward through an extradimensional passage into the 23rd-floor NSpaces lobby. There was the usual flash of bright pink as he slipped through negative matter, but Prester hardly noticed these things anymore.

"Good morning, Mr. John."

"Good morning, Rosha." Rosha was part sciapod. Prester could tell by the size of his feet, the length of his stride, and his knock-kneed walk—those legs had not been separate for many generations—and the frizzy orange locks that passed for hair. Rosha's teeth weren't sharp, but Prester had discovered centuries ago that this was a private cultural custom and not a species trait. Prester often wondered if Rosha knew what he was, how his people had stomped across the land, flattening Mongols, Hittites, and Bi-Garunds alike. Few now remembered the sciapods, though their genetic influence still dappled America.

"Milk, sir?"

"Please."

"Frothed?" Rosha asked, smiling.

"Too early for that," Prester said.

Rosha hopped in three bounds from his desk to the lacto-matic, then walked with both legs, more carefully, following Prester into his office with the day's 3Q reports and a double-skim hot.

"Evansville needs another two score of movable holes, and a Dr. Humbert called on a personal matter."

Rosha ticked from foot to foot like a metronome as he waited for a response. Prester guessed he was dying with curiosity about Dr. Humbert and his business but knew better than to ask.

"Thanks, Rosha."

Rosha ticked a few more beats before hopping out. The door and windows coalesced into solidity behind him.

Prester made calls, read reports, and moved three or four projects off his "to be done" stack. And then Evansville. They needed at least fifty more movable holes after being shorted in the last shipment. He had an email and two phone calls out to corporate trying to muster even a dozen, but all were in use, and production was down because of a shortage at Negative Product.

The lines of Prester's door darkened. That was odd: no one had called, and he had no appointments. They slid out from a central point to form a rectangle about six and a half feet tall. Then it opened without Prester's authorization. Out of it stepped Henry Beck, VP for NSpaces Southeast, and a rep from Human Resources. She was pretty. Sleek black hair curling at the neck, neat but with a few strands carefully loosened.

"Henry!" Prester smiled. Something was clearly wrong, but he saw no need to make his guests feel awkward about it.

"Hi, Prester." Henry shook Prester's hand, decidedly not smiling. "We need to talk."

"Sure, sure. Have a seat."

"This is Griffiths. She's from Human Resources."

"Yes, I think I've seen you around. Prester John." He took Griffiths's hand and stopped himself from bowing to kiss the back of it, stopped by an ongoing reminder of a new time that had buried those long-expected courtesies. She was staring at him with a look he couldn't read. Fascination? No.

"Prester, we've gotten a complaint this morning. Have you heard about it?"

"Only from Evansville. About the shortage of holes. I don't suppose production is coming back online anytime soon?"

"No. No, Prester, this wasn't that type of complaint. It was a complaint that concerns you."

Prester leaned back in his chair. He hadn't often been surprised by bad news. He had, at times, been surprised by betrayals—by Jesus, by Lonk—but Prester in the last few hundred years had learned to stay ahead of bad news, calculating his reactions and anticipating results. Now, he was trapped by an unanticipated outcome.

"Apparently there was an incident last week."

Prester's mind flashed a high-speed replay of the prior week. Every phone call, every interaction with every customer. They had all seemed happy or at least content. He'd missed something, and it was coming at him faster than he could forecast its trajectory. It pinned him to his seat, like a movie where you know something bad is about to happen but you've lost track of what should be a perfectly predictable plot. Prester watched Henry Beck's mouth, trying to catch the sounds before they plumed out in vibrations that could either mean nothing or change his life forever, and forever meant more to Prester John than to most.

"The incident involved Sharyn Henderson, from marketing." Henry Beck paused, waiting for Prester's response, but Prester only stared, riveted to Henry's mouth as it sounded out new, unfamiliar words. "She's filed a complaint that you made inappropriate advances."

As Prester expected, he was completely blindsided. "Hnh," he said flatly, realizing as he said it that this wasn't the reaction Beck expected.

He remembered what must have been the incident now—he was in the 22nd floor kitchenette preparing an espresso with two lumps of curdled cream when Sharyn walked in. She was only a couple of years out of college and had moved quickly into key accounts. Collaboration was her strong point—bringing out the best in coworkers with a solid mix of high expectations and personal charm. She said hello, and he looked up and smiled. She walked toward him, but then not toward him after all and instead to the coffee machine.

She was wearing a miniskirt (did they still call them that now? Prester couldn't keep up) and a black silk blouse—not salamander silk but a tasteful knockoff that only someone with 1,800 years of familiarity would notice. The first few buttons of the blouse were undone, all the way down to the bottom of her sternum. He couldn't help noticing this, but only from the periphery as he forced respectful eye contact and asked what she was working on.

"It's this B2B pitch to fast-food conglomerates," Sharyn said, opening the coffee tin and scooping a portion into the filter cup.

"What's that about?" Prester asked.

"We're pushing out kiosk locations where walkup consumers in metro cities could open a hole, maybe NS-11 or NS-12, direct to the cashier at a brick-and-mortar site and place an order, pay, and receive product, all through the hole. The hole would stay closed and secure until the next customer arrived. Solves the problem of squawky call boxes and exhaust fumes, promotes walkable communities, and boosts sales penetration area."

"Nice," Prester said, genuinely impressed. "That's a perfect application of the tech. Did you come up with that?" He caught himself glancing at Sharyn's chest when he looked down, stirring his coffee, and a thought slipped into his mind of how the light brown shade of his coffee was almost the color of the soft skin of Sharyn's upper chest, but it was an accidental thought that he quickly dismissed.

Sharyn smiled and started the machine.

"No—I sure wish I had," she said. "That was Kathy in accounting, so she gets one of those NIdea bonuses. But it gives me something new to push, so I'm not complaining."

"Exactly," Prester said, and they both smiled. Then Sharyn jolted, and a stricken look came over her face. She put a hand in front of her cleavage and backed up three paces, staring in horror at Prester.

"You okay?" he asked.

She turned and walked quickly out of the room. That had been the end of it, and Prester had given it only a moment of thought as he rinsed the stirring spoon, turned off the now-whistling espresso machine that Sharyn had abandoned, and went back upstairs.

"Prester?"

"Sorry, Henry. I . . ." Griffiths from Human Resources was looking at him with that look. Anger? Hatred?

"Do you remember the incident?" Henry said.

"No, I mean, I remember we were talking and she left the room suddenly, but I never found out why."

"We reviewed the video, and I want to show it to you."

Griffiths dropped a tablet on Prester's desk like a gauntlet and lightly, with absolute control, touched Play. It was high-resolution black-and-white surveillance-camera video from the kitchenette. No audio. Prester and Sharyn talked. She put coffee in the filter, she turned the machine on, and as Prester stirred his coffee, the sun seemed to go down in the window behind him. His shadow lengthened along the floor, crossing the four feet of space between them, and as Prester smiled and chatted and stirred his coffee, the shadow moved up Sharyn's legs, up her miniskirt, and was for a moment lost in the blackness of her blouse. Then the shadow could be seen again, emerging at the edge of her blouse and shifting the weight of one breast in a firm caress. Sharyn stepped back and left the room as Prester continued stirring his coffee.

"Can you explain how you did that?" Henry asked.

"I didn't do anything," Prester said, knowing as he said it that it was only partially true. It wasn't wholly him. It wasn't wholly not him, either. "I'm clearly stirring my coffee."

Henry picked up the tablet and handed it to Griffiths. "We wondered about that, too, and Human Resources did some research. Ms. Griffiths, can you read Prester some of what you found?"

Griffiths called up a document on the tablet and began reading in a harsh monotone. "Since 1763, there have been seven medically documented cases of umbraic distinction, in which the umbra forcefully removes itself from the object body, typically from the underpedal epidermis. In all seven cases, the object body was that of a patient with hypergeriatric syndrome advanced in age beyond 350 years. In six of the seven documented cases, the umbra, acting of its own will, fully separated and then inflicted some degree of harm upon society or the object body, with one exception in which the umbra was assigned janitorial services for the patient's funeral home until being dismissed for ineffectiveness."

"Thank you, Griffiths," Henry said. "As you know, NSpaces has a policy of equal-opportunity employment that covers hypergeriatrics. There's Jensen in capital holdings, for instance."

Prester thought about those "hypergeriatrics"—old-men, and old-women. He knew some of them, but he himself preferred living under the radar. There was too much to explain, too much baggage. Besides, all they ever wanted to talk about was the past.

"And of course, Prester, if this is some sort of disease that's outside your control, that's something we can work on, and obviously we have policies about preexisting medical conditions. NSpaces gladly offers its employees a full array of flex-time and telecommuting opportunities."

Prester wondered if one of the seven cases Griffiths had read about might be Thomas Bond, who in the late 1800s had served as a surgeon for the London Police. Bond was about 525 at the time, and Prester had known him a century earlier in Europe. And he knew about Bond's shadow and the trouble it caused. When Prester read in the American newspapers about an elusive murderer called Jack the Ripper, and about Bond's careful psychological profile of the killer, he felt certain that the profile was in part autobiographical, a deep self-analysis of the basest nature of his kind old friend. Bond eventually got his man, though the account of the death of Jack the Ripper never made it into the American or British papers. In 1901, Bond had drained a bottle of laudanum and thrown himself from a sixth-floor bedroom window. Prester felt certain that the shadow had landed first.

"But the thing is, NSpaces also has a policy against lying on your employment application. Prester, your personnel file says you're fifty-three years old. That isn't true, is it?"

Prester couldn't shake the look from Griffiths. That look. It wasn't curiosity. It wasn't affected boredom. It was a look he finally understood: It was contempt.

"Well, this is all very sudden, and I suppose, yes, I am older than I stated, but . . ."

Contempt. Only contempt.

"Prester, we're thinking you should take some time out of the office, you know, so we can clear all this up."

They were firing him, and Prester knew it. Not at once, of course. First, they'd have to get him out of the office—on administrative leave or short-term disability or whatever they could come up with. Then they'd suggest he might be more comfortable in another environment, or maybe spending more time at home. And if they had to, they'd offer a severance check. There was no use fighting it. The decision was made, and the only way Prester could avoid making it worse was to keep anyone else from being inconvenienced. Especially Sharyn Henderson. God!

Poor girl. Prester thought maybe he should write her a note. No—letters never seemed to solve anything.

"Of course, Henry," Prester said. "I'll forward my accounts to you and get back in touch once it's all cleared up." Prester knew this wouldn't be necessary, but switching the conversation to logistics seemed like it would make things less awkward.

"Yes, yes. That'll be for the best, you know?"

"Okay." Prester smiled. Poor Henry. Prester imagined what it must have been like when management sat him down and explained the situation, and that Henry would have to be the one to get rid of him. Prester had no illusions that Henry was distraught over this or that their friendship was anything more than a business association. He couldn't tell whether Henry blamed him for his shadow's actions or not, but it was clear that Henry wanted to be anywhere other than in that room having that conversation.

"OK. Well, we should get back," Henry said. He got up and opened his mouth to say something, but closed it and nodded for no apparent reason.

"Thank you, Henry," Prester said, filling the silence for him.

Griffiths turned away at once and preceded Mr. Beck through the wall.

Prester would not see them again, though Henry did sign a letter written by some secretary under the secretary under Griffiths, to the effect that Prester's letter of resignation was accepted. Prester wondered who had written that letter of resignation, but ultimately he decided it didn't matter. He was thoroughly resigned, regardless of authorial authenticity.

In the following weeks, he began having more dreams like the one about Sharyn Henderson. Only they were about fluorescent strip clubs and the alleyways behind them, and harshly lit motel rooms and somehow becoming repulsively, impossibly close to the couples inside. Prester would wake the next morning and remember these dreams and notice his languid shadow collapsed under the sunrise, and feel an unexplained burn across his feet.

Knowing what he knew about Thomas Bond, Prester began staple-gunning the shadow to the pads of his feet. Any time the shadow tried to pull away, he'd add a staple, so that spots of blood dappled the sheets and the carpet where he walked.

The first time he did it, he felt the shadow's voice.

"You disgust me," Prester said.

Then you disgust yourself.

"Maybe I do."

Not my problem.

"Yes," Prester said. "It is."

Why do you say that? You think you can control me? You think I can't break free whenever I want and do whatever I want? You think these staples can hold me back?

"They're not meant to hold you back. They're meant to let me know. And it if happens, I will know, and I will stop you."

You're wrong.

"We'll see."

The shadow stayed attached, but all else drifted away: his career, his income, and, he was becoming convinced, the love of his wife.

"So this thing, this shadow that groped that woman, you're saying it's not part of you?" Mina had shouted. He'd just come home from work for the last time, carrying a cardboard box of framed service awards, milk cups, and a surprising number of just-in-case moist towelettes. The box was at his feet, which were bleeding from the first stapling, which was the first thing he'd done before telling his wife. She was pacing the room now, waving her hands as if she held one of the cigarettes she'd quit smoking a decade earlier.

"It's part of me, yes, but the worst part."

"So without it you must be some kind of angel, then, right?"

"No, it's not like that," Prester said, staring out the window at the gathering night. They were two hours into the conversation. He was trying to help her understand.

"So it's part of you! So you wanted to grab that woman's breast? Who else have you wanted? Who else is going to get the benefits of your dirty little ventriloquist act?"

"Okay, first, yes, I had a fleeting thought about Sharyn, but it was fleeting. Surely you've had fleeting thoughts—glanced at attractive men."

"Don't turn this on me! I wasn't the one who made a pass at a coworker."

"You know what I'm trying to say. I didn't want to be with her, I just had a thought about her, or my shadow did and there was some sort of feedback—I don't know."

"You're avoiding my question, Prester. I want to know when this is going to happen again. I want to know whether I can be in the same room with you and that . . . thing. Is it going to touch me? Does it have a name?"

He wanted to say that he wasn't avoiding her fucking questions, he was trying to answer them, in the fucking sequential order in which they were fucking posed, but instead he took a mental breath and tried to shelve questions 57, 59, and 60 so he could first address 61, then circle back to question 59, which bore a striking resemblance to the previously addressed question 14.

"It won't hurt you, Mina, it can't," he lied. "In most respects it's gone," he lied. "I didn't know before that the shadow was becoming distinct. Now that I know, I can pull it back in. I worked on it today as soon as I had a chance, and it's almost a normal shadow now. I can control it and keep this from happening again."

"Bullshit," she said, crossing her arms and holding them in tight. "I'm not an idiot, Prester, I know how to do research and I've read the files. This isn't something you can control!"

"Don't tell me what I can control," he said, raising his voice for the first time, slightly. Mina's pacing stopped. "The research said, what, onset at 350 years? I'm five times that old, and this is the only emergence."

Mina began pacing again, slowly this time.

"So it's not sentient?"

"No more than I am," he said. She looked at him and he smiled. "No, honey, it's not." He lied, but it was working. "I can control this."

"So why the staples?"

"Just a precaution, for now."

"You and your precautions," she said, finally smiling. "Does it hurt?"

Prester suppressed a laugh. Does it hurt. Of course it hurts, it hurts like hell. Does it matter? Hadn't he endured physical pain far worse thousands of times? "No," he said. "Not once you get used to it." The latter had more truth than perhaps anything he'd said that night.

He didn't like to lie to her. But she could never truly know what it was like. He could control it, his shadow, at least to an extent. The shadow was just another part of him that he couldn't share.

She knew parts of his story. Of what he'd endured to get to where he was. She knew of his failure at the Tigris, of the ruin of his Asian empire, of his rise to power in Abyssinia and the slow decline of that kingdom, of his role in the Redshell Revolts. But there were things he'd done, that he'd had to do, sometimes wanted to do, that she wouldn't understand. And that was no longer him, and that, too, she wouldn't understand.

And now he'd have to start over, rebuild it all, like he had done generation after generation.

Or not.

The sunset crashed to a close on the horizon of the sea at St. Brianna Island, giving way to the steady howl of stars, seeking lovers, like fireflies. Constellations rose and fell in a nightly dance.

The sound of it sickened Mina.

She shifted in her chair. She didn't like Adirondacks—not these, anyway. When Prester had ordered them, he'd promised to either get cushions or pay the extra money for pushwood, which had a negative magnetic charge to keep the body's weight off the hard slats of the chair. He did neither and never apologized. He probably didn't even realize what he hadn't done, Mina told herself, but that only made her more angry. He never seemed to want her advice. She sighed.

"What?" Prester said.

"Nothing."

"I'm tired," Prester said. "Long drive. Are you ready for bed?"

She was. She stood and drifted in, pausing at the pyrorium in the hallway to check the salamanders, which were still restless as they waited for their new coals to glow orange. One was mottled gray, the other was white, and the white looked at her with sad eyes—kind eyes that betrayed understanding without audible communication. Mina touched the pyrorium and gently ran her hand down the warm glass.

Prester followed Mina inside and shut the door twice before the lock clicked. He'd have to clear that mildew.

THE SQUEALING BOAR
C. 210 A.D.

THE SECOND PERSON GJONA-JA KILLED wasn't so much a person as a blur: a face, then a flash of blood. A man? A boy? He never noticed. That wasn't what he was looking for. He was looking for something else, something in the eyes of Khurta-ra.

Just days after the killing of Rayka, Khurta approached the boys, who were teasing a hillside stream by throwing rocks into its path. The stream would stop, confused, then roll up an embankment to avoid the stone, and the boys would drop another. Mist might rise off the water as the stream grew agitated, creating little whirlpools of anxiety. It would try another path, then another, as the laughing boys dropped more stones and pebbles. The stream was just barely aware. A larger creek might already have spiked out needles of water to drive them away, but this one merely trickled in hapless circles.

"Gjona-ja!" Khurta bellowed.

It was the first time the man had used the boy's name, the first time he'd spoken directly to him. Gjona dropped his stone in the wrong spot, letting the stream meander away, and stepped toward Khurta. In his thick fur coat, boots, and silver-white kalpak, Khurta looked like a great bear.

"Yes, master?" Gjona was the odd boy out in using "master" for the men of the tribe instead of the usual "father," an honorific that could also imply parentage. Gjona had learned at an early age that it was a word he could never use.

"Tomorrow Khali and I go to hunt boar," said Khurta. "You will join us."

"Yes, master!"

"Bring your club and your meal."

As Khurta walked away, the boys stood in attentive silence, for fear he might turn again and change his mind. When he was out of earshot they jumped in victory.

"Your club," said Khali. "Do you have a club? A real one, I mean."

Gjona did a mental inventory of his mother's yurt, but all he could recall seeing were small, light toys he'd played with as a child. On the Steppe, a man would pass down his club to his son. They were clubs of long-cured wood, solid with bands of metal or spikes driven into them to add weight. Gjona had no such weapon.

They spent the remaining daylight scouring the hillsides around the camp for a suitable branch, something fallen but not yet weak with rot. Gjona found one, a walnut branch that in places was as thick as his leg, then rushed home to get a hand axe and back again to chop it down to a reasonable size. This he carried home, and all night, long past Tana's retirement to sleep, Gjona carved the branch, carefully rounding the ends despite the sap pouring over his knife and his fingers. There was more sap than he expected, and it was making a mess. The sap bubbled and steamed as he blackened the ends of his club in the smoke of the fire. The salamander watched, amused, but did not offer advice. The next morning, Khali woke Gjona with a kick. He had fallen asleep at the fire, the club still in his left fist. Khali laughed as Gjona tried to let go. The tacky sap pulled at the skin of his palm. It was stuck fast.

There was no time to heat water to liquefy the sap, even if he could. Gjona dressed for the hunt one-handed. They ran for the horse corral, Khali loaded down with a satchel of food, a water skin, his club, and another satchel that held cord, ropes, and flints. Gjona carried his club in one hand and nothing at all in the other. In the darkness before dawn, Khali didn't notice until they were almost at the horses.

"Where's your food?"

Gjona had forgotten everything but the club.

"I'll be fine."

"We'll be gone all day. What are you going to eat?"

"Boar," Gjona said with a smile.

The boar of the Karatau had short black fur like that of a wolf, and a tight mane running down their spines from thick skull to flashing tail. They were about the size of a wolf, too, but much broader in the chest than in the hind, and that broadness was solid muscle. Most fearsome of all, and what made the boar most remarkable as a creature of legend, were the tusks, jutting out from either side of its upper lip and curving backward. While the boar was, indeed, a grazing and rooting animal, it carried territoriality into a whole other realm of hatred. And the boar had a ruthless method of attack. It would charge forward, butt its victim with its head, then tear into the unfortunate interloper with its tusks, shaking violently. The tusks would rip away the victim's flesh within moments. Little could be done to stop a boar once this aggression took hold, and hunting parties often ran to save their own skins instead of stopping to defend an unlucky comrade left behind.

The men in the hunt stuck together; they'd send the fastest of the boys out to find and rustle up a boar. The boar was fast in a sprint but couldn't handle distance, especially after being woken in the middle of the morning. So while the boar was distracted trying sleepily to run the boy off, the men would surround it, then fill its hide with arrows. To keep the boys from getting lost as they wandered, each one was given a spool of silk cord that could stretch for what Prester now reckoned to be about two miles.

That day, while the rest of the group was still finishing breakfast, Khali and Gjona wandered off together. They dared one another over sharp, craggy paths instead of going around them, stopping at wide walnut trees to disappear and startle each other. Then Gjona spotted a boar.

It was the size of a pony, sleeping in a rooted-up mess of leaves and moss. He tapped Khali on the shoulder and pointed it out, unsure how to proceed, since they were supposed to be back at camp resting. A smile widened on Khali's face. He motioned for Gjona to follow him back to the camp. There they found another boy, Ular, who was easy to trick. Gjona distracted Ular with talk of his new club, showing off the freshly seared ends. Khali, meanwhile, made sure that Ular still had his hunting cord tied around his waist, then fished the other end out of the boy's pack and disappeared into the woods with it.

"You did that just last night?" Ular was asking Gjona-ja.

"Yeah, I didn't have much time."

"I bet that sap made a mess."

"It wasn't bad." Gjona shrugged.

While they talked, the cord slid slowly away. Once it had been still long enough, Gjona stood up.

"Hey, do you want to see the snipe nest we found?"

"Sure," Ular said.

Gjona led him toward the boar, still chatting about the merits of his club and how he planned to wrap it with iron bands.

When they were about ten paces from the boar's den, Khali shouted, "Boar! Boar!"

The boar woke with a grunt.

Khali was running toward them, waving his arms frantically. The boys did an about-face, running as fast as they could to outpace the boar's initial charge. They should have been able to get away, but every few paces a fresh burst of enraged squeals stood their hair on end. They ran again, and again.

At first Gjona and Khali ran ahead of Ular, laughing and sneaking glances over their shoulders at the terror on his face, but Gjona's laughter turned to fear when he realized the boar wasn't giving up.

"Why is it so fast?" Gjona yelled.

"It must be getting mad!" Khali shouted back. "The cord—it's caught on the tusks. We have to cut it!"

The charging boar was closing in on Ular fast, tethered to him by the cord that was tangled on its tusks.

"You did that!" Gjona-ja yelled. "You cut it!"

They were making too much noise. The men would hear. But they wouldn't reach them in time to save Ular. What would Khurta say if the boy was mauled?

Khali had no weapon. Gjona had his club, but that was only because it was stuck in his left hand: the wrong hand, as it turned out.

This was badly planned, he thought.

Ular cried out for help.

Gjona veered off, ducking behind the thick trunk of a tree. He let Khali and Ular run past him, then waited for the boar's approach. His breath came in shallow pants like the snorts of the galloping boar. When the animal was almost upon him, Gjona swung out low with his club. The wood connected, smashing into its front legs.

The boar slammed maw-first into the earth. It squealed in rage and pain as it tried to scramble up and attack, to clutch and rip and tear and shred, but its legs bent the wrong way. It sank to the ground again, and might have stayed there; but Ular's cord yanked tight, and its thrashing began anew. Gjona heard a yelp from over the hill as Ular hit the ground on the other end.

The men were closer now, shouting. The cord: it would give them away. Khurta would know.

Gjona leaped onto the boar's back. The creature squealed and stabbed at the air with its tusks, but its strength was waning. Gjona dug his knees into its sides, tucked his club close to his chest, and unlooped the cord with his free hand. Just as the cord disappeared into the forest, the men reached him.

"Hit it, boy!" Khurta-ra shouted. "Hit it!"

For a moment Gjona couldn't think. Then he understood the use of his club. He smashed it down on the boar's skull once, twice, a third time. The animal groaned, shivered, and lay still.

Gjona scrambled up, trying to conceal his hope. Khurta-ra came to survey the boar's crushed legs and Gjona's bloodied club. It was a glance that lasted thirty forevers, but it was followed by a quick smile that brimmed with pride. Gjona straightened, and without thinking—to the men's embarrassment, and later his own—he bowed to Khurta like a servant presenting a meal.

Ular's run had taken the hunting party deep into the forest, away from their usual grounds and uncomfortably close to areas no one from their tribe had explored, at least not without a war party. And this was no war party: five boys and ten men, equipped only for hunting.

But they had to dress the boar. So they set to work, singing songs of the bravery of hunting heroes as they taught Gjona and the other inexperienced boys how to gut the animal. Gjona nursed his clenched fist and his clenched stomach. He hadn't eaten since the night before, and he regretted now not grabbing a loaf of bread before leaving the village.

One of the men stopped what he was doing and looked up. The work paused for a moment as everyone followed his gaze.

Twigs snapped in the distance.

Thirty paces away, a man bolted from hiding. One of the hunters jumped to his feet and gave chase. The other men scrambled for their weapons and followed, with the boys running after. Gjona saw the first man plant his feet and let loose an arrow that pierced the neck of the intruder. The man fell to the ground, and by the time Gjona caught up, he was dead. The hunters whispered a debate on what to do. It was settled by Khurta, who told Khali, Ular, and Gjona to go cording again, only this time they were looking for men.

The three went off in the direction the man had run, Gjona bearing left, Khali in the middle, and Ular bearing right, dragging their cords behind. Weaving among the rocks of the hillside and the thick walnut trees, Gjona ignored the chittering birds overhead and most other signs of movement, immersed in worrying over whether he'd be found out. If Ular told of the dangerous trick they'd pulled, or if Khali bragged about it, Gjona would be shamed for having made out that the kill was of his own design. And he'd bowed to Khurta. Bowed! Trying to impress the man, he'd made himself look simpering and weak. Like a whore, like the son of a whore. Always needy, always relying on the good will of others instead of his own strength. He wouldn't have been like this if he'd had a father. His father would have known what to do. His father would have made him strong, whoever his father was.

Three sharp tugs told Gjona to come back. They'd called it off, that or one of the other boys had kept a sharper and less whorish eye and found something. Gjona retraced his steps as someone on the other side wound his cord back onto a spindle. His gut began to churn. One of the others had found something, and he had not. Only let it be Khali. At least if it were Khali, he could be happy for him.

He approached the men in time to see Khurta clapping a broad hand on Ular's shoulder. Ular had found the rest of the strangers.

When all three boys had returned, Khurta whispered the plan. Their enemies were a party of scouts, it seemed, moving along an old path through the forest and marking the trees with cuts from their axes. There were about a half-dozen of these scouts, all riding fine horses and wearing fine garments, likely with excellent weapons as well. Khurta wanted two things: for these men never to return home from his clan's summer grounds, and to take possession of their horses and anything else worthwhile.

A steady rain was beginning to fall, rattling through the leafy branches overhead, and the scouts were hurrying to make camp. Their guard was down; they would be easy prey for Khurta's party if it were mounted on stolen horses.

"If we go down the ravine, we can take the horses without being seen," whispered Khurta.

He pointed out the tamest-looking mounts to the boys; the men were to handle the others. They crept forward to the lonely ring where the horses were tied. Gjona approached his assigned horse, which shied and stomped. Unlike the other boys of his age, he wasn't an experienced rider. Teaching horsemanship was a duty for fathers.

"What are you doing, boy?" whispered one of the older men. "You're scaring him. Give me that club."

Gjona struggled to pull the club out of his cramping left hand. The sap must have loosened, because this time it worked. He gave it to the man to hold while he mounted. Without thinking it through, Gjona took the wooden pommel in his left hand and swung himself over. He then took the club in his right hand and realized he now had one hand freshly stuck to the saddle and the other to the club. Before Gjona could reposition and find the reins, Khurta-ra was galloping forward, leading them all into the attack.

The scouts were unprepared, their camp in disarray. Khurta and his men descended on them like wolves on baby rabbits. While the other boys held back, as they had been instructed, Gjona's foot slipped and he kicked the horse forward.

The war-seasoned horse, with no reins to control him, galloped past Khurta and toward the fleeing men. Gjona saw Khurta was watching, so he gripped his club tight and swung it hard, clipping the top of one scout's head. The club bounced up in a spray of blood as the man fell to his hands and knees. The horse was now separated from the group, so it turned and ran back toward its brothers, on a path that led straight past the dazed, kneeling man.

Khurta was watching.

The scout was almost a full span to the side, but Gjona leaned far and swung hard. The man looked up at the last moment and seemed to make a sound. And then the face was gone and there was no sound.

When the horse settled, Gjona looked frantically for Khurta. The remaining scouts had been killed as they tried to flee into the woods. The skirmish had ended in cheers almost before it started. Gjona, on his reinless, wandering horse, struggled to turn and see what was happening.

"Stop!" Khurta shouted from somewhere behind—whether to the horse or to Gjona wasn't clear, but the horse took the order as its own.

And then there he was, Khurta-ra, walking over with a wide, proud grin.

"Well done, Gjona-ja," he said.

FRIDAY NIGHT: THE FUNERAL OF BEATRICE JOHN

T HE SOUND OF PRESTER JOHN snoring was like the groan of an old woman waking from anesthetic in delirium and lingering pain. The old woman seemed first to be wishing the IV and bedrails away, then whining in horror at the stitches across her belly, then finding comfort in the presence of a friend or oxycodone. Mina found it maddening as she tried to lose herself in a history book, Daniel Boorstin's *The Discoverers*. She wasn't looking for references to her husband, but there one was, jumping out at her from a discussion of Prince Henry the Navigator's explorations of Africa:

> These advances down the coast brought new rumors of the famous but still unseen Prester John. While Prince Henry's first objective was to move into the unknown, another objective, his chronicler Zurara reported, was "to know if there were in those parts any Christian princes, in whom the charity and love of Christ was so ingrained that they would aid him against those enemies of the faith."

"Charity and love of Christ." Not the Prester she knew. But she had known about his past almost from the day they met, in 1991, at the funeral of Beatrice John.

Dr. John was an anthropology professor at Alabama Polytechnic Institute. She had directed Mina's master's thesis, on the role of women in quelling the Redshell Revolts through both sexual and maternal influence over the crabs, in varieties natural and genetically modified. She had been helpful and patient, even while challenging Mina to draw on her own history to inform her observations. History, Dr. John said, was "the coalescence of multiple personal experiences, including those of the historian." Then Beatrice John's own history rolled on to a dismal end, trapped inside a nursing home in that final year, spending dark hours and cold months under stainless cotton sheets. Mina got a phone call from the history department's secretary, and the woman seemed taken aback when Mina cried out and began sobbing. Her father paid for the trip back to the States, a last effort at kindness in a relationship that was long past being improved by the attempt. That was how Mina found herself standing uncertain and alone in Auburn, Alabama, at the gates of a cemetery dotted with tombstones that bore the pretentious epitaphs you only find in a town full of professors. ("There is an end, my love. There is an end.")

She walked past the statue of Milton carrying the head of Dr. Taylor Littleton. She walked among wisteria vines—bent and pruned for decades to spell out the names of beloved deans, twining into T's and I's and close-enough attempts at K—and eased into the gathering crowd, where she traded awkward nods with familiar people she felt she should know. She watched as Dr. John's coffin was lowered clumsily into a hole by a Cyclops in a splitting tuxedo and undersized hat. It was desperate, Mina thought. A pathetic end for a great woman, surrounded in burial by stone-faced colleagues and a few students. Even the Cyclops, trained by the morticians to show perpetual sympathy and understanding despite lacking the capacity to feel either, looked weary. Only one guest stood out: a man at the foot of the grave who looked to be about forty years old, tan and wearing a faded black suit that could have stepped right out of the 1930s. His full, thick, dark hair spiked straight out in several places where the wind had bothered it. His features were somewhere between Asian and European—from southeast of Russia, Mina thought—and his eyes were gray. He didn't appear sad or shaken enough to be a family member. He was too old to be a student and showed no interest in joining the faculty, who were clumping together in numbers for safety from the whims of emotion.

The cemetery Cyclops suddenly dropped the coffin the last couple of feet; one side caught on the red clay wall, and Mina, horrified, heard Dr. John's body roll inside.

"Surry," the Cyclops muttered, looking over at the man in the old suit.

But the man looked into the Cyclops's eye and just smiled, gently.

He must be in so much pain, Mina thought, that he was numb to it now, unable to muster any more tears, and that brought Mina to tears again, and she held a now-damp handkerchief to her face to keep her sobs silent.

After the funeral, the stone-faced professors all shifted and looked off in different directions. They quietly fiddled with watches and programs and keys, long before any of these things might reasonably be necessary. On some psychic signal, perhaps a whistle too high-pitched for Mina's ears to register, they took a collective step away, then another, and soon drove off in a fleet of Toyota Corollas, dyed black for the occasion.

The man in the faded suit remained behind. He did not cry, not even now that he was alone. He seemed resigned to his loss, whatever that was, but not terribly saddened by it. Mina approached him, her face a wreck of smeared makeup and tears, eyes red and swollen, but knowing she would obsess about this for weeks if she didn't at least try to find out who he was.

"I'm so sorry for your loss," she said. "She was a great woman."

"Yes," the man answered. "She was that."

He stared at the hole as the Cyclops filled it, dumping too-large shovelfuls of clay onto the coffin lid. It dented and popped back with each splashing blow, bouncing up small pellets of red dirt and dust.

"She was your mother?"

The man only smiled, that sad, faraway smile.

"I'm sorry. I should leave you alone."

"She was my wife," he said.

Mina backed a step away.

"When I met Beatrice, everyone called it a scandal," he went on, seeming not to care whether she stayed to listen. "I looked as I do now. She looked about sixteen. Her friends—they would lure in the young soldiers returning from war, young soldiers with scabbing bayonet wounds and still coughing mustard gas. But she chose me," he said, smiling at the memory. "They called her a gravedigger."

Mina hadn't met an old-man since she was a child in Madagascar, where they were common and often ended up as sages or tribal leaders. He was an old-man. That made sense. He wasn't an age fetishist or a swindler out to plunder whatever pension Dr. John had stored away. He simply hadn't kept up with his wife's advancing age. And, it turned out, he had lived for a time in Abyssinia. He smiled when Mina speculated that his time in Africa might have extended his life.

He seemed kind, Mina thought, and polite, especially for someone who had just lost his wife. By comparison, Mina was out of control. As they talked, she'd begin crying at the memory of Dr. John, and over her guilt at not having stayed in touch. With each burst of emotion, Prester seemed concerned and helpful. Only years later did Mina rewrite that bit of historical analysis: It likely wasn't concern so much as curiosity.

They had coffee, then dinner, and then, when Prester discovered that Mina had not yet made arrangements for a motel room, they went back to the Johns' home on Burton Street. He had extra rooms, and he assured her that this wasn't an overture, though Mina had to admit to herself she was flattered by the idea that it might have been.

Mina had never been able to figure out where Dr. John lived, and now she understood why. Burton Street had long ago been closed off for the development of new student apartments, but the portion sustaining the Johns' home had been set aside as extradimensional space, retaining much of the flavor of the original street, minus the houses chopped up into student quadplexes and stained with keg party debris. This Burton Street was turn-of-the-century neo-Georgian with some Craftsman mixed in, full of well-fed squirrels and well-aged trees.

Prester opened one of the wood-and-glass double front doors. A breeze helped him along, sending strands of Mina's loosening hair across her face. A central hall with fifteen-foot ceilings ran from the front door all the way to the back, in what had once been a dogtrot. The grand hallway opened into rooms on either side. Between each set of doors was displayed a collection of artifacts and related drawings, each focused on a theme, primarily historic in nature.

A tattered flag on a rotted pole was the centerpiece of a display on the Redshell Revolts. There were 1930s-era research-quality photographs of dissected crabs, victims of the mutation experiments that led up to the conflict, some fitted with tools or housekeeping objects instead of claws: toilet bowl brushes, measuring cups, cat litter scoops, toothpicks. Some crabs, if you could still call them that, were nearly unrecognizable, angry screams trapped in their glooming eyestalks. There was also a pistol, cased but apparently functional: a black steel semiautomatic with wood grips.

They briefly discussed Mina's thesis on the role of women in the revolts. It was a good distraction from her sadness, getting worked up as she fleshed out the argument, citing the examples of strong central figures such as Linda Bruckheim and Virginia Abernathy. Prester smiled and seemed to appreciate her passion. He didn't debate with her, pushing dismissive arguments the way her father would, but instead asked encouraging questions.

Another wall held a collection of pottery and stonework from pre-Mongolian central Asia. A centerpiece of well-preserved leather braces and a hefty club, blood-stained and battered, led Mina to the conclusion that this collection of artifacts—focused on weapons rather than art—must be Prester's and not Dr. John's. There was a stately felt hat: a kalpak, purple, with threads of white silk and gold forming mirror images of a gryphon clutching a stone in one claw. The only art in this section was a series of drawings—front, back, and side angles—of a sciapod. Mina had never seen one drawn in such detail and had certainly never gotten a chance to look at one in person for any length of time. In the drawing, the single leg began at about the ribcage and extended a labeled sixteen inches, stopping at a massive knee and then tapering to a twenty-inch calf that ended in one wide, flat foot. Seven toes splayed out from the front, the center toe being about twice the size of its neighbors, and a heel, about the size of a grapefruit, planted firmly in the ground. Not far above the leg, wiry, toned arms jutted out, ending in bony hands with untrimmed fingernails. The sciapod's head was typical enough, lacking the sharpened teeth of a leader but sporting matted lengths of unwashed hair. Such creatures would have been fearful harbingers as they hopped along the plains, the drumming pound of feet and flashing bounce of hair sending enemies scurrying from their homes long before the sciapods arrived to take their plunder. They were beautiful, and now they were gone, wiped out through genocide and forced assimilation.

"I wonder if this is really what they were like," Mina said, not expecting an answer.

"More or less," Prester said.

"More or less what?"

"That's more or less what they looked like, as I recall."

Yes, he would know, wouldn't he? Mina thought of the work they could do, of the history books they could write, together, with her perspective from scholarship and his from personal experience.

On the opposite wall was a large glass case containing a book made of golden plates. The plates were engraved with some sort of hieroglyphs that Mina didn't recognize. Beside the book was an odd pair of crystals held together by silver cloth. They resembled glasses, but Mina couldn't imagine anyone being able to see through them, and she wondered at how ridiculous Prester would look wearing them if he tried.

"It's a beautiful book," Mina said.

"Yes," Prester said.

"What is it? What language is it in?"

"I'm not sure, actually. I've never tried to read it. But it belongs to a man I know, and I expect he's going to want it back one day."

"Your friend has interesting tastes," Mina said with a laugh.

"I didn't say he was my friend."

"Oh," Mina said. "I'm sorry, I . . ."

"Beatrice tried to read it once. She spent a whole week peering through those damn stones, praying for a vision. Ended up with a monthlong headache."

Set in a frame above the case with the book and the glasses was a daguerreotype of Prester, looking exactly the same as he did now except with a ridiculous brimmed hat, standing beside a ragged man dressed for the open range. Behind them was a goat about the size of a horse looking dully at the camera. "Prester John, Daniel Tucker, and 'Emma'; Rochester, New York; 1852."

Another collection Mina recognized at once: Abyssinia. There were weapons and pottery, reeds and tools. On an altar purificator rested a calcified white loaf of sweetcake with a cross in the center. Beside a large piece of broken emerald shaft was a yellowed map folded to show the country, at the center of which was the profile of a man sitting on a throne, holding a green scepter. *Hic longe lateque imperitat magnus princeps Presbiter Ioes totius Africae potentifs Rex*, read the inscription.

"A Christian king of the east. So that was you?" she said.

"More or less," Prester said. "There were exaggerations, misunderstandings."

"I'd love for you to tell me about it, one of these days."

"We'll see," he said.

Past the collections from America and Abyssinia, at the end of the hall, close to the kitchen, was the Johns' salamander pyrorium. They had only one, a white. As Mina walked up, she almost overlooked it, but then it rose to greet her from a pile of white-hot coals. It—no, she—lifted her head and peered carefully into Mina's heart. Mina felt her sending out test echoes, soft murmurs, questioning and sympathetic. Understanding, commiserating in the loss of Beatrice John. The feedingwoman and the teachingwoman, yes (the white said) you both knew her. Knowingness and apologytaking for probingtime. Respects. Mina felt these things and felt her heart moved with a warmth that now rolled in a welcome embrace through her body. She bowed slightly in kindness and smiled. The salamander bowed in return.

"She likes you," Prester said. "That's good."

"I suppose so," Mina said. "Have you had her long?"

"Yes, I think I have."

"What's her name?" Mina asked, lightly stroking the place on the glass where the white had pressed her chin.

"Name?"

Prester woke. He did this too often now, unable to capture a full eight hours of sleep, or even four. He had two options: He could try to fall back asleep, or he could cause himself to slip out of time. The second was easy enough. It took an act of will to slow his mind enough to stay anchored in the present anyway, so skipping ahead several hours, or even several months, wasn't difficult. The difficulty was in knowing when he'd come out of it. There was always a danger he'd wake to a cleaning lady in midwinter, with Mina having gone back to Georgia a year earlier. So sleep it was. Meditation often worked. He could never meditate without falling asleep. He stared at the ceiling and took deep mouth breaths, then nose, then barely breathed at all while he listened to the sound of his heart. Controlling one's body was one of the first lessons an old-man had to learn. The necessity of it extended well beyond falling asleep.

"I want a child," Mina had told Prester one day over lunch, in a downtown Auburn diner run by owners just bohemian enough to serve proper vegetable soup. "I want us to have children."

It was 1993. They'd been engaged for a few weeks, and for the last of those Mina had been debating whether to tell Prester she'd stopped taking the pill.

"Prester," she said again. "When we're married, I want us to have a child."

In between mouthfuls of soup, Prester rolled the green beans around on his spoon, spinning them back into the broth. "I didn't know you wanted that," he said, finally.

"Well, I do." It wasn't the reaction she'd hoped for, but it wasn't a surprise.

"You don't want children," Prester said rhetorically. "You have your research and your book and your swimming."

She laughed. "Well, first," she said, "I love swimming, but it isn't high on my list of life goals. The book comes out in December, and I can start research on another one after the baby arrives."

The book, *Undone: Pre-Giamite Empires of Central Africa*, was all but finished, with only minor edits still to come.

The book was her idea—inspired by his stories of what Abyssinia was like when he arrived. She riddled him with questions night after night, and even as the sun battled its way into morning, she'd bounce around the room with new theories to explain the political climate Prester had faced and what his sudden presence must have done to redraw the regional lines of power. She was so happy, so excited. And Prester, like a dried sponge pulling water into itself, soaked up her passion. That passion led her to *Undone*, and if he could only nudge her to apply that to a second book, they could bypass this whole distracting business of having a child.

Mina knew this, too. She knew that if she were to have a child, she would need to do it now, before starting a new project.

"You don't want children?" Mina asked, taking a sip of sweet tea.

"I've had children," Prester said.

Mina stopped. "What?"

Prester looked up at her and chewed his bread.

"You've had children? You never talk about them."

Prester wiped his mouth and placed the napkin back on his lap. This conversation again, he thought. He didn't like to speak of it, but it seemed necessary. Why? Can't they know how old he is and figure it out on their own? Obviously his descendants weren't running around holding reunions in great-great-great-whatever Prester John's honor every ten years. Obviously he was alone. "They died," Prester said, trying to subdue his annoyance.

Mina searched his face for signs of hurt. "I'm so sorry, honey."

Prester smiled. First the obvious question, then the show of pity. For Mina's sake, he reenacted the old liturgy. "Most of them went with old age. A few by disease or ill fortune."

"How many did you have?"

"A few dozen. But they were mostly girls."

"Prester!"

That's right. It mattered now. "It was a different time, Mina. It was nothing to have girls."

"But you had boys as well."

"I had a boy." Prester stiffened in his chair, wondering when the waiter might return to check on their meal. He wanted more crackers.

Mina looked away. She didn't like it when he talked like this, about the time when women were bred and used and killed according to the whims of men. But Prester didn't think that way. He had changed over time. Hadn't he? "So you consider your line dead because all of your descendants are from women; is that it?"

"Well, that could be the case, if that were the case," Prester said, now confusing even himself. "But it wouldn't matter. None of my children had children." He drizzled cooling soup from his spoon into the bowl. "Some of them, when they died, I was the only family they had left."

Prester couldn't run away from it. Even still, 1,700 years later, he felt as if he were holding a dying son in his arms, sobbing to himself, "Never again." He wondered how it would be if he broke down and told Mina about that, about his only son. She might understand. He saw himself blubbering the words, whispering, maybe crying as the pain tore into him once more. What would it take, how many more questions would she ask before they turned down that road?

"Besides," Prester said, presenting one aspect of the truth, "I'm not sure I can have children anymore."

But Mina's mind wasn't there. She was writing a different narrative from the scraps of history Prester had dropped on the table. Prester could have children. Prester could have dozens of children. So maybe things would change, maybe he'd be more open to the idea, once the book was out, once they were married, once they'd had more time together.

They married, and Mina waited a year, then another, waiting month after month for a child to come until her cycles seemed harbingers of empty lifelessness or gory death, depending on how much her hopes had been worked up in the weeks before.

Prester was in Britain for a demonstration on wardrobes when Mina went for her first infertility consultation. (The white salamander saw this and she knew, and she wanted with wholebeing to tell the woman of the pointlessness and pain, but want and ability were long ago sundered, and she could only mew in sympathy for what she knew was to come.) The doctor was patient. He ran all the tests and made all the best recommendations. Prester considered paying the doctor to leave him out of it, but finally he submitted to humiliating himself to appease Mina. Centuries earlier, Prester had, through the same concentration he used to keep his mind in the present, or to lull it to sleep, willed his seed to be sterile. Now it had become involuntary, like breathing or digestion. Some minor part of his mind kept his semen free of sperm (as he understood the biology of things), and it would likely take a further act of will to undo the process. But he would not do that, and his decision wasn't up for debate or even explanation. Not even with Mina. So he let her think it was his fault, and there wasn't anything he could do—and, in a way, there wasn't.

Slate mildew grows thick on the door jambs of homes without children. You can stay married five years and you hardly notice; the mildew grows a bit and disappears at the first scent of weeping milk ducts. But after ten years, after prayers and treatments and countless unwanted menstrual cycles, you begin to see it: Spots of mildew at first, tiny slate-gray spots around the sticking parts of the frame. Fifteen years on, the spots connect, lace together like years of quiet afternoons with nothing between you and your mind but the sick drone of TV news. The laces mesh. Thicken. The mildew grows dense and dark, becoming something more than itself. Sentient. Angry. After that, a door will hardly open without a solid shove.

One evening Prester came home to find her crying on the floor by the toilet, the water streaming red. He sat by her and pulled her heaving and shaking into him and stroked her wetted hair. She stiffened as she waited for him to say all the wrong things he always said: "We don't need children, Mina." "It's okay, Mina, we have each other." He considered repeating these things. But after all she'd been through, it was too late for her to hear the truth. Instead, he held her, rocking her in silence, listening to her sobs. "I know," he said. "I know, I know."

RED PLUMES OF HOT SILK,
C. 215 A.D.

GJONA-JA FOUND SOME SOLACE IN growing a beard. It wasn't much of a beard yet, but it was better than Khali-ro's, which was blond and patchy.

"Father says I should try spreading blood on my cheeks," Khali said. He nursed the bare spots in his stubble as the two of them loitered against the face of a boulder, watching women on the scrubby hill above them clean silks in a great bonfire.

Gjona laughed. "And if that doesn't work, try goat urine."

Khali hit Gjona in the chest with the back of his fist. Gjona let him do it and staggered over as if winded. The women looked down in mature disdain. Gjona and Khali knew better than to stand around watching women work, but they enjoyed picking out their next mates from amid the sea of thrashing arms and clenched thighs. Whether that mate would be too annoyed with them to go along with the proposal wasn't yet on their horizon.

"What about her? She'd be feisty enough," Khali said, lazily pointing toward a tall brunette whose arms were almost black from her few years of handling the smoldering silk.

"Hrm." Gjona chewed the stem of his fennis stalk. In raw form, the plant had a sedating effect. "She's run me off too many times already."

"Well, leave her alone then, grandmother."

Gjona pushed Khali over hard enough that his hands hit the ground. Khali was only kidding, but it was a sore subject with Gjona, who, having been raised mostly by his outspoken mother and an inthinking salamander, endured a lot of jibes for not taking more women by force.

Khali pushed him back, but Gjona just resumed chewing his fennis stem and staring at the fire, at the women dragging silks soiled by food, by dirt, by shit, and by blood up the hill and tossing them over the flames.

Billows of purple smoke shot out from under the sheets and cloaks, followed quickly by lashes of flame, as if the flames were trying to catch the smoke and pull it back before it funneled off to drag trails of violet wisp across the sky. Looking at the women work, you'd think they would be set ablaze, but being covered in salamander silks themselves, they were mostly safe. Wherever they weren't covered, years of practice kept them clear of danger.

"You heard, this morning? Another girl?" Khali asked, more to draw Gjona out than to share something he didn't know.

"Yeah."

"But you don't want to talk about it."

"What should I say? Four women, four girls. I've tried standing up, tried the coal ash, tried the sliver moon. Still girls. If one of them can give me a son, she'll be my wife."

Khali pulled a fennis stem from his belt and crossed his arms to put it in his mouth, not intentionally mirroring Gjona but doing it just the same.

"I guess I should tell you what they're saying."

"What's that?" Gjona said, stopping in mid-chew.

"That your seed is weak," Khali said. He puffed up to mock the bluster of old warriors. "Does he have a salamander's teat for a cock, that he makes the milk of women and not the seeds of men?"

Gjona smiled and shook his head. He didn't want to let it bother him, but it did, and Khali knew it. "So, what do they say I should do?"

"You don't want to know."

"Probably not, but tell me," Gjona said.

"They say among themselves, the old warriors, that you should kill the infant girls, to make room at their mothers' breasts for the chance of more sons."

Gjona watched the logs under the fire, mingled with orange-hot coal. "They really used to do that?"

"That's what Father says. It hasn't been done in a long time, so most folks think it's an old story, but Father says it's true."

"So, what does Khurta-ra think I should do?"

"He doesn't say."

"Hunh." Gjona knew his friend was lying. Khurta-ra was saying something—something Khali didn't want to share.

The brunette with black arms ripped a wide sheet out of the flames and whipped it in the air, tugging it this way and that. As it billowed over the flames in a dance-like frenzy, the soiled parts flaked and smoked away. The cloth began to shimmer under the solid rays of sunlight and Gjona squinted against the reflection. Finally she whipped the linen toward herself and spun it above her head, a cyclone of silk whirling into a smooth roll of perfect fabric, clean and hot to the touch.

"They can say what they want," Gjona said. "I'm not killing babies."

Later that night, after he returned, spent, from the yurt of the girl with the blackened arms, Gjona went to the white salamander to seek wisdom. He knew now how to care for her and how to milk her, though he was too old for this chore of boys and women. He sat on a stool next to the brazier and dropped some coals to the outer corners, then sloppily shoveled away some of the spent ash, leaving too much behind and on the floor, and not enough in the ash bowl. The white turned to him, and in her waving nod and glassy eyes he felt compassion and sadness and a concept he could not yet follow but most assuredly understood: Waitwatch, take care.

So, in a manner of speaking, Gjona waited.

As he waited, the girl with the blackened arms was no longer the girl with the blackened arms; they healed up in a matter of weeks. Then she was the girl with the big belly and then the woman with a baby girl the size of a calf.

As he waited, he sired another daughter, and another, until he began to lose count.

And after a time, Khali-ro's beard came in, thin and blond, then full and brown. All Gjona could ever grow was a thick stubble. Then, one morning during a hunt, sitting in the haze of morning with still-green ribbons of cloud strung across the sky whispering their song of dawn, Gjona saw that Khali-ro's beard was tinged with grey.

"Khali, your beard is old," Gjona said in surprise, touching to see if it was merely streaked with ash.

"Of course it is." Khali knocked Gjona's hand away in an ill temper. "I am old."

Gjona stared in smiling disbelief, transfixed by what seemed to him a new look for his friend.

"We're all old, Gjona. Except for you."

Gjona sat back and looked around him at the scouts tending the fire and the hunters sitting and talking of serious things on the outskirts of responsibility. The friends he'd grown up with, Ular, Pesak, Khali and his dutiful younger brother, and all the others, they were no longer scouts, were they? They were all warriors now. And it occurred to Gjona that he and his friends were now the oldest hunters in the group—that they indeed were the "old hunters" now.

Gjona laughed in disbelief. "We are not old!"

"You are not old," Khali said, lowering his voice in the urgency of saying out loud something he'd long kept to himself. "Do you even have a gray hair? You still run like a scout, you eat like a bear, and you fight like a tiger."

It was true that Khali had slowed down, but Gjona thought Khali was just letting the younger hunters have a chance now that he had taken a wife. The younger hunters, though, were now approaching the age of leaders.

"Do I really look that young?"

Khali looked at him with what Gjona could only call fear, for himself or for the tribe he couldn't tell. "Gjona, seriously, you look no older now than you were for the 92nd Effusion," Khali said. "Are you doing something strange? Is it magic? Is it why you can't have a son?"

"I'm not doing anything!" Gjona said, trying to laugh off Khali's seriousness. "Maybe you're all getting old because you've settled in with women and have a bunch of kids swarming your feet. That's what'll kill you, you know."

Khali didn't laugh. "And if you would settle with a woman, Gjona, men wouldn't say you're sleeping with their wives."

Gjona stopped smiling. "They say that?"

"Yes," Khali said. "Is it true?"

Gjona said nothing.

"It's a dangerous game, Gjona. You can beat a friend at ordo or kill some stranger in battle, but you know the saying: 'To betray a man with his wife is to tease a gryphon with new flesh.'"

Gjona stood. "Don't lecture me. You may look older than me, but I'm not a scout. I'll do what I want with any woman, and anyone who doesn't like it can say so to my face." Gjona left the circle.

"You act as young as you look," Khali called after him.

Gjona slowed as the comment pierced his spine, felt it shudder up and down his back in waves of alienation, but he continued to walk away.

Back at the encampment, Gjona continued the argument, only this time with Tana-ja.

"Why should I be careful? Why should I settle with anyone?" he demanded of his mother, who had pestered him long enough with questions. "My friends have sons. You had a son. My father, whoever he is, had a son. None of these women can bring me a son. Why should I settle down and wait for one woman to give me a son if she can't prove herself first?"

"You should be careful, because the white told you that you should be careful. I have learned to trust her judgment."

"You just want me to settle down because you want another woman around here to help you bake bread."

"Well, all your friends have wives, don't they?" Tana-ja answered, dropping bits of flour into her kneading-bread with bone-knobbed fingers that dripped with flesh so loose it was hard to tell where the dough left off and the fingers began. Only the old purple scar across the palm of her left hand stood out amid the flour and brown dough. It was a scar from another time.

"My friends are old men!" Gjona said. "I spend half my nights pleasing their wives because they aren't strong enough to do it themselves. And their wives aren't much younger at that!"

"You are old," she said, muttering. "As old as them, older than some of them, whether you look it or not. You're going to die without bringing me a proper daughter, without bringing me anything closer to grandchildren than the bastard offspring of your rutting."

"Oh, don't worry about me dying before you do, old woman, I will see to that," Gjona said, smiling, as Tana smacked her bread and gave him a scornful look.

Gjona thought of these words, these and many others that he

and his mother had shared over the long years of baking bread, weaving silk, and cleaning ash, as he placed the last rocks on her grave some two dozen years later. Even after his argument with Khali, Gjona didn't think often of the passage of time, not in those days. No one did. Except perhaps at those moments when a revered woman died of old age and the tribal elders gathered around the stone-pile tomb to pay their respects and to think on their own mortality—their gray beards, their weakening backs—and that man they grew up with who now looked only slightly older than their children. A shock of straight, bristly brown hair. Legs and arms straight and strong. A body without scars, despite all the blows from the blades of his enemies and the cuts from his kills. This was not right, they decided. Something must be done.

One night, within the moon of Tana's passing, Gjona was awakened by the voices of three women arguing outside his yurt. He opened his eyes, put his hands behind his head, and stared out the tunduk above him, past the colorful tufts of felt to the lazy stars that swirled beyond.

"You had him last night—it's my turn!"

"I did not; he wasn't with me. And if he wasn't with one of us, then he was with her, the whore."

"You're one to talk, after you kept him in your bed most of last week while your sick husband was all but dead one curtain away. The only reason you gave him up was your husband disappointed you by getting better."

"I'll cut out your tongue!"

"Stop it," the third one said. "The ayil kenesh is going to go on all night. If we do this right, Gjona may visit us all before sunrise."

Gjona smiled and bellowed from his bed, "I've had none of you hags for six moons or more, and I've no desire for any of you again. Get away from my yurt with your bags of bones, and be glad your men give you a place to rest them."

Gjona stifled his laughter and listened to the affronted cursing of the old women in their scurry from his door. He rolled over to sleep. But as the broad grin relaxed from his face, he began to think about the ayil kenesh, a meeting of the tribal council. What ayil kenesh? These were the elders. What were they meeting about? And why so late? He rarely joined in these councils. They too often substituted deliberation for action, and Gjona was too much in love with the hunt and the migration to waste hours discussing how best to go about them. Still, the elders usually told him they were meeting even if they didn't expect him to come. Gjona pushed the line of thought from his mind. But the further from sleep he traveled, the more he yearned to see how much more waking he might need to do. He wrapped himself in a fur and went out into the night.

The tribe was now camped on the banks of a creek flowing into Lake Kumsuat. This afforded the people both a barrier from enemies to the south and an ongoing challenge to keep them wary, for an angry creek could wipe out an encampment overnight, and with these waters flowing from the feet of the Karatau range, they were particularly moody.

On nights like this, though, with the waters dreamily at play under constellations so bright they kept the moon awake, the sound of trickling water quieted many voices, and also silenced Gjona's footsteps as they sought out the meeting place. Perhaps this meeting had to do with Tana-ja, he wondered. Her death had brought few mourners, but it left Gjona rootless in the tribe. He had children, but all daughters and none legitimate, and it occurred to him how easy it would be for the leaders to cast him out. Who would object? What bloodlines tied him here? Who would defend him if he came under the elders' disapproval? Not the chief. He was old now, far too old to do anything other than nod at their suggestions. He should have been killed off and supplanted long ago, but he'd earned respect from all those around him, and now there was nothing for it but to wait for him to pass on. Khurta-ra was long dead, and Gjona found both sadness and comfort in the knowledge that he was gone. The man could have been a father to him—might actually have been his father for all he knew. He could have accepted him more fully than he did, but instead treated him as little more than a ward over whom he had some influence.

Gjona heard a girl's startled cry as he rounded one elder's yurt. It was Shali, the daughter of Khali-ro, with whom Gjona now realized he hadn't shared a meal in many years.

"What do you want, Gjona-ja?" the girl asked.

"How do you know it's me?" he said from the shadows.

"Everyone knows Gjona-ja is always somewhere he's not supposed to be."

She made him smile. Shali was young, taut, sleek like a foal and almost as skittish. He could see in the angle of her shoulders the urge to flee, but in her feet (her soft and small feet dug hard into the ground) the determination to stay and fulfill her duty. She didn't seem to know what to do with her arms, first folding them across her chest to hide it from this man who presented himself alone in the dark in nothing but furs, then dropping them back to her sides with fists clenched in a show of strength. The result was a comical one that reminded Gjona too much of his unclaimed daughters trying to appear older than they were. Shali, in fact, was younger than a few of Gjona's daughters. This sobering notion tipped him back to his purpose.

"And are you supposed to be here, alone in the dark, Shali, daughter of Khali-ro?"

"If my father tells me to stay here, here is where I stay."

"And why has Khali-ro put his daughter out of the yurt in the dark? Are you bait for wandering boars? Or have you done something to offend your family?" Gjona walked slowly forward, like a black tiger, taking care not to scare off his prey, wondering how much younger this girl was than his daughters and how much, after all, that should matter. Then he saw the rope. Coiled a few feet from the girl was a knotted rope about an inch thick, rising straight up about three spans. After that it stopped, disappearing into some other space—a space where Khali-ro and the other elders must be holding their deliberations.

"That's not your concern," Shali said, but her voice wavered. "You should leave now."

"But it is of interest to me if it interests me. And it does interest me that a mere girl should tell me, one of the tribal elders, what time I should retire!" Gjona put some bite into his words, forcing Shali's head a few notches lower. His mind shifted. He was still thinking of how he might coax her to his bed, throw her down, find out for himself how protective Khali had been of her purity. He could feel his shadow filling the dark space around him, reaching to the edges and almost to the sky. But he was calculating now, trying to put his thoughts ahead of his actions. He'd always acted first, but in this moment he saw some advantage to plotting things out ahead of time. He came closer to her, letting his furs glide in the wind across her thighs, breathing down into her quivering face. "I find that you interest me very much."

Shali bolted to the rope—had she been a colt, her bray would have pierced Gjona's ears—and yanked three times. Khali-ro's head appeared from nothingness.

"Gjona!"

"Khali, you old thief! Your head should be hanging from this rope, not sitting on top of it. What's happened to the rest of you?"

"Don't joke with me when you're standing next to my daughter in the middle of the night! What are you doing to her?"

Khali was spitting down the rope in anger, and Gjona feared he might actually fall and break his neck. "Don't worry, Khali. I came here to see you. I only stopped to admire your daughter because a simple man such as myself can't pass a ripe apple without at least smelling for the sweet flesh inside." Gjona looked to Shali and she ran off, clearly no longer needed. "I will come up, then, if you wish." Gjona spoke as he climbed and was pushing Khali's head aside before it could voice any objection.

Atop the rope with no ending was a yurt without walls—without walls, but sparse draperies of red silk gave the impression of enclosure. It was not unlike the chief's black yurt, only smaller and with no brass brazier. Twelve leathery old men sat on the floor around a torch, beneath a thick mesh of flattened apple branches. They wore felt kalpaks fringed with the gray tufts of their hair, which plumed also from their noses and their ears as if senile white wolves were trying to creep from inside their bodies. They looked down at Gjona the way wizened men of authority always look at insolent young scouts who need to be put in their place, and Gjona could see that they intended to treat him this way. All of them, except the chief, had been his childhood friends. Had they been anything less, and had Gjona been carrying his sword, he would have hewn them to pieces where they sat and left them there, taking the rope down with him. In fact, the muscles of Gjona's right arm twitched to reach for the sword that should be at his side, and muscle memory easily might have gotten the better of the men in the room. But Gjona reminded his arm that he'd left his sword behind, and that was, in the end, for the best. They were blind. They saw that his body was young and assumed his mind was the same. But he shared their guile; he shared the wisdom they had gained from long years of wrestling against the world. Let them think less of him, and let them be strangled by their own ignorance.

The only thing they had that Gjona didn't was knowledge of what precisely they'd been talking about before he entered the room. He could guess, but it didn't matter. Gjona, who had been in the room only long enough to take two breaths, was tired of waiting.

"Gjona-ja," Khali began.

"Don't trouble yourself, Khali-ro, I won't stay long. I know you men have much to discuss, and as I've said before, I don't have the strength of mind to join you. But it was happy fortune that your daughter was chosen to mind your rope tonight, for it is in her interest that I now speak."

The elders looked from Gjona to Khali and back. Gjona guessed what they intended to tell him, but he could see now he'd said at least enough to gain a stay of exile.

"If I might first quench my thirst?"

Pesak, the son of Purna the midwife, poured from the pitcher into his own glass a full draught of milk and leaned over the torch, smiling broadly, to hand it to Gjona. Pesak had always enjoyed a good show.

Khali gave him an irritated look and waited as Gjona enjoyed his milk in expectant silence.

"Many thanks."

"My cup is yours," Pesak replied with a bow.

"You and your house are too kind."

"We are all sustained by her milk alone."

"So it has been, and so shall it always be."

"May the Effusion find you wet with her milk and—"

"Gjona!" Khali interrupted. "What is it you wish to say?"

"Great sirs." Gjona paused to wipe the milk from his beard and see how long he could tax their patience. He wiped his hand on his furs, then shook them to dry them out. "It has recently come into my mind that although I have trained half the scouts in our tribe, such that they can speed out and back with hardly the notice of their masters, much less their prey . . ." Gjona motioned to the elder next to him that he might borrow a pillow, took the pillow, and found a comfortable position on it before continuing. ". . . and although I have slain so many of our rivals in battle that if my arm could carry a mark it would be more black than brown with the scars . . ." Gjona took the torch, adjusted the branches below it, and repositioned it upright, doubling the illumination of the room so that the elders' eyes were, for a moment, useless. ". . . and although I have led our men into the hunt for decades, and have slain massive beasts for our table, and have built more yurts for our families than I have owned myself . . ." Gjona paused this time just to look each man in the eye, some to the point of forcing their eyes down or away, until finally his met those of the chief, who seemed almost to be smiling back at him. ". . . it comes to my mind after the death of my beloved mother that some in the tribe may wish more of me than all these things that I have already done on their behalf. They might wish me to populate the tribe with legitimate sons who can carry on my good works after I lie under my own heap of stones. Some might be impatient for me to make a choice from among the fine women of this tribe and take a wife who might share in the glory of my sacrifices and efforts for others."

Khali was transfixed. Gjona could see behind his twitching eyes the shuffling labors of thought as he worked out what this would mean for him and his standing.

"So I have decided, Khali-ro, that with your blessing I will take your daughter Shali as my wife for the modest dowry of three fine goats. I will not seek your salamander, not out of any question of its virtue but out of respect for Shali, who is far too dear a treasure herself to require a dowry so great."

Gjona waited for the reaction. The elders were turning the idea over in their minds. If he were matched, perhaps he'd cause less havoc in the camp; and who indeed would train the scouts if he were to leave? Gjona as an ally in battle would be far better than Gjona as an enemy from another tribe, and as this notion hit them,

Gjona smiled inside, knowing the seed he planted had borne fruit. They all seemed to be waiting anxiously for Khali to give consent.

"Gjona."

"I will take your daughter into my bed tonight."

"No!" Khali cried, rising from his pillow as quickly as his bones allowed and pointing down at Gjona. "You will not take her tonight. I will speak to my family first. If they are agreeable, you may have her tomorrow night. And with two goats, not three."

"I will take her tomorrow before sunset, and with three goats."

Khali looked around the room to assure himself that this bargain left him in good standing. "Agreed."

SATURDAY MORNING: HELL

MINA CAUGHT HERSELF SMILING UPON waking from a child's dream of waves, freshwater waves too young for malevolence that rolled up from the depths and crashed across her body, leaving her dripping and laughing in a pool of rushing bubbles. There were waves like that in Madagascar, in lonely pools caught between mountains, where the water lingered just a moment near the shoreline before the waterfalls pushed it away again. The falls plunged just a few dozen feet, not enough to attract tourists, but enough to make a young teen want to spend the better part of her days lying naked in the sunlight and foam.

She opened her eyes and looked over at her husband, still deeply asleep, and studied his face, which seemed sickly now, even under the rising glow of a sunrise glancing off white sands. She wanted to find something there, some boyish piece of him still alive while he slept. Instead, she found only the yellowing stubble of an overnight beard. Drool trickled down the seam of his lips, making a cold puddle under his 1,800-year-old face. He was trapped. Trapped in age at forty, maybe forty-five, his hair still a shock of unkempt brown tufts, his skin leathery and tan, while the world around him died and renewed itself over and over again.

And behind it all the shadow, quiet now but still there, like a sleeping bear that had killed its own cubs and shat in its own den, then fallen into hibernation expecting everything to be okay while it slept. Mina frowned.

She pushed herself out of bed. Her sleep-wobbly legs shimmered across the carpet as she walked, flashing in and out like a cell phone signal on an uncharted highway, distracting her as she tried to brush her teeth. She leaned harder on the countertop, forcing weight into her body, and rolled her eyes at the mirror. It seemed silly, brushing her teeth. There was no long-term risk of gum disease for suicides. It didn't seem right, though, to let herself go, as if this was about depression or anything. This was the right thing to do, the sensible thing to do, given the alternative.

Mina had been dealing with PED—psychomorphic equilibrium disorder—most of her life, but only this year had she begun to see the signs of Stage 2, which came with a confirmed diagnosis and a better idea of her prospects, if you could think of it that way. Sometime in the next five years, maybe ten depending on her emotional state, Mina would fade into nothingness. First she would enter a state of glassy translucence, then recede entirely into spectral invisibility, floating limbless and helpless on the wind. One minute she'd be solid and firm. The next she'd stumble over a fading foot or drop a glass through transparent fingers.

She had long since gained control of the Stage 1 PED symptoms, a tendency to melt during times of intense emotion and re-solidify afterward. Melt had scared Mina since her childhood: liquification of her body from the outside in. The doctors thought it was vernix when Mina was fresh from the womb, but then some fingers dripped away, and surgeons had to mold new ones through genetic duplication. Ever since, her parents had warned Mina against feeling too strongly, letting her emotions run too hot. Mina remembered times when she was a toddler and her mother would catch her—running and squealing and dripping wet, staining her clothes and the carpet—and hold her and calm her, rubbing her down with ice packs as she screamed, with laughter or anger, to be set free.

That hadn't been a problem for many years. She'd gotten very, very good at self-control.

Doctors, therapists, scientists had nothing to offer. She'd talked to every specialist she could find since the day Dr. Humbert told her she was fading. It was only a matter of time before her legs vanished, then her arms, her torso, her head. Where would she go? Would she still exist, disembodied but alive and powerless? The doctors thought it would be comforting to tell her they suspected she'd survive. Survive. Spectral. Forever. It was only a matter of time.

The horror of it made her wake in the night, screaming, thrashing around like she was being eaten alive by the cold steel of absolute nothingness. Sometimes when she felt overwhelmed, crazy with anger and fear, she would begin to melt again, her arms dripping under her fingers like warm ice cream. Would that be so bad, to melt into the floor rather than fade like a ghost? There was no point discussing it with Prester. He'd only offer some bit of practical advice, some suggestion for how to deal with things, some linear strategy for coping with unknown probabilities. Certainly not compassion, or reassurance, or some tearful expression of how much he needed her and feared losing her. Mina laughed inside at the thought of that. She tried to love him. She tried to do anything other than stare at her slowly fading hands. But what's the point when the end brings emptiness?

Mina pulled herself away from the mirror—she kept doing that, getting caught thinking about it. No point. Just get dressed, make breakfast, go to Hell to buy their final day or two of groceries, and carry on until it's time. Thinking about it won't help anyone with anything.

When Prester John dreamed, he dreamed of mornings that started off wrong at NSpaces. One recurring narrative had him arriving early, ahead of everyone else. He walked long, echoing corridors full of stagnant air in which curls of yesterday's cologne and cigarette smoke hung suspended like half-cherries in a Southern Methodist Jell-O casserole. But when he got to his office, the phone was already ringing with the screams of clients behind schedule, looking for missing shipments that Prester had never heard of. And then he'd look down at his desk, which he was sure he'd meticulously organized the night before but which was now in chaos: papers everywhere, some dog-eared, some crumpled, some on fire, some being consumed with a cup of milk by Rosha, who was chained to the wall and leering, paper pulp dripping from his lips. Nothing was in order. Too many loose ends. Then the outlines of the door would appear, and the door would open, and then Griffiths from Human Resources. He'd wake, breathing hard, before she got a chance to give him that look—the look of contempt.

Almost nine months since his last day of work, he was still dreaming about it, still waking up from it. But that was better than several alternatives.

Prester sat up in the bed and looked around him. Mina, once more, wasn't there. She used to wake him on weekend mornings, mewing like a salamander, her eyes bright with adoration. Now she'd leave him lying in bed for God knows how long while she started the day on her own. Prester wiped the drool from his face, wondering how that happened, and went to the bathroom to urinate and shave. Mina was gone from there too, which was just as well. She could no longer stand the sight of him naked, it seemed. Every time, she'd wander away, sometimes with an excuse, sometimes not, never lingering when he was changing clothes or showering. Maybe his body was a painful reminder that he couldn't give her children. Maybe she was afraid. Maybe she didn't really believe him—that he couldn't control his shadow then but that he could control it now. Or maybe she couldn't bear to watch his morning ritual of staple-gunning the shadow to the bottom of his feet.

It hadn't been like this with the others, or Prester didn't remember it being this way. Beatrice remained grateful, grateful and practical to the end—the final nights of silent smiling, holding vigil for hours as all thought and memory slipped from her. And even after, when Beatrice was nothing more than a breathing, beating shell, Prester held her limp hand for days and watched as her breaths slowed and stopped. She was grateful, not just for the education Prester had supplied and the financial backing for her low-salaried teaching positions, but for his sticking by her as she wrinkled and hunched into something far less (physically) than what he'd met seventy-four years earlier. She had told him once that he could leave, that it didn't make sense for him to stay with her. He told her he didn't mind, and he didn't. She was a good companion. Before her, there was Shali-ro, dutiful and patient but wholly self-sufficient, with no more actual need of him than of a horse or a grinding wheel. But Mina, Mina was neither grateful nor unneeding. Mina—once so dynamic and brilliant—now seemed resigned, and nothing Prester offered seemed to go any distance toward a solution.

Now they were only going through the motions.

There was a time when going through the motions was a solution. When Prester rallied the armies of his empire and marched them to the west, down into Persia and across Babylon to the Tigris, his soldiers were chomping at the bit to reclaim the Holy

Land, but he'd failed. And following that failure, exiled in Abyssinia, he tried doing nothing, but that left him subject to the whims of his court. The only solution, then, was to go through the motions, to survive, to pick at the edge of prosperity without pursuing greatness, without teasing failure once more. He'd been steadily walking that path for over 800 years. What did it get him? A pathological, separated shadow pursuing carnal misdeeds and a wife who no longer loved him. No. Going through the motions was no solution.

There could be no solution except suicide, and that was one they could both live with.

Prester dressed and walked to the hall, pausing to look over the salamanders, checking the flame color, the heat, their general behavior for any signs of trouble. As usual, the white closed her eyes and shimmied, contorting her thin pink lips into what could be mistaken for a smile. It was an amusing trick, and she did it only for Prester. He smiled at her and she shimmied again.

She shimmied and opened her eyes to find him gone. The morninglook was over, but he'd be back tomorrow. Tomorrow to feed her with prettythoughts and glances. The woman was kind. She took care of them, Prester's white and her own gray, but the man had long been with her and she with him, and there were many milkers and cleaners. There were even many salamasires: the mottled gray, the blue, the streakingblack and another blue before him. But there was always the man and his morninglook, and that was all the white needed. She rustled to the corner and dug her nose into the ash to find a live coal. She swished her tail to fling the colding embers aside, clouding the pyrorium with small torrents of ash that lifted and fell and burned away, fanning the dying coal back to a warmer shade of orange. The coal rolled over her back, and a tingle of warmth surged through her body. The mottled gray salamander looked at her with tired indignation. He was old now, and he did not understand her digging like a pup. Had she gone mad after all these days? He placed his head back down on his rock, vexed. The white curled up around her glowing-coal and put her mind to the woman. The woman wasn't sure, and that bothered the white. The man needed that the woman be sure. He needed that she be more than she was, the white decided, and she was becoming less than she was all the time. She would have to become more, for him and for her. The white purred gently and sadly, sending out tiny waves of sympathywarm—barely audible, barely felt over miles of distance and time—to the woman and to the man, that they might find peace.

Island stores made Mina uneasy. The aisles were tight, the selection was limited and overpriced, and the floors too often had rivers of mud coming from the vegetable section. With the energy of an automaton she detangled a cart and pushed it into Hell. She skipped the first circle (they'd brought plenty of toilet paper and napkins) and went directly to the second: fruits and vegetables. A woman cut her off and led a string of shouting children in front of her cart. Mina glared, but the look went unnoticed. Just as well. Sometimes it's nice to go unnoticed.

At least the island had that going for it. There was no one to stumble over at the grocery store, asking "How are you?" Because what was Mina supposed to say to that? "I'm dying. You?" Then, inevitably, they'd have some kind of overactive spleen or ticky eyelid they'd want to show her and talk about how much they'd endured. "But nothing like what you're going through, of course." On the island, no one knew who Mina was. She could be Julianne Moore or Lizzie Borden or St. Mary, wandering through the second circle of Hell looking for iceberg lettuce and tampons. No one cared.

But she wouldn't need the tampons, would she? The plan was they'd kill themselves that night, and she wasn't due for several days. All she needed was enough for their last meal together. One final trip.

Mina left her cart at the edge of a long row of ready-to-harvest carrots and trudged up the leafy plant rows. The iceberg was wilted on the vine, so she cut off a big head of romaine and returned to her cart. She heard shouting to her left. A large woman had stumbled on the gourds and landed on a watermelon, cracking it. Manager crabs and stockcrabs scuttled up from the back and insisted she pay for the melon, but she refused. Several more large crabs emerged from the back. Claws clicking, they dragged the woman off the vegetable field to a pair of metal swinging doors with rubber edges. Mina wondered what went on back there. You would hear occasional screams and laughter, and sometimes brimstone smoke would belch from a dusty air vent. Another Mina in another time would have run after the woman, made excuses for her, and helped her back to the aisle. Or she would have cried out and demanded the store's humans do something. But now, this Mina looked away.

By the ninth circle, her feet were killing her. She wanted to take off her shoes, but there was no way she was going barefoot around all those chickens. Inland, people thought of chickens and ducks and geese as fluffy soft things, the source of down comforters and feather quills. They didn't think of the chickens pecking at blankets of their own excrement. They'd never seen how a drake would snap the head off a straggler duckling, as Mina had seen one do during a romantic stroll with Prester.

Mina used to like birds. As a child growing up in Madagascar she'd had a pet roc named Urtyylk, though the name never suited him. He was small for a roc, about forty hands tall, but plenty big for Mina to ride on his back across the sky, along the shore, hunting horses and baby elephants. Mina would never let Urtyylk kill them, though once she let him take a sheep. They were gliding across the south side of the mountain and spotted a lone sheep in a meadow. It seemed to be waiting there for them, assigned to stand in clear sight on a green plain just in case some large predatory bird was in need of a snack. Urtyylk angled into a dive and glanced back to see if Mina would stop him. She considered it. She should have stopped him, but she did not. Instead, she watched in a daze, curious what it would look like. Would there be blood? Would the sheep scream? Would it even know it was dead?

The roc bore down, silent as a falling leaf. The sheep never looked up. Urtyylk, soaring only five feet above the ground, speared it silently with his lower beak. There was a *phlumph* and explosion of white wool over Urtyylk's head, then Mina's body, then, as she looked back, a trail of white fluff that hung in the air behind them and landed softly on the meadow. She felt some pity for the sheep, but seeing the roc fully live out its place in the natural order of things—it was thrilling. She felt alive and more deeply a part of the greater world of pleasure and suffering than ever before.

Mother would get nervous about the flying, afraid Mina was diving too deep, getting too close, finding too much to love about the big, shaggy bird. One day Mina came home laughing, almost crying with joy after diving with Urtyylk in and out of Lake Victoria's waterfalls, far across the straits from Madagascar. She stumbled in the back door, giddy. Her mother stormed over and wiped Mina's brow, then held up the yellow stain of melt on the blue towel in accusation, screaming how could she be so careless?

She rushed Mina into the freezer and kept her there for hours, while Urtyylk was scolded and struck across the beak for taking the child too far from home. In the freezer, Mina kept laughing, feeling the gummy slickness on her arms gradually thicken and congeal back into form. She sighed with love for her bird. Then, letting the cold seep in, she set. Her smile drifted away. She asked politely for Mother to open the door.

These chickens, pecking around their feces for crumbs of grain—these were not Urtyylk.

"I'll take this one," Mina said to the butcher.

"The yella one?"

"No, this white one with the brown beak."

"Ya sure?" the butcher asked, taking the brown-beaked bird by the neck. They always asked that.

"Yes," she said, and at that he whisked the bird over his head, snapping its neck in the same motion. He swung the bird a couple more times to ensure its demise before landing it on the table, cleaving off the head, and draining the blood into a dark hole at the side. They were careful in Hell to do these things humanely. The butcher began plucking, and in no time he was hidden in a cloud of plumage, as if an autumn fog had descended upon him, or the fluff of a lone sheep speared by a roc. Gradually the cloud settled; by then he was working at the legs.

"You want broiler, parts, bones and skin?"

"Parts. Boneless and skinless, thank you."

Mina turned away. She didn't like to watch this part.

A youngish couple was looking at her from down at the steak pens. The man had faded reddish hair, with too much of it tufting out the neck of his orange golf shirt. The woman was Asian, with long black hair and a thin yellow sundress. Surely she had on a bikini underneath? They waved. Oh, God, Mina thought. No one knew her here. No one was supposed to know her here. Who were these people?

They rolled their cart toward Mina, who tried to act islandy.

"Hi," the wife said.

"Hello," Mina said with a polite smile. "Do I know you?"

"We haven't met. I'm May Gog, and this is my husband, Reggie. We live across the street from you on the bay side."

"Oh!" Oh, God, Mina thought. They've been watching us.

"You just came in last night?" May asked.

"Yes, we come every fall," Mina said, wanting to add, or when we want to commit suicide. "And you?"

"Actually we should have left by now," Reggie said. "We're usually gone by Labor Day, but we stayed over for the Crab Festival. Do you go to the festival?"

Mina hadn't been to the Crab Festival in years. She and Prester used to go, long ago, when things were different. They almost dressed up one summer but decided against it at the last minute. People often dressed up for the festival, as 1930s beachgoers or crabs or even St. Brianna herself.

The history of the island started with a young woman named Brianna, whose family operated a lighthouse there in the early 1800s. Brianna was a true beauty and, had her family lived anywhere less remote or had she been less resolute in her devotion to both Morning and Evening Prayer, she would have caused a great many duels and broken hearts. One afternoon, Brianna was spearing grouper from a shallow sandbar when a pair of waves reached up and attempted to deflower her. Being a virgin daughter of Christ and not enthralled in any case by the idea of making love to the Gulf, she objected. The waves persisted, lunging at her with hard spears of saltwater. She dodged them and ran and cried out in anger. They persisted, and she cried out to God. The rejected waves, now spiteful, lifted Brianna in a bed of splashing foam, for her family and all witnesses, man and crustacean, to see, then slung her out a fathom into the Gulf. There she sank, unspoiled but helpless, to rot for weeks on a saltwater bed.

Crabs found her. They were a tribe of wandering crabs not even native to that part of the Gulf. Moved by her beauty, even as her body bloated and flaked at the edges, they could not consume her, and instead lifted her on their backs and hauled her carefully out from the waves. They came ashore during the well-attended beach wedding of Brianna's sister, who, upon seeing the green, rotted, but glorious body, immediately dropped to the sand and gave birth to seven sons. The church refused to beatify Brianna for this miracle, insisting that Brianna's sister must have entertained seven boyfriends in the weeks before the wedding, but that didn't stop the tribal crabs from recognizing Brianna's sainthood and becoming Anglicans. They established their own mission church and then an island parish, renaming it St. Brianna.

The festival carried the history forward, presenting reenactments of the wedding with an all-crab cast, parades, inflatables for the kids, stage shows, look-alike contests, and food vendors. The first few years the festival had been fun, but now Mina found it mostly obnoxious. Still, something about this couple's enthusiasm in the face of such a ridiculous tourist show made Mina smile.

"No," Mina said. "That's not in our plans this year. But it does look like fun, doesn't it?"

"We're doing it for the first time," May said. "Reggie's going to molt!"

The molting competition was something to see, even for Mina. Human males were genetically altered, only temporarily of course, to grow massive, dark red crab shells. Then, at the finale of the competition, each man would molt, his shell breaking off to reveal a soft blue underbody. The man who could give the most impressive display of either bravado or comedy won some sort of coupon for oil changes or a bucket of golf balls at the driving range.

The Gogs giggled, or pretended to, and Mina discovered that she hadn't laughed in a long time. She smiled.

THE BOAR HUNT,
C. 280 A.D.

T HE FIRST CHILD BORN OF Gjona-ja and Shali-ro was a girl, a little piglet of a thing with soft violet eyes and coos that felt like the warmth of a heavy fur in the dark night of a snowstorm. This meant little to Gjona, who was doing his best not to be angry. He felt betrayed, in fact. Tricked. What good was it to lay out his life before the elders and the tribe and this woman if he couldn't get a son from his tribulations?

Gjona wandered out away from the camp to nurse his anger. As he walked, he was followed by Tobo-da, the son of Ular, the same one Gjona had so nearly killed in a foolish boyhood prank. Tobo-da often followed Gjona on hunting parties, and he followed him now, whether out of curiosity or habit Gjona wasn't sure.

"Are you following me, boy?"

"Yes, old hunter."

"I'm not old," Gjona said.

"Still, I follow you," the boy replied.

They walked in silence for a while, the land shifting from sparsely wooded plain to thick forest, then to the hills and mountainsides of Karatau, and soon Gjona noticed the land growing clearer. The sun was coming up, and he turned to see Tobo stumbling behind him, half-asleep, his eyes all but closed.

"Boy," Gjona said firmly, knowing better than to yell in these wilds.

Tobo blinked hard and slapped his still sparsely bearded face awake.

Gjona reached out and grabbed his arm to silence him. He heard a rustle. Then the grunts of an adult boar, probably female, probably near her den at this mark of the sun. Any moment, the boar might notice them and charge. Gjona remembered the trick he'd played on Tobo-da's father and considered tossing Tobo forward and running back to the camp, ignoring the boy's screams. But the boy had followed him, and that was not a thing to be scorned. Gjona took note of the boy's club, the simple club of a scout, a wooden beam with a few brass studs pocked into the thick end. He traded him for his own, much sturdier weapon, which was wrapped in iron bands and varnished with once-sticky sap. He looked hard into the boy's eyes.

"I'll flush out the boar and run it toward you," he whispered. "Wait in silence. As the boar passes, swing hard at its legs. Not its head, its legs. Understand?"

"Yes." Gjona sensed fear in the boy, but there was none in his jaw or his arms. The boy backed into the nearby bushes, never taking his eyes off Gjona.

Gjona listened for the boar, heard another snort, then walked steadily toward it. The boar was further away than he thought, and more deaf than he expected. He began clearing his throat loudly, hoping now just to end the frustration of waiting.

"Boar!" he shouted at last. "Come to me!"

That did it. A scuttering of leaves came from his left, and a snorting breath. Gjona ran back the way he came, with the boar only a few paces behind him. He glanced to his side as he passed Tobo, who had the club cocked back for the swing. Gjona turned only after he heard the crunch of the boar's forelegs and the squeal of its pain.

He ran back to the scene. As the boy desperately tried and failed to crush the boar's skull with Gjona's club, Gjona pulled out his dagger and flashed it down the boar's hide, spilling its blood across the path.

The boy looked to Gjona in thrilled pride. Gjona smiled at him. Then, after the dying gasps of the boar faded away, they heard muffled squeals.

Together they abandoned the carcass and followed the sound to a den packed with half a dozen rooting boarlings, not more than a hand's length each. Gjona, using the same blade that dispatched the sow, stepped into the den and one by one grabbed each boarling by the hind legs and gutted it. Tobo followed his lead. Watching him, Gjona thought of how it would be to have a son: to have a boy follow him and do as he did, learning and growing in his image. Tobo would make a fine son, he thought, ripping his blade through a boarling's soft hide. When they were done, the den was a massacre of blood, flesh, and fur. Gjona considered whether to take their skins back to the encampment, but decided it was too much trouble. The great boar, though, Gjona and the boy dressed and carried off, and the tribe was much impressed by their trophy.

In the months that followed, Gjona taught his technique to old hunters and scouts alike, and hunting parties soon made it a priority to flush out and kill all the boars they could find, including the sows and boarlings. A generation later, wild boars no longer dwelt on the Kyrgyz Steppe.

It was a worthy distraction from the shame of siring yet another girl.

When next Shali was ready to make a child for Gjona, she urged him to consult the white salamander. Many of the young women of the tribe had been visiting Gjona's salamander in those days, seeking advice and consolation in their barrenness. The white seemed to be better at this sort of thing than salamanders from other families. Gjona would come home from a hunt or raid to find a half-dozen of them in his yurt, clamoring around the brazier. Upon his return, they silenced themselves and filed out, as if he had business to conduct with the salamander himself. He did not.

"I have no reason to speak with her," Gjona told Shali one day over a meal of oat gruel and butter. He scooped it up with a slice of cold bread.

"She may have something to say that you need to hear," Shali said. She looked at Gjona knowingly, as if pushing him toward a knowledge he was supposed to have already. It confused and therefore annoyed him.

"Am I a woman, that I should seek counsel from a salamander because you can't give me a son?" he shouted. "You seek the white's guidance."

"I have," Shali said.

They spoke of the salamander as if she weren't five paces away, shifting around in her ashes, absorbing their every word and more. Absorbing their meanings and thinkings before they meant or thought them. Gjona munched his crust, more loudly the more sandwiched he felt between this daughter of a disloyal know-it-all and the too-loyal know-it-all hanging from the uuks.

"What did she tell you, then?"

"She told me nothing. She asked for you."

Gjona sopped up the remaining bits of his meal and pretended to be checking the bowl for more. What did the salamander want with him? She was a scold, perpetually nagging him to do things that were not in his nature. He didn't necessarily think the white was wrong; he was just weary of the endless burdens she stacked on him. But the salamander could not be ignored forever.

"All right, then," Gjona said, standing up. He walked over

and stood before the brazier. The white leaned across the rim to meet his arrival. She ceremonially arched her back and lowered her head in honorgreetings. Gjona came nearer to the brazier, his heart clouded by resentment, and watched in annoyance as the white rose from her genuflection, fluttered her lids, and shimmied. Happiness at his presence exuded from her, filling the yurt with a warmth that made Gjona smile inside. He reached for some fresh coals and placed them around the edge of her brazier so they'd be warm by the time they reached her. She sent him graciousthanks and opened her mind to his need.

"I want a son."

Yes. You have daughters.

"I have one daughter."

You have many daughters. Daughters in pain.

Gjona set that aside. "So, will you not give me a son?"

You will have a son.

Gjona's face lit up with pride. "When?"

Soon. But not of mydoing. Be happy; be warm; be slowintime. Not all goodnesses are allgood. Not all badnesses are allbad. Wait-watch. Be slowintime. Take care.

Gjona bowed to the salamander and rushed to Shali, who was lying on the pallet feeding their daughter. An hour or more had passed, which was not unusual when consulting a salamander. He dropped down beside her and covered her face with excited kisses. "Soon, she said! She said we'll have a son soon!"

Shali laughed at his enthusiasm and put her daughter aside in a bundle of felt and fur. "Yes, husband. We'll have a son soon."

The salamander watched the couple over the edge of her brazier in patient contentment as their mating lifted into a fury, then slowed and became still. The woman then resumed nursing her daughter. The white pulled the newcoals down to meet the warmers and heaters. The master would not bring coals again for some time. Too much quickingness and angerheart. But he would see, and having heard her once, he would someday know.

When next Shali was heavy with child, the midwife administered her undivided attention. Shali was the only woman in need of her services anyway, with so many other women unable to give birth now. The few women who were lucky enough to carry a child were showered in attention and luxuries in hopes that whatever they'd done right might continue. The tribal elders noticed as well, marking the dwindling population of children with frowns and muttering.

Gjona's son came. Even before Gjona was let into the yurt or heard Shali's shouts of relief, he felt the waves of sympathetic happiness surge from the salamander. Gjona took the boy in his arms and would not let the midwife finish cleaning him. He sat on the floor, cradling the pink little thing, its insistent arms groping, its penis a small proud nub. This was proof, then, of his manhood and the destiny of his line. He would live on in children and grandchildren and grandchildren of grandchildren. Gjona bowed close to his son's ear and whispered, "You shall be a strong man, a great man, the envy of your people." His voice wavered, and a tear dropped from his face to plink upon the child's broad new chest. "And I shall love you and teach you and honor you till the day you place me under my stones." He covered the boy and held him close, rocking back and forth, shaking with joy.

After a time, the midwife returned and demanded that Gjona let the baby go back to his mother—he must be hungry now. Gjona brought the child in and laughed with Shali at the tears that had left clean streaks down his dust-cragged face. He placed the boy at her breast and laughed again as the child gulped loudly at his mother's milk. The boy opened his eyes, and they flashed a bright purple.

"What shall we name him?" Shali asked.

"Perhaps in honor of your father, Khali?" Gjona said. "Khala-ja. Yes, he would have liked that."

"Yes," Shali said. "He would have. It's sad he didn't live to see his grandson born."

Gjona rubbed his hand over the soft coolness of his son's head. "And neither will I," Gjona said.

"This one is not like the others. He will bring you grandchildren. Just look at him. This one will sire a whole clan of sons."

Gjona stared at the boy and thought of grandchildren. Then, slowly, he saw that he and Shali were talking of two different matters.

"What do you mean?" he asked.

"Just a mother's wish for her son."

"You mean that I should live long enough to know his children?"

"No, that's not what I meant. But won't you?"

He thought about it. "All my childhood friends are dead or dying. I may look young, but my time is surely coming. Having a son now is more than I hoped for. I beg the Great Salamander to allow me to raise him until he can carry a club and go into the hunt. But to live long enough, now, to see the sons of a babe—it's impossible."

Shali grew quiet. She stared down at Khala-ja and began to weep.

"What is it?"

"I do not want to be a widow, Gjona. I do not want to see you die."

He lay down beside her and stroked the hair from her face, and the tears from her eyes. "Shali, Shali. What did you expect? I look young, but I'm older now than your father was when he died. I can't have more than a dozen years left. We'll enjoy them together, but you can't hope for more than that."

"Don't tell me not to hope!" she said, looking at him hard. "I can always hope."

He smiled and allowed her that.

She held his face in her hands and kissed him and cried and stared into his eyes and kissed him again.

She was often like this, speaking of their love as something grand and important that made her talk of them being together beyond birth and beyond death, as if that meant anything. It was far more to her than mating and marriage, having children and sharing meals. Gjona didn't quite understand. Centuries later, Prester John would begin to, if only for a very short time.

They turned from one another to stare at their son.

"Shali," Gjona said. "What did you mean, 'This one is not like the others'?"

"Your other children. Your daughters."

"What daughters?"

"Gjona, I know of your daughters," she said with her eyes lowered in deference. "You are father to most of my friends. Everyone knows."

"Those? Those are not my daughters," Gjona said, scoffing. "Those are the offspring of my youth; I lay no claim to them."

"Nonetheless, they are your offspring, just as this one is. But I think this one will beget children."

Gjona felt the strings in his mind flutter and connect. This one will beget children. A story here of a barren girl; there another, from some weeks before; there another. And matching memories of those girls' mothers, wild and lonely, pawing at Gjona's loins behind closed curtains. So many daughters, and not one had borne a child.

"Barren?" Gjona said. "They are all barren?"

"Yes. Did you not know this?"

"No." He sat up in on the pallet and tried to count them all and account for their families. Shali did not have to count.

"The whole tribe knows this, and many old women's secrets with you have been revealed in the empty wombs of their daughters," she said with a tinge of a laugh. "It all happened long before we were joined, so I don't hold it against you. But no one has told you?"

Gjona collected images in his mind of longtime friends, gray now and hobbled, looking away from him in pain; of young women he felt no attachment to giving him bitter expressions for no reason he could understand. They all knew, and they thought he did as well.

"So, my son, he will be without children too?"

"No, Gjona," Shali said in words full of more faith than knowledge. "He is a boy. It will be different for him."

"Yes," Gjona said to her, though not believing it himself. "It will be different for him." His joy turned away, like an apple sweet on one side and rotted on the other, and he wished now for some way to carve out the core.

It was in this time that Gjona began to think. He would spend what he reckoned was only a morning (but others later insisted was several days or more) wandering the hillsides with a stick, striking the grass one way, then another, considering in his illiterate way what this meant: not to have grandchildren, nor great-grandchildren, nor any descendants past the first generation. Sometimes he would begin this thinking when wrestling with Khala-ja or teaching him to sharpen a blade. Almost at once, it seemed to him, Khala would fall asleep or be carried away. Lights would dim and flash, and voices would become low murmurs, sometimes punctuated by quick bursts of sound.

As the years wore on and Gjona's wanderings grew longer, more of his friends died, and then, at last, the chief. Soon, even the women who claimed to be his daughters showed streaks of gray in their hair. Like a long roll of precious silk billowing over a bed of red coals, the idea opened in Gjona's mind that his death should have come long ago. If he had not yet died, he began to wonder if he might die at all. Would he live through yet another generation? Another after that? What would he do with so many tomorrows? Tomorrow was not a boar to be slaughtered or a battle to be fought. Tomorrow was a seed one stares at with no idea what it might grow into. Gjona would as soon throw it away as spend his time nurturing it into discovery.

In thoughts such as these he'd ride into the foothills of Karatau and find company in the wonders that increasingly seemed to surround him. His horse took ill and collapsed under him. Gjona tried to tend its sickness but could only watch as the beast broke out in lesions that bubbled across its flesh, which withered on the bone in a fantastic show of nature's cruelty. Another time he stood watching as a branch sprouted leaves and buds, then popped out apples, first green, then swiftly turning to red like pale curtains dipped into thick dye. And just as quickly, the apples dropped to the ground and shrank into rot. Gjona turned from the spectacle of beauty and sighed. It was getting dark, he noted (not having noted before that it had been pitch dark and light again hundreds of times since he'd gone into the hills). It was time he got home.

The encampment was not where it was supposed to be. Only the outlines of the place remained in stunted circles of grass. When the tribe moved, they never ranged far from Lake Kumsuat, so Gjona began walking the rim. The horizon was a wheeling ring of rainbow and darkness, with brilliant lines arcing overhead where constellations should have been. In what seemed less than a day Gjona was on the northern edge of the lake, looking out across the

Kyrgyz Steppe. There was the encampment of yurts, only a mile or two to the east. Gjona cursed himself for not noticing it before.

He walked across the plain of yellowy scrub to the yurt he recognized as his own. He pulled back the flap and found a man inside, tending to Gjona's white salamander.

"Who are you?" Gjona demanded.

"The ghost returns!" The man put the white down and looked Gjona over as he brushed the ash from his hands.

Instinctively, Gjona hung his long-idle horse whip on its place beside the yesik, though he wondered if he should have kept it in his hand.

"Wait here a moment and I'll fetch Mama."

"Mama?"

"Yes, Father. I'll fetch her. Come, sit down."

Father? He looked at the man—a bearded man, hair brown like Gjona's, eyes a sparkling purple. "Khala-ja! Is that you?" Gjona stepped forward. "You've grown!"

"Yes, yes, Father. It's still me. Everything will be fine. You sit, and I'll fetch Mama. She's busy weaving but she'll want to see you."

"No, wait. Wait. Stay with me, Khala." Understanding returned to him, of other homecomings and other explanations. He had been gone too long, gotten distracted again, and now he had been gone for a season or more, perhaps years. "What were you doing?"

"Milking the white. She's been sour of late."

"Milking? Why are you doing the work of women and children?"

"It's not woman's work, or child's work. It's work that needs doing. The white is heavy with milk and my hands are idle, so I do what needs doing."

"Why aren't you away at war, or on a hunt?"

Khala smiled at him like a young scout smiles at a senile

fool, like Gjona had smiled at the tribal elders atop the rope with no ending in the yurt without walls. "The borders are safe now, thanks to you. There's no need for more boar hunters, thanks to Tobo-da's men. They have no scouts to teach and nothing better to do than hunt all year round for meat without enough mouths to consume it, or perhaps milk the salamanders."

Khala was much older now than Gjona could fathom. He was almost as old as Gjona looked. "So, you have no sons?"

"Nor daughters." Gjona could hear the bitterness in his voice, but Khala didn't linger on the matter and looked away to his duties. "Come here, old man," Khala said with enough good humor in his voice to keep Gjona from being insulted. "Let me show you this 'woman's work.' You may have need of knowing it once Mama and I are gone."

"Gone? Where are you going?"

Khala led his father to the milking table, and the salamander bowed at a respectful angle to Gjona, who returned the bow out of long decades of muscle memory. Khala gave him a pair of gloves—battered gloves of hide and wool, fraying at the edges and worn down from long use.

"With this arm, pick her up and hold her gently. No, like this."

Khala firmly but respectfully moved his father's arms into position, setting his hands and fingers in the right hold to keep the salamander at ease and produce the most milk from one effort.

"Ha! I remember this now from when I was a child. It's been a long time, though."

The white looked up at him and purred.

"Father," Khala said. "We would like you to stay this time."

"Stay?"

"Yes. Stay with us. Not wander off again to stand in the hills like a bearded rock. We want you here, with us."

"You have no need of me. There is plenty of food, as you say, and men so idle that they now draw their own milk. What, am I to be your milking woman?" Gjona chortled with laughter, spilling milk on the table and annoying the salamander.

"Careful, you might hurt her," Khala said, setting things right again. "I mean that we want you here with us, Mama and I."

Gjona looked at his son. The man was not a hunter, not a leader, at least not yet. He was milking salamanders, even! Nevertheless, Gjona felt pride in what he had wrought. This was a man who was sure of himself and free, strong of heart and brave in his words. He was a man Gjona wanted to know better.

In what seemed a fluttering of days, Shali died, then some of the daughters. All of them without children. The clan was getting smaller by the year. There were fewer mouths to feed but also fewer hands to feed them, and they often turned to Khala and Gjona to lead the hunts. The salamander had told Gjona to wait, to watch, to be slowintime. Once he thought he had done so, had been as patient as any man could be; now he wondered if that was true. Had he cursed the clan by not thinking before he acted, never thinking?

At last Gjona found himself once more cradling his son in his arms, only now Khala was withered and gray, his mouth gaping with sounds that might have been love or gratitude or the mere wanderings of a senile mind. Khala-ja's arms bent across his chest and shook with uselessness. When finally they stopped shaking and Khala's amethyst eyes went blank, Gjona curled down over his son's body, rocking back and forth on the floor of his yurt. In his grief he made a second vow to his son: Never again.

SATURDAY AFTERNOON: WHAT IT TAKES TO REMOVE SLATE MILDEW FROM THE INSIDE OF A DOOR JAMB

PRESTER'S BACK WAS IN NO condition to do this the right way, so he made sure there was plenty of lighter fluid. He hadn't seen his can of it around in so long that he wondered whether it had evaporated. Once, in the days when men still carried a Zippo and to smoke indoors was just falling out of favor, Prester and Mina had attended a party where a bored guest filled an ashtray with lighter fluid and set it on fire. This was on the coffee table in a living room, of course. They all turned to stare at the rising flames, including Prester, who, like most everyone else, was trapped in confusion over what to do. An attempt to blow it out might shoot liquid flame across the table and onto the carpet or, worse, onto a guest's lap. It occurred to Prester that the best course might be to let it burn. The fuel would be spent, and the flames would diminish into a cold black char with no damage to anyone or anything.

Amid the shouting and scrambling, Mina disappeared and came back with a glass Pyrex bowl, which she turned upside down and placed over the ashtray. Competence. Absolute purpose and beautiful competence. Mina smiled pertly and bowed as the guests applauded. The flames went out. So did the guests who had lit the blaze. Prester watched as they were dragged from the room, with

Mina following, yelling at everyone to leave the men alone. He listened to the cheer of the mob outside as the men were stripped, beaten, and made to carry one another home piggyback. Prester agreed with Mina—the punishment was too harsh.

Slate mildew, however, could not be smothered with a Pyrex bowl. There was a new spot on the door jamb and a new trail of lacy gray leading to the next, spots for every unfertilized egg that drifted, dejected, from Mina's body. Every year, the mildew got thicker and the door harder to open. Left unchecked it might enclose the door altogether, leaving Prester and Mina no way out, except perhaps through a window or extradimensional portal. This time, Prester would have to take action: He'd have to clean the door. He walked downstairs and rummaged in the shed between the concrete piers for the blowtorch and duct tape. This would need doing before Mina got home; there was no point making her feel worse. Sure, they were about to die, but he wanted things to be just right, and there was no need for a jag of depression and anguish to hang over their suicide. Ajax powder, mothballs, staple gun. Staple gun? Where had that floated in from?

"Stop it," Prester whispered. His shadow dropped its head and put the staple gun back where it was. It was supposed to be a joke.

The trick to scraping off slate mildew is to mix nonoxynol-9 with the lighter fluid. Prester had brought some with him for just this purpose and had been careful not to show Mina. He mixed everything in an old paint can and smeared the mixture onto the wood, smothering the mildew in a clear, greasy sludge. He went to the pantry for his blowtorch and a box of baking soda. Lighter. Where was a lighter? Prester rummaged in the scissors drawer and found only rotted ideas and paper clips. On the shelf above the washer were some barely worn sneakers and several jugs of detergent with a quarter-cup of liquid in the bottom of each, but no lighter.

"Ah," Prester said, and walked by the fireplace, grabbing a tall container of wooden matches he'd never used. The idea when he bought them was to have long nights at the fireside with Mina. Wine, maybe a hookah, then sex by light of the flames. But they never seemed to find the right moment.

By the time Prester got back, the nonoxynol-9/lighter fluid mix had dripped in globs down to the floor and was seeping into the carpet on one side and between planks on the other. For a moment Prester thought about just cleaning it all up and trying again next year, but then he remembered he'd be dead tomorrow, so that was no good. He laid the match container on the gas can and wiped up some of the excess near the floor with the front of his shirt. Prester took one of the matches and swiped it against the bottom of the container. Nothing. Must be old matches, he figured. On the fourth strike, the match lit, and he held it to the door jamb. The jamb lit up with a *foom* and a flash. The mildew curled and smoked and wisped as the flames neared the ceiling. Prester reached for the baking soda and realized it wasn't ready—it was a new box, unopened. He quickly ripped the top off, wasting just enough time for a bit of the ceiling to blacken, then tossed half the contents of the box across the door jamb. He shook more into the flames, and when the box was all but empty, the flames were gone. The mildew flaked now in a powdery ash. Prester blew the ash away, and when he was done, it was as though the mildew had never existed at all.

Prester was locking the metal shed doors when Mina came home, rolling down the pebble-and-shell driveway and onto the paved carport under the house. He walked around the corner to greet her and help unload the groceries, feeling awkward now, as if she'd caught him at something.

"How was Hell?"

"Not too bad," Mina said. "You needed toothpaste, right?"

"No, actually, but that's all right." Prester took the heaviest bags, more out of lasting habit than conscious deference.

She walked ahead of him up the long outdoor staircase. Reaching the top, Mina noticed how easily the door opened. She knew what the slate mildew meant, and she knew that even if he didn't clear it off only for her, Prester couldn't leave a stuck door behind. Not in a house that had once meant so much to them.

"Thanks, dear." She smiled. He hadn't seen her smile that way in months.

"You're in a better mood," he said, setting his bags on the countertop.

"Yes, actually. You're not going to believe who I met today."

"Who?"

"The neighbors across the street: May and Reggie Gog. Nice couple. They're normally gone by this time of year, but they stayed for the Crab Festival of all things. They're nice."

"Hnh."

"I invited them to dinner."

"What?"

"I know, I know," Mina said. "But we can do that after dinner, right?"

Prester put away the couscous and marshmallows, then crushed some of the rotted ideas when he shoved a box of salamander vitamins in the drawer. He was angry, but he wasn't sure whether this was worth the argument. "Mina, honey, how is that going to look? 'Gosh, it was nice to meet you. Thank you for coming. It's been a lovely evening, but now if you'll excuse us, we ought to be killing ourselves'?"

"What was I supposed to do, be rude?" Mina said.

"Well, it's not like you're ever going to see them again."

Mina nearly cracked the pickle jar shoving it onto the shelf. The pickles were still lucid, and they rolled toward her, frantic with worry they might be spilled out across the yawning stove below. "Let's just have this one nice dinner, enjoy some company for a change, then we can do it after they leave."

What he wanted to say was that he wanted dinner with her, alone. A quiet dinner, maybe a long talk about their life together, remembering times when they were happy, and then their death could be the passionate, perfect closure of a romantic evening. Instead, he'd have to endure small talk with some unknown couple, then rush through the suicide. Wait, this wouldn't work.

"Don't you think the police are going to find that suspicious?" Prester said.

"What?"

"The Gogs will be the last ones to see us."

"Oh."

"Yes, and then there could be an investigation and a trial and the Gogs could end up on death row in exchange for your 'one nice dinner.'"

Prester began collecting plastic bags and stuffing them violently into one another.

"Will you stop doing it that way?" Mina said.

"What way?"

"Putting the bags inside one another like that. It makes it impossible for me to get at them."

"We're going to be dead in less than eight hours! Will you please refrain from nagging me about grocery bags?" Prester looked around, newly aware of what they were doing. "Wait—why did you buy all this stuff?"

"I told you. We're having dinner tonight with the Gogs."

To hell with not fighting. To hell with the niceties and the deference and with trying to make this a gentle slipping away. He wanted to shout at her, curse her, and itemize the inconsistencies she'd introduced that would now lead to nothing but confusion and an upsetting of the plan. But then it came together—a new plan.

"Hunh," Prester said. "Maybe this can work." He absently tied the bags in loose knots so Mina could more easily pull them out. "We could kill ourselves before the Gogs get here. They'll arrive, find us dead, and call the police. That way you don't have to cancel our dinner plans, and the Gogs won't be accused of murder."

It was brilliant. Prester smiled.

Mina looked at him in horror. "Absolutely not!"

THROWING THE HORSE WHIP,
C. 500 A.D.

A FTER THE DEATH OF HIS wife and child, and as his barren daughters began to pass into darkness, Gjona spent years at a time wandering the foothills of Karatau, coming down to seek out the encampment as it suited him. The people became accustomed to his intermittent presence and unrelenting youth. He was what they might have called an anomaly, had there been such a word in their nonliterate tongue, a harmless anomaly that came down from the hills on occasion to milk salamanders and tell fantastic tales of fighting the ferocious tusked boar, which even now was fading into myth. A few generations after the death of Khala-ja, as the population of the tribe began to rebound from what they now called the barren season, Gjona decided it would be best to cut back on the time he spent wandering the hills. This was partly so his horses would not die of starvation or exposure before his return, and partly because he was finally getting used to the passage of time and how it was different for him. The people, in turn, understood now that he did not grow old, though he was older than anyone could remember—older even than the elders and certainly the chieftains.

As the tribal brothers became accustomed to him, even friendly with him, they egged Gjona on to make the challenge to become chieftain. In these days, leadership was determined by a careful balance of strength and popularity. Anyone could be toppled and replaced by a strong warrior, but a beloved leader could rally the people around him, making any attempt to oust him a move against the will of the people as a whole. Many of Gjona's friends over the years had made attempts at leadership and found themselves, in the slice of a blade across their necks, less than worthy.

Generation after generation of Gjona's friends pleaded with him to make his challenge for the chieftain's black yurt. The population was growing with renewed vigor, which meant they needed more food and more land. Gjona all but led the war parties in rolling over competing tribes, taking their currant stores and countless skeins of silk. But with time he became more reserved and began to lead from the middle, if not from the back. He began to see there was little point being blessed with long life if it's taken away at the point of an Aktobe spear. Most injuries didn't bother him long, but what of a crushed chest or severed head? And how long might he live if he played things more cautiously? Several more generations? A hundred? And what would he do with these long stretches of time, other than milking salamanders and wandering the hills?

Gjona set his mind to careful observation of the chieftains, one after another. A few inherited the black yurt from feeble, beloved old men, strong of mind, too respected and protected to be challenged in their final seasons. But most chieftains took the yurt by force. Gjona saw how they fought, their tricks and talents, from a hidden blade to a modest shift in balance. Finally, there came a generation of bold men who had no sooner popped up and bloomed from childhood than they persuaded Gjona he could have the black yurt with little more effort than it took to flay a deer. They prodded him, and, after another year of careful observation, he agreed.

Gjona had been watching this chieftain, Ishkin, and his family. He'd seen Ishkin as a child take blows to the head and arms with a grim laugh, and use his sword to nick and piece away bits of flesh from his opponents in long battles before finally growing weary of the game and slipping in for the kill (which, in fact, was the way he had risen to his current position). But this Ishkin, as a child, then even as a man, had fought back tears any time he was punched in the belly. His liver was weak. So Gjona, instead of a sword, selected his finest club, the one with iron bands just above the center of balance, and walked into the black yurt, the club in one hand, his horse whip in his teeth. In those days, when entering another man's yurt, hanging one's horse whip over a cord near the yesik was a sign of friendship. To enter with the whip between your teeth, as if you were fighting over a goat carcass in a game of kokboru, was something else altogether. Gjona took it one step further. Ishkin was sitting up on his pillows, smoking from a hookah, only half-attired in new silk and rabbit fur, as his young wife sang to him of green-feathered quail among the miyzam flowers. He looked up first in surprise, then in fear as Gjona took the whip from his mouth and threw it on the ground next to the hookah. The chieftain rose, and Gjona, rather than offering a ceremonial bow, offered instead a ceremonial turn of his back, then walked out into the middle of the camp.

The few who had seen Gjona with the whip in his teeth had spread the word, that what had been expected for decades—generations even—was about to take place: The salamander milker from the mountain was making his challenge.

In hushed commands, the chieftain ordered his women to get him dressed and armored in leather jerkins and brass bracers. Ishkin was surprised not so much by the challenge as by the challenger. Gjona was a fixture. No one knew when he'd been born or how old he might be. He had simply always been, like the earth or the oldest braziers or the river. To Ishkin it was as though the very soil of his youth had risen up against him.

Gjona stood in the clearing at the center of a widening circle, holding his black club with both hands, waiting for the chief. The ones who had encouraged him a year earlier jockeyed for positions in his line of sight and smiled at him and nodded. The only blank spot in the thick circle of spectators led directly to the closed ye-sik of Ishkin's yurt, and the eyes that weren't on Gjona were on that ornately decorated tapestry, which showed a raging boar far more fearsome than any even in Gjona's memory. It was midsummer, and the sun was hot, dripping lines of liquid yellow from the skies, the beads of it popping in searing bubbles on the skins of those too shortsighted to dress for the outing. Gjona wore a light, unbleached tunic and thick wool pants, but his leather girdle was wide and he wore his hard leather boots, suspecting he might have need of them if his club failed.

The tapestry yesik burst open, and Ishkin stormed out, carrying Gjona's whip in one hand and a sword in the other.

Gjona was concerned about the sword, but not offended. "You carry a weapon that wasn't challenged," he shouted to Ishkin.

"I owe you nothing," Ishkin replied. He threw the whip at Gjona's face, then rushed forward.

Gjona lifted his club to knock aside the whip, and Ishkin made his first cut an inch deep across Gjona's arm.

Gjona swung back to regain a safe distance, knowing he would have to finish things fast. He feinted twice more, to put the chieftain off his guard. Ishkin's blade struck hard on the club, but this club had been seasoned by years of blood, fire, and rain, and the young sword barely nicked its surface. Gjona then allowed Ishkin to swing and hit, making a cut on his forearm where no scar would stay. The chieftain sliced him again, then again. Gjona put considerable effort into making these three strikes appear deeper and more painful than they were. This made the chieftain hopeful, and hope is a fickle ally. So much like Rayka, laughing and jabbing carelessly, or like the boar, charging ahead in anger without thought.

Ishkin was now slashing and teasing in a game of overconfidence. Gjona was playing a different game. He pretended to stumble, making easy bait of his head, and the chieftain swung hard—too hard, leaving his torso exposed. Gjona had the strength of a wood-splitter and sunk all of it into the blow he landed in the chieftain's belly, right where the liver hid quaking in fear. He felt the crack of ribs as a plume of blood-spattered air burst from Ishkin's lungs. The chieftain dropped to the ground, heaving and whimpering.

Ishkin would have been dead within an hour, but this was a different time. Where Prester John might walk away, allowing that hour to do its work, Gjona-ja had no such patience. In one full-bodied blow of his iron-banded club, he crushed the skull of his predecessor.

Usually, when a new chieftain won his challenge, many of the people shouted from sheer excitement that something new was happening; another portion wept with happiness, comforted to have their kin atop the mountain; while a smaller handful ran for the hills, certain that the new chieftain would soon chop the heads off the old guard. But this—this was different. This man was more part of the earth than of the people. Gjona-ja was the old-man who would not die. And now, this piece of earth, this tree in the landscape, had stepped forward to lead. No one fled to the hills. No one cried with the happiness of coming riches. But they shouted, they screamed, they yelled to welcome a new era. This was no chieftain—this was a king.

Gjona panted and grinned, standing at the blank center of the crowd. No one was brave enough to step forward to pat him on the back or pick him up above their heads as was the custom; no one was familiar enough with him to offer congratulations—not even those who had encouraged him and now looked at him, sheepish below their cheers, more in fear than in pride. As Gjona began to understand, awakening to this new reality, he grew sober. He watched the blood of the chieftain flow out, thinking of another time, another boy whose blood was sucked into the dust. This death too would make a mark, in its way, a mark of leadership. And a mark of that depth would leave a scar that could never fade.

There were no raids of neighboring clans that winter, or even that spring. The tigers stayed in their forests, and the lake waters dared not leave their banks. They waited, held back by some change in the smell of the sky, and it came from Karatau, from the black yurt of Gjona-ja.

When the raids did resume, they were like the onrush of a great river held back by stones, with the loosening of one pebble setting off a flood. In the next winter, and the next, and so on for years to come, clouds of horses rolled over neighboring encampments, and those sent back tributes, offering whatever it took to make peace and join hands with Gjona-ja.

Early one spring a generation later, a man in orange silk came riding up from the south. His ten-strong guard carried spears with flat copper blades and held aloft shifting standards adorned by long golden dragons. There had been no envoys from foreign nations for as long as Gjona could remember, though he had heard of them in his travels. The consensus among the strands of gossip flying from yurt to yurt—strands so thick they obscured even the coming of the envoy—was that this had something to do with

Gjona's rise to power.

Gjona made sure the delegation was welcomed at the rarely used saray, well fed and comfortably housed. He would meet with them in the morning; for the time being he remained shut up in the black yurt, awaiting the arrival of a concubine. Gjona had given up having offspring—he would not allow that again—but not on the pleasures of women. He found some unexpected advantage in being more present in time, one of them being the ability to pull out at the last moment and spill his seed onto the sheets or on a garment or, even better, into a woman's mouth, and in recent months he found these pleasures far more plentiful and fine than they had ever been before.

He felt a tug in his heart, a familiar one but not welcome. He spoke without turning to the white salamander.

"What now?"

They come.

"Yes, they come," Gjona said with resigned curiosity. "Who are they?"

They come in seekingstealth and hidingmind.

"Are they dangerous?"

No. Not to you. Not to he whom they do not seek.

"Then why are you worried? Why are you pestering me?"

You must understand. You are not he whom they seek. You can never be. You must understand.

Gjona turned to look the salamander in the eye. It hurt, to make the white feel his anger, though the white never seemed to hesitate to hurt and anger Gjona. The white looked back, knowing the angerhurt, but not re-emanating the spearingpain. She only returned understandinglove and counsel. That made Gjona's anger all the more painful.

"I'll decide what I am and what I can be. Do you hear me?"

The returning sympathy of the white was too much. Gjona

stepped away from the hanging brazier and waited impatiently for
the concubine's arrival.

She came wrapped in a single uncut lion fur, the mane of it
curling under her soft brown neck. This was Bayan, the daughter
of Baytosk, who was slowly becoming one of Gjona's trusted men.
Sending his daughter to the black yurt was an unmasked effort to
solidify that trust, and it didn't take much effort on Bayan's part
to impress Gjona-ja. She turned and rolled down the yesik for the
night, then closed the inner doors.

"Lash them," Gjona said. Such security wasn't normally necessary, but with foreign visitors in the camp, Gjona couldn't be
foolhardy.

Bayan turned in a single motion that melted into her easy
footsteps, and the edges of the lion's pelt drifted apart. She came
closer to the fire, the lights of it illuminating shards of beauty. Under the pelt, which she now dropped to the floor, Bayan wore a
sheer white silk gown, cinched at the waist by a brass belt of three
large circular plates. The largest, in the center, showed two lovers
sharing from the same currant, their hands gently intermingled as
their mouths drifted toward the same bite. Bayan came closer to
Gjona, who was sitting at the center of the yurt before a smoldering fire, his own purple robes shifting with his growing interest in
Baytosk's offering. Bayan approached and cautiously stroked her
chief's chin, and neck, and chest, taking care to give pleasure but
not to overstep. Gjona dropped his head back in ecstasy. He hadn't
had a woman—fully—since Shali, and now he mused on the prospect. What would be the consequence? Another barren season;
would it be so bad? Would it be worth the pleasure?

As Gjona mulled this over, his mind dazed by the shivers
Bayan was causing to roil through his body, he came to the idea
that the will of a king is the will of the people, and if it can be the
will of the people, why can it not be the will of the body? The will

of the flesh? He would have the flesh, and command it by his will not to bear children. Like a stallion that never produces a colt, he could mate without mating, create seed that bore no fruit. It would take only an act of will. He grinned at the thought and looked down at the beautiful, adoring young woman. He lifted her up and tore away the silk, leaving it to hang over the edges of the brass girdle. She let out a shriek, half in fear and half in excitement, as Gjona chased her to the bed and threw her down upon it. He dove into her without pause, realizing all at once that Bayan was still a maiden but not caring one way or the other, and he had her fully, willing their mating to become all things except fruitful.

Exhausted, he collapsed onto the bed and drifted into sleep to the gentle sound of Bayan's excited attempts to quiet her breathing.

The next morning, Gjona woke to hear Bayan washing herself. She was quiet, but Gjona had had generations to study the vagaries of sound, and the sound of water trickling over a woman's loins, even so softly as this, was one he could never sleep through. When she had finished, she created a makeshift tunic for herself from the spare linens, then lingered near the bed.

"Yes, I am awake," Gjona said. "You may wash me now."

Gjona stood and allowed Bayan to wash him, but nothing more—his mind was opening now, and he wanted it steeled for the envoy's visit. He mustered in his mind all that he had been told of the south. The Silk Road, the Cyclopes, the mountains into which travelers climbed only to their death. These images told him nothing of politics or customs. He needed to know more, but there was no spy with feet fast enough to grant him that knowledge in the time he might be able to detain this visitor. Even as Bayan dressed him in fine breeches and layers upon layers of silken finery, Gjona felt naked before an oncoming crowd of questions and negotiation. He felt the pull from the hanging brazier, but he ignored it. Not now.

Gjona summoned into the black yurt his two closest allies, Baytosk and Chim-dur, to stand on either side of him. Baytosk was a powerful man—not in stature necessarily, though he had been a solid warrior in his youth, but in wealth and influence. He had accumulated through inheritance, dowry, and dealmaking a herd of three dozen horses. These he loaned out in exchange for the promise of this favor or that, or food, or finery. Baytosk was light-haired like his daughter and took no pains to conceal his riches. The other ally, Chim-dur, lacked such advantages but had long been eager to offer his advice to Gjona—advice born of foresight and intelligence, not of conniving and the pursuit of mutual advantage. He was slighter than Baytosk, and what little hair he had hung in shaggy gray strands beneath a simple brown and white kalpak that he never removed. He was generally unkempt, barely presentable enough to have a place inside the black yurt. Outside, warriors were stationed for the occasion, six on either side, with ceremonial clubs in their hands and sharp blades hidden in their belts. And before them were children, as many as the women could gather up, strewing miyzam petals and singing songs of sweet milk and rainbows. All others gathered around the passage to see what would become of the envoy.

"I hope our chieftain's night was pleasant?" Baytosk said.

"Yes, it was pleasant," Gjona said impatiently, trying to keep his focus on matters more important than the deflowering of Bayan. "What do you know of the envoy?"

"That he also had a pleasant night," Baytosk said, smiling.

"Ah," Gjona said. "Good, good. What do we know, other than that he enjoys a fine welcome from our tribe?"

"He's from the palace of Zhizhi, built on the Talas River by the Khitay, who have occupied the valley since the exile of the Baltay some generations ago," Chim-dur said. "The Silk Road is theirs, from Xi'an to Samarqand."

Baytosk interrupted. "They likely don't want their commerce disturbed by a rising power to the north. So they come to make treaties or issue a challenge. Or they wish to exact tribute from us, in salamanders or silk."

"It is said that the silk of the Khitay is spun from worms," Chim-dur said.

"Worms? From the earth?" Gjona said.

"From moth larvae. It's a crude silk that doesn't withstand fire."

"What good is that?" Gjona said. Neither Chim-dur nor Baytosk had an answer, but in the bewildered silence they felt a sense of pride flow out from the brazier.

"We won't give tribute, though we may send gifts," Gjona said. "We will make no treaty, though we may give some assurance of friendship. We will listen, and we will consider."

"Yes, lord," Baytosk said, drawing a sharp look from Chim-dur at the word "lord."

Gjona was taken aback as well, but he did not respond. Lord. He liked the sound of that.

"Send for the envoy," Gjona said.

The envoy came with eight of his guard following. He was a curious sight, with narrow eyes and long, plaited hair, straight, fine, and black as coal. This hair was obscured on top by a hat that fit tight against his head like a potter's cap, embroidered with gold strands in markings as alien to the people of Karatau as any other writing. The orange silk of his robes was familiar to them, though he wore it in a strange way, with billowing material bunched around his legs and waist—surely he was not so large—and sleeves designed for a man with arms three times as long. Some of the children giggled and whispered that he must be wearing his father's pajamas, and his father was a Cyclops. These were quickly chastened by older siblings who knew better than to laugh at such a ceremony.

As the envoy came down the path, his guards stepped to the sides and took places in between Gjona-ja's guards, which at first the old warriors found disconcerting. But as they reflected on it, they began to feel proud to stand shoulder to shoulder with foreign soldiers who wore such fine red-banded armor and whose strange helmets were inlaid with smooth ebony.

Baytosk met the envoy at the yesik and closed it behind them after they stepped inside.

The envoy stood at the threshold and gave a low bow, which Gjona only slightly returned. Then, with a startling flourish of his sleeve, he produced a golden rod with a hook on one end, made to look like a horse whip, and hung it on the cord by the yesik. Gjona smiled at the nicety of the symbol. The envoy stepped forward.

"Greetings to Gjona-ja of Karatau, from Lord Zhizhi Chuan, keeper of the Talas River valley, the Talas Alatau, and the Kyrgyz Alatau, and the road to Otmok Pass. May your days be plentiful and prosperous."

"Welcome, envoy of Zhizhi Chuan. May the milk of the Great Salamander flow freely in his lands."

Chim-dur's eyes went wide and he raised his head. Gjona caught the glance and paused in his salutations. He warily skipped the bit about the finery of her silk. "May his horses be swift and his fennis grow sweet."

The envoy appeared confused, but smiled at the intent behind the unfamiliar greeting. "I am Xua, messenger of my lord, come to confer with you on simple matters."

He turned his head to the brazier hanging on the opposite side of the central fire. The white was up on her front legs, peering at the guest and flicking her tongue.

"Ah! A salamander of the Kyrgyz Steppe. These are rare south of the Talas Alatau. May I approach it?"

Gjona wasn't sure he liked the idea. He would rather the white stay out of this, but there was no polite way to say no, now that the question was posed. He regretted not pulling down the silk curtains over her, so at least he could make some excuse of her being asleep. Even as he tried to concoct an excuse in his mind, he was impelled by waves of sudden hospitality.

"Certainly," he said.

Xua walked to the brazier with Baytosk close at his side. He leaned over as if to touch her; Baytosk gently put a hand on his arm to discourage that. Baytosk was ready, in fact, to tackle the envoy and risk his life to stop him touching the white, but for a man of Xua's experience in diplomacy, a simple touch sufficed. Xua stood in smiling silence, and Gjona recognized the respectful movements of the salamander as she greeted him in her way. He sensed the emanations of speech between them but could not feel what was being conveyed. When the envoy straightened up again, he was, to Gjona's relief, still in a convivial mood.

"Remarkable creature," he said.

Chim-dur frowned, out of Xua's sight, at the reference to a salamander as a "creature," but decided perhaps he'd correct the envoy in private rather than disrupt the discussion.

"Please sit," Gjona said, motioning to the designated pillow. The envoy took his place.

"On what matters do you come to Karatau?" Gjona was not yet learned in the subtle paths of diplomacy.

Xua smiled at the crudity of Gjona's approach but dared not bring it to his attention. "Lord Zhizhi bids me greet you in friendship and congratulate you on your command of this encampment and other outlying lands. He hears that your reach extends from the Karatau over the southern edge of the Steppe, covering lands where many nomads now travel only at your pleasure or in fear of your advance."

Xua paused as a nameless woman in white silk stepped out of

the shadows to offer him currant wine. He bowed to her in thanks, and Baytosk did the same, though he was unaccustomed to bowing to servants.

"My lord Zhizhi bids me assure you of a stable friend in Talas, who takes pride in your growing kingdom to the north. He bids me assure you of the strength of his armies, of his brigade of Cyclopes, his regiment of archers, his battalion of Quaabite swordmasters, and he offers you the peace of knowing that your southern border is secure."

Gjona's heart quickened. This was no assurance; this was a warning. This was an old warrior demonstrating to a scout that he could snap the youngling's neck with a turn of his fist.

Xua sipped his hot wine and looked patiently into Gjona's eyes.

Chim-dur jumped in to cover the lack of response from his chieftain. "My esteemed envoy, your assurance is of great comfort to us, as is the news of your lord's pride in our conquests to the north. By that, then, can we also be comforted to know that this pride would only grow with further conquests along our northern borders?"

"Speaking for my unworthy self," the envoy demurred, "but with some confidence that I might understand the will of my lord Zhizhi, I can say that news of further conquests to your northern borders would be to us nothing but pleasant tidings."

Gjona was glad to hear this, but felt sick at the thought that he was now being granted permission to hunt by a huntsman who had never set foot in his forest.

"I find that the clearest understanding is reached in the briefest of discussions," Gjona said, standing up.

The envoy rose with a look of surprise in his face. He glanced down to his currant wine, with some consternation that he would not be able to finish it.

"Is there more that your lord wishes to discuss?" Gjona asked.

"I suppose there is not," Xua said after an unexpected pause. "Only, may we remain here another day, to enjoy more of your fine hospitality and to rest our horses?"

Gjona smiled in easy welcome. "Of course, my friend Xua. You may stay a week if you like, and permit me to seat you at my table tonight."

"Yes, yes, this will be most agreeable." Xua turned uneasily, not accustomed to being rushed out of a room, and confused by the strange mix of hospitality and dismissal. "Only one more thing, if I may. My lord Zhizhi has heard for some years now of a boy of great renown—of unsurpassed strength and skill. We have been most eager to greet this boy but have been unable to locate him, and many years have passed since these tidings first reached us."

"Is this so? Who is this boy? Perhaps we have him here, playing ordo in the courtyard," Gjona said.

"His name is Manas." The envoy looked deeply into Gjona's grey eyes. "Manas, who was born clutching a black clot of blood, who made the sun and the moon to change places, who holds the stone that brings storms to the land."

Gjona was struck by the description, feeling some frustration that he hadn't heard it before and some jealousy that such a child could be born near his borders. "He sounds like a most worthy boy."

"Worthy, yes. Worthy of many things," Xua said.

"We shall discuss this further, then."

"Yes," Xua said, no longer able to comfortably linger. "My thanks Gjona-ja, Lord of Karatau." He bowed again, and while Chim-dur and Baytosk returned the honorific, Gjona did not. He smiled at the envoy, who took his golden horse whip and, bowing again, backed out of the black yurt, with Baytosk as his escort.

Gjona stared at the yesik as it dropped shut. "Chim-dur, do you know a boy named Manas?"

"No."

"Has there ever been a man of this tribe, or a family, named Manas?"

"No, not that I recall. The Manas he speaks of, it's a legend of the people around Talas, told in song. That a boy would be born who could replace the sun with the moon and moon with the sun, who was born standing on his feet with a black clot of blood in his hand, who could unite all of the people to stand against the Khitay."

"I see," Gjona said, staring at the still-wavering fringe at the bottom of the yesik.

"But I'm told that this legend of his birth has been sung for hundreds of years, and the song grows with each singing," Chim-dur said. "Had Manas been born, he would be dead now. Many times over."

Chim-dur waited on Gjona, who continued to stare in silence. His gaze drifted to the tapestry on the next kerege: the tapestry of the world. It showed the Great Salamander, stretched across the top of the lands. From her teats flowed four rivers, one of them the Talas, across mountains and plains and into wide white seas. The flow of the Talas was but one, and the other three were unnamed, except in myth. The mountains were unknown, the plains untrod. The tapestry itself had been woven generations ago and gifted to Karatau by some other envoy from some other tribe where the salamander was known and revered. It was not from the Khitay.

"Don't tell the envoy."

"Sir?"

"Don't tell the envoy that there is no Manas here. But don't tell him that there is, either. Tell him nothing."

"What do you propose?"

"Nothing yet, not until I know more, until I have a better sight on the horizon and the hunt. But I do think it might serve me well to be Manas."

SATURDAY AFTERNOON DRIFTING INTO EVENING: CORRESPONDENCE

THE DOOR SLAMMED AS MINA walked out, leaving Prester holding his loosely tied bag of bags. The door didn't stick this time, Prester thought proudly, but he placed the bags on the counter and sighed, running his hand through the bristly cowlicks that traversed his hair, wondering how he'd get her to come around and stop acting a fool. With the specific intent of forging ahead, Prester began preparations for the suicide, which was going on as scheduled that night, Gogs or no Gogs, whether Mina damn well liked it or not.

He opened and unfolded the shower curtain and draped it over the sofa. They would have to do the shooting there—no need to leave a big mess—and they'd use their old sofa instead of the new one, just in case a bullet went through the back of a skull and the curtain. But that shouldn't happen, because he'd made sure to get the bulletproof shower curtain and not that cheap plastic kind with rubber eyelets. Most women would appreciate his thoughtfulness in this regard, the careful attention to detail he'd honed over 1,800 years of experience, Prester told himself, but Mina likely wouldn't notice. She never looked for the details, only the motives—always digging for what-he-meant-by-that, when all he ever really meant was to get the details right. Because details matter.

Prester would shoot Mina first, then himself. When they came to this decision months earlier, Prester kindly offered that Mina could do the shooting; or they could each shoot themselves, taking turns, and Mina could go first or last. But she said she didn't want to touch the gun (she'd never liked them, always thought they were too dangerous). And that was just as well, because otherwise Prester would have to teach her how to use the thing, and that would be a nightmare.

Why did she have to make this so damn complicated, Prester asked himself, carefully placing candlesticks on the card table. He wanted to slam them down but didn't, because they might break. Inviting company. Buying groceries. Ruining their last night together. Now the investigators would think they weren't planning this, and that one or the other was a true murderer. Now he'd have to explain it all in a suicide letter, which is what Prester had been trying to avoid. He hated letters. They had a way of committing a man to something he could never back out of. And then it would be your name attached to a promise—a name that could never be cleared if something went sideways.

Prester thought it out for a while, pacing slowly in the living room. There was no way around it. He hunted for a pen and paper and came across the chicken left to brine in a pot full of salt water. Dinner for the Gogs. There would be no dinner for any damn Gogs, he told himself. He took the chicken out of the pot, dried it off, and put it in the freezer. There was a pen in the scissors drawer and there was paper next to the salamander pyrorium (Mina kept a record of the mottled gray's forced belch times). Prester sat for about half an hour, staring out the window at the swirling hydrogen ribbons in the sky, before he could think of a way to begin. Who would find the note? The Gogs? They wouldn't read it, surely. The police? Of course, the police.

Dear officers,

My name (that is, I, the deceased male) is (for all present purposes) Prester John, and beside me is my late wife, Mina Deitasy John. No doubt you would like to identify the decedents (that is, us), determine cause of death, assign motive, and close the case with the utmost speed. With the first issue addressed, I can save you some time by pointing out the bullet wounds to our skulls. You can find the bullets therein or on the shower curtain. As for motive, I have lost my job, my reputation, and the passion of my wife, after an unfortuanate incident involving my shadow. My hope is that you will find my shadow attached to my feet, and my further hope is that it is as deceased as I am. If it is not, please shoot it or imprison it or whatever it is you do with these things. My wife, I'm afraid, is (that is, was) dying of psychomorphic equilibrium disorder and has no wish to spend her remaining years adrift with some low-density cold front, as is the fate of many fellow PED sufferers. We have decided it best for all parties to end our lives quietly and with as little burden on the rest of the world as possible.

Your only remaining concern should be the involvement of Mr. and Mrs. Gog, whom I have not met while still alive, but whom my wife regrettably invited to dinner tonight. Please express to them our sincere apologies. In recompense for the trouble we've caused, we'd like them to take home the chicken in the freezer, along with any other groceries they might like. The Gogs had nothing to do with our deaths (assuming nothing unforeseen has happened), except in that we stumbled upon a convenient way in which someone (that is, the Gogs) might alert you to our bodies before any undue decomposition sets in. You may bury us where you like, as we have no remaining family or friends. You may notify our creditors in Kensington, Georgia, that they are welcome to my car and my wife's funds, stored in Cotiers Bank in Antananarivo, Madagascar, account #520673.

Yours,

Prester John and _____

That would be nice, Prester told himself, and left it out with a pen on the coffee table so he wouldn't forget to have Mina sign it.

Outside the beach house, under the late afternoon haze, the waves played a game of plummet and spike. A particularly boisterous one whirlpooled to the seabed to snatch up a young crab, which it yanked through forty feet of seawater and sling-shot screaming into the air.

Seventy feet up, the crab lost consciousness and fell back to the waves, which now rippled with laughter.

Mina walked a half-mile along the beach, shoving her ankles hard into the sand, before she calmed down enough to slap her newspaper on a table under an empty public umbrella and sit. She was livid. He always had to be like this, the bastard. He couldn't shift his plans for just one night, to have a nice dinner with a new couple. The Gogs would be mortified.

She lay back on the chair and tried to read her paper. The asshole. She wanted to get to the sudoku—that would clear her mind—but she flipped through the headlines first. Something about plans for a local adequate-facilities tax. Another person on trial for murder using the "shadow defense." That sounded familiar, Mina huffed. Then something about a large eagle spotted over Rhodesia. The article said a group of rail workers on lunch break heard an echoing cry and looked up to see an eagle the size of a house flying overhead. "We couldn't believe it," said Maribu Ntognan, age 152, a ferrous-mining engineer. "We ran to the work shed to get a gun or a camera or something, but when we came back, it was gone." Local experts disputed the reports, saying Inyani workers often consumed hallucinogenic Nutter Butters on lunch break, and reports of mythical beasts were often the result.

All seven workers were detained for questioning.

A giant eagle? It was obviously a roc, Mina told herself, just like the one she owned as a child. No eagle could grow to be the size of a house, and if anyone had taken the time to interview the witnesses properly, they'd have been told of the blue pin feathers, the five-taloned legs, and the tinge of orange in the eyes.

Daniel Rostica was the reporter. Mina, already fuming from bickering with Prester, dug in her purse for a pen and wrote a note in the margins: "Don't you know a roc when you hear of one? — Mina John."

She waited a few minutes and stared angrily at the sea looping and surging toward her, waves flying over her head and pulling back into themselves. They knew better than to douse the beach-goers, but often splashed playfully within inches of a little girl's ponytail or punched out suddenly toward an old man's crotch. Mina found it relaxing, and gradually her anger ebbed. The doctors, Prester, and now this idiot reporter, they seemed in league to make her crazy with frustration. All of them jumping forward with presumptions of knowledge and solutions to all problems, babbling like ghosts trapped in an illusion of life.

A response formed on the margin atop Mina's as hers faded into the background. "Thank you for your interest in reading the Tallahassee Federalist. We've received many comments on this report, and we regret our failure to acknowledge the similarity between the animal allegedly sighted and the mythical roc. Please be assured any follow-up reports will acknowledge the similarity. Thank you, Daniel Rostica."

Mina wrote back before the response could fade out. "The roc is not a mythical beast."

The response was immediate. "Thank you for your interest in reading the Tallahassee Federalist. We've received many comments on this response, and we regret that some readers object to our characterization of the roc as mythical. Please be assured that any follow-up responses will refer to the roc as 'allegedly mythical.' Thank you, Daniel Rostica."

These men—all of them the same. She'd be trapped in a forever of silence, watching as they twirled about with wooden swords and blanket-capes, pretending to be something more. She felt the numb fading of the hairs on her arm as her body took another step toward insubstantiality. No, not this time. She wanted this one to see. She flipped to the feedback directory on Page 2 and wrote in the margin next to Daniel Rostica's name, "Hello. Can I ask you a couple of questions about that great article you wrote this week?"

A few moments later he responded. "Sorry. I was on the phone. Which article?"

"The one about the roc."

"Yeah, thanks. I've received several comments on that article and I promise that next time . . ."

Mina scrawled over his response before he could finish. "I know you think I'm crazy, but I used to own a roc when I was a girl . . ."

Daniel didn't let her finish either. "You're that Mina chick, right? Don't you bird nuts have anything better to do than harass the shit out of people trying to do their jobs? I have five stories to work on, eight calls I have to return before 6 p.m., and an editor who's ready to put me on a PIP because I can't get any fucking work done because of your bored ass spending all day writing on the newspaper! Go volunteer at a flamingo shelter or something."

Mina replied, "His name was Urtyylk."

Daniel waited a while to respond. "Okay, fine. Tell me about Urtyk."

"Urtyylk. I raised him from a fledgling. When we bought him from the hatchery he was all fuzz and beak, about the size of an adult penguin." Mina wrote to the edge of the page, then started back at the beginning, chasing her earlier words as they faded ahead of new script. "They banded his beak shut, but we cut the band at once and he never bit me. He made this noise, kind of an alto squeak, when he was hungry. I fed him live fish from our pond and afterwards he'd waddle to me and climb up on my chest. He'd wrap his neck around to the back of mine and try to sleep there, and sometimes I'd let him. His molting fuzz smelled like perfume, but rich and musky. I'd breathe deep and feel his heartbeat on mine, pounding out rapidly and finally easing off to match my own. Later, when he was bigger, as we'd fly over cliffs and climb sea waves and drop into rocky green valleys, I'd remember that downy hatchling wrapped around my chest. He was real—very real."

Mina drifted. The waves rose and leapt, over her head and around her body, playfully trying to get a scare out of her. But she was somewhere else, somewhere high and soaring, her eyes closed against the glare of the sun off a closing wall of clouds.

Urtyylk had let Mina ride him early, long before she'd finished her six months of formal lessons. He'd only been flying a few months himself. Mina was up on his back, cleaning his collar. He seemed as surprised as she was when he hopped out of the barn, trying to escape the swabbing brush. As he did, he lifted briefly off the ground and seemed to suddenly realize how easy it would be to carry her. Urtyylk hopped again, flapping a few times to see if Mina fell. She was terrified—no harness, no stirrups—but she didn't order him to stop. Instead, she grabbed tight to his collar and dug in with her heels. She was so giddy, so gloriously happy. Fear that she might fall off was the only thing that kept her from dripping away into a slick mess atop Urtyylk's back.

Two hours later, a child walking by on the beach poked Mina with a stick.

"Lady? Hey lady, are you dead?"

"Hm?"

"Are you dead?"

Mina blinked and heard again the roar of the waves. It was darker now—one side of the sky deep blue and the other fading into brilliant reds and purples. "No. No, I'm not."

"Oh. Were you sleeping?"

Mina smiled. "I was flying."

"Why are you dripping?"

Mina stopped. She swiped at a wet bead dripping down her neck. Yellow.

She jumped up and dabbed at the melt, trying to staunch it but realizing it was too hot and had gotten too far. She started walking, anything to change her emotions, and the child called after her, "Are you crying yellow?"

Angry. She must get angry. That was the only way to stop it, she told herself. She was clutching the newspaper. Whatever response Daniel Rostica made had long since faded.

She scrawled barely legible words next to his name as she kept walking. "You don't believe me because you're afraid. You like to pretend that what the workers saw was something normal like a phoenix or whooping crane, but you know in your gut what those men saw was a roc. You know that records of the roc were wiped out after the government culling began. That's the story you should write. Coward."

The "coward" part didn't help her point, she knew, but it helped her get angry, and every bit would help.

Mina folded the newspaper and went quickly back to the house, taking short, harsh breaths and trying to forget.

As she walked, the sky darkened and the waves calmed. It began to rain—a damp, thick rain, the kind that could capture words as they flailed in the air between speech and hearing and crash them to the ground with an unsettling thud.

Mina rushed up the rain-slickened steps. The whole afternoon had passed, and the Gogs would arrive in half an hour. She struggled to hope that Prester had snapped out of his stubbornness and had the actual foresight to make dinner.

The house was dark except for a flicker of candles by the plastic-curtained couch. Surely, Mina thought, surely he started dinner. She saw the note on the coffee table and the gun lying next to it. It occurred to her that Prester might be dead. No, she told herself. He couldn't be dead. Prester John would never kill himself and leave candles burning. She walked to the table and picked up the gun. It was cold, which was a good sign. She'd never held a gun before. It was heavy, and too big for her hand. She picked up Prester's note.

Typical Prester, she thought, covering all his bases. Then she got to a line she didn't expect. "I have lost the passion of my wife." What the hell did he mean by that?

Mina sat on the couch. It crinkled with the pull of plastic over stitched denim. What did that mean, that he'd lost the passion of his wife? When had she stopped being passionate? She was passionate, at least as much as anyone else. No less so, at any rate. She rolled it around in her mind until answers no longer came, only angry rebuttals that swelled up inside her, about how passion should be earned, and love has to be given freely, and how can she feel passion when she's going to die a cold death, and since when does passion have anything to do with sex anyway? Then she read the part about the chicken in the freezer—dinner was nowhere close to being ready—and the end of the letter: "Yours, Prester John and . . ."

The pearls of melt congealed and sucked back into her body, leaving her cold but whole. She felt her arm again completely: the hairs, the skin, the muscles cooling and tightening down her arm, her hand, and her index finger, tight now on the trigger of the gun.

"Prester!"

She walked through the dark house, turning on lights along the way in the living room and hall (the salamanders blinked in confusion) and bedroom, then jumped with surprise when she saw, through the window, Prester pop up on the other side of a chair on the deck, backlit by murmurs of lightning.

"There you are!" Prester shouted.

She slid the heavy glass door open. "You! You bastard! You uncaring, self-obsessed bastard!"

The anger in her words stained the falling rain red. It dropped to their feet like congealing blood.

"Are you still throwing a fit?" he asked, no longer trying to hide his frustration.

"What are you doing out here?"

"I'm trying to enjoy the last few minutes of my life," Prester said, "but those minutes keep growing. I've been waiting more than two hours for you to finish your tantrum so we can kill ourselves. Where have you been?"

Prester's words came out an icy blue, turning the shafts of rain to cold sleet.

"I fell asleep," Mina said.

"You fell asleep?"

"Yes, I fell asleep. Or something. I don't know. Stop asking me questions!" she shouted, waving the gun at him.

Prester hadn't noticed the gun. Fear stabbed his body, along with the urge (conditioned into him since the invention of small firearms) to dive out, jab the tendon above her armpit, take the weapon, and kill her. Or jump backward and propel himself off the porch rail to the carport below. Or calmly say, "Honey, put down the gun." But then it occurred to him that he was about to kill himself anyway, so really, there was nothing to worry about.

"Are you going to shoot me?" he asked.

Mina looked to the gun in her hand. She dropped it.

"Mina!" Prester shouted, but the gun hit the floor without going off. "Goddamnit! Are you trying to break it?" He picked up the gun like a wounded kitten, checking it for signs of damage, brushing sand off the sides.

"Prester, the Gogs are going to be here in less than thirty minutes."

"Then you better hope the gun's not jammed, because if it is, it'll take at least half an hour for me to clean it properly, then we'll have to kill each other after they arrive." He wasn't serious—he'd never do that to strangers—but he was trying to make a point about her carelessness.

"You wouldn't dare!" she said.

Prester thought of all the people he'd killed, in duels, in wars, perhaps in cold blood, and he laughed.

She hated that, his little inside jokes. "It's not funny. You can't do that."

"Why not? Who are these Gogs to you anyway? Why are they suddenly more important than us?"

"They're not, but why are you in such a rush?"

"Because we had a plan, we had a schedule," Prester said. "We had committed to this. Tonight."

"Well, I don't think we should kill ourselves solely because you had it marked on your calendar for the evening."

"You know that's not what this is."

"Do I? Is this your decision or our decision?"

"Of course it's our decision." Prester looked at her, and a pair of misted glass doors creaked slowly open in his mind. "You don't want to do this, do you?"

"No," she said, sitting down. "I don't know."

"No, you don't want to do this, or no, you don't not want to do this?"

"I said," Mina repeated, the words drifting like snow from her mouth, "I don't know."

Prester crossed his arms and scratched an itch on his forehead with the barrel of the gun.

"When I talked to the Gogs today," Mina continued. "I don't know, they were someone new, someone who didn't know about what happened . . . before . . . and we were just chatting, and Reggie said something stupid, and I laughed. And I realized I hadn't really laughed since . . . the incident? No, since my diagnosis. And I felt good, and then I made plans for dinner, and it felt really good to be planning something fun, with somebody who didn't have anything to do with that . . . that cloud."

Prester tried to speak calmly. "So. You think having dinner with these people will (a) cure your PED, (b) restore our careers and reputation, and (c) revive our marriage."

"What do you mean 'revive our marriage'? And what did you mean in that note about losing the passion of your wife? What the hell, Prester?"

"You think everything's been good for the last couple of years?" Prester said.

"No, maybe not, but . . ."

"When was the last time we had sex? When was the last time . . ." he was going to say "you even kissed me," but the words wouldn't emerge from his throat.

Mina dropped her head into her hands. How was this suddenly about sex? After a while she looked out at the beach. It was dark behind thick rain. Turtles were lined up with flashlights escorting the newly born back into the waves, the waves obnoxiously teasing, then peeling away again with laughter.

"Prester, I'm tired."

He looked at her and sighed. Once in a moon she'd open herself to him like this and say things that had truth in them. He couldn't stay mad when she was like this, and it half-hurt, half-thrilled him to feel connected again, to feel that he was necessary and wanted.

"I know, honey." He sat beside her on the long chair and put his arm around her. "It'll be over soon, all this fear and pain. It'll be over. I'll take care of it for you."

Mina looked at him, amazed. "That is not what I was talking about!" She stood up. "God, Prester! I mean that I'm tired of arguing with you! I'm tired of arguing, and I'm tired of you assuming you know what I'm thinking all the time! Talking to the Gogs today . . . I've been living in a fog for almost a year. No, I don't know how to fix it, but does that mean there's no other solution?"

"So now you don't want us to kill ourselves?"

"No, damn it, no. I don't think I do," Mina said.

"That's the whole reason we're here!" Prester stood. "We've been planning this for months—you can't change your mind now!"

His words became shot through with yellow, splashing Mina with a sickly stain.

"Yes, Prester, yes I can, and I have," Mina said, lowering her voice, almost laughing as she talked. "I don't want to kill myself; I want to have a nice dinner with the Gogs, and maybe in some crazy fantasy of some alternate-universe Prester John, maybe sit down with you tomorrow and have a long talk about whether this whole thing is such a good idea."

"No!" Prester started pacing, charging at her and pointing on every other pass. "This was planned! We talked about this again and again. The house is sold, my job is gone. This life is over. The decision has been made, Mina! I've covered the couch, even written a damn suicide note to keep your precious Gogs from going to jail for murder. You and I are going to kill ourselves exactly as planned!"

"Fine! Do it, Prester!" She stood up. "Blow my fucking brains out right now on the porch if that's what you want!"

He raised the gun to her face, just above the point between her eyes—teeth gritted, blood pulsing in his temples, ready to pull the trigger. He shook the gun up and down a few times and pointed it firmly at her again.

"Can't do it, can you?" Mina laughed. "I should have known. All this time, all the things you've said you'd do or been expected to do or wanted to do that you couldn't, and now you can't do this either."

Prester knew she couldn't see his face clearly behind the rain dripping down his cheeks, couldn't hear the falter in his voice. "When I kill you," he said, "I don't want it to be because I'm mad at you. I want it to be because I love you."

He dropped the gun on the cushioned chair. From the rail he looked down at the stone drive, bits of rock splashed with the reflected colors of the moon. His lip quivered; that was unexpected. He fought it back under control.

Mina stood next to the cushions and the gun, unmoving, throwing the words around in her mind.

The doorbell rang.

THAT WHICH IS NOT MANAS,
C. 520-527 A.D.

I N THOSE DAYS, PRIOR TO the system of pulleys and mo-
tors that makes the current Silk Pipeline possible, there was
the Silk Road. Spread out at intervals of about six feet—close
enough that they could talk to one another but far enough apart
to make the system practical—a line of slaves and peasant workers
passed skeins of silk hand over hand from Xi'an through western
Khitay, into the mountains, through Talas, Samarqand, and Persia, then to Constantinople, where it was considered too logistical-
ly difficult for the human chain to continue, and the skeins were
disassembled and folded for trade with the West.

In exchange for this silk, goods were conveyed in the other
direction as well. For a time, there were attempts to get the workers to toss goods to one another back up the road, but after several
mishaps involving gunpowder, porcelains, and child prostitutes, it
was decided that any goods moving in the other direction would
have to be transported by cart. This gave the added advantage that
the Silkies, as the human conveyers came to be called, could be fed
in the process, as part of the commercial arrangement. A feeder
was assigned to each cart, and his job was to toss a loaf of bread
or a water skin at the foot of each Silkie, of course without stopping the cart. Mishaps in this system were rare and were quickly

brought to the attention of the Silkies' communication network, wherein messages of alarm would be shouted down the line far faster than any marauder could stop them. These messages could easily be mangled over the course of their multiple iterations, however, so within a few years the Silk Road conveyors developed some clear words of notification, the primary ones being: "hooker" (the skein has broken up the line and a piece is moving down with steel hooks connecting the broken ends together), "dropout" (a Silkie has fallen out dead or dying and a replacement is needed), "mother" (someone has attacked one of the Silkies and military assistance is needed), and "bite me" (food is needed on the line). So while many messages could go up and down the line, some of them being twisted in the retelling —from rumors of war and state secrets to recipes and sciapod jokes—a yell of "Hooker!" or "Bite me!" would fly immediately up or down the line, bypassing all other conversation. One estimate gave the network only two days to get word of a dead Silkie from the Otmok Pass to Constantinople.

As simple as it sounds today, establishing this system was difficult in the early days. There were plenty of slaves to be had for the line, and pulling silk hand over hand is a much preferable assignment to, say, being servant to a liturgist or cleaning out sewage carts. The difficulty came in clearing the path of predatory beasts and hostile half-breeds, in particular the sciapods. In these days, sciapods hadn't yet acclimated to the presence of man. As likely as not, on any sunny day, a sciapod could be found lounging on his back with his single foot propped over his body for shade, never minding that his bare and unbifurcated ass was exposed to half the world. On a sunny day, a traveler might find a dozen or more of them, foot in the air and ass-forward, scattered over a field doing nothing more than drying the rotted pits between their toes. These sunny-day revelries were interrupted by the arrival of the Silkies in the mountains of the Kyrgyz Alatau, where the sciapods lived, and the creatures scoffed at all attempts to bring them into the line. After a few attempts at reasonable exchange with a race to whom reason seemed as alien as two-legged pants, the Khitay organized a band of Cyclopes to do the job for them. The sciapods' main method of attack, stomping their enemies flat, was of no use against giants three times their height. The Cyclopes, by contrast, enjoyed picking up what to them were harmless curiosities and, in dumb fascination, trying to turn their single legs into two. It was a gruesome sight, for the Khitay and the sciapods alike, and the horror of it was enough to drive the sciapods north into the desert of the Kyrgyz Steppe, where over the years they dug encampments into the ground, making a sort of inverted Kyrgyz Alatau for themselves. This sciapod stronghold was the only region of the lower Steppe that never became part of the Karatau kingdom.

Many years passed before the late summer when the sciapods of the Steppe were first taught to pronounce the name of Gjona-ja.

The season brought cool breezes off the river by nightfall, along with the sounds of restless waves, enjoying their remaining weeks of frenzy. Soon the chill of night would make them sluggish and slow, too slow to lash out beyond the banks, too slow to spike high into the air. Then would come the freeze and the long stillness of dead, blue winter.

Bayan's lion-fur cloak, more matted now than the last time she visited the black yurt, flipped open in this light wind to reveal the white silk of her garments. Her father had sent her, just as before, only this time as a woman, learned and strong, not as a child being thrown into womanhood. Her instructions were to make the most of an opportunity to forever tie the future of Baytosk's family to the fortunes of Gjona-ja. She knew better how to accomplish this than she had ten years earlier, and that it took more than gentle hands and compliant thighs.

Bayan pulled back the yesik and found the inner doors already open. She let her robe drift open and stood, awaiting Gjona-ja's notice. The king was lying on his bed, with only a linen draped over his loins, scratching with a gold-handled dagger on a platter of soft wood. The room was dark, with more of it in shadow than should have been considering the blazing fire at the center of the yurt. Gjona didn't look up, but it was clear to Bayan that he couldn't have failed to notice her arrival. She closed the inner doors.

"Don't lash them," Gjona said, without stopping his work. "More are coming."

Bayan turned. "More?" At first she spoke with surprise, but then moved closer to him, her robe open, giving tease and seduction to her voice: "I am sorry, my lord, but I am not dressed for company."

Gjona glanced at her attire. "Yes, you are."

Bayan pulled her robe closed and moved slowly toward the table. This wasn't the way it was supposed to be, at least not the way she had been led to believe. Was this to be a competition between herself and other women of her standing? On the table were the half-eaten remains of dinner, and she recognized the menu of quail, chatma, and peppers as the one she'd enjoyed only an hour before. It must have been provided by the house of Baytosk for just this occasion. She passed the hanging brazier of the salamander, who bowed respectfully, and she felt a sense of comfort—sympathywelcome—though certainly not from the occupant of the bed. Gjona was ignoring her, continuing to scratch on the platter, the shavings of which were scattered over his chest.

"My lord, I came here to be of service to you. If you don't have need of my service, I don't wish to be in the way."

"In the way of what? Leave me be for a moment to think, and the others will arrive soon enough."

What others? Bayan was torn between fear and annoyance. She was no maiden, Gjona had seen to that, but she had taken care in the years since then to protect herself from brutes and unworthy men. Gjona was above them all, but he was still a man and might still be a brute. The sooner she knew what was to happen, the better.

"My lord, may I help you with what you are doing?"

Gjona smiled and kept scratching. "Do you know the strength of silk, the properties of steel, or the economic policies of Samarqand?"

"I know silk will tear one way but not in another. I know that steel has its uses beyond the making of needles."

Gjona kept scratching at his platter without looking up. "Very well. What if I told you there was a line of silk—not the silk of our salamanders, but of worms—that stretches from where the sun rises to where it sets?"

"I would say that is a long line of silk," Bayan said.

"Yes, yes it is. What if I told you this line moves from the east to the west, and that it moves by a road south of here, near Talas. You've heard of Talas?"

"Yes, I know of Talas, and I know of the Silk Road as well."

"Ah, good. What else?"

"I know that this silk on their road is crude and plain, not as smooth as ours, and without color. And their silk can burn."

"Exactly." Gjona said. "Their silk can burn." He kept scratching for a long time without saying anything until Bayan shifted, and he seemed to remember she was there. "What else do you know? Tell me of the politics of Talas and its defenses and its people."

"I know that what politics is for men, love is for women. And I know that you haven't told me enough about your problem for me to help you solve it."

Gjona let out a laugh and put down the platter. "You're a clever one. Oh, you're Baytosk's daughter, aren't you? Bayan, is it?"

"Yes, Bayan." She was relieved and infuriated.

"Come, let me see you."

Gjona set the dagger on the bed alongside the platter, then motioned Bayan to him, pulling aside her robe.

"Ah, I remember this. A pretty image." Gjona traced the figures on the brass plate of her belt. They were angled toward the currant, their hands intertwined, and their features less distinct from one another the closer he came to her body.

Bayan took a gamble and rolled away from him. "My lord, I fear there has been a misunderstanding. You said someone else is coming. Who?"

"I don't know, exactly. One or two more of you. Isn't that why you're here?"

Bayan cautiously pulled her robe closed. "I had thought I would be alone. I had thought you wanted to see only me."

Gjona laughed as if she were toying with him, then frowned as he realized she was serious. "Yes, there must be a misunderstanding. If I wanted only you, I would have sent only for you. I did not send for you at all, in fact. Did your father send you here?"

"Yes."

"To drive home what bargain? He has accounts of my herds, of my horses, of my silks, of my lands. Does he also want accounts of my arms and legs?"

"I do not know, my lord." Bayan edged away and found herself standing in front of the brazier, looking into the eyes of the salamander, which emanated softly. "I think he wants a match."

"A match? Is he mad?" Gjona laughed and fell back onto the bed, causing the dagger and wood to fall to the floor. The laugh pierced Bayan's heart. The salamander quickly filled the wound, pouring in worthiness and stronging and keepingup. It gave her the courage to say what she said next.

"Do you not wish, my lord, to consider me for a bride? No one of the tribe can recall that you have ever married or begat children, and surely it's time that you do so. Am I not worthy to stand by your side and to give you sons? Will you not give me the chance to show you I am a worthy companion?"

"Turn away from that meddler in the steaming pot," Gjona said, now in anger. "I'll tell you for your father that you're a fine woman, and there's no insult in my encouragement that he find some other suitor for his pretty daughter. His lord has no wish to be a suitor for anyone and no need of heirs who won't outlive him. I'll tell you for yourself that if I wanted to fuck someone worthy of being my adviser, I'd send away my whores and cut Chim-dur a new hole."

Bayan knelt and picked up the dagger and plate, glancing over the design carved into it. She handed both to Gjona-ja.

"I'm sorry, my lord, for the misunderstanding. May I go?"

"You may."

Bayan left the yurt, not bothering to close the inner doors behind her. She rushed down the path, holding her robe closed tight under her arms. Halfway to the courtyard she heard voices and turned to see two women, lower than her in both age and nobility, lifting aside the yesik she had just closed.

Despite her anger, Bayan felt the pride of having conducted herself well. The only regret nagging her mind was unanswered curiosity about Gjona's carving: A man standing atop a hill, with figures marching down each side. On one side they were linked to one another by a long, smooth groove, and on the other by what appeared to be flames.

A Silkie's work didn't require the utmost concentration. Half-day shifts standing in one spot, in overnight chill or daytime heat, in rain or snow, pulling the line of silk hand over hand, was an act of singular endurance but not of intellectual prowess. Still, the presence of shouting children and nagging wives near the Silkies' line was frowned upon. Older sons, if sensible enough, were permitted to relay messages, but they were encouraged to go away again as soon as their errands were complete. In rare cases, when the time was right, they were told not to return to their mothers. In the northern reaches of Persia, between Merv and Nishapur, a boy named Rasham was still beardless when his father bade him stand and watch.

"Watch that old man there next to me," the father of Rasham whispered. "Do you see how slow his arms move? Do you see how slack the line is that I give him and how taut it is after? This man is not long for the line."

Rasham looked at the man on his father's "give," and his father was right. The man's face was pitted with age, his eyes hollow. His arms moved like the branches of a dead olive tree in the wind.

"Rasham!" his father whispered in excitement. "He has no children. You could have his place on my give."

Rasham smiled politely at his father, unsure whether this particular career choice was right for him. On the "take" side stood a young man only a few years older than Rasham. His beard was new, but his eyes were glazed. He seemed weary of a task he had only just begun, one that would continue until he too had a taut line on his give.

A shout rose up on the east side of the plain and screamed toward Rasham's father, louder as it came: "Bite me!"

"Bite me!"

"Bite me!" his father yelled.

"Bite me!" the old man croaked.

"Bite me!"

"Bite me!"

It continued down the line, repeating into the distance toward Hecatompylos, whence a cart would be expected within the hour.

"A tale," the young man on the take side said, with little excitement.

"A tale," his father responded.

"A man from Merv took his flock of fat sheep past the Road one day. At the end of the day, the man returned with a wool coat. The next day, the man from Merv again passed the Road, this time with his entire store of grain, and he returned with a loaf of bread. On the third day the man from Merv again passed the Road, this time with his only wife, and he returned with a loaf of bread."

The men looked at each other, pulling their line in matching pace, until Rasham's father said, "This is a broken tale, is it not?"

"I thought so myself, and if you cannot repair it, I shall send it straight back."

"Send it back," his father said.

"Send it back," the man replied. Then Rasham heard him relaying the tale back toward Merv, a week's march to the east. Presumably somewhere in between, the tale would be repaired and sent back down the line in a manner that made sense.

In this way Rasham was introduced to the line, to its singular purpose, to its network of commands and stories and confusion, to the timing of the two daily shifts. And when the day finally came when the old man fell, his father did not yell "dropout," because Rasham jumped into the old man's place before the silk could touch the ground. The old man lay in a gasping heap under Rasham's shadow for some hours before his swapout noticed and sent a boy to carry him off.

Many years later, when Rasham's hands were as smooth as

glass from handling the silk, when they had attained the brilliant orange hue of a Silkie to match the burnt tan face of a man living under the sun, he heard the command coming down from Merv:

"Hooker!"

"Hooker!" his father shouted.

"Hooker!" Rasham replied.

"Hooker!"

"Hooker!" repeating into the distance.

Rasham knew now from experience that a "hooker" would take a half-day from Merv, two days from Samarqand, or four from Talas. In this way, the Silkies could gossip over who might have broken the line and gauge which portion was weakest in the pass.

A few hours later, though, new words, then new phrases came flying down the line, and by nightfall they developed into full sentences.

"Smooth." "Finery." "Gold." "Holy silk." "Spun from gods." "Light and thin." "New silk, cool to touch." "Coming silk is pure, soft."

By the fourth afternoon, the line was abuzz with rumors of a new silk after the hook. Rasham could tell it was getting close because the line became taut. The Silkies were slowing down in their excitement over the change, the first change in the fabric that any had seen since the Silk Road was formed three centuries earlier. Rasham grew fearful that the distraction would cause a break.

"Pace!" he yelled at his father. "Pace!" his father shouted up the line, and the silk quickened as others got the message and hurried things along. Rasham was later remembered among Silkies for his quick thinking.

Then Rasham saw it. Great brass hooks glinted in the afternoon sun at the top of a hill near the horizon. Then the silk. It shimmered; it sparkled. Rasham struggled not to blink as the line of new silk flowed down the hill with a brilliance that seemed an emanation of its own essential light. Rasham felt his pace fall apart as he gloried in what was coming. Too slowly for his own desires, but at the same speed as the silk that had moved through his hands for almost a decade, the brass rings arrived, and with them the new silk. Rasham's hands came alive with sensation.

"Gjona-ja!" his father relayed to him. The silk was like water, or oil, only dry—so smooth, so beautiful. "Gjona!" his father relayed again.

"Jon!" Rasham yelled in surprise.

"Jon!"

"Jon!"

"Jon!"

As the word passed away, Rasham realized he had broken it. "Gjona-ja," not "Jon." What did it mean, anyway? But it was too late, and if Rasham's father noticed his son's error, he was either too ashamed to point it out or too distracted by the liquid gold pouring through his fingers.

Gjona-ja sat at a low-burning fire in the center of the camp, which was now within arrowshot of the Silk Road, at a point a day's ride west of Talas. On the opposite side of the fire was an old woman wearing a tall, veiled, conical hat. It was midday now, and the wind fluttered the veil to shield her face from the sun, as though at her command. She rocked with the rhythm of her words, moving her hands in a strange series of gestures, in part to convey her meaning and in part to help her remember. She had been chanting the story, and Gjona-ja listening since the break of dawn.

> *He is at all times the perfect man,*
> *he is a lion saved by a king.*
> *Look deep into this man's inner world:*
> *it is wider indeed than the earth.*
> *No one could live fighting with him,*
> *no one would dare to approach him;*
> *he stands among those famous lions,*
> *he is the lion Manas.*

The old woman had been brought from one of the camps to the east, a camp now allied with Gjona-ja. It was said she was a Chinigi Manaschi, or true speaker of the tale of Manas, a tale that took three days to recite if told each day from the rising to the setting of the sun.

> *He caused fear across the face of the world.*
> *He laid waste the seven gates of Xi'an.*

The woman paused as Chim-dur walked his horse close to where Gjona sat.

"It's done," he said.

"Will there be enough silk?" Gjona asked.

"Enough to last us three seasons if we were to stop now. But we will not stop now."

Gjona looked across the valley to the now-broken line of Silkies, who had begun pulling from his reams of carefully folded salamander silk. These sat stacked in carts alongside the line in a rainbow of shimmering greens, oranges, and purples, woven together in fades that lasted several spans each. They were moving it down the line toward the west, to Samarqand, to Merv, to Constantinople. About twenty paces to the east, across the gap in the line, over the bodies of some half-dozen Silkies who had refused the commands of Gjona-ja, lay a discarded pile of silk, this one white. The dogged Silkies were still pulling it in from the east, piling it ever higher on the ground. Though beautiful enough on its own, it was a dull heap of refuse compared to the finery that now moved in its place.

"And now?" Chim-dur said.

Gjona walked back to the fire. "Please, honored Chinigi Manaschi, do continue."

> *Death is at hand*
> *for those caught in the path of this lion.*
> *You should have seen this hero in battle!*
> *He was a fortress of iron.*

Gjona-ja reached into the fire and took out a branch that was cold on one end and blazing orange on the other. His shadow was strong now, between the fire and the midday sun. It sank deep into the earth, making the ground under his boots cold to the touch. He handed the branch to Chim-dur. "Now," he said.

> *Manas tied his belt tight,*
> *hit his horse with a whip,*
> *grabbed the spear in his hand,*
> *and shouted his wrath.*

Chim-dur mounted his horse and rode down toward the pile of crude, white worm silk. There, to the horror of the still-working Silkies, he threw the torch into the pile. It exploded in a blaze so intense that the surrounding brush scorched black. Many of the Silkies who saw what was happening jumped away from the line; many did not jump fast enough. The flames shot up the line, riding the silk eastward and on into the horizon, burning toward Talas, the Otmok Pass, and then to Xi'an.

The Manaschi watched this, but though her hands shook, she did not waver in her tale.

> *Behind him the forty chieftains cried out,*
> *calling his name, "Manas!"*

SATURDAY NIGHT: DINNER
WITH THE GOGS

YEARS AGO IN A DESPERATE moment, Mina had learned a recipe for ten-minute grouper in salamander milk with parmesan egg noodles and broiled asparagus. The trick was to have grouper on hand, a steady supply of salamander milk, and access to a handful of fresh asparagus stalks. Luckily, they were at the beach, not far from Hell, and the salamander was lactating.

That was the only option now that the chicken was frozen and the Gogs had arrived, soaked from the rain.

After initial pleasantries at the door, Prester escorted them, dripping rainwater across the linoleum, to the dryer in the laundry room downstairs. That bought Mina enough time to make it look like she and Prester weren't completely unprepared.

"They'll be dry in a moment," Prester said, coming into the kitchen. "Can I help with anything?"

"Yes." Mina was washing asparagus and breaking off the stems. She was too rushed to tell him Yes, you can help by thinking for ten seconds outside yourself, by considering other people's feelings and whether their way of making decisions just might be better than yours. By just not, for ten seconds, being Prester John. Instead, she settled for "Kill the grouper."

Prester reached into the fish bucket next to the refrigerator and pulled up the seven-pound grouper by its wide mouth. He slapped it on the chopping board. As soon as its mouth was free, it began its supplication: "Fisherman and better man, please spare this poor fish. I have done you no wrong that you should take my life."

"Fish, I have no quarrel with you," Prester responded from rote obligation. "But you live to die and I eat to live. Thus it has been and always will be."

"Oh fisherman and better man, my flesh is but meager and not worthy—"

Prester chopped off its head.

Mina huffed. "It's bad luck not to let them finish."

"I've heard it before," Prester said, filleting with one hand and tossing guts out the window with the other. The gulls would have a feast as soon as the rain stopped.

In the asparagus-scented silence that followed, Prester wondered if he should have put on some music.

"Hello!"

The Gogs arrived upstairs, lingering uncomfortably at the threshold of the kitchen.

"Hello again," Mina said. "I'm so sorry that we're running behind getting dinner ready."

"Not at all, not at all," Reggie said, grinning for no reason.

Reggie Gog was about what Prester expected. A tall man and muscular. The type bred to play high school quarterback, who actually manages to make something of himself in college. It can be a lethal combination for a woman prone to swooning, and in Reggie Gog's case it took the form of an obnoxiously chiseled jaw and red hair fading toward a duller gray that Prester predicted would soon disappear in a bitter series of auburn washes. The weaknesses, though, were clear: Gog lacked subtlety, and that was a terrible flaw in Prester's mental log of historic catastrophes. And then there were his knees. Despite a handshake that could pop the boil on a Cyclops's ass, Gog had underdeveloped muscles around his knees, a lack apparent in his awkward gait. Prester felt sure this had led to many years of painful injuries, any of which could be quickly revived with the strike of an elbow or even a knuckle jab into the soft cartilage just under the cap. Prester often squirreled away such knowledge about his guests and acquaintances, though it had been a few hundred years since he'd found any reason to put it to use.

May Gog was Mongolian. Prester looked away from her quickly.

"I'm sorry if we came too early," May said, taking a chair at the bar that separated the kitchen from the dining room. "We wanted to get here before the storm got worse, because frankly I could hardly get a word out on the way over here, and thank you so much for letting us use your dryer. Ours is an early model, you know the kind you had to sit in and use the nozzle? But we'll have to get one of these new ones like yours. I love that you can stand up inside it—so much easier. I hope we didn't interrupt anything?" She glanced nervously at the shower curtain–draped couch.

"No, nothing at all," Prester said. Northwestern province, probably of the Kaprokta tribe. She wore a breezy cotton dress, gathered at the waist by something low-hung and shimmering gold. Cockle shells? No, surely not. Prester wanted to know, but he feared being caught in a stare.

Mina took the fish from Prester. "Thanks, honey." He couldn't tell if she was playing nice for company or making a small overture toward reconciliation, so he played it safe and responded only with a smile.

Once lime and butter were foaming in the pan, Mina placed

the fillets and sprinkled them with pepper.

"Smells great!" Reggie said.

"Yes," Prester agreed. He looked at Mina hopefully. No reaction. Realizing the parmesan was still unshredded, Prester jumped at the chance to be useful.

"You know what it smells like, Reggie, it smells like those margaritas we had at that place in Tallahassee next to the bar with that funny name, the Sit Down Bar?"

"Shut Up."

"Yes, the Shut Up Bar, and they had signs that said, 'Shut up and drink your beer!'" May laughed. "Oh, that bartender was a terrible woman, but I think it was just an act. My God, was she ugly. No makeup at all and her hair just a mess. She really could have looked all right if she'd only taken care of herself. And they had that jukebox that had two or three Steve Miller songs on it, and I'm fine with Steve Miller, but someone put in about thirty dollars worth of quarters and hit those same three songs over and over, and a little Steve Miller goes a long way, you know. But the restaurant next door, Tres Margaritas or something."

"Dos Margaritas," Reggie said.

"Yes, Dos Margaritas—but you know two are never enough!" May laughed again. "So, they served fish, and they served margaritas, so yours kind of smells like that."

Mina looked up, unsure if May was talking to her.

"Your fish."

Prester smiled.

Mina caught up to what May was saying. "Oh, yes."

"Because margaritas have lime," May clarified.

"Yes," Mina said. Prester was grating so carefully to avoid flaking cheese onto the counter that he would still be at it when dessert was served. "Thanks, Prester, I'll finish for you," she said, confiscating the cheese and box grater.

"Thanks," Prester said, pleased by the signal that Mina was no longer mad at him.

"You know, I could use a margarita right now!" May said with a chuckle.

Prester wandered over to check on the fish. Mina had a bad habit of overcooking seafood, so he tried to help her by keeping an eye on it.

"Nice house," Reggie said.

"Thanks," Prester replied.

"Do you own it or rent?"

"We own it."

"How long have you had it?"

"About fifty years."

"Fifty?"

"Sorry. I mean five. I lose track of time."

"Move over, honey," Mina said. Prester stood aside so she could put the pan of asparagus in the oven and set the timer.

"Have you checked the pasta?" he asked.

"Timer," Mina said.

"What about the fish?"

"Timer."

"Looks like she's got the bases covered!" Reggie said with an unwarranted laugh.

Prester smiled.

"We own our house too," May said, looking around the dining and living room area. "Of course I tried to talk Reggie out of it, because the worst thing you can do if you want to enjoy a beach house is to own it. Then you have to spend every vacation replacing broken dishes and cleaning carpets."

"And unsticking doors," Prester said.

"Your doors stick?" Reggie said.

"Sometimes."

"Well, Reggie insisted we buy a house, so we did, but I'll be damned if I'm going to replace the furniture every season just because someone spilled wine on a chair or burned a cigarette hole in the carpet. And the carpet, oh, my lord! One time a few years ago—I think it was three years ago, wasn't it Reggie? Or was it two?"

"I think the carpet thing was four years ago, because that was the year you had the plantation shutters put in."

"That was three years ago, wasn't it?"

"Four."

"Okay, four then."

Prester stole a glance at the fish. Not burning yet.

"So there was this renter who must have had some sort of fire in one of the bedrooms—maybe they were grilling in there, I don't know—but when we got back we found this big scorch mark about three feet wide on the floor next to the bed!"

"My heavens," Mina said.

"So we had to have the whole carpet rubbed down with fennis oil just to get it back the same color, and in the right light you can still see that scorch mark."

"What happened to the renter?" Mina asked.

"Oh, well I don't know. The property management company worked it all out, made sure they paid for the damages, but they certainly never came back to our house."

"Maybe it was self-immolation," Prester offered helpfully.

"I certainly hope not!"

"Or spontaneous combustion. That's not as rare as some seem to think."

"Prester!" Mina hissed.

"So I just keep everything sealed in plastic," May went on, "for when renters are here, including the carpet and the appliances, then we uncover it for when we're here, and I've been able to keep the same furniture now for about twenty years. Of course, it's not very stylish, but it sure beats buying new all the time, doesn't it, Prester?"

Prester looked up from pondering the idea of self-immolation. "Hmm?"

"The plastic on your sofa—is that for when renters are here?"

"Oh, that? No."

Prester was studying the fish, which was just turning brown at the edges. The timer ticked down toward zero. Mina gave Prester a look of warning, but he wasn't sure if it was about the plastic shower curtain, the increasingly intriguing idea of self-immolation, or his involvement in checking the fish, so he said nothing.

All three timers dinged at once.

Reggie and May backed out of the kitchen and dining room as the Johns became a blur of Mina setting plates and Prester trying to assist, with Mina resetting behind him all the way.

The Gogs jumped to accept glasses of pinot grigio from Prester, and shortly afterward he managed to refill their drinks without Mina's assistance.

"There we are," Mina said, taking her seat. "Dinner is served."

"This looks fabulous, Mina," Reggie said.

Prester pushed his fish around on the plate, checking for doneness.

"I hope it's okay," Mina said. "The grouper assured me he was Gulf-born at the market, but you can't trust anything these Hell fish say."

May laughed and leaned in. Prester offered a close-lipped smile, noticing how the soft weight of May's breasts shifted forward under her dress. Images of countless Mongolian concubines in sheer silk blouses dancing atop ox-horns twirled to the front of Prester's mind.

"So, Prester," Reggie said. "Mina tells me you're in surreal estate?"

"Yes, yes I am."

"What exactly do you do?"

"Personally, I dealt mostly in spatial pockets—movable holes, double-opening doors, that sort of thing."

"Really? I love those things," Reggie said. "Especially the spatial pockets. We used to have a whole warehouse full of paperwork, a huge security risk too, but we had Rooms To Go install a spatial pocket for us and transferred the whole thing in there. Now we carry the entire archive in a briefcase, and when we need anything we send a librarian inside and whammo, you got what you need."

"Good, good," Prester said.

"So, is that where you work, Rooms To Go?"

"No. I worked at NSpaces."

"Ah. Don't think we ever used you for archives."

"You probably wouldn't have. My department specialized in alternate-dimension fantasy estate. We were on commission to build our fifth Xanadu when I left."

This wasn't exactly true, but he was baiting a response from May, who only looked up and cocked her head in a smile as she chewed her fish. Maybe she wasn't descended from the Khans. Or maybe she was ignorant of her history, a trait Prester found distressingly common in this century of too-broad education and literacy.

"Now, you said 'worked.' You win the lottery or something? You're a bit young to be retired."

"Not really," Prester said. "I'm retired."

"Are you retired too, Mina?" May asked.

"Not exactly. I've never really worked in an office. I . . ."

"That's wonderful!" May said. "You know, as soon as we had our first child, I wanted to be a stay-at-home mom, but Reggie just wouldn't let me. Always telling me I'd turn into one of those hopelessly bored people who waste their lives away waiting for things to happen, like their husbands coming home to tell them fascinating things about the stock market and the next company party." May bounced her fork. "So I've mostly worked in sales, finding shops I like and offering to help out. One time I worked as a psychic at a bookstore and coffee shop that sold crystals and smudging wands and the cutest little figurines of dragons. So I was the psychic there, and you would be amazed at the things people would tell me! Agh, my God, you wouldn't believe it! Then, what do you know but the owner has one of those 'born again' thingies and turns the whole place into a Christian bookstore and purse shop." May laughed again, broadly, and the other three made an earnest attempt to accommodate her. "But anyway, now that both our kids are grown and out of the house—we have two, Tre and Jeanie— Reggie makes enough that I can kind of float around depending on what's out there. Oh, Mina, this is delicious! I might just have to start selling fish!"

"Thanks," Mina said. "So, you're psychic?"

"Heavens no!" May laughed, then (it seemed to Prester) paused with a momentary lapse into self-reflection.

"So, do you have children?" May asked.

"No, actually we don't," Mina said.

"Oh."

Forks clinked. May seemed overly aware of the sound of asparagus softly crushing in her mouth (Prester himself was happily aware of it). She swallowed a particularly large piece just to subdue the sound of her own chewing.

Silence is a grand thing. Prester thought so, anyway. He likened it to the right use of spatial pockets: a place to go where you can reflect on what's been said and decide how you want to proceed. Or whether you want to proceed. The great turmoils of life come not from deliberation and silence, but from rushing to a decision, and people who rush to decisions have a tendency to never shut up.

"Me, I'm in wildlife control," Reggie blurted in a cracked voice.

See? Prester told himself. That's why.

Species Control was an international agency. In the United States its bureaucracy touched federal, state, and local levels of government, with a mandate to keep flora and fauna from over-populating and with a complicated system of funding that seemed to keep it outside any clear authority. That made it much easier for them to, for example, quickly eradicate entire species: mosquitos, pit bulls. The problem was that over the years other species had disappeared as well, species less obnoxious, such as Canada geese, selkies, and non-GMO corn. People seemed to remember these creatures having existed, but suddenly they found all records of them gone. The only remaining references to foxes, for example, were in fairy tales and folklore, though if you spent any time in a nursing home you'd find plenty of residents who remembered seeing them in zoos if not in the woods. The same was true, some said, of manatees, polar bears, and, in Mina's case at least, rocs.

"My area deals with rodents and other small mammals, mostly," Reggie droned on proudly. "Our team handles pandemic customization filters. We just wiped out a subspecies of panda badger that was wreaking havoc on shiitake mushroom farms."

"Extinction," Mina said, the hairs on her arms going stiff and cold. "You do extinction."

"Well, yes, in a way. If you want to call it that. We control wildlife that's gotten out of control."

"Wildlife that's gotten out of control because you've made the predators extinct?"

"Well, I suppose that's one way . . ."

Reggie's uncomfortable conversation with Mina drifted into the back of Prester's mind as he noticed the line of shadow that drifted down May's ear to crash hopelessly into the crossing of her clavicle.

"I mean, imagine if we still had gryphons, for God's sake, swooping down and gobbling up livestock, or even children off of playgrounds."

From there, the line shot to her delicate shoulder, then plunged down her sternum into the dark crevasse between breasts that glistened in the humid summer evening, perspiring beneath the drying cotton. Her soft skin was alive with the musk of beach water and fresh with the scent of lime from butter-sauteed fish.

"I'm sorry, Reggie, I don't mean to challenge you, but I don't see how anyone can work for a company that manufactures a deception through selective extinction and then destruction of historical records."

Prester took a long sip from his wine, letting the curve of the glass bend the light as it came cascading toward him from May's breasts. He teased himself by blinking hard and taking a relaxed bite of asparagus, looking around the drab room, then back at the glorious display.

"Well, it's a bit of a complicated thing to get into over dinner."

"No, no, I want to understand this," Mina said.

"It's not destruction of records," Gog said. "I mean, those rumors—if they're even true—although, frankly, I hope they are, because it makes perfect sense . . ." He trailed off, leaving everyone confused.

Prester imagined his tongue following the line down between May's breasts, across her belly, and splitting then—not yet, not yet—down her thighs and around the backs of her knees.

May's leg shot up and banged the table. "Ow! Something bit me!"

Prester realized what was happening and stood up quickly. I was just daydreaming, he told himself as he went to turn off the light behind him that had flung his shadow under the table. Just to be sure, he also turned on the overhead light behind May's chair.

"I'm sorry, folks, really I am," Prester said. "We have some Tuskegee moths around here, and they kind of go crazy whenever this overhead light is turned off."

Mina wasn't buying it. She watched Prester's movements, looking for his shadow, and wasn't surprised to see he was shuffling to keep it under his feet as he returned to the table and sat down.

"Tuskegee moths?" Reggie said.

"Yes, you haven't seen them?" Prester said. "They developed in the late seventies at the university. Mostly harmless, but they kind of grab you with these claw-like legs—feels like a bite, but it's really a grab."

"Really?"

"Yes, Reggie," Mina said, staring at her wine glass and idly turning it by the stem. "You should kill them all."

Reggie stared, then scooped in a mouthful of fish. "This sure is delicious," he mumbled.

May, still edgy, peeked under the table. Prester pushed hard on his shadow to keep it still. He could feel the shadow erection fading, pulsing back to a gray disk on his crotch.

"You know, speaking of crabs," Reggie said, "you two really ought to go to the Crab Festival. It's a blast. And the food is out of this world."

"Reggie's going to molt," Mina said blankly.

"Well," Prester said, standing. "I think we've had a toddy too many. Tell you what, we'll come out to the Crab Festival Monday and cheer you on."

The Gogs stood, May still looking around the floor for the Tuskegee moth.

"Oh, you don't have to cheer for me," Reggie said. "I can molt with the best of them."

"Nonsense," Prester said. "In fact, if you don't hear me whistle from the stands, you better come back here quick, because it means something terrible's happened and the missus and I are both dead!"

Prester grinned proudly; Mina closed her eyes and grasped the table, trying to stay solid. Reggie and May smiled just enough to make everything seem okay.

The Gogs made a gesture toward helping to clear the table before gathering their things and heading down the stairs, across the pebbled street, and into the warm glow of their house. Prester watched from the door, unmoving, angry, and wishing his shadow dead. The staples on the pads of his feet were digging sideways and causing old wounds to bleed. He stormed to the closet and found a flashlight, then flicked it on and off at the shadow, which wavered in pain and finally submitted into an exact silhouette.

Prester came back out into the hallway just as Mina was turning off the lights.

"Mina."

She gave a pained look and held up her hand. Then she drifted past him toward the bedroom. When Prester came to bed, she turned away.

THE COLOR OF SCREAMS,
527-528 A.D.

T HE GREAT CITY OF TALAS was built in about 400 A.D., in the valley between the Kyrgyz Alatau to the north and the Talas Alatau to the south in what is now Kyrgyzstan, astride the river that bore its name. To the west was Chach, then Samarqand, along the road to Constantinople. To the east was the Otmok Pass of the Silk Road, leading to Yining and eventually to Xi'an itself, until that road was consumed by the Great Fire of Manas.

The Khitay built Talas, but Talas was not a Khitay city. It lacked the grand wooden pagodas, the ebony columns, and the facades that were dragons, forced into deep hibernation. Instead it was composed of hundreds of yurts arranged at the whims of tribal leaders. First they clustered in rings, forming a labyrinth of circles like a forest of squat trees. Then in a grid, so that one could see from end to end of the encampment along any given line. One leader had the sense to arrange the yurts in a single wide circle, but the clearing at the center was so broad that communication from one side to another was less reliable than a Silk Road rumor. So the Great Yurt was built in the middle, thirty feet high and a hundred feet side to side. Then, the great-grandfather of Lord Zhizhi Chuan decreed that the Great Yurt would be covered not with felt but with brass poured over the kereges at the hand of Scythian giants. The brass Great Yurt became an architectural standard for the whole of Talas. Soon, overeager giants and Cyclopes were pouring brass on every yurt in the valley, some prematurely. In places they left behind fields of brass statues, horrified Sogdian merchants trapped in time, holding their arms up to yell even as the brass dripped into their throats.

In 527, the year of the Great Fire, many of these giants still remained around the Talas Alatau, working on orders from the Great Yurt. As the smoke cleared along the eastern Silk Road at the northern edge of the city, word came that the sciapods had found favor with Manas. Ten thousand of them, lured out of hiding in the southern Steppe and armed with long-handled Kypchak-forged swords, pounded the earth for miles on each side of the Otmok Pass, seeking giants to kill. They had never used steel weapons until Gjona-ja, but soon found these could reach where feet and clubs could not, even to the fat bellies of the giants, spilling their entrails from one end of the scorched road to another. The sciapods were no longer afraid.

When the giants were gone, Gjona turned his attention to Talas itself.

From the camp where his men had re-established the road with salamander silk on one side and a trail of charred destruction on the other, Gjona sent scouts to the nearby villages in the lowlands west of the Talas River valley. Word of the arrival of Manas preceded him, and his army entered most villages unopposed. He sent messengers ahead to announce his coming, then rode in atop his black, silk-robed horse, at the head of long columns of cavalry, wearing not the ceremonial costume of later days but the true armor of a warrior who might meet the blow of a sword.

Approaching one such nomadic tribe, the Neshun, he received extravagant offers of surrender and tribute, along with an invitation from the chief to share a meal. With Gjona's two advisers still encamped at the Silk Road and no leaders of battle willing to stand in his way, and with a growing annoyance at having to wear armor everywhere when it hadn't yet been needed, Gjona was in a reckless mood. He left his army behind and rode into the camp alone, with only a courier and a manservant trailing unarmored in his dust.

The people lined the path to the yurt at the center of the camp. The yesik was black but festooned with blood-red flowers. Gjona dismounted and walked between two rows of armed men, and he was reminded of another entry, not so many years ago, by a man in orange sleeves that dripped to his toes, bearing veiled threats and false humility. Gjona smiled to himself and vowed to be no such man. The yesik was opened for him, and Gjona stepped inside.

The light was dim. As he reached to his right to hang his horse whip, he heard someone say *trayik*, a crude dialect word for "begin." Gjona felt the air in the room rush with movement as two beasts leaped toward him. But in an instinct born of decades hunting boar, and partly also from a desire to have his mettle tested, Gjona braced his mind and did not move. The beasts stopped short, their eyes and bared teeth flashing at him, then at one another, uncertain what to do with prey that wouldn't run. Then he could no longer see their teeth. They sniffed at him, and one reached up with a great white-and-orange paw and batted lightly at his chest, pushing him onto his heels with the force of seven hundred pounds of muscle and bone.

His vision adapted to the firelit room. The tigers lost interest in him quickly. One sat grooming the dust from its paw while the other watched the chief, who was standing now in the center of the yurt with his eyes wide.

Gjona smiled. "Good day!" he said brightly, and stepped between the tigers to approach the chief. He had his sword, and he considered killing the man. But would the tigers then attack? And what of the seven soldiers he could now see in the shadows? The man had tried to kill Gjona, but where was the fault in that? He was cunning. He'd make a good ally. And he'd managed to train tigers for battle, though not well enough to attack someone who wouldn't run away.

Gjona stopped short of the fire at the center of the yurt. "Your tigers don't seem interested in killing me. Maybe they know I'm not here to kill you. Maybe they know better than you that I'm not your enemy."

"I—"

"Now, what if your men step out of the shadows and attack me? It appears I have two new friends. What will these new friends think of that?"

"I'm sorry, my lord. I—"

"Let's you and I start again. My horse whip hangs on your cord," Gjona said.

The chief quickly bowed and blurted, "Greetings, my lord Gjona-ja, from the people of Neshun."

"Greetings, Durya, chief of the Neshun," Gjona said, returning the bow.

Both men rose, smiling.

Durya extended an arm to a place by the fire, where there was a pillow draped in red silk. Gjona sat, and the tigers lay down near them. The men in the shadows quietly left.

"We have many things to discuss, my friend Durya—what I can do for you, what you can do for me. But first, Durya, chief of the Neshun, people of the plains on the borders of Talas, tell me about your tigers."

The following winter, Gjona's new army held the Road to the east and west, cutting off the city of Talas from the string of merchant caravans that normally kept the Khitay rulers fat and rich. Instead, all their wares went to Gjona-ja's army, which stayed well fed over the winter and grew in numbers as more of the Kyrgyz people abandoned the starving city to join its ranks.

That spring, a half-dozen nomadic tribes moved to the mouth of the Talas River valley to join Gjona in the ongoing siege. When the miyzam flowers were fully in bloom and the Khitay rulers were throwing yarn against stone trying to call for salvation from Xi'an, a caravan moved away from Gjona's camp and toward the city. The caravan preceded an army of over a thousand men, shepherds on horseback and hunters wielding clubs and swords and curved bows, all of them smiling with pride over being part of something bigger, something more important than they'd ever taken part in before. Ahead of them were six wagons draped in black, escorted by nervous horsemen carrying only long whips. And at the front was Gjona-ja, his armor still unscratched, his gray eyes focused on one goal: the shining brass spire atop the Great Yurt of Talas.

As Gjona's caravan approached the scattering of farms and dwellings at the outskirts of the city, the people were more excited than afraid. These were not strange men in orange sleeves with dragon flags and an unknown speech; these were their own people, the Kyrgyz people, and they were here not to conquer but to restore. This, perhaps this, could be Manas.

Gjona met no resistance from the Talas soldiers who'd been sent to block the road. Instead they lined the road with their outstretched heads, helmets removed, awaiting either mercy or death from the prophesied hero in black. Gjona passed them by and felt alive with the vibration of the word coursing through his body: Manas, Manas, Manas.

He arrived at the Great Yurt. The yesik was more of a massive wooden gate, which was opened now by the still bare-necked soldiers who'd until recently been in the service of the Khitay. The entry hall echoed with gloom, and Gjona could hear fearful whispers inside. He motioned to the horsemen escorting the wagons, and they removed the black silk veils that had covered them and opened the tigers' cages.

"Trayik," Gjona said.

The inner walls of the Great Yurt soon flashed orange and black, and then with that strange color of screams—a bright yellow infused with horror, sharp at the edges and flashing gold—and finally with red, everywhere red.

SUNDAY MORNING: THE CUP
OF SALVATION

A NEWLY BORN SUNBEAM INCHED ACROSS the side of the bed that Mina had left empty. It rippled over the folds of white sheets, speeding and slowing with each dip and rise. The organic thing that awaited it looked curious: heaving and wet, with jagged contours along its top. But as the sunbeam rose closer to Prester's eyes, it sensed something else, something behind the organic, something that couldn't easily be rolled back and replaced, something that did not want to go. The waiting shadow grinned with hate. The sunbeam bent and contorted.

As it tripped over Prester's left eyelash, he blinked awake and felt that he had heard the sound of a particle scream. He rose from the bed and tightened the blinds, killing the young light within the room, not knowing how much it had wished for death.

Mina was gone. Prester's heart skipped three beats ahead as he turned to the closet and saw that her clothes were still there, as were her face wash and makeup bag. The burst of panic subsided, but it angered him, even more so as he recalled her cold dismissal of the night before, and more again as he tried to recall the last time his wife had woken him with the press of lips against his cheek.

He dressed and walked out into the kitchen. He opened the

shelves and let his eyes roam blankly over the food—too much food, all going to waste after their suicide. But what did he care if their money was wasted on food or clothes or lottery tickets? There was no one to leave it to. Staring at the food made the lump of semi-sentient grouper roll like a lead ball in his stomach. No, no breakfast. He walked to the window, where new sunbeams burned in, working at his skin to wake it into new warmth.

When he heard the voice, he almost didn't recognize it. It was soft, distant, whispered. Perhaps it was the rising dawn or the stress on his mind, but Prester felt honored to hear it: "Prester. We should talk."

He hadn't heard from Jesus since the creation of Mormonism. This time, for the first time, it was an invitation and not a barging in. Perhaps now, perhaps this time, he might get some explanation. It was worth trying. After all, there was nothing left to lose.

Prester grabbed his sandals and walked out the door, letting it slam behind him and leaving Mina to sit ignored and hurt on the shower-curtained living-room couch.

Prester hadn't set foot in a church in about 700 years, not since Abyssinia anyway, where the churches were of his own design. They built them the way he wanted them built and preached what he wanted preached, not because he told them to but because they were obedient to God, and if God walked Abyssinia, his name was Prester John.

So going to church now wasn't easy. Things had changed. And he had changed, or so he told himself. But he felt an intense urge to do it anyway, and whether this was spontaneous or the handiwork of God didn't seem to matter. The Abyssinian parishioners wouldn't have seen any difference, Prester thought with a smile.

No point fighting it.

Driving out Carapace Road, he wasn't even sure where to go. He felt certain he'd seen a church or two over the years as he passed through downtown St. Brianna. They certainly littered the sides of Highway 98 on the way to the island: roadside shacks of white clapboard that made Jesus seem angry and desperate, a poor, white-trash Jesus with a pastel three-piece suit and greased hair. Prester didn't like him that way. Instead, he traced the streets of St. Brianna, trying to see around the Crab Festival preparations to the buildings on either side. There were storefront churches, full of charisma and ease—fluffy-haired Jesus in red silk. There was an old Catholic mission. A Salamandry. Crustacean Church of Prophecy. Lutherans. Prester was surprised by the number of churches downtown that he'd never noticed until he actually began looking for one. Finally he saw a stately white brick sanctuary—Methodist. That would do.

Prester parked across the street in Hell's lot and walked into the church, too late for the start of service. They were singing "Let Us Break Bread Together on Our Knees" and lining up to kneel at a rail for grape juice and saltine crumbs. He walked down the side aisle, past pews full of dutiful old women and bored teenagers, and then May and Reggie Gog—he almost stopped in surprise, but had the sense to turn his head and scoot by unnoticed. He wasn't ready to discuss what had happened at dinner, and he was far less enthused about getting trapped in a Methodist service.

Jesus saved him by opening an office door; Prester dodged inside.

"Hello, Prester!" Jesus leaned forward and hugged him.

"Jesus," Prester said stiffly. "How are you."

"Good! Come in, please."

Jesus's demeanor hadn't changed. Still the warm but outlandish response to someone he hadn't seen in almost two centuries, acting like they'd just met for milk the week before. He was white this time, with short hair, and he'd shaved the beard (or willed it away or whatever he did for personal hygiene), leaving a fashionable soul patch. Prester imagined Jesus thought this made him look hip.

Jesus smiled. "Actually, I keep the goatee to put young parishioners at ease."

Showoff, Prester thought. Simpering, self-satisfied, pedantic showoff.

Jesus chuckled. "Have a seat, Prester, please."

Prester found a chair, one of those modern Dutch things that claimed to offer the best in ergonomic support but was about as comfortable as a campfire log. Jesus didn't have a desk, from what Prester could tell. He had an Ikea chair with a matching coffee table that featured a haphazard litter of magazines: manga, *Redbook*, *Popular Mechanics*, *Highlights*. The walls, or what there were of them amid the floor-to-ceiling windows, were chessboarded with signed publicity photographs: Kurt Cobain, Wendy O. Williams, Ian Curtis, Don Cornelius. They had glib salutations like "Jesus rocks" and "What a friend!"

"So, Prester," Jesus said. "Did you come here to admire my office?"

Prester begrudgingly sat down and crunched his hands together. It wouldn't matter. But if it would get Jesus to talk, he'd play the game. "*Deus meus, ex toto corde paenitet me omnium meorum peccatorum.*"

"How about less Latin and more specifics?"

"Fine. I have been covetous; I have been deceitful; I have held anger in my heart."

"And against me, no less," Jesus added, in a playful, mocking tone.

Prester looked at him hard. "Yes, in fact."

Jesus smiled and said, "What about lust?"

"That wasn't me. That was my shadow."

"So, you toss that in with covetousness, I guess?"

Prester darkened in face and mind, debating whether to pursue the argument. "If that."

Jesus rubbed at his goatee with his index finger. "Okay, Prester. You're forgiven."

Prester felt a rush of warm blood fill his chest and head. His scalp tingled and his eyes fluttered while he shook his shoulders to contain it.

"Cracker?"

"No thanks," Prester said.

"So," Jesus said, producing a Ritz and breaking it in half, crumbless. "I'm thinking you didn't come here for confession."

"I came because you called me."

"I didn't call you," Jesus said.

"Yes, you did. You said, 'Prester, we need to talk.' You summoned me, and that's why I'm here."

"No, I didn't."

"Yes, you did."

"Prester, I don't lie."

Prester wasn't sure if it was the absolution or just the mystifying presence of Jesus, but he felt confused now. He knew he had heard a voice.

"I'm afraid you're mistaken about the source of that voice. But I'm glad you're here, and I'm thinking you're here because you want me to talk you out of it."

"Talk me out of it?" Prester said.

"Talk you out of the murder of your wife, your suicide, that sort of thing." Jesus's eyes smiled brightly as he popped the first bit of cracker in his mouth and then proceeded to talk with his mouth full. "You know that it's wrong—unjustified. It can never be justified, really. Life's a gift to be cherished and protected. There's no return policy."

"I'm not a depressed twenty-year-old, Jesus. I've been doing this for 1,800 years, and I've done what you wanted, for the most part."

Jesus coughed. A bit of cracker lodged in his windpipe and he produced a glass of Shiraz to wash it down.

"For the most part," Prester repeated, defensively. Jesus worked to clear his throat, standing and pounding his chest, drinking more wine. "If you didn't want me to turn back from the Crusade, why didn't you freeze the Tigris? Or provide boats, or part the waters or something? If you were so intent on me going to war, why did you send me all that way just to make the passage impossible?"

Jesus flashed his eyes at Prester and continued to cough and grumble.

"Do you know what it is, Jesus, to lead men to war? To rally them for miles through dysentery-ridden filth? To inspire them to march past or even upon the bodies of their kinsmen on the road to Jerusalem?"

"Or piled in the doorway."

"That was not my doing," Prester said.

"So you say." Jesus cleared his throat once more. "Wine?"

"No."

Jesus sat. "You think I let you down at the Tigris," he said. "What, do you think I changed my mind? Or that perhaps I wanted the crusaders to die waiting for your arrival? Or that I sent you there to destroy the empire your armies left behind, or to ensure you'd establish a new one in Abyssinia?" The compassion in his voice dripped like salt water into a gaping wound. "Or that you failed some great test of faith?"

Prester said nothing but thought a great deal.

"It's not that easy, Prester, or that complicated. I told you what to do; you didn't do it."

"You know what would have happened if I had gone on to Jerusalem," Prester said, sharpening his tone. "You know what my men would have done, what the sciapods would have done."

"You should have done what I asked you to do. You should have waited at the Tigris."

Jesus sat smiling at Prester. His calm silence made Prester feel ashamed of his anger, then both annoyed and embarrassed by his shame.

"You have a right to be angry. Be angry. But what would lead you to make that mistake, to be so sure of the outcome?" Jesus asked.

"Tokmat—"

"Tokmat? And why would you believe the words of a dead man?"

"Aren't you a dead man?" Prester said, half-joking.

"No, Prester. No." Jesus gave him a grave look, then smiled. "I am risen."

At these words, Prester felt his shadow pull up inside him, like the blooming of a flower in reverse, like the lurching of testicles against your groin at a splash of cold water. And he felt at ease, calm, at peace. He hated Jesus for being able to pull that trick, even now after all these years.

"So, are you still obsessed with this futile idea of suicide? Or does this mean you're ready for your next task?"

The parts of Prester's mind that weren't laid open like the most recent issue of *Popular Mechanics* on the coffee table, with its center spread on hydroelectric power genarators, were placid, unmoved by outside noise. So much so that the notion of a new commission was as alien as it was acceptable.

"Task? What task?" Prester muttered.

"I want you to kill the Gogs."

THE BALSAM PALACE,
527-613 A.D.

O VER THE NEXT FEW YEARS, Gjona rebuilt the eastern Silk Road and reestablished trade with Khitay, but on his terms, on Kyrgyz terms, and this brought new life to the trade with Constantinople. Gjona-ja now owned the Silk Road, end to end.

This eased the way for his path to conquest. The tribes and villages north and south of the road had long been ignored by the Khitay—shut out of commerce so the Eastern rulers could focus on silk. But now alongside the silk were bags of goods tossed up and down a second line of Silkies. Among these goods were packs of fennis seed and spices for kazi sausage. From Maveranahr, the eggs of a basilisk, which when eaten poached can cure tremors; from Jetysuu, a pink salt that tastes of apples; from Khorasan, caged crickets whose chirp is said to soothe anger and turn enemies to lovers. More slowly the Silkies handed off jugs of distilled spirits made from beetle dung or poppy seed, and bars of red gold that burned the flesh off the hands of thieves. With these goods now moving up and down the line, Gjona had only to ask to gain tribute and supplication from Khorasan, Bactria, and the entirety of Sogdiana.

As for the Great Yurt of Talas, Gjona made a point of expanding its decor to include the cultures of all the kingdoms with which

Talas could now establish trade. The inner walls were rebuilt of apple wood and banyan of India, traded at the cost of many leagues of salamander silk through a new southern branch of the Silk Road. These walls were so heavily inlaid with Persian turquoise, sealed into the crevices in the final stages of construction, that some appeared more gem than wood and had a soothing effect on those entering the palace. A constant supply of Sassanid balsam burned in every room, and intricate pipeworks built into the walls and ceilings allowed the spiced fumes to travel throughout the structure, concentrating in the upper rooms to which Gjona alone had access. The drifting balsam smoke at times invaded the surrounding dwellings, breathing such tranquility that old feuds were set aside and grudges forgiven. For this reason, the people of the valley, and then beyond, called it the Balsam Palace.

This soothing effect was lost on Gjona-ja, who sat each week on a wide throne at the center of the Great Yurt, receiving tributes from the corners of his growing kingdom and growing restless over what might come next.

It didn't take long for word to reach him of dead King Jesu—the rumor that a religion had been built around this king, whose kingdom had grown inside other kingdoms, attacking them from inside like gnawing mites or worms. The worms of Jesu had eaten the Sassanids, leaving their leaders beholden to a sort of proxy king that was called a pope.

At first it was only words, and words mean little. But then came the spies. Three of them, traveling without guards, without weapons, along the Silk Road from Constantinople.

"They claim that they're priests, and they've come to tell you about Jesu."

Chim-dur was getting old now, having overseen the conquests and the palace renovations and the expanding borders of the new empire, and Gjona could see that he would soon need another advisor. This one was running out of time.

"Should I bring them in?"

"Where are they now?" Gjona asked.

"At the stable, unpacking their goods. They seem to be planning to stay."

"Hm." Gjona was wrapped in furs, sitting on his throne before a low fire. One arm of the throne was carved of ivory into the figure of an eagle standing atop a sphere. The other was carved of ebony into the figure of a lion, also perched on a sphere. Two spheres—one black, one white—like the sun and the moon that only Manas could reverse in the sky. Gjona found his fingers tracing the feathers carved into the eagle's neck.

"They're dressed in rags. They're travel-weary and brought no tribute or provisions. They must be hungry. Should I feed them?"

"Feed them to what?" Gjona asked and looked up with a grin.

Chim-dur appeared to be considering the options.

"What of the horses?"

"They are fine horses, just as we heard: each with eight legs. They rode in so quickly they were at the gates before we could arrange a greeting."

"And are the horses the tribute?"

"They did not say," Chim-dur said. "And I think they would have."

"What have they said?"

"They said they are here to share the story of Jesu with the great king Gjona-ja, whose kingdom, though overflowing with majesty and wonder, is but a goat in the desert compared to that of Jesu, the king of all kings."

"The king of all kings?" Gjona said with a laugh. He found himself gripping the lion's mane in the arm of his chair. "A dead lamb god, the king of all kings?"

"The king of all kings."

"Hm," Gjona said. "Kill them."

"Yes, my lord." Chim-dur turned and walked out toward the stables. Along the way he signaled for two guards to follow him down the flame-lit halls, out the massive front doors of the yurt and into the stable, where the priests looked at Chim-dur with glad expectation.

"Kill them," Chim-dur said to the guards. Then, as an afterthought, "Spare the horses."

As he walked away, he listened for the sound of shouts or screams. But he heard only a rush of urgently chattered Latin followed by the dull thud of wood crushing bone.

A generation passed before Gjona heard about Jesus again. There were no more spies, no more roving priests, though he did hear reports of priests traveling along the Silk Road to Khitay. Fine then, Gjona said, let the spies of Jesu meet the teeth of a flying dragon instead of the thick end of a club.

Most nights, Gjona walked the rounds of his palace, visiting the halls and inner rooms of his guests and tributes. On any given night he might walk in on a game of chance involving bones and blades or step into a parlor where an audience gathered to hear wine-readied stories lively enough to make them almost sick from laughing. Some nights, he'd open a door to find lovers inside who often asked him to join them, and some nights he did. Some nights he'd step into the mirror room, where the walls were hung with forty mirrors, one for each parcel of his new kingdom; looking into them Gjona could look through the eyes of the forty Kyrgyz kings. These eyes might show him other games, other loves, other meals or battles, some to amuse, some to sicken, some to bore, and some to excite. There were so many doors, and after so many years of so many nights, Gjona often became weary of opening them. He'd find himself back in his private tent, his yurt within a yurt, sitting on his pillows and eating a meal out of habit more than desire.

Many of these nights he'd spend calculating his next conquest or the strength of his borders. The empire was at peace, and peace made him restless. Baytosk and Chim-dur were long dead, and even Bayan was now a doddering old woman whom he supported out of lingering obligation. There was no one now he could trust short of the nagging salamander in the brazier, who upon sensing its arrival in Gjona's thoughtstreaming pushed a pulse of lovingthanks to the master, that it might ease his fears.

Fears? Gjona tried to ignore the salamander. He would have shouted at it, were it not for the presence of a servant who was kneeling at a table nearby, clattering platters of bread and wine. The lamb's meat laid out for dinner was old, slick and tangy. This was the fault of the steward—incompetent and lazy—who should know better than to let the stores run so dry that the king was left to eat the remains of better meals.

Gjona was worried. In the fifty years since the taking of the Silk Road, he had also taken all of Sogdiana, and as his reach extended he heard more rumors of Manas. The rumors served him well, as most conquered people thought him to be Manas, and Gjona did nothing to correct their mistake. At times he even began to think of himself as the prophesied hero—but if he was, where were the powers? It was said that Manas could call down lightning with a stone, lead a gryphon into battle, or cause night and day to change places in the sky. And if he was not—then where *was* Manas?

At the same time, there were strange things happening on the borders. Khitay was in check, but to their north were rumors of "khans" too strong to be conquered. And to the west, Constantinople pushed back along the new Silk Road with stories of that dead king, said to be more powerful than any Manas or khan.

Gjona took out his worries in violence against his meal, ripping greasy flesh from lamb bones. The clatter of the servant fumbling brass plates interrupted his fuming.

"Will you be quiet? You've all the grace of a lowlands goat on a mountainside."

"A servant must serve, just as a master must lead."

"Tch." The man was a fool.

But despite himself, Gjona thought on the words: A servant must serve, as a master must lead. The master does have a role, just as a servant does, Gjona told himself. Perhaps in the carrying out of those roles, we see what makes a man. Is the obedient servant more a man than the weak master? Then Gjona heard the servant's words anew. The servant had responded without any courtesies.

"Servant, you'll address me as 'lord' or you'll address me from the end of a pike, and without the benefit of any body parts below your neck."

The servant refilled Gjona's cup.

"The king, it seems, is in a state." The wine reached too high, spilling over onto the pillows, seeping into the fabric. "And yes, you should be angry at the steward. He did, after all, send you spoiled lamb and molded bread. But maybe if you forgave your steward, he wouldn't be so afraid to come to you with news of rotted stores."

Gjona picked up the bread. The servant was right—it was molded, dotted with black spots that could very well be lethal in large quantities. But Gjona couldn't remember having spoken any of these thoughts aloud.

"And how do you know I'm angry at the steward?" Gjona said, continuing to eat so as to appear undaunted.

"I know you, Gjona-ja," the servant replied. "I have known you for a long time. I think we have some common interests—enough common interests that it's time you got to know me better."

Gjona reached behind him for his sword, but it wasn't there. The servant stood calmly, with a sort of smile on his face. His arms were at rest, with his fingers laced together at the waist. He wore ratty brown cloth, with a soiled towel over one shoulder, torn leather sandals, and long shaggy hair pulled back from his face. His beard was unkempt and twined in knots, his face unclean. He was a dog, Gjona thought, a clever dog playing dangerous games with a king. Gjona tried to remember where the bread knife was.

"We won't settle this with blades, or fists, or clubs, not the way you settled things with the three priests from Constantinople."

Gjona remembered them, the spies he had killed, who had brought the eight-legged horses they still bred as treasures of the kingdom. "Those were not priests," Gjona said. "Those were the spies of some dead king, looking to build their fortune from my coffers." The servant was a madman, and badly fed enough that Gjona was sure he could beat him to death with one fist, but this madman seemed to know things he shouldn't. Gjona wanted to know how.

"No, Gjona-ja. They were priests." The servant turned and walked to the sideboard. He took a pitcher of water and poured it into a basin. "They were good men I sent to help prepare you for my coming. And you met them with mistrust and death. Why would you do that?"

"Why not?" Gjona said. "Even if they weren't spies, I don't need emissaries with empty hands. They were beggars, then, and I treat beggars the way they deserve to be treated."

"So a person seeking aid is a beggar?" the servant asked, washing his hands in the basin. "A person of no use to you isn't worth your mercy?" He dried his hands on the towel at his shoulder. "Be careful of such words, even of such thoughts, Gjona-ja. Regret can be a heavy burden."

"Who are you?" Gjona demanded, standing and knocking his wine onto the now-soaked pillows. He remembered the prophecy and was for a moment struck with fear. "Are you Manas?"

The servant laughed. "No. Are you?"

The question stung in way it shouldn't have. Manas was a story, a legend the people used to give themselves hope, a warning the Khitay used to keep the people under control, a trick to ease the conquest of Gjona-ja. So why should he feel shame at the servant's question? He looked at him again. Only the white salamander had ever spoken to him this way. Only the white could make him feel anything like remorse. But the white had grown silent. Then he remembered.

"The Coaler. You're the Coaler."

"Yes, Gjona-ja," he said, smiling. "In a way, I am the Coaler. But I am also the dead king. I am the lamb. I am the bread. I am the servant."

"You're saying you're the dead god the priests talked of? Jesu, the one on the cross?"

"I am."

"But you're dead," Gjona said, smiling at the madman's idiocy.

"No, Gjona-ja. I am risen."

Gjona looked hard into the man's eyes and saw expansive fields of dark brown, fields devouring the sky over lush valleys, over rich kingdoms, over mountains as old as creation, stretching past wars and powers and into the souls of men. They pierced now into Gjona's soul, exposing an unbearable fear he hadn't felt since before he stopped dying. What was this man? A dead king? It couldn't be true, but it felt true in a way that made everything else seem unreal. Gjona felt the floor moving closer.

Jesus stepped forward and put a hand on Gjona's shoulder. He wiped the hot sweat from Gjona's forehead with the damp towel. The coolness of it tingled across his skull. The bread, or the lamb, or both—it had gotten to him. That was it, that must be it.

"Let's sit down, shall we?"

"Yes," Gjona said, no strength left in his voice, all of it spilling down onto the floor, washing away from him like the waters gush from a woman in birth. He felt weak, exposed.

Jesus kicked a dry pillow under Gjona and they sat together at the center of the yurt.

"Gjona-ja, king of Talas and the Silk Road, I have a task for you. My desire is that you should make yourself useful in a great many things, to carry forward the building of my kingdom."

Gjona looked at his unscarred arm and thought of his friends, his wife, his long-dead son. "So this is why I don't die? Because you find me useful?"

Jesus held back a laugh. "It's not that simple. But it starts with you, Gjona. It all has to start with you, inside you."

Gjona didn't understand. His head felt light, as if he were a dead man galloping on a horse, his head bobbing madly side to side. He no longer wanted to understand; he wanted only to comply. "What do you want with me?"

"I want to forgive you."

"To forgive?"

"To forgive you for your cruelty in the name of power, for your mercilessness amid calls for compassion, for your dispassion in the face of passion."

As Jesus laid out Gjona's sins, they became clear to him—that these were wrongs he had done to others. Still, some things had to be done in the rise to power. Some things were required of a king.

"Yes, Gjona, you told yourself this, but in your heart you knew these things were wrong." Jesus took a small loaf of bread from somewhere inside his garments and pulled out a chunk. The mold was gone, and the bread was white. "And for this I forgive you. Bread?"

CHRISTOPHER SMITH

Gjona ate the bread. Its cushiony sweetness filled his mouth. After he swallowed it, he felt full, without discomfort or sleepiness, nourished in a way that could sustain him forever.

"Let me tell you a story, Gjona-ja. There was a man from Merv traveling the Silk Road—before you burned it—leading a lamb to trade for a coat. Along the way, an angry river lashed out and took his lamb, pulling it down into the depths. He returned with no livestock, saddened. On the second day, the man from Merv carried upon his back a bushel of wheat to trade for bread. Again, the river lashed out and ripped the wheat from his back. He returned with no stores, dispirited."

Jesus produced a chalice of shining gold adorned with bejeweled silver bands, so bright it chased the shadows from the cobwebby corners of the room.

"On the third day, the man from Merv walked hand in hand with his bride, a beautiful young woman. Again, the river lashed out and took the woman, drowning her thrashing below the current. But this time, the man returned whole and at peace."

Gjona stared in silence.

"Well, what do you think of my story?"

"That the man wanted his wife dead."

Jesus smiled. "No. Well, maybe. Never trusted him myself. But my point is this: It is only when we have given up everything that we can become anything."

Jesus wiped the inside of the chalice with his towel, then stood and walked to the low table. He filled the chalice and returned.

"Wine?"

"Yes." Gjona drank the wine. A warm quenching sensation spread through his limbs, pushing out a cold that seemed now to have been with him so long he'd forgotten it wasn't part of his being.

"Now go in peace to love and serve me, and with my blessing.

Rule this land not as Gjona-ja, but as Presbiter Ionis, as a king and priest of both power and righteousness, and, in time, the savior of Jerusalem."

As Jesus said this, Ionis had a brief vision of a perfect kingdom, of a kingdom where people lived in order and justice, of an end to chaos, and of Gjona—Ionis—on its throne.

When next Ionis was aware of himself, Jesus was gone. The chalice was still there; Jesus had left it behind.

SUNDAY MORNING, PART II, BUT MOSTLY SUNDAY AFTERNOON: THE RISE AND FALL OF SAM BRUCKHEIM

P RESTER HAD NEVER DONE THAT to her before. In all the times they'd argued, Prester had sulked, yelled, even thrown a pillow once, but he'd never ignored her and walked out as if she didn't exist.

Mina had been sitting on the couch wondering how she'd get it through to Prester that she no longer wanted to die, or at least that she was no longer sure—that she wanted to wait a while and talk things out. She wasn't angry at him anymore, not really. Mina could see things from his point of view, and she knew Prester well enough to see that he'd made his plans and was ready for implementation. Steering him away now was asking for trouble. But this was big, too big to go along with simply in order to make him happy.

Prester came in, walked to the kitchen, opened a cabinet, closed it, and walked to the window. She told him they needed to talk, and he left. She was too stunned to follow. Something must be terribly wrong—maybe with his shadow, maybe with their marriage—and he was either too embarrassed or too angry to discuss it.

Mina wandered the house, catching herself staring for long minutes at the sky or the dishes or the shower-curtained couch or the burn marks around the front door. She thought of May banging her knee on the underside of the table and of what the shadow must have done to her, how it must have touched her. She thought of Prester's words—"I want it to be because I love you." She didn't like her thoughts; she didn't like where they took her and how they made the hairs of her skin shimmer with transparence.

When she couldn't stand the silence and loneliness anymore (where the hell was Prester anyway? She wasn't about to sit in the house all day waiting for him), she dressed (she had five clean outfits; which ones would she never wear again?) and left the house, unsure where she would go, but certain she wanted to be anywhere else.

When Prester first proposed suicide, it felt like he was only saying what they were both thinking. But was he? Or was he drawing on some unknown powers of the old world to manipulate her into agreement? They'd argued so many times since he lost his job, intricate fights that lasted a week or more, beginning in a quiet moment or unkind look and building from sniping into tearful charges, countercharges, and challenges for rhetorical justification. Then would come numb days of exhaustion where it really didn't matter anymore who was wrong or who apologized first so long as the fighting stopped. She couldn't be sure anymore what was really in her mind and what came from his. Prester had some 1,750 years on her; how could she know if he was up to something? What if, as she had asked herself again and again for the last several weeks, what if he intended to kill her and walk away? Would he do that? How would she know he hadn't done it before, a dozen times, every time one of his wives got too old to give him an erection? Every time he "lost the passion of his wife," as he put it.

She walked into town, down pebbled streets toward signs of life—actual life, not the hum of TVs and computers in darkened beach-house dens. A little girl's laughter sparkled down the street as she and a friend sat on a patchy front yard making false teeth out of saltwater taffy.

Pebbles flashed by along the ground, streaks of reflected iridescence in blue, green, violet. Pebbles dug up from long saltwater trenches now filled with car tires and scallops. Pebbles, then stones, cobblestones of the downtown street. Gray at first, gray with the dulled weariness of being on the outskirts, waiting for something more than gas stations and street signs to add color to their lives. Pawn shops. Churches. Hair salons. Strip clubs. Any development would do. As Mina breezed closer to town, the stones grew fresh and clean with pride in this-great-city-of-ours. But that would change. It always changed on festival day. A crushed cigarette here, a coffee-cup sleeve there, and soon the stones would be smothered in streamers, candy, sandwich wrappers, maggots, and the filth left behind by proud, stupid Cyclopes waving tiny flags emblazoned "St. Brianna Island." Mina was glad for once that her legs had become ethereal from the calves down.

She was still again. So still, so quiet. Things moved past her. People. Some turned and looked into her glassy eyes. That's okay. Things flew by. Squirrels. Newspapers. Brown sleeves for coffee-to-go with catchy phrases: "Headlines are easier to write when you're not saddled with content." Headlines. "Rhodesians spot big bird." That was a headline. Mina drifted a bit, her feet now insubstantial. She bobbed down the street, dragging along the sidewalk with each gust of salt-infused sea breeze. A nice couple came into view, happy playdolls of a couple with bendable legs and matching smiles. They were happy in their construct of caretaking and extinction, two sides of the coin flipped into Adam's unworthy hand by a male God imposing male dominion.

"Mina?"

Bendable legs that went places and bendable arms that did things, important things, and mouths that didn't move but surely said things of substance, and made smiles that grew into concern.

"Mina? Mina, are you okay?"

Mina blinked.

"Oh dear, Reggie. I think she's having a fit."

Mina realized that she had stopped for God-knew-how-long in front of a shop downtown. The Gogs laughed in uncomfortable relief that she wasn't comatose.

"I'm sorry," Mina said in a distant whisper.

May put her arm around Mina and walked her to a nearby bench. She didn't notice that Mina moved her legs only as a pretense; her body was floating across the concrete. "Okay, you just come sit down here and rest a minute in the shade. You'll be just fine."

Yes, Mina told herself. I'll be fine. She looked at her watch. She must've been standing there for forty-five minutes. Her skin was pink with the onset of translucence.

"Mina dear, how long have you been out here in the sun?" May asked. "You look as pale as . . . well, I don't know what, but you need to get out of the sun."

Reggie gave his wife a look. "May, please."

"Don't May-please me. I can say what I want and Mina knows what I mean, don't you Mina? Good grief, if he had his way he'd have me up on his arm with his hand up my ass making up the words for me, wouldn't you?" May sat down next to Mina, rubbing her softened hand, pushing the blood back into her veins, pushing her veins back into reality.

"Maybe later, dear," Reggie said, drawing an exasperated look from May. He disappeared into a nearby milk shop.

"What happened, honey? Are you all right?"

"I'm fine. Just had a . . . moment. It happens sometimes."

"Oh, good." May dropped Mina's hand and began fiddling with the makeup in her purse.

That was settled, she seemed to be thinking, and Mina considered whether she should be offended at how quickly May moved off subject. She was a funny little woman. Ebullient, charming, not particularly smart, but Mina had more than she needed of that from Prester. May was married to a horrid man, but Mina could look past that. In another life, if she weren't about to die, she might consider May a friend.

"It's so good to see you today!" May said. "And I'm so sorry if Reggie was a bother at dinner last night."

Mina considered her words. Disappointed? Horrified? Disgusted? "I was just surprised," she said. "About his job. But I suppose everyone has to do something for a living."

"You don't have to pretend with me, Mina. I know Reggie can be frustrating sometimes, particularly with his line of work, because it's a difficult topic for so many people with it being controversial and all, because not everyone thinks that sort of thing is a good idea, you know, and that's what makes it controversial. And that's what I told Reggie this morning when we were doing yoga, that it's just not the sort of thing you bring up in front of people."

"You do yoga? Together?"

"Yes, I just love yoga, don't you? Reggie and I do yoga every morning before our walk, to loosen us up and everything. I was telling him it's just not the sort of thing you bring up. But he said it's his job, it's what he does, it's who he is, and how can you not talk about that when you're meeting people? So, well, I don't think we ever came to any kind of agreement about it, but we yelled at each other for a while."

"I hate that you argued about us."

"Psh, we yell at each other all the time. It's the only way to get a word in with him the way he goes on, anyway. But in any case, we're both really sorry about that and we'd love to get together with you two tomorrow at the Crab Festival. Maybe we can have lunch or watch the parade together. Isn't it exciting, all the decorations?"

Reggie came back out from the milk shop and handed Mina a tall styrene cup of ice water. "Here, this might help." He turned to May. "You know they wanted to charge me $4.25 for that?"

"No!"

"Yep, $4.25. And that was after I had to wait in line for an old lady trying to order milk with Pepsi in it, and of course they don't sell Pepsi."

"Why did she want milk with Pepsi?"

"I don't know," Reggie said. "That's what she wanted. That's what she said. Milk with Pepsi."

"What would that even taste like?" May said.

"Creamy, I guess, and sweeter than Coke."

"Hah!" May blurted. "Sweeter than Coke!"

The ice water in Mina's throat sent ripples of cool moisture down her arms and legs. She sipped carefully, worried she might get a headache from the sudden drop in body temperature—or maybe that it might spill out of her body if any parts were still unreal. She could feel the gaps closing, though, and her skin stitching back together into something resembling wholeness.

"So I told them hell no I'm not paying $4.25 for water, and if I was near my sink I wouldn't be paying at all. So the lady said well you're not at your sink are you? So I told her my poor friend out there on the bench is about stone-dead and drifting, ready to float off their pavement. So unless they wanted a dead body hung up on the underside of their awning the day before the Crab Festival, they'd better give me a damn cup of water."

"Reggie, I have money for the water," May said.

"Well, so did I, but that's not the point! The point is, why should I have to pay for water?"

"Didn't you get that money I left for you on your dresser from my purse? I hate it when you leave the house without money. I never know when you're going to end up needing it and have to call me to come find you to give you cash. Nobody on this island manages to take credit cards, it's just exasperating."

"May! That is not the fucking point! I'm not going to pay $4.25 for water!"

"Well, you shouldn't!"

"I know!" Reggie turned to Mina, and for a moment she was so shocked by the outburst she was afraid he might yell at her, too. "Hey, how are you, are you okay?"

"Yeah, I'm fine," Mina said.

"You sure?"

Mina looked at him and May. They were fine now. The fight was over. He'd said what he wanted to say, and she'd said what she wanted to say, and it was over. And now, here he was, done with May and ready to deal with Mina, and suddenly Mina didn't want to be dealt with like another problem for the big hero in a line of problems to be solved. She was ready to throw the water in his face, to call him a condescending, empty waste of a man. But as she looked up, she saw in his eyes true sympathy. To those eyes she could say, "Actually, I feel awful, could you carry me back to my house?" and he'd do it. What he did for a living was despicable, and that he could go back day after day knowing what he did made her feel ill. But here he was, being oblivious to all of that and just trying to be nice. She couldn't help it. She smiled. "Yes, I'm fine. Thanks, Reggie."

"Listen, I'm sorry about last night. We kinda got off on the wrong foot."

"The foot in his mouth," May said. "Hah!"

Mina was exhausted. Between the fading and the fight with Prester, she had no more capacity to spar with Reggie or anyone else, or to make them feel better about the ontological corner they'd backed themselves into. "Let's just not discuss that," Mina said.

Reggie looked deflated. He'd expected something more conciliatory, more bendable and smiley.

"Well, listen, Reggie needs to get going, because he's got to be there at two and it's already ten-till. He's got to have some genetic testing and preliminary injections for the molting competition tomorrow."

"Yep," Reggie said. "Better go."

"I was going to go with him to make sure everything's okay, because you know how these crabs are and I don't want him ending up with a permanent shell or claws, hah! But really I'm not sure I trust them. I heard once about a man who tried to sneak melted butter onto the island? And do you know they had one of those awful Cyclopses hold him down while they injected him with grouper roe, so by the end of the day he had fins and everything? And then they actually ate him. The Cyclopses did, I mean. Because those crabs, you know they won't eat anything that hasn't already rotted on the seabed, and there wasn't nearly enough time for that. So I was going to go with Reggie, but I think I better see you home, because you still look a bit worn down."

Listening to his wife, Reggie's expression changed from happy humor to uncertainty about the genetics work, and he seemed to be looking for a polite, manly way to ask May to come hold his hand. Mina smiled at the thought of him enduring the modifications. She wondered if there was anything that could be done to implant memories along with the carapace. Memories not just about the extinct, but the memories from within the extinct as well, of living inside their reality, of being, touching, smelling, and feeling in the world. All those things that we seem intent on conquering in our toy-sword quest for dominance.

"No, it's okay," Mina said. "You two go along. I'm fine now, and I'm meeting Prester soon anyway."

"You sure?" Reggie said.

"Definitely."

"Well, all right then," May said, taking Mina's hand again and turning toward her dramatically. "We'll try to catch up with you tomorrow at the festival. You take it easy."

The Gogs walked away down the street, toward the hospital and genetic alterations center, holding hands.

Mina was left standing in front of the milk shop. She could hear the steamers whistling and frothing inside, making sweet cream lattes and chilled lactose fluffs. It was a Brother Borshky's, one of two on the island. The chain had started in the hills of North Carolina, where a group of monks had been given a special license to sell their salamander milk—normally prohibited, but the Salamandrite monks had special friends in the North Carolina legislature, and they proved to be friends worth having. From a few downtown shingle signs in Asheville to a sprawling franchise with Atlanta diocesan headquarters, the monks had turned their one-salamander operation into the vast Brother Borshky's chain, with tens of thousands of locations all over the world. They served things like double-pasteurized, lactose-free skims with a shot of curd, and were serviced by regional cathedrals that resembled livestock farms, with shrine/milking stations for the hundreds of salamanders at each site. It was an impressive operation, which the monks insisted drew the favor of the Great Salamander herself.

Near the alley next to the milk shop, a sour scent roiled from the garbage cans, the stench of weeks of molded-over cream residue in rusting metal pails. The smell was strong enough to rouse Mina into walking again toward the heart of downtown.

The closer Mina got to the city center, the more frantic was the activity around her as the town prepared for the Crab Festival. Signs for molting clubs and eye-stalk polishers were plastered in store windows. Hunched-over street cleaners with sandblaster toothbrushes formed long lines across the road, shoulder to shoulder and eyes mostly downcast, raising them in unison to give dirty looks to anyone who didn't leapfrog over them quickly enough. Droning, stupid questions rolled off the thick tongue of a Cyclops who was slowly, gingerly hanging banners across rooftops.

It was too much.

Mina slipped into a museum—the St. Brianna Memorial Museum and Conference Center—and took deep breaths of air-conditioned room freshener. She hadn't been inside the museum in many years, not since the days when she and Prester first visited the island, taking in all the touristy sites before settling in as near-residents.

The lobby was cool and dry. Red carpet covered the floors and walls, all the way up to a dark wooden ceiling. Long, drooping chandeliers struggled against walls and floors that drank light faster than it could be emitted. Plate-glass display windows glowed along the narrow hallway ahead; a wooden donation box separated her from them, yawning for coins. The box had been finely painted, at one time, in a pure white that stood out amid all the dark reds and browns of the room. At the corners it still bore the glimmer of unsmudged brass that matched its hinges and long-fastened latch.

Mina dropped some coins in the box, which got down from its pedestal on squeaking wooden legs and toddled ahead of her to the first exhibit, an old colorized postcard image about twenty feet tall that showed overdressed swimmers being fondled by saltwater.

"Please step this way, and do not tap the glass," the box said to Mina, as if she were a crowd of fifth-graders. "The tour is about to begin." The box paused and seemed to be trying to collect itself. Its spiel had started too late, and it wasn't sure whether to skip ahead or start over. It resigned itself to following the script. "St. Brianna Island is known for its playful waves and long, white-powder sand beaches, but its original claim to fame was as a sanctuary for politically marginalized redshell crabs." The image was from the 1920s, before the revolts. It seemed to show the waves as playmates on the beach rather than the annoyance that Mina knew them to be. Propaganda had changed.

The box waddled to the next window, behind which a living, naked old man sat on a tall steel stool. "The crabs' story began in the late 1920s, when industrialist Sam Bruckheim, having chipped a tooth on a malformed crab claw, began a campaign for genetic modification of the North American crab."

Mina looked for the eyes of Sam Bruckheim, but they were cast down, maybe upon his liver-spotted knees. He looked cold, but he was not shaking. The donation box pushed a button on the wall, causing Mr. Bruckheim to startle, then make a forced grin, showing a broken front cuspid.

He looked away from the window despite his grin, and he seemed to keep grinning even as Mina moved hesitantly to the next window. What a horrible thing, she thought, to be put on display like that. He had aged a lot since she last visited. Then, he'd had a look of anger, of defiance. Now, it was something else. Resignation. Surrender.

"At first, the modifications seemed a boon to the crab community. Their claws were larger and meatier, their coloring more brilliant. But Bruckheim's eccentricities began to show themselves."

Behind the next window, in front of large photos of deformed crabs with shoes growing from their feet and hats from their antennae, was a taxidermied bright red monstrosity that seemed to combine a duck with a dustpan. It had claws.

The box continued. "As the population of willing volunteers for modification dwindled, Bruckheim and his teams began kidnapping crabs from the seabed and forcing them into laboratories. This led to the Redshell Revolts of 1934 and the subsequent

Castigation of Sam Bruckheim Act, which, along with generous contributions from patrons like yourself, provides ongoing funding for the museum to this day."

The next window showed an empty room with steel walls. A panel opened inside, and Bruckheim appeared again, stepping into a room he'd been forced into for more tours on more days through more years than he could count. Cupping his gray-tufted genitals with his hands, he walked to the center of the room, turned to face Mina, and squatted on the floor, waiting. Another panel opened on the other side, and a half-dozen bored crabs scuttered in, holding cricket bats. Bruckheim didn't try to run. He curled up in a ball, covering his head with scarred and bruised arms while the crabs closed in, then beat him lazily with the cricket bats.

"How long has he been . . ."

The box held up one twig of an arm. "Please hold your questions until after the tour, thank you." It tottered on to the next exhibit, leaving Bruckheim to his tormenters and Mina still watching.

"Today, the redshell crabs have a large sanctuary on the eastern side of St. Brianna Island, where they remain hard at work on their own natural selection process to undo years of Bruckheim's experimentations."

The box droned on. Mina could hear the grinding of crab mating processes in the next exhibit, with the music of Barry White in the background. But she stayed there, in front of Bruckheim, watching them work. There was no pleasure. They seemed only to draw up enough energy to swing a claw forward and get in a hit, then drop away to find enough will to swing again. Had they been trying, they might have been able to hurt him much more, but they didn't seem to care. And what about Bruckheim? Why did he stay? Why did he cooperate? He was a sick, old man. Could it be that he enjoyed it?

She waited and looked carefully for his face, hoping perhaps she'd catch his eye and then she'd know what it was that drove him, day after day after day, into the steel room to cower naked before the cricket bats. Then, just then, he saw her staring, and he drilled at her with his eyes—old, bloodshot eyes with the lower lids dripping away like centuries-old slate mildew or the sagging teats of a hiero-salamander. There was no masochistic pleasure in them. If there had been, it died long ago. There was only routine. Only knowing that the same thing is done today as was done the day before and will be done again tomorrow.

His eyes were blue but tinged with grey, tinged with Prester's eyes, tinged with the drudgery of centuries and the yawning dread of centuries to come. The decision was made, yes, but it was made for a reason, and it must have been a long time coming. Prester John was ready to die.

Mina imagined Bruckheim not beaten and dragged and sustained but left to drift, a half-dead, forgotten specter floating up against the ceiling in a milkshop corner like an obscene Mylar balloon, his hollow eyes screaming out into silence, her silence, her nothingness, and the eyes became hers. Her eyes, her body, her eternity, another wispy cobweb of unlived life, slipping away, one layer at a time. Bruckheim had gone from a man of will—deranged will, but strong—to a passive object. But she, she could choose—choose not to wait for some medical breakthrough or gradual transparence. It was in her power now, and she could say for herself when it would be over. Why not? Why was she doubting herself, now? The life that lay ahead was only slow torture, perhaps not a life of being beaten listlessly by crabs, but torture still. At least in suicide, in action, there was power.

They finished. The crabs scuttered back out, dragging their bats behind them. Bruckheim stood and walked back through his door, looking only at his yellowed toes.

What a relief, Mina thought. What a relief it would be, for both of them, to die.

She felt solid. She could hear the firm stamp of her heels as she walked past the glass cages and toward the door. She dropped the cash from her wallet onto the clean square in the dust where she knew the talking box would return.

And as she smiled and wiped her cheek, she was surprised to see that the drop sliding down her face was absolutely clear.

SARCALOGOS REX, 615-1136 A.D.

THE NEXT EMISSARIES FROM CONSTANTINOPLE, who arrived in about 615 A.D., were received with more courtesy than the first. These three priests were met with a great banquet upon the emerald table: rabbit with currant sauce, kazi sausage, quail, and, in tribute to the homeland of Presbiter Ionis, roasted fennis with salamander's milk.

They were not beaten with clubs, nor were their horses stolen. In fact, their mounts—strange, ugly, spitting beasts with large bent backs and necks like snakes—were taken from them and slaughtered, and they were given an upgrade: the offspring of the eight-hooved stallions that their predecessors had brought to the kingdom.

A bit to the priests' dismay, as they hadn't been told they'd never need them again, their mud- and shit-stained traveling clothes were burned and replaced with fire-refined silk. Their skullcaps and hairbags disappeared in favor of custom-made wool kalpaks, folded by the virgin daughters of Ionis' chief generals. These daughters were then offered to the priests for marriage. Some months passed before the clergy accepted both their unexpected permanent assignment to the court of Presbiter Ionis and the bonds of matrimony to local families.

In exchange for teaching their new sovereign the finer points of Christianity—beyond his new daily habit of eating bread and drinking wine—the priests were given full access to the library. They seemed more excited about the library than about the wives, and they quickly made themselves a nuisance with requests for more wisps, more tables, even a hole in one wall for the admission of light and fresh air. When they began insisting that Ionis learn to read, however, he marked the butt of his emerald scepter on the throne. Nothing more was to be said.

With the priests' help, Ionis gradually worked to reform his court into the Christian kingdom Jesus had called for. The priests taught him the commandments and several other key instructions regarding the uncleanness of bleeding women, unblessed food, and serpents. Within only a few generations, Ionis began to see himself as the shepherd of a growing flock, wiping out disloyal subjects like rooting boars or dangerous rocks, according to God's law and not his own whims.

Following in the tradition of the Hebrew kings, in about 800 A.D. Ionis began sitting in judgment on civil and criminal matters. At the first opportunity, he commanded that a disputed goat be cleaved in half, from tongue to tail. The goat was not happy with this judgment, but Ionis was not to be challenged in his own court, and the goat was silenced. The same judgment was applied to various rabbits, monkeys, and other disputed creatures, and would have been applied to a slave if not for the last-minute howling intercession of the priests—descendants of those first emissaries—who insisted that applying the equal-cleavage precedent to humans would be a violation of God's law, and that in fact Solomon never intended to carry out his ruling in the disputed infant case. Ionis thought it weak-minded of an emperor to issue a judgment he had no intention of executing.

The dead lamb king seemed to smile fondly on Presbiter

Ionis, for in the centuries that followed his conversion, the Ionian Empire—the Grand Diocese, as Ionis liked to call it after learning a smattering of clerical jargon—had swallowed the Dahae west to the Caspian Sea, the eastern remnants of the Sassanid Empire including Nishapur and Herat, the Hephtalites in the south from Kesh to Balkh, the Rouran and the Uighurs to the east, and in the north, as far as the gryphon could fly, lands beyond those of the sciapods and Quaabites. The Umayyads, Abbasids, Jou-Jan, Qarluq, Kypchaks, and Oghuzes, not to mention the Kangui, Kurgans, Sogdians, and Kyrgyz, were all under his dominion.

As the diocese grew, more bishops ordained more priests and curates and second curates, and as they grew in number, they grew bolder. The priests had long cautioned, with increasing insistence, against Salamandrism, arguing some nonsense that the world was created not from rivers of milk that flowed from the teats of the Great Salamander, but in a garden using ribs and dust. Ionis at first laughed and warned them against repeating these claims to a people who already struggled to accept that the courtesies normally reserved for guests should be extended to all of one's neighbors, and that to steal a man's wife was as bad as to steal a guest's horse. These ideas were hard enough without challenging the sanctity of the household salamander. And after all, Ionis told them, what did it matter how the world was created? But over the generations, the priests began to be more vocal about the salamanders, and one day in about 950 A.D. a messenger arrived in the Grand Yurt with a letter in need of the signature and emerald seal of Presbiter Ionis.

"Read it to me," Ionis said. He was busy carving the tiny figure of a boar out of the larger figure of a lion, which had been carved out of the larger figure of an eagle, which had been carved out of a block of apple wood. Carving had become Ionis's favorite way of passing the time while he listened to courtesies.

"My lord?" The messenger seemed dismayed, and Ionis got the

immediate impression he'd hoped Ionis would sign the letter without knowing what it said.

"Read it."

Ionis almost drifted off listening to the first few pages of the priests' encyclical, which was titled "On the Propriety of a Christian Household." There were long passages about the designs of tapestries, about washing in only non-sentient water, about the creeping things that creep upon the earth, and then this:

> ... that salamanders, being kin to the denizens of hell, and breathing hellfire upon their very lips and living in the very flames to which our Lord cast the Enemy, should be excommunicated from each Parish of each Diocese and wherever possible put out of the homes of the families of the righteous. The exactment of this encyclical will be verified upon clerical visits, wherein any family housing such a beast shall no longer be considered one in communion with the True Faith.

Ionis was awake now. He was standing on the dais of his throne, looming a foot and a half over the messenger, who could no longer read because his hands were shaking. This was no Jesus. This messenger was a slight man of the people: dull black eyes, dressed enough like a monk to be known as one of them, but without any vestments of authority or respect. He had as much right to deliver such a message as a goat to demand justice. Just before Ionis could grab the messenger by the neck, he felt warm clouds of green humming toward his mind, pulling him away from wrath and into soothingkind and patiencewait.

"I don't want your soothing," he whispered.

"My lord?"

"Not you," he boomed, ripping the parchment out of the messenger's hand. "Get out." The messenger turned and walked, and then as he began to run, Ionis shouted, "Wait. Stop." He had another idea. He'd send back a message—a messenger leading a battalion of soldiers to split their skulls.

Soothingkind and calm. Patiencewait.

"You hear what they want to do to you? To all of your kind?" Ionis whispered to the salamander. "First they want you excommunicated and next they'll want you killed. You want me to sign this?"

No. Nosigning. But calmingthoughts. Calmingthoughts and carefulmaking. These falsepriests and notCoalers, notCoalers and idlewaiting and troublemaking.

"Idle, yes." Ionis uncrumpled the paper and looked at the writing. He didn't know what the characters and words meant, but he saw what it took to make them. They were carefully drawn, with patience and precision. Each section began with a letter painstakingly illuminated with flowers and fish or spirals of vine, inlaid with emerald dust and lined with liquid gold. This had taken weeks, perhaps months, to write out.

"They need something to do."

Ionis wadded up the page and walked toward the cowering messenger, then stuffed it in the man's mouth, grabbed him by the collar, and marched toward the presbytery. A band of seven soldiers rushed in behind Ionis as he walked, and he allowed them to follow, though he felt certain he wouldn't need them. He kicked open the door of the rectory and tossed through it the messenger, who fell to the floor and coughed out the wadded-up encyclical.

"I bring you tidings from Presbiter Ionis!" the messenger blurted.

Ionis smiled. He'd have to keep the messenger.

"Assembled curates of the Grand Diocese," Ionis began.

The two dozen men had been sitting around a long table covered in books and parchment and bright bobbing wisps tethered by string. The men jumped to their feet.

"Upon receiving your beautifully written encyclical, I was inspired to write another, on many, many more pages, on the proper relationship between curate and priest—and emperor—using as ink the blood pouring out of your necks."

The soldiers stepped forward, but Ionis held up a hand.

"But the subject of your encyclical—one of the creeping things that creep upon the earth—pleaded with me to have mercy, and to consider that you might be overly taxed with too much time at your disposal, and that maybe instead of slitting your throats I should find some better use for you."

Ionis walked to the table, and the priests backed away from it. He put his hands on it and looked around, thinking of Jesus with his disciples—only at this table, they would *all* betray him if they could. They needed something to turn their minds. Something to turn them from connivers to mendicants.

"My brothers, I want you to pray for me."

"To pray?" one of the older curates croaked.

Ionis imagined the curates hogtied with their hands clasped together, being roasted naked on a pile of salamander coals, but that wasn't what he had in mind.

"Yes, to pray for me. Starting now, right now, you will hold the Mass of Presbiter Ionis. You will celebrate Mass in my honor all day, every day, and all night every night. You will not rest, you will not sleep. You will celebrate the Mass and at its conclusion you will begin again."

"And after that?" the older curate asked.

"You begin again," Ionis said. "And again and again. I find myself in need of much prayer."

The curates looked at one another.

"Here, I'll help you get started. *Gloria Patri, et Filio, et Spiritui Sancto.*"

The curates joined in, hesitantly. "*Sicut erat in principio, et nunc, et semper, et in saecula saeculorum. Amen.*"

"Good, good. I'll leave you to it then."

When reports came back a few days later that the curates had begun collapsing in exhaustion, Ionis issued an encyclical of his own. All curates of the Grand Diocese would celebrate the Mass of Presbiter Ionis every day in three shifts, so they might have time to sleep and eat. To vary things, each day of the week they would pray for a different bishop and king, for now Ionis had divided his Grand Diocese into seven smaller dioceses: Maveranahr, Jetysuu, Bactria, Dahae, Khorasan, Gandhara, and Sogdiana. When the priests from the outer dioceses objected to this workload, Ionis added more. They would also pray each month for one of the twelve dukes of the Grand Diocese, and each day for one of its 365 counts. As the complexity of the structure grew, the clergy began to see its wisdom and soon retreated so far into daily Mass that Ionis forgot their names.

The ordination of his empire that began with making diocesan bishops of his kings felt right, so he extended it, starting with his first cook, who was made a prior and king. His marshal would be abbot and king, and his chamberlain bishop and king, then his butler archbishop and king. His steward would be patriarch and king. For himself, Ionis reserved the title of Presbiter, having been told that a show of humility is far more exalting than putting great titles upon oneself.

By 1110, Ionis felt his Grand Diocese complete, and in celebration of this, he held a year-long Mass. The first week consisted of the Introit, which called for a seven-day procession of bishop-kings from each diocese of his empire to the Balsam Palace and cathedral. During the second week were the three-day Kyrie, three days of the Gloria, and a Collect lasting an entire day, calling for God's favor upon each carefully itemized aspect of the kingdom, from its flocks and its silk to its armies and scholars. The Epistle lasted some four weeks, as did the Gradual. For the Gospel procession, the entire body of several thousand worshippers paraded outside the walls of Talas, into the hills, around the city, and back into the cathedral in a weeklong trek. After a four-week reading of the Gospel (one week for each Evangelist), Presbiter Ionis was called upon to deliver the Sermon. This he accomplished in one day while the tables were being set for lunch, and by the time the Credo started, the vast majority of the worshippers didn't realize they had missed the Sermon. Those who did hear it recalled something about a man drowning his wife. By midsummer, it was time for Communion to begin, and this process lasted ten weeks, with every member of the Grand Diocese expected to make pilgrimage to the cathedral to receive the host and wine.

Amid all of this, there was a rush on baptism, with hordes of families bringing children stacked by the wagonful to the banks of the Talas River for the sacrament, rumored to be officiated by Ionis himself. When he finally got word of the rumor and arrived at the riverbank, entire families were being washed away and drowned by waves that were only too glad to accept the unwitting sacrifice. The crowds stampeded and flowed back again with each new set of frantic cries for help, like waves of life lapping the water. Ionis arrived to see the final grasps of hands flailing in the current as yet another group slipped under the delighted waters. There was a child lying in the black sand, crying, orphaned and helpless. Ionis picked him up and decided that as priest on duty it was up to him to give the child either last rites or baptism—in any case, some sort of sacrament was called for.

Ionis looked hard into the face of the child, who was just old enough to speak, and demanded, "What name do you give yourself?"

The boy stopped crying a moment and blurted, "Tokmat."

Ionis marched directly into the waters, which then humbled

themselves into placidity.

"Tokmat, I baptize you in the name of the Father."

The child began screaming as Ionis dunked him under the water that had consumed his family.

"And the Son."

On the second dunking, the child was coughing too hard to scream.

"And the Holy Ghost."

The "Amen" from the crowd, echoing across the Talas River valley, shocked young Tokmat into quiet submission.

Ionis turned to hand the child off to someone, but there was no one nearby. So to avoid any liturgical gaffe, he tucked the boy under his arm like a bag of dead rabbits and strode back to his yurt. Along the way, he nodded to a line of young priests, who rushed in to begin baptism for the rest of the crowd. Amid the hundreds of people praying and dunking and amen-ing at once, any who could discern under what name they'd been baptized could consider themselves truly blessed.

During the final weeks of Communion that followed, young Tokmat was left with nothing better to do than to toddle after Ionis like a dog awaiting scraps, which was, in fact, how he was primarily fed. The priests and courtiers who tried to remove him were met with sudden shouts or a disruptive chase, until finally Ionis told them to let the boy be, and Tokmat spent more time lingering in the shadow of his master than most.

As the final act of the yearlong Mass, Ionis himself delivered two days of the weeklong benediction. All agreed it was a fine service. Those who didn't were never heard from again.

After this, Ionis retired to his personal sacristy to change out of the sweat-, wine-, and filth-stained alb that he'd been wearing for the whole year. A woman was waiting there for him. She wore purple veils over a sparse red garment, accented with golden bands and jangly bracelets and anklets. Her presence wasn't unusual; Ionis would often call for a concubine to await him in the sacristy, but this time he hadn't called for one. It must have been a surprise gift arranged by his steward, and Ionis was grateful for the thoughtfulness.

"Ah, good," he said.

"You expected me?" the woman asked.

"No, but I'm glad you're here. Help me with this." He raised his arms and lifted his neck. She came forward and unwound the golden stole, which was embroidered with white salamanders chasing one another's tails. Ionis had insisted upon this design over the objections of the Constantine and Roman theological scholars.

"I don't mind them, really."

"Don't mind what?" Ionis said.

"The salamanders," she said, loosening and pulling away his cincture.

Ionis looked down as she peeled open his mildewed alb.

"You're a mess. Would you like me to wash you, Ionis?" she asked, looking up at him with wide eyes the color of bear cubs, the soft brown of silent woods, the deep brown of fertile earth, of sustenance and everlasting life.

"Jesus!" Ionis grabbed up what was left of his alb, crammed it against his nakedness, and backed away.

"Yes," she said.

"You're a woman!"

"So you say," she said. "I am many things, Ionis. I am the Coaler, I am the Servant, I am the Lamb and the Priest and the Victim."

"Good God," Ionis said, lashing the alb around his waist.

"That too," she said. "It was a fine service, by the way. Though I have to say your sermon was lacking."

"I'm sorry . . . my Lord."

"It's fine, Ionis. You're fine. It's okay," she said with a gentle smile.

"Very well, my Lord." He was torn between fear and annoyance. He'd spent five hundred years building a kingdom on the might of Jesus Christ, and now the embodiment of love and power and peace had come to him in the form of a beautiful whore.

"I'll accept that as a compliment," Jesus said.

"Why have you come?" Ionis said.

"First, to tell you that I love what you've done with the place, with the Grand Diocese, as you call it. It far exceeds what I thought you'd make of it."

"Thank you, my Lord."

Jesus walked to a nearby trunk, opened it, and removed a fresh white alb, which she shook out and brought to Ionis.

"The visiting Latins and Constantines have told you of Jerusalem, of its place in my kingdom, of the promise that it will be restored?" she said.

"Yes." Ionis took the alb and put it on over the one wrapped around his waist, then stepped out of the old one.

Jesus smiled. "Jerusalem is now safe in her mother's arms, but the lands around it have been too long in the claws of the Saracens. I want the Holy Land back, and I want your help."

"How?"

"You will bring your armies to join with those of Emmanuel of Constantinople and Frederick of Rome, to drive the Saracens away from Jerusalem and protect the Holy Land."

"My armies. All of them?"

Jesus nodded.

"But—the mountains, and the desert, and the river."

"Don't be coy with me, Ionis." Jesus looked sideways at him and smiled, teasing him and batting her eyes. "The mountains and desert will be nothing for you. And the river, the river will be nothing for me. Did you know there were once two rivers?" Jesus held up a cincture by the middle, ends dangling side by side. "The Tigris had a twin, the Euphrates they called it. And it separated the people of God, in exile in Babylon, from their home in Jerusalem."

"What happened to it, this twin river?"

"I destroyed it," Jesus said, tossing the cincture at Ionis. "Or he did, or we did, depending on how you want to look at it. In some ways, that was before my time."

Ionis wrapped the cincture around his waist and tied it off.

"So I will make a deal with you, Ionis. Go to the Tigris. Wait there for me, and I will freeze the river solid so that your armies may pass over. Then you will march toward Jerusalem and destroy the Saracens. Will you do this for me?" Jesus walked up to him and raised her fingers, tickling Ionis under the chin.

"Please stop that," Ionis said.

"Very well," Jesus said with a laugh. Then she grew serious. "But will you do this, Ionis? Will you do this for me? Will you do this for God?"

He looked down at her: glazed with scented oil, big doe eyes accented by paint, lips reddened and full. She was more beautiful than he could have imagined, and his mind was ripped between conflicting versions of adoration.

"Yes, my Lord. I will march to Jerusalem."

Ionis sent word quickly, to stop the bishops from leaving Talas before he could convene a daylong announcement of the plan for a mustering of all the armies of the Grand Diocese, for a crusade of tens of thousands to Jerusalem. The announcement took only a day, but the planning would take the next twenty years.

And what came next began with a letter, and the letter with a word, the word with a character, and the character with a stroke.

The brush hairs bulged with ink, desperate for the release of a drip onto the crisp parchment below. Born of the ooze from an eel's gizzard mixed with the oils of crushed fennis seed, the ink had served no purpose thus far apart from darkening the inside of a dark vial in a dark jar in a dark box in a dark cabinet. Until now. A portion of the ink, too long on the brush, too close to fulfillment, emanated thoughts of a rebellious spatter upon the clean parchment, but the wiser whole held it back. At last the brush lowered and touched the paper. The ink spasmed in glorious union, fusing itself to the thirsty fibers of the page, becoming more, becoming meaning, in itself and in communion with the nearest stroke, its neighbor, and the character as a whole. The ink could not see beyond the character, but if it could, it would have found the sentences well worth its patience.

Dear Friends in Christ,

Hail to your Eminences Manuel of Constantinople and Frederick of Rome, rulers of the Western world, from Prester John, King of the Eastern Lands, of Quaab and of Gara, of Kyrgyz and of Buryat, of Kabul and the Steppe. Word has reached our kingdom of your great need in defense against the Saracens, enemies of our Lord and defilers of the Holy Land and of the Sepulcher in its Glory. You may be astounded to know that a king of the East shares with you in the one true Faith, but so it is and so it shall be forever, if our trust in God remains unspoilt by the ravages of the unconverted. You should know that we are greatly grieved to hear of the losses of Aleppo and Edessa, and our mind is set to restore these lands to your Eminences, upon whom the Lord has entrusted its care and keeping.

So I say to you that before the next Salamandric Effusion, we and our armies will issue forth to your aid, bringing with us the might of the Eastern kingdoms to wipe these invaders from the Holy Land. You should know that we have at our command 25,000 Quaabites, men strong in stature and skilled in clubbing the enemies of their brothers, with death coming upon a single stroke. We have also 10,000 Garunds and 8,000 Bi-Garunds, archers of such skill that they shoot their arrows doubled, striking targets at distances limited only by the sight of their fiery red eyes. You should know we have also sciapods, some 40,000 strong, quarrelsome beasts but numerous, who have but one leg and one massive foot, so large they may lie on their backs in the desert sun and shade themselves with it, but more often employed to flatten their enemies, for what they lack in wisdom they balance in ferocity. These beasts are denied the faith and seem bound only to follow those capable of turning their savage wills to a noble cause. We have also Hittites and varied men of the hills and plains east of the Great Mountains, and these men also, some 30,000 in number, we bring with us to your aid and defense.

May we together drive back the invaders, and may Christ visit upon you comfort and solace as we bide our time before the coming of our great victory.

Yours in Christ,

Presbiter Ionis

"Excellent, my lord," said Tokmat, now his steward, peeling away the letter to dust-dry the signature. "That will put comfort in Manuel and Frederick's hearts and bring courage to their armies. Christ Jesus will surely bless you for it, in this world and the next."

Ionis sealed the letter in the wax of melted emeralds with a stamp that showed his scepter, fashioned from an eagle's claws, and handed it to a missionary priest. He sat back in the ermine-lined fur of his chair; warmth surged through his body. Not since entering the Black Yurt with his whip in his teeth had Ionis felt such purpose, such power in having a mission to accomplish, a job to be done. But this was bigger. This was right. This was to be his path. He didn't need the salamander, now dancing a circle of joy from her nearby hanging brazier, to tell him through her emanations or ridiculous head-bobbing that this was the path that would lead him to glory. This was to be his purpose.

SUNDAY EVENING:
MISFIRE

PRESTER SAT IN HIS CAR watching the purple-crested sunset bring sharp focus to the homes and trees and liquid horizon around him, to the other parked cars and the streetside garbage cans and the pastel-blue clapboard house of the Gogs. It wasn't a well-designed house, he thought; the bedroom windows were too near the street. The headlights of every passing car would surely fill the room with light, and who would want that? Prester would have had curtains installed—thick curtains with solid liners.

Reggie and May Gog. Why would Jesus want them dead? Jesus had tricked him into a shithole of existential wonderment and then pissed on him with mission, so deep being the wonderment that the mission seemed nothing—a trifle he'd gladly undertake in the crisis of the moment. But now, looking back over things, he saw more clearly and couldn't make sense of the mission. Kill the Gogs. Why? What had they done? Or was it something they were about to do? Prester wondered if it was even his place to question the mission. The last mission Jesus sent him on had destroyed his empire, turned his people into roving nomads again, made a mockery of his letters of allegiance.

"Everything," Prester muttered to himself, sitting in his car parked outside the beach house. "Everything I do is wrong."

The Tigris, Abyssinia, Khala-ja, the shadow and Sharyn Henderson—disasters, all of them. And now, this insanity of killing the Gogs. None of it made sense. It had to be a distraction, something to put him off the suicide, not a genuine task with purpose.

Only when we give up everything can we become anything, Jesus had said. He would be a powerful king and the savior of Jerusalem, Jesus said.

No. It was all senseless, punctuated only by personal failure and a never-ending barrage of accusation. Senselessness. Senselessness and yawning time.

The house was dim when Prester finally opened his front door, though it wasn't quite dark outside. His keys rattled in the ceramic key bowl that should have broken long ago, and the *schurr* of crashing waves filled hollows in the drone of an otherwise silent house. The hallway alone glowed with the flames from the salamander pyrorium. The salamanders turned to follow Prester's passing to the bedroom, and the white's narrow eyes betrayed a sadness that made Prester suddenly alert as he opened the bedroom door.

"Mina?" The room was thick with steam.

"I'm here," she said.

He walked to the bathroom. She was lying back in the garden tub, the water clear and swirling. Her skin shimmered with reflected candlelight. In one hand she held a sweating glass of white wine. She slid over to one side of the tub, making room for Prester, and on his side of the tub—on a dry pedestal within arm's reach—lay the gun.

"Welcome home, dear," she said softly.

"Are you sure?" Prester asked, looking at the gun, then Mina.

"Yes," she said, smiling. "I'm sure."

Prester smiled back. "Okay."

He stepped back into the bedroom and sat to unlace his shoes. This was it, then, he thought. Time to put an end to everything. Two bullets, and in the tub there wouldn't be much mess. Again Mina's absolute competence overwhelmed any plans Prester could have come up with. He wondered at her change of heart, but he knew better than to probe too deeply into its cause. If she wanted him to know, she'd say so.

Mina felt a growing excitement now that Prester was home, an excitement she hadn't felt in many years. This would be the end, the end she'd wanted for so long. Free of her momentary doubts, she felt actual joy at the prospect of not being damned to fade away. She held back her anticipation and tried to break the silence. She didn't want Prester thinking too much. She wanted to reassure him that she was thinking clearly, and that this could be done in simplicity and honesty.

"So," Mina asked. "How was your day?"

"Fine," Prester said with a long pause. "I saw Jesus."

"Oh? How is he?"

"Good," Prester removed his shirt and pants and frowned at his toenails. He hadn't clipped them in weeks. To be discovered dead with long toenails. Would the embalmer clip them? "How was your day?"

"Fine," Mina said, staring at the beads of sweat dripping down the bulge of her wine glass. "I went to that museum downtown. They still have Sam Bruckheim there."

"Really? Is he still alive?"

"Yes, apparently so. He's likely to live a long time. The crabs beat him, you know."

"Hmm." Prester remembered Bruckheim, the madman who started the modifications. Officially, anyway. Genetic modification had been going on for decades before then, only with rubber gloves, siphons, and castration. Bruckheim really did nothing more than incorporate the nonorganic. Prester had never held it against him. Bruckheim was flawed and vulnerable to conceit like the rest of humanity. Besides, everyone needed a function.

"I think they do it daily. The beatings, I mean," Mina said. "Can you imagine? Trapped in a cell for all those years, every day going to be beaten the same way by the same things?"

Prester stood naked in the bathroom doorway.

"Is that what it's like, Prester? For you?"

He climbed into the tub. "Ooh, hot," he said. The water was just at the cusp of what he could endure, just enough to keep the tingle of heat ongoing. Prester put aside Mina's question, which was another of those probing questions like "What are you thinking about?" that sent him into spirals of self-obsession. He relaxed into the sting of hot water against his testicles and chest. Mina reached over and passed him a glass of warm red wine. It felt almost cold by comparison.

"You opened a bottle for me?"

"Well, I wanted one and I thought you'd want one, and since there's no one to leave the bottles to . . ."

"Except the Gogs," Prester said, frowning.

"Except the Gogs. Do you think they'll be the ones to find us?"

"I don't know. They'll be the first to notice we're missing, anyway."

"Yes."

Prester tasted his wine. It was the 1921 Chateau d'Yquem, and he almost choked. "You opened—"

"Surprise," Mina said. "I know it was your last bottle, but when are you going to get a chance to drink it again?"

"Well, I suppose you're right." He hadn't tasted it since their tenth anniversary, when he snuck a bottle into the Opryland Hotel. Prester always found the selection there limited.

The ceiling flashed with rays of purple and green as dusk crashed across the sky. Back home in Georgia, the clouds fought back, smothering the colors in dank gray billows. But here on the beach they were outnumbered. Each night, shrieking, brilliant spears of violet chased them away.

Prester sipped his wine, testing the contrast between the coolness in his throat and the heat on his chest, losing the comparison amid the haze of rising brain temperature.

"I had a talk with Jesus today."

"Yes, you said you saw him."

"Well, we talked for a while, and of course he's not enthused about the idea of our suicide."

"I suppose he wouldn't be," Mina said.

"In fact, he wants me to do something."

"What now? Haven't you done enough already?"

"Apparently not," Prester said. "He wants me to kill the Gogs."

Mina leaned forward with a start, sloshing wine into the water. "What? Why?"

"I don't know. He didn't say."

"Well, that's ridiculous!" she said. "You can't just kill the Gogs. You're not going to do it, are you?"

"I guess I hadn't completely decided. Until now."

Mina thought back to the stories Prester had told her, of his brief childhood, the battles he'd fought, the Silk Road, the crusade, Abyssinia. But that was long ago, and another man, she told herself. Not her husband. She stared at his solid, smooth, scarless face. No wrinkles, no worry lines, no sagging of the eyes. He glanced at her, and in those gray-flecked eyes she saw that he could do it. He could kill, if he wanted to. Even now. "You can't."

"Don't worry, I won't. This is it, anyway. We've decided."

Mina kept staring. He hadn't made up his mind. How could he even consider it?

"Mina, if I were going to kill them, I would have done it already. Or I'd be telling you now to wait a moment while I go kill the Gogs," he said with a chuckle.

She didn't laugh.

"Seriously, I wouldn't do that. I promise." It was easier this way, to make her believe. The Gogs were no different from any of the other people he'd had to kill over the years. Only the date had changed. But for Prester, it wasn't the fact of killing that held him back, it was the source of the commission. It was the prospect of once more being made a tool of divine will.

Mina softened. She'd have to take his word for it. "So, why does Jesus want them dead, anyway?" Mina said. "Reggie's in Species Control, but so are about a thousand other people. Does Jesus want all of them dead?"

"You did meet the Gogs in Hell."

"Where else would anyone shop for food? I meet a lot of people in Hell; are you supposed to kill all of them?"

"I don't know," Prester said. "Maybe it's a test. Maybe the Tigris was a test."

Mina swirled her wine, thinking about what he didn't say but implied—that he had failed that test, and things might have been different if he hadn't. "Maybe."

"It doesn't matter," Prester said. "I'm done with Jesus."

"Was he angry? About this?"

"Angry? It's hard to say. He said it would be giving up. But it's none of his business, is it?"

Mina sipped at her wine, mulling the notion. Is it giving up to take your life into your own hands? She felt power again at the thought of ending it. This wasn't giving up, she decided; this was taking control. She finished off the wine.

Prester sat, swirling his around, then drank it all, slowly, breathlessly. He'd carefully considered the ramifications and had made his decision, and if Mina was over her foolishness and was ready to do this reasonably, there was nothing to hold him back. Certainly not another commission from on high.

"Well, then," Prester said. "Are you ready?"

"Yes."

Prester dried his hands and picked up the gun.

"Prester," Mina said. "I want you to know I'm sorry."

"About what?" He ejected the clip and set it on the pedestal. He racked the slide and let the chambered round bounce across the tile floor.

"About doubting you, the last time. About making it difficult for us to do this before. I wasn't sure if it was what I wanted, and I wasn't sure if you really wanted it, or if you were just doing it for me."

"It's okay, Mina. I wasn't angry with you." He reloaded the magazine and racked a new round in the chamber. Sounded clean.

"Yes, you were," Mina said. "But that doesn't matter. There's something else. In your letter, you said you'd lost the passion of your wife."

Prester looked up at her.

"I've thought a lot about that since then, and at first I thought it was unfair. I thought it was about sex."

"Mina, you know I would never want you to do anything that you—"

"I know, I know, you meant something more. I think I've been ignoring you, Prester. At first I thought it was the PED, but I think this really started with the shadow."

"That wasn't me, Mina."

"I know, Prester. I know that in my head. But inside, I think I still saw it as your fault. And even if it wasn't your fault, there was still this thing that was always with you. I'm sorry." Mina began to cry. "I'm sorry Prester. That was unfair, and it hurt you, and I'm sorry."

Well, you're not wrong, Prester wanted to say. You ignored me and it hurt and I don't want to think or talk about that, and I just want to get this over with. "No, Mina, you could never hurt me," he lied.

"And you've been alive for so long," she continued as he winced. "And you've been dealing with this for so long, and I should've realized that you need this to be over too. You've been taking care of me, but I didn't take care of you."

Prester smiled. "I don't need anyone to take care of me."

Mina laughed a little. "Yes you do." She paused a moment, then laughed harder. "Remember that time we went running on that trail near Stone Door?"

"You'd remember it better than I do."

"Since you were out cold half the time. You tripped on that root and dropped face-first onto the biggest rock on the trail."

Prester watched the sadness fade from her face as it brightened into the joy of remembering the story.

"Or that's what I figured, anyway," she said. "I just remember hearing this thud and I looked back and it was like you'd just gotten tired and laid down to take a nap." Mina laughed harder, then changed her tone. "Good God, I was scared, though. Turned you over and your face was covered in blood. I yelled at you and shook you, and you were out cold. I could barely get a pulse.

"It was close to dark, and there wasn't anybody out there, and of course this was, what, 1995? So we didn't have cell phones, and we were miles out on the trail. I couldn't leave you out there alone. All I could do was curl up around you and try to keep you warm overnight until the sun came out. I was so worried about you." Her face grew sad again and serious.

"And then I woke up," he said.

"And then Prester John wakes up," she said. "Hours later, in the middle of the night, nothing but stars in the sky, absolute silence, freezing cold, lying in the dirt—you sit straight up, look around, and roar out, 'What the fuck?!'"

They both began laughing, and as they laughed they looked at one another and Prester tried to remember the last time they'd laughed like that.

"And I pulled you back down and whispered in your ear what had happened and that everything was going to be okay."

"So maybe that one time," Prester said, smiling, "I needed you to take care of me."

"Maybe that one time," Mina said. "Because I love you."

"And I, you."

They smiled at each other in the silence, and Mina remembered the gun in his hand. This was a good moment, a right moment.

"Are you ready?" he said.

"Yes." She took a breath and closed her eyes.

Prester swung his arm around, placed the tip of the gun against Mina's temple, and pulled the trigger. It clicked.

Mina opened her glistening eyes wildly, breathing hard.

Prester looked at the gun, turning it in his hand to check the safety. No, the safety was off. The bullet was in the chamber. He raised the gun to try again.

Mina pushed the gun away and climbed onto Prester, kissing him. Her tears wetted his cheeks. When was the last time she cried like that? He remembered a night, twenty-odd years ago, when he told her he loved her, and her tears dripped down his neck. They felt cold as trickles of ice. Mina reached down and caressed his cock for the first time in the better part of a year. Her breasts were slick and hard as they glanced across his chest. The gun fell from his hand. Prester was relieved that it didn't go off when it hit the floor.

Later that night, as Mina slept, Prester climbed out of bed, put on his bathrobe, and went to check the gun. He took it outside, near the garbage bins. He ejected the magazine, cleared the chamber, and blew a few times down the shaft. Nothing seemed out of order. He reloaded the gun, pointed it at a trash bin, and pulled the trigger. A shot blared in hazy green waves, shaking the palm trees and setting off a car alarm a few streets down. Something in the trash can screamed—a leftover bit of grouper, perhaps. The lights came on in the Gogs' house. When Prester heard the police sirens, he ran back inside.

THE BISHOPS' CRUSADE, 1138 A.D.

F ROM THE MOMENT OF HIS baptism, Tokmat had been a servant of Presbiter Ionis. No one knew his people. They knew his face, smooth black hair, and tawny skin, and most assumed he came from the eastern regions of Jetysuu, from one of the tribes that had paid a high price for holding off first the Khitay and more recently the Mongols. But none of that mattered after his baptism. As soon as he was old enough to be of use, Tokmat was put to service as a kitchen boy and then as an apprentice to the chief cook and prior in the Balsam Palace. As he became a man, he focused his energies on inventories and cupboard stock, so much so that when the chief cook overdosed on cumin (it was a difficult addiction in those years, and many culinary artists fell sway to its hypnotic effects), Tokmat was the only one among the staff who knew fennis meal from gunpowder.

But he also knew his place wasn't to lead the kitchen. He was a second, always a second, and he needed a better first. Eventually, the only one left above him was Presbiter Ionis himself, the Emperor of the East, Ruler of the Grand Diocese, so he focused on serving him, soon at the expense of other advisers and even of Ionis's then-steward, whose advice Tokmat began to see was only self-serving. That steward would arrange schedules to put his tribesmen at the front of the line, ensure trade deals benefiting courtiers who lobbied him with favors, even serve himself the leanest slices of ox meat before the platter made it to Ionis.

To excel, Tokmat knew instinctively, was to put the interests of the master first, regardless of uncertainty, of danger, of fear.

All three of these were hard at work on Tokmat as he galloped past the last stragglers of the main caravan to the Holy Land. He was riding in the opposite direction, with his fingers white on his reins, and he had to tell himself to stop clenching his jaw for fear his teeth would crack. All he had to do was deliver a message. He'd done it before, but he was alone this time, and that might make a difference.

Even from a quarter mile away, Tokmat could feel the pounding of the sciapods' march. The stutter of shaking rock rattled through the legs of his horse with each hoofstrike. Dust quivered atop the ground, dust that had only just settled after the passing army stirred it up minutes before. In the distance a scattering of soft thuds cascaded into a single thunderous one, over and over. The sciapods were marching in time, each giant foot slapping onto the earth in synchrony with some 40,000 more. If only the Saracens knew what was coming, they'd already be scurrying back to Egypt and Arabia, Tokmat thought.

The two caravans—more accurately, a caravan and a stampede—were traveling west across Persia, and they were just past Nishapur, staying on the northern rim of the Dasht-e Kavir but several miles south of the Silk Road to avoid disrupting trade. As it was, Tokmat heard that the Silkies were having trouble staying on their feet as the earthquake moved west.

As Tokmat neared the stampede, he better understood one reason at least for their rhythm. If all the sciapods rose and fell at once, there was a break in the cloud of resulting dust. Not much of one, but enough to allow their heads to rise like exploding flowers above the brown cloud to see what was before them. Organizing such a dance of thousands to a halt would be impossible, so Tokmat wheeled his horse and began galloping, slowing his pace until the sciapods' leader, Lonk, had caught up.

Lonk was tall for his race. His leg extended about four feet, with the lone kneecap three feet above the ground. He had red hair knotted at increments with river stones and the occasional dried flower. His long weapons, rusted with dried blood, bounced in a hard leather pouch slung across his massive chest. He looked into the eye of Tokmat's horse and grinned with mangled teeth.

They could kill him so easily. They could kill him at a touch, maybe even by accident. But he was the baptized of Presbiter Ionis, and that alone gave him courage to speak.

"At the next ridge," Tokmat shouted, pointing forward, "we rest for the night."

"No rest," Lonk said. There was no need for Lonk to yell, with his natural voice booming over the din of the march. "We still go."

The salamanders could make communication easier, establishing psychic translation between the Kyrgyz and the sciapods. But once the Kyrgyz discovered the sciapods could learn a smattering of human language, they no longer sought translators. Most of the time.

"With great respect, my captain," Tokmat said, risking a fall by bowing awkwardly toward Lonk. "While your strong army may not need rest," he made a muscle and pointed behind him, "some of our men of the tribe of Dahae, they ride like the grandmother of my wife. They hobble and pant like a dog in the desert!" Tokmat pointed forward and made a mocking, panting mime. "They grow so weary, if they were to break wind, the force of it might knock them to the ground!" He had no idea if Lonk understood the joke, but he laughed hard to convey the point and bring Lonk into a jovial and agreeable mood.

"Hah!" Lonk said. "Okay, we rest for you! For you grand-mothers."

Tokmat laughed more than he might to ensure they were on the same page, then made another horseback bow and spurred his horse to speed on to the main caravan. The horse needed little spurring.

That went well, he thought. That went well and I'm not dead, and maybe being alive is well enough.

To Tokmat's right were the foothills of the Alborz, dark blue snow-traced peaks that pierced victoriously into sullen grey clouds. To his left was Dasht-e Kavir, a vast salt desert flat to the visible horizon, broken only by man-sized pillars rounded by centuries of wind. Tokmat was told these were what was left of Lot's wife and her family, dozens more than were written about in Scripture, who had all been turned to salt. This was their punish-ment for merely looking back, and Tokmat—riding alone between two great armies on a mission from God to restore Jerusalem—wondered if the prohibition might still be in effect.

He passed the tail end of the march, with the most ragged horses and dilapidated wagons, those from the northern reaches of Dahae, who hadn't fully seen the benefits of the Silk Road econ-omy. He rode to the front, past some men trotting in shifts because there weren't enough horses, past horses that seemed half-starved and driven only by the hope of water at the next stop. At the front of this group was Masata-Eenhi, bishop and king of the Dahae, on the back of a well-fed horse, clad in light armor.

"Greetings Bishop Masata!" Tokmat called as he approached the king. "The Lord be with you!"

"And also with you!" Masata called.

Tokmat rode closer, and it was far easier to keep pace with this second leader. Masata wore no kalpak. His wavy brown hair splayed out from under a steel helmet engraved with designs of branches and nuts unfamiliar to Tokmat. His men carried axes and long pikes, and it was said they could upend a horse, or perhaps a sciapod, when working in a group. Masata himself carried only an ax, bladed on one side and sharpened to a point on the other, strapped to his side with thick leather. It seemed more ceremonial than military, with a finely carved handle and no trace of a scar. But it looked heavy enough to split a skull, and so did Masata.

"We'll break just over the next ridge, then ride on past Rayy tomorrow," Tokmat said.

"Good, good," Masata said. "Some of my men have been panting like dogs."

Or like grandmothers, Tokmat told himself.

"They haven't eaten well the last few seasons, and it begins to show," Masata said, talking as much to himself as to Tokmat. He suddenly looked up. "They will be ready to fight, though! They will fight, and they will be strong by that time. We're rationing well for that, don't you worry."

Tokmat sensed he'd stumbled into a debate that had started without him. "I'm sure they will be, Masata. Presbiter Ionis has every confidence in the Dahae, its bishop and its people."

"Thank you, steward and patriarch," Masata said. "That means more than you know."

Tokmat rode on in silence, then looked back at the men. They were more than tired. Some appeared thin, even gaunt, some sickly. Their thick beards served to hide the hollow of their cheeks. And it wasn't only a few. Tokmat began to see that most of the soldiers from Dahae were shambling atop their thin horses like puppets in a parade.

"Masata," Tokmat said, "how goes it with the Dahae? Is trade well? Are you able to bring goods that will trade on the Road?"

"Yes, yes. We bring fine wood, mainly. Timbers from the ula trees, green pepper, wool and black sand from Kara-Bogaz-Gol. All of it is highly treasured, and after the tithe we would have more than enough, but last season a flight of gryphons roosted by the sea and fed on many flocks of sheep, and then with the ula blight, there has been little left for the people, and of course the tithe has remained the same, which we understand."

Tokmat looked over. "The tithe?

Masata turned white and stopped his horse. "I'm sorry, my lord, I had forgotten." He dropped his voice to a whisper and leaned in, with terror in his eyes. "I had forgotten. I didn't mean to—I am so sorry, my lord. Please forgive me."

"What tithe?" Tokmat said.

Masata bounced his jaw, but no speech came out. Then his expression changed. "Exactly, my lord! Exactly. What tithe? Exactly. What tithe? Ignore me, my lord, I don't know what I'm talking about." He was sweating now, his hands trembling on the pommel of his horse.

This was more than confusion by a tired old man. This was something Tokmat didn't know, and there should be nothing in the Diocese that Tokmat didn't know.

"Masata, I think you and I should talk. I think you should tell your men to carry on."

In a wavering voice, Masata told his captain and curate to bring the men back in line before reluctantly riding away from the caravan to have a conversation with Tokmat from which he might not return.

They peeled away from the easy, even plain on a path of their own, north toward hills that too quickly became blue-headed mountains and mountains that too easily became star-frosted sky,

sky that would grow dark as it had always grown, with the darkness that lay hiding behind all skies.

One hour and one sunset later, the Black Yurt was assembled. It took a few weeks of patience on Ionis's part to train a new generation on how to properly assemble a yurt. Many had been so long in the Talas valley that they'd lost the art, at least the art as Ionis remembered it from a few hundred years before. When he was satisfied with their work, he dismissed them all, then he hung the brazier himself. The brazier, three feet in diameter, was made of iron coated in gold, and it hung by three brass chains from an uuk in the roof of the yurt. Ionis filled it with coal. The salamander was still in the pouch at his side, and he raised the pouch to the brazier, letting her stay warm inside while she blasted the coals with red tongues of flame.

And when she was satisfiedyes, she wrigglewayed onto the heatingcoals and curledasleep thanking into peace.

"Wait a moment now," Ionis told her. "We have guests coming."

No guests, no helptalking. Curledasleep yes.

"Just a moment. I promise," he said, packing up the traveling pouch. "You'll be curledasleep soon."

Two hours later, Lonk was almost as sleepy as the white salamander. They were now reviewing strategy and whether a flank attack could be done with surprise.

Lonk was muttering in a complicated guttural grumble that sounded more like a badger ripping into snake eggs than anything resembling speech. But the salamander was there, and Ionis didn't need to understand with his ears.

It would never work, and I will tell you why, Lonk said. The might that we bring to the battlefield is not merely in the strength of our legs or the resolve of our minds, but in the terror incited by thousands of massive feet crashing at once toward the enemy. This is a tactic designed to weaken the mind ahead of our assault on the body.

"Yes, I know," Ionis said. "But this is an enemy that has never seen nor heard of you. If they see and hear the rumble of your feet hitting the ground, they're more likely to be curious than afraid. We should save the tactic of fear for the second battle, and use surprise in the first while we can."

I will not debate the merits of this with you any longer. If you wish us to flank the enemy, I have no objection to that strategy. But it will avail you nothing, as there will be no surprise. They will hear our rush toward them and be just as dead when it is over as they would have been before, only, perhaps, if you are correct, mildly surprised in their death.

"They'll hear you coming either way. Only my way they won't see you, which will scare them even more."

And by my reckoning if they see us they will be more terrified, so perhaps—

The white salamander stopped translating as the yesik pulled open. Tokmat and Masata stepped inside.

There was a flash of dull orange around the room as the white tried to translate greetings across four minds at once, causing all but Ionis to grimace with nausea.

"That's enough, thank you," he told her.

Now curledasleep. Yes.

"Greetings, Bishop Masata," Ionis said. "Sit."

"Greetings." He took a place on a pillow, then looked nervously to Tokmat.

"My lord, I have troubling news," Tokmat said.

The white had nestled down into the coals, but became interested and opened one bulging eye. She translated to Lonk, who was about to hop out of the yurt but instead leaned back to hear more.

"I was speaking with Bishop and King Masata about the welfare of his people, and in the course of our talk, he made reference to a tithe," Tokmat said.

"A tithe."

"Yes, a tithe. It seems that Bishop and King Nanevande of Khorasan has enacted a tithe on the outlying parishes of the Diocese, exacting of them a tenth of their profits and yields on behalf of Presbiter Ionis—profits and yields which Nanevande, he told them, had been entrusted to collect."

Ionis leaned back and clapped his legs. "Hah! That devious bastard! That's worthy of Baytosk himself. Tokmat, I've told you of Baytosk, yes? He tried to get me to marry his daughter, who was a pretty thing, too, and brilliant."

"Yes, you've told me, lord."

"So, end the tithe and make Nanevande give back what he can. I can't fault him for being smarter than you, anyway, Masata." Ionis stood up.

"There's more, my lord."

Ionis sat down again. He should have known. Every time there was bad news, Tokmat called him "my lord."

"This has been going on for several years now, a few decades actually. And the reason we hadn't heard about it is that Bishop Nanevande made them keep this a secret. He did this by telling them that you yourself wanted it to be a secret. The riches would go to Nanevande's family, which was to inherit your throne."

Ionis was no longer smiling.

"This family was to inherit your throne because you could not have children. And you could not have children because, well—"

Tokmat stopped, but the white translated to Lonk what Tokmat was about to say.

Lonk roared in laughter, looking around the room at the other kings of the lands, who should enjoy the rich joke as much as he did. None laughed, and Lonk let his laughter subside into a happy grin.

Ionis, unmoving, stared at Tokmat, who lowered his gaze and continued. "The kings were told that if this were revealed, you would be so angry at any who revealed it that you would have them and their family tortured and killed."

Ionis drifted into himself. This wasn't supposed to happen. This was supposed to be the Grand Diocese, an empire built on the power of the Prince of Peace, ruled by bishops—righteous men ministering to a new kingdom. How could Jesus let this happen? Ionis himself had blessed the sacrament he'd placed on Nanevande's tongue. He wished now that the wafer had been an orange-hot coal, or that he'd grabbed that extended tongue and ripped it out of the man's throat. He was considering these options when Tokmat spoke up.

"My lord?"

More time had passed than Ionis intended, and Lonk was now nodding into sleep. This was the way of it. This was the way it had been done before the Grand Diocese, and nothing had changed.

Ionis stood. The others did as well, except for Lonk, who now blinked his eyes open.

"This man who is supposed to be my heir. What is his name?"

"Not yet a man," Tokmat said. "Nanaivandak—the king's son."

"Send seven men back to Khorasan and have them kill Nanaivandak, along with the rest of Bishop Nanevande's family. Put Khorasan directly under the authority of Talas until we return and can sort things out."

"Yes, my lord."

The fire was still flickering between Ionis and the wall, but he could see his shadow rising beyond him along the rug-covered floor.

"Bishop Masata," Ionis said. "Why did you keep this secret?"

"My lord, I . . ."

Tokmat spoke up. "He thought he was doing your will, my lord."

Ionis slapped Masata across the jaw, sending him stumbling backward into a kerege pole, causing the yurt to shake and the brazier to sway.

"Then why did you tell it now?"

The shadow was rising now up the kerege, darkening a felt tapestry spiraled with green and purple waves.

Ionis walked to the swaying brazier and stilled it with a touch of the brass chain, which was searing hot now. He let the pain edge into his finger, bringing his mind to life in a way it hadn't been for many, many years. Hanging on a kerege opposite the brazier was, among the many skins keeping the warmth inside, the still-furred skin of a goat.

"Tomorrow, we will not travel to Rayy. We will celebrate our journey with a game of kokboru."

"Yes, my lord," Tokmat said. "Only I don't think we have a goat."

Ionis pulled his finger away and watched the smoke drift, the skin pull together, and the wound fade from blood red to pale flesh.

Kokboru is known by many names—buzkashi, kokpar— and in some ways it united the Grand Diocese more than Christianity. Two teams on horseback gallop across a wide field fighting over a goat carcass, carrying it or often dragging it to a goal on either side. The game takes a toll on the carcass, which by the end of an event lasting hours or even days is little more than a furry sack of broken bones.

For the celebration of Presbiter Ionis's crusade, two circular mounds were dug out on either side of a flat stretch of land, and each bishop nominated a player.

When all was arranged, Ionis had the bishops assembled and, in answer to Tokmat's question, walked toward them with the goat skin and a length of rope over his shoulder. He walked up to an increasingly dismayed Bishop Nanevande, dropped the goat skin over his head, and slammed him on the ground. Amid Nanevande's muffled shouts, Ionis himself wrapped the goat skin around his head and tied it around him down to his elbows, cinching it tight with the rope. As Ionis worked, Tokmat explained to the stunned bishops what had been revealed the night before, and once he had, their objections were silenced.

Ionis picked the man up and led him, stumbling blindly in confusion, hands flailing under trapped arms, to the center of the field. As they walked, Ionis whispered in his shrouded ear, "*Misereatur tui omnipotens Deus, et dimissis peccatis tuis, perducat te ad vitam aeternam.*"

He blessed Nanevande with the sign of the cross and yelled for the match to start.

As the sound of hooves and the shouts of the bishop became one with the cheers from Ionis's army, his shadow grew large on the hillside, swelling toward the ridge that separated their camp from that of the sciapods. At the top of the ridge stood Lonk, looking down on the spectacle. Their eyes met. Lonk gave a look that Ionis didn't understand, and a gesture of anger. Then he turned his back and hopped away.

MONDAY MORNING: NOTES

M INA WOKE UP FEELING MORE solid than she had in years. She could see her feet, clearly defined with arches and toes, and they made full contact with the floor as she walked—actually walked—to the basin to wash up.

Prester was still asleep. Soon he'd begin drowning in the drool that filled his side of the bed. He'd cough and sputter, then shake like a sickly brown chow. But this time the thought made Mina laugh inside, where yesterday she'd turned away with disgust.

Was it the sex? she asked herself as she brushed her hair, which was softer and fuller than before. Come to think of it, they hadn't had sex in months. It did make her feel closer to him, but she wasn't buying that it had solved everything. Maybe it was the thrill of having been one misfired bullet away from death? She had to admit the excitement of that. He was willing to do it—willing to kill her. But he'd failed, or the gun had, anyway. But was the gun really jammed? Could Prester have faked that—was that why it was so easy for him, because it wasn't real? Maybe he really wanted to live. Would he admit that?

Mina's cheeks flushed yellow. She wiped off the excess and washed her face with cold water. She'd have to get her mind off things before she drowned in a pool of herself.

257

Prester would be awake soon, and he'd want to carry on with the suicide. Mina found herself unsure. She might be doomed to fade, or she might not. She felt solid now, and maybe that was the solution. If being with Prester when things were right again between them made her solid, would that be enough? Would she want to rely on him—on them—that much? She wasn't sure if she could.

A newspaper flew through the wall and re-solidified just before crashing onto the breakfast table, knocking over Mina's juice and a container of ground cumin. She went to the hall and opened the salamander pyrorium. They scurried out and had a feeding frenzy, sucking up the spilled juice and gurgling with pleasure.

The lead headline announced: "Turtle Hatchlings Killed After Mystery Gunshot Scares Driver."

"Awful," Mina whispered.

Farther down the page, the picture of a wild-eyed Rhodesian caught her eye.

MYTHICAL ROC OR MYSTICAL COOKIES?
Engineer Claims He Saw Extinct Bird

By Daniel Rostica

Maribu Ntognan had been taking soil samples in a sun-drenched, rocky slope on the side of Mount Inyangani in Rhodesia, a typical day for this 351-year-old ferrous-mining engineer.

But the day became far from typical when, during lunch break, a shadow rolled across the plain below. Ntognan and his crew looked up to see a giant eagle cross the sky.

"This was not no eagle," Ntognan insisted in a phone interview early Sunday. "This was urtaah." Urtaah is Inyani for what is known in classical mythology as a roc: an eagle so large it can carry away elephants to feed its young.

Early reports on the incident suggested this might have been a hallucination or hoax. But a growing number of people claim that what the engineers saw was no Nutter Butter–inspired daydream but a survivor of the U.N.–backed Species Control program, and that the engineers' sighting is making headlines only because the government didn't act quickly enough to silence them.

"Witness and evidence tampering have been going on for at least as long as Species Control," said Jereme Trask, president of the Society for the Protection of Living Rights. "The problem is circular: No one can prove the evidence tampering is happening because there's no longer any evidence."

No U.N. or Species Control official would comment for this report.

"The roc is just like the unicorn, platypus, and lemur. All of these species once existed, but we don't remember their existence except in myth, because the government doesn't want us to remember," Trask said. "If you doubt that, ask yourself exactly how many species Species Control has eliminated. Most people can remember only the mosquito and the pit bull, and the pit bull wasn't even a species in itself. Awfully short list, isn't it, for an agency that's been in existence for over 75 years?"

Trask claims his group has found documents suggesting Species Control is preparing an extinction program for the eastern ridge salamander, a move that could have international ramifications, particularly for Central Asian cultures in which the salamander is revered as a religious symbol.

Mina's salamanders looked up at her and smiled weakly, their eyes heavy with the sadness of foreverknowing. The white took a deep breath and wafted cumin-laced plumes of smoke from her tiny slit-like ears. The mottled gray shook his head and finished off the spilled juice, then shimmied slowly back to the pyrorium, vexed.

Mina took a pen and wrote in the margin, "Thank you. — Mina."

Almost immediately, Rostica replied. "Hey, you set me on the idea. Interview in NYC at UN next week w/ man named Gog who knows more about roc thing. Want to talk to you before then about pet roc. OK?"

A laugh jumped from Mina's throat, and she covered her mouth. Gog? It was too weird. How could it be Gog? That was a hell of a coincidence.

Rostica's words faded, and Mina chased them with her own. "Gog? At Species Control?"

"Yes," Rostica replied. "Reggie Gog. Know him?"

It couldn't be a coincidence. Thousands of people worked in Species Control. Why would the expert on rocs suddenly want to be her best friend? Could Reggie be following her? Maybe this was about her memory of Urtyylk.

No. That was silly. Black helicopter paranoia. Could it be Jesus, setting her up for Prester's mission? Or was she losing her mind?

She looked again at the margin. The note was there, though fading. It was real. This was real.

Prester coughed, and Mina heard a splatter of drool hit the wall as he shook his head. He'd come out soon. He'd come out with his gun and want to kill her. How could she explain this? And she'd have to talk about Urtyylk again, and if Gog was following her, Prester would really want him dead then. She folded the paper back to the front page, away from her conversation with Rostica.

The white salamander looked around now for more juice, but the mottled had finished it off. She sauntered slow-legged toward the pyrorium and listened for the oldman, who was waking in his wetness. He'd soon walk by and give his morninglook. She needed that. She'd waited every morning since her waking centuries ago (but time, what was time?) for the oldman's morninglook. It fed her, kept her complete. The mottled didn't understand. The mottled was vexed, always vexed. But the white would wait for the oldman's morninglook and feel whole again. There—the sound of the wetness and the cleaning and the blood. She used to watch it when she was in the oldman's matingroom, but she no longer was in the matingroom. And the drying and the stumbling and the door. There. There he was and he looked at her and smiled. She slanted her eyes in deeppleasure and her skin shimmered with warm wakingagain. He walked by, and she melted into an ecstatic late-morning trance.

Prester walked to the kitchen and put his gun on the counter. "Good morning, apricot," he said with a smile.

She smiled back and lifted her head to accept his kiss. "Good morning." Apricot. He used to call her that more often.

Prester dug some Honey Os out of an overhead cabinet and poured himself more than he normally would. No point holding back on the sugar now, he thought. Or the milk. He sat down and opened the newspaper.

"Last night was nice," Mina said.

"Yes," he answered. "It was."

There was an article about the shooting.

> Three turtle hatchlings being led by their father to the Gulf were killed Sunday night when a Crab Festival visitor veered off the road at the sound of gunfire.
>
> The hatchlings, ranging in age from 5 to 7 days, were run over on the side of Palmetto Boulevard as they were making their initial crossing, according to police reports.
>
> The driver, Eaton Stanfill, 45, of Valdosta, Georgia, said he veered off the road when he heard a gunshot. Stanfill, a veteran of the first Gulf War, said he knows

gunfire when he hears it.

"You don't forget a sound like that," Stanfill said. "I panicked, and my first thought was to get off the road. I can't believe I ran them over. I'm just so sorry. I didn't see them."

The turtle father indicated through sign language to police that he did not have a flashlight with him because his batteries had run down. The Tallahassee Federalist does not identify turtles because their names cannot be correctly rendered in print.

"I think it was my fault."

"Hm? What is?" Mina said.

Prester looked at the gun on the counter and wondered if he should be worried. There would be an investigation—into Stanfill, certainly, but possibly into the neighbors. The police would go door to door, asking questions about guns and sleeping hours and locks.

"The gun, it jammed . . ."

But this might work, Prester thought. If the police came to ask questions and the Johns were dead, the police would handle everything without having to bother anyone else, and their bodies would still be fresh. Maybe, Prester caught himself thinking, it would even make it easier to kill the Gogs. If the police were out here anyway, they might discover all four of them at the same time. More convenient that way. Of course he couldn't tell Mina.

But what if I don't want to kill the Gogs?

Is that up to you?

Prester wasn't sure if that was his thought or one from Jesus.

"It's okay, Prester," Mina said. "Maybe that was for the best, maybe it's better that we waited." Mina looked at him, hoping for some bit of agreement. "Anyway, today I'd like us to have one last day together. Do something just the two of us."

One more day. Prester wondered if he could simply blink and reach the end of the day without having to go through the motions. He'd done it before, for days, months, years at a time. But one more day with Mina, a day like the night before, truly with her again, together. That would be worth waiting.

"We could go to the festival," Mina suggested.

"This is festival day?"

"We haven't been in so long. Remember the year when the fireworks hit the water tower?"

"Ha! And everyone's tap water fizzed green for months."

"Let's do it. Let's go."

Prester saw the excitement in her eyes. "Okay. One last day," he said.

"One last day." She went to the bedroom to change.

When Prester returned to the Honey Os and his newspaper, he noticed words forming on the underside of the front page. He opened to Page 2, next to an article about an eagle sighting.

"I need to talk to you about Gog," the words said.

Jesus. He wouldn't give up. Prester figured Jesus had to know about the suicide. Did he cause the gun to jam? A little delay-tactic miracle, to push Prester into obedience? Is that what this was about? Prester picked up a pen lying nearby.

"I don't care about Gog," Prester wrote. He bounced the pen above the paper, trying to decide if he should say what he was about to say next. "Handle Gog yourself."

Prester had never done that before—told Jesus no. He wasn't sure what would happen next. He wondered if Jesus might strike him down, turn him into a leper, drive him mad. It wouldn't matter. After the tricks and betrayals, there wasn't a way for Jesus to reach him now, not anymore.

"Mina?"

Prester's eyes lit up as the four letters and a question mark scrawled in a dirty threat across the page. Mina. He'd threaten Prester with Mina.

Prester threw down the newspaper and stood, toppling his chair with a crash onto the tiled floor and hitting the hanging lamp with his head. His shadow danced a fast waltz across the kitchen. He grabbed the gun. "Jesus?"

The room was starkly silent. There was no response.

"I know you hear me!"

"Prester?" Mina called from the bedroom. "Are you okay?"

The salamanders' heads craned above their low rocks. Outside, the Gulf's waves paused in midair, tongues of salt water suspended to listen.

Prester's mind raced in angry prayer. Okay, I'm not obedient. Fine. Not a leader. But if you want me as a tool of your will, you won't do it by dragging Mina into this. I won't lose everything—I won't lose her. Prester stood over the chair with the gun in his hand, chest heaving, and then he stopped and laughed at the thought of shooting Jesus in the chest. He put down the gun, calmed his breathing, and carefully set the chair back upright. Good. Very good, Jesus. But it won't work. I'm not a child to be manipulated. Not anymore. Just give me a good reason to kill Gog, and I'll do it. But I won't kill him unless I know why you want him dead. If you don't like it, set aside for Prester John his own oven in hell.

"I'm okay!" he yelled to Mina.

Again the room was hollow, silent, and Prester wasn't entirely comfortable with the prayer that still rolled inside him like live meat in his stomach. But inaction had always served him best. Wait it out, he told himself. Wait it out, and all the untold motivations will rise to the surface—shards of glass buried in the dirt, that's all they were. They would surface.

Prester slid the gun into the small of his back, a trick he'd used during the revolts. Mina would know. She would see him wearing jeans with an untucked shirt and know immediately that he was hiding a gun. But Gog would not. Just in case.

"What happened?" Mina said, walking in and putting in a final earring.

"Nothing," Prester said. "Just toppled a chair."

She walked toward him. "Are you ready?"

"Yes," he said, slapping his front and back pockets to check for keys, cash, wallet, and phone.

Mina glanced nervously at the newspaper, open to the article about the roc, but the margin was now blank. She picked up her purse. Prester followed her out the door, shutting it behind him. It closed smoothly, as if oiled, and the bolt of the lock slid into place like it lived there. The room relaxed, salamanders glancing and nodding at one another, the cereal bowl dissolving into the table. Only the newspaper still seemed uneasy. "Mina, you there?"

TAPESTRY OF THE WORLD, 1143 A.D.

S MOKE POURED INTO THE SKY above the eastern bank of the Tigris River. Below the smoke lay the charred remains of villages and the charred bodies of those who once lived in them. From these black stains on the sea of brown sand, trails of discarded loot led back to a massive encampment of thousands of Central Asian yurts, looking ominously out of place in the desert landscape.

The sprawling camp had been constructed haphazardly over the course of five years, during which temporary arrangements gradually became permanent. Yurts were set up side by side and then connected to each other, overlapping until they seemed one. Felt and hide roofs had been patched and not replaced, kerege walls lashed together instead of rebuilt. Openings had been hacked into the kereges, sometimes mutilating tapestries that must have been centuries old.

Every yurt-room seemed to contain heaps of half-sorted goods: Piles of saddles. The machineworks of a catapult, taken apart and stacked high. Atop casks and trunks teetered layers of parchment maps, scrolls, letters, manuscripts, and blank paper, all brown from dust. Barrels of water and wine, half-open bags of meal, dried fruit, and smoked meat. Then there were the women:

the mound of them four feet high just inside the door to the dining yurt, their bodies withered in the desert heat but not fully decomposed. Even in death they suggested beauty. They wore silk garments draped in sheer veils of purple, red, orange, and blue. They wore bracelets and anklets and necklaces of gold chain with gold amulets and trinkets. They wore headbands and slippers of leather. And each had the calcified remains of a piece of steak sticking out of her mouth.

In the next room, a thin stream of mote-filled light illuminated an altar bearing the chalice, paten, and gold-inlaid Gospel, all of them coated in a layer of dust. Behind them a massive wood and gold crucifix loomed from the shadows.

Inside what remained of the yurt of Presbiter Ionis was a massive wooden chair on a dais. Onto one arm was carved an eagle, and onto another a lion. But the chair was empty. To its left, next to a cot-like bed, was yet another pile, this one of blankets and fur, but this pile had a head, and it had eyes: gray eyes staring at a wall, trying to make sense of the tapestry that depicted the entire world. At the top was the Great Salamander, who had four teats, from each of which milk flowed upon mountains and valleys. The easternmost was the Indus, feeding princedoms and powers Ionis never felt obliged to challenge. Then the Talas, the widest and most holy of the rivers, pouring between the Alataus to bring life to the people. Then there was the Volga, which fell under Ionis's command, though he often wondered at what cost he'd crossed the Urals to take it. And at the furthest west the Tigris, which fed the Saracens and separated Ionis from the Holy Land. Its milk flowed down the Zagros Mountains, across Nineveh and Babylon, then into the Gulf. What power could ford this river? What power could freeze its course and allow the army of Presbiter Ionis to cross, if not the power of Jesus? Yet still it flowed freely down the tapestry of the world.

Tokmat entered the room. He stood for some time before speaking. "My lord?"

Nothing.

The last five years had been more than a challenge to Tokmat. He was a lifelong servant to Presbiter Ionis, and to serve is to obey, certainly, but that is only part of it. If the master issued a command, comply; if the master was hindered, clear his way; if the master was drunk, hide the indiscretion and see him safely to bed; if the master was wrong, find a way to put the blame on yourself. The path to excellence lay in always putting the master's needs first, especially when the master wasn't sure what he needed. Now, Steward and Patriarch Tokmat had to find a way to bring his master back.

"My lord?"

The mound shifted, and a voice croaked. "Yes?"

"Are you in want of anything, my lord?"

"No."

"My lord, I must tell you news." Tokmat bowed.

"Has the Tigris frozen?" Ionis asked blankly, watching the milk of it flow out of the Salamander and over the Caucasus, Alborz, and Zagros. He knew the answer already, and he knew the answer would not change.

"No, my lord. The river has not frozen," Tokmat said. "I must tell you that your men are leaving. Quite a few of them, my lord."

"Yes," Ionis said. "I expected they would."

The long silence following his words didn't seem to bother Ionis, but it left Tokmat unsure whether the next bit of news would be taken as calmly.

"I am leaving, my lord."

There was silence, and Tokmat wondered if the mound might explode, leaving Tokmat's blood splattered across the yurt. It did not.

"You too, then?" Ionis replied.

"No, my lord, I am not abandoning the crusade. I am leaving to find a solution, to look for a way around the Tigris."

"There is no solution."

"I will find one," Tokmat said.

This was in the fifth year of the vigil of Presbiter Ionis. In the first year, he had celebrated weekly Mass using the very chalice Jesus had bequeathed to him. Those were heady days that tasted of the glory of coming triumph. They would march into the Holy Land, unchallenged by any but the bravest or most foolish of heretics, and claim the entire region in the name of the Prince of Peace. They would be granted lands and riches, and for Presbiter Ionis there would be power beyond imagining.

In the second year, when the Tigris failed to freeze or even drop below the temperature of bathwater, Ionis began to worry, hearing word of a man named Khan entering his eastern lands at Jetysuu, which were unprotected now since all his armies were camped at the Tigris. It didn't help that Jetysuu had been starved by Bishop Nanevande's tithe, and the few soldiers of that people who were left now looked to this Khan as almost a savior. Ionis began to hold Mass every day.

In the third year, he gave up on Mass and took to prayer alone: earnest, repentant prayer, filled with terror that something had gone wrong—that he had misunderstood. Was this the right part of the Tigris? Was he supposed to be fighting the Jews instead of the Muslims? Did he have the wrong Holy Land? In these months, he felt his shadow tugging at him, restless and angry, ready to move, to act, to be. But then it stopped, and Prester began to wonder if that part of him had died, or if perhaps it had gone its own way.

In the fourth year, Ionis was too distracted by the effort of keeping his men from revolting, from killing one another, or from settling down with the women of nearby villages to worry about the trappings of religion. And then there was the massacre of the concubines, after which Ionis had to put one of his strongest captains to the sword. And then he received word that Talas had been taken. The Balsam Palace had been set ablaze, with a great man by the name Ambaghai Khan holding the torch. The people had succumbed, and the Grand Diocese was no more, all of it now in the hands of a horde of savages from the east. Manas was nowhere to be found, though the Manaschi continued to sing songs of his glory.

At the beginning of the fifth year, Ionis gave in and let his men do as they pleased. With no home to return to and no crusade to fight, they scattered like plague rats into the doomed villages of western Persia.

Always with Ionis, though, had been the sciapods—the cruel, embittered, but fiercely loyal sciapods.

Tokmat had been gone a few weeks, and Ionis had no idea when he would return. All he had now was Lonk, whose frustration grew with each meeting, and the white salamander, who seemed intent on advising him to wait for Jesus, despite everything that was going wrong.

When Lonk stepped into the yurt, clouds of dust billowed with each fall of his foot. He covered his loin with a stiff, cylindrical cloth, and Ionis sometimes wondered if Lonk might be a eunuch—maybe all sciapods were. Ionis didn't like to think about it. Lonk's arms, long and low, dragged his weapons along the ground in a traditional sign of his status as a king who no longer required self-defense. His bejeweled sticks of braided red hair flew wildly around his head as he flashed glares during the long days of strategy negotiations in Ionis's yurt. Two broken leaders, stranded on the shores of the Tigris.

"Do you want to leave too?" Ionis asked, staring at his tapestry. Tokmat was gone, and likely not coming back. Why not Lonk as well?

Lonk began his grumbling mutter, and Ionis felt the warm orange glow of meaning flow from the salamander and into his mind.

No, I have no intention of leaving. We made a covenant, you and I, to journey together into these blood days and accomplish this mission for your god, to work together under the terms of our allegiance.

"Yes, we agreed. And the mission has failed, so the covenant is yours to break."

It is a covenant. (Lonk growled as he said this, and his eyes went wide.) It cannot, by its very nature, be broken. How can you not understand this? Look at me, Presbiter Ionis. Look at me!

Ionis turned toward Lonk.

How can you betray one another, steal from one another, and then kill one another in punishment—you remember your disgusting trick with the goat skin—cheering the death of your own in a game of your devising? And your men, they murder women for sport. You are your own people. (The translation seemed to break down here, with that sciapod concept difficult for the salamander to convey.) I am not your people, and I yet I keep this covenant between us. Your people are leaving you now while you do nothing.

"And what do you say I should do?"

You should take action. Go back to your kingdoms, establish a new kingdom here, travel north or south to ford the river or use your resources and ingenuity to build great boats or a massive bridge upon which to cross it. You wait for a miracle from your god to freeze this river, but what god would do such a thing when it is wholly unneccesary?

"Because Jesus promised that he would," Ionis said. "That was his covenant. He will keep it. How long will you keep yours?"

Lonk growled and beat his rusted weapons on the ground, creating small clouds of dust. He was angry over the implied challenge to his honor; but Ionis no longer cared. He wanted them to leave—all of them—while he sorted things out.

The next day, Ionis stood looking over the Tigris valley at the last, loosely organized streams of men, flowing away from him like black creeks toward distant settlements, smoke rising here and there, screams echoing across the hills. Lonk hopped forward, demanding that Presbiter Ionis look at him. Behind him ranged battalions of sciapods waiting desperately for a command. Lonk suggested many things: that they should join the raids, or corral the other regiments, or fall on their swords, or set off for home, abandoning all honor. Ionis turned away.

"Do what you will," he said as he walked into his tent, leaving Lonk to hop a furious dance all by himself.

Lonk came back the next evening, trailing the cold sting of dry air into the still, humid yurt. He entered dragging not his sword but a long horse whip, which he threw at the ground. It had been a long time, but the meaning wasn't lost on Ionis.

"Gaa!" Lonk shouted, and the salamander rushed to keep up with the translation.

Ineptfailure ofaman—ifthatiswhatyoucallyourself—youcall yourself PriestandEmperorandLeader andknow nothingofleadership!

Lonk gave up on his translator and used the words he knew Ionis would understand.

"We are our people! You are leader no much!" Lonk spit as he talked, flailing accusations.

Ionis stood, looking up into the spray of anger, his ears ringing with the bellowed words.

"You living more. You stink time. You time short!" Lonk rushed at Ionis, finally lifting one rusted blade and swinging it at his ally.

Ionis ducked, took Lonk's arm, and wrapped it once around Lonk's neck. He was tempted to swing a leg out and trip the sciapod as he'd learned to do centuries ago on the Steppe, but he wanted Lonk's compliance, not his undoing.

"We are our people," Lonk growled under the strain of his own arm on his neck. "We want you leader more!"

"I don't want to leader more," Ionis whispered calmly in Lonk's ear as the sciapod struggled and hissed. "You are your people. You leader more."

Ionis shoved him away, and Lonk swung his head at his king, eyes smoking with hate. Then he hopped out of the tent and down into the field, where he called for his people to break camp. They were going home, leaving behind the human who'd promised them glory in battle and redemption from a grim past but delivered only senselessness and yawning time. They left Ionis to wallow in it.

In the grand yurt of Presibter Ionis, there hung a brazier. Upon this brazier was a pile of hot coals, and upon these coals rested the white salamander, almost unseen, burrowed into gray ash. When she slept, the room slept, and when she woke, the room woke, and when she raised her head and looked toward the door, Ionis knew that someone was coming. But he did not turn. It didn't matter.

Tokmat walked into the room to find Presbiter Ionis sitting upon his stool, staring at the tapestry, just as he'd been when Tokmat saw him last.

Pain and shame, shame and pain. Bitterloss weaving with disappointedness in hanginghead sad.

Tokmat saw the increasing glow from the brazier, and he turned to see the white salamander rise up, the ashes drifting down her body. She didn't normally communicate with Tokmat, leaving servant conversations to Ionis, but Ionis was quiet now, too often quiet, and the salamander had to communicate with someone.

And you with ideas, and you with hopefulness, and you with youranswers.

Tokmat could feel the salamander stretching out tendrils of questions, their marks floating in the air like wispy crosiers, searching and yanking, closer to him each time. He moved toward the brazier. One gray crosier wrapped around his mind and penetrated deep inside.

Solutions, a path, awayout for him, for your masterliving? Yes, your masterliving. You need him and want him leadermore, like the sciapodking, like the one you think a monster?

Tokmat recoiled at the comparison to a sciapod. He had heard the news from Lonk as they met on the road. He was disheartened by the loss of armed strength, but he couldn't say he was sorry to see the sciapods go.

No, this is notyou, notyou. You bring answers for your masterliving. You bring hopefulness.

The salamander grew still for a moment, then blinked and stared hard at Tokmat, who felt his mind emptied now of everything but the gray crosier. Then the salamander found something, and its eyes bulged wide.

You! You will hurtbetray. Bloodred seed inside you, bloodred seed growingfestering, bloodred seed to hurtbetray. Do not do this.

The crosier pulled back. Tokmat felt relief, but also rejection, shock. He would never, could never betray Presbiter Ionis.

The salamander nestled down into the ash again. Tokmat found himself reaching into the bucket on the ground nearby. He plucked three coals to place by the salamander's side. She lashed wisps of flame that made them glow instantly red, then curled up around them and let the crosier fall away. Suddenly the salamander didn't want to be in Tokmat's mind any longer, nor anywhere near him.

"Well?" a voice said. Tokmat remembered Presbiter Ionis.

"My lord?"

"What did she say?" Ionis turned his head halfway toward Tokmat.

"She said . . ." Tokmat thought better of sharing the confusing warning. "She said she wanted me to freshen her coals."

"Her coals?"

"Yes, she wanted three more coals."

Ionis was silent for a moment, and then he laughed. "The Grand Diocese is gone, the army has disbanded, Christ himself has forsaken us, and the white salamander wants three fresh coals. Then what of me!" he shouted.

Ionis threw off his blankets and charged past Tokmat toward the brazier. Ionis grabbed one chain and shouted into the glowing dust.

"What of me? What will you have me do? Brush out your ash? Would that bring you comfort as my empire crumbles? Is that your advice to me now?"

Whiffs of rank smoke rose from his fist as the pattern of the chain seared into his palm.

The salamander rose again and waves of calm poured out of the rattling brazier, pushing down on Ionis's shoulders until he let go of the chain and dropped to the floor, his red-printed hand still smoldering.

If the salamander was speaking to Ionis now, Tokmat could not hear. The glow from the brazier moved around the room as it swung like a fiery pendulum or smoking thurible. Tokmat knelt by Ionis and kept him from falling further.

"My lord, are you all right?"

Ionis turned his head slowly, almost drunkenly, to Tokmat. "Do not call me that. Do not call me 'lord.' Do not utter that word in my presence." He spoke with deep bitterness, but Tokmat felt certain it wasn't meant for him.

He helped Ionis back to his feet and toward the throne, but Ionis directed him instead to the cushions on the floor nearby.

"Wine."

Tokmat went to a low table and found an ewer and goblet. He brought the goblet back, and Ionis drank in silence without regard to Tokmat's presence.

"So, you have returned?"

"Yes, m—" He stopped himself from repeating the forbidden words. "Yes, I have returned."

"You said you were leaving in search of a solution."

"Yes."

"And what solution have you found?"

"Better than a solution, a plan. A plan for you to sit upon a new throne, in a new land—a land rich in treasure, people, and creatures, a Christian land that is neither Rome nor Constantinople, where there is now no king."

"I have no interest in being a Christian king."

"Still, you might easily go there and rule, expanding your empire."

"What empire? I have no empire. I have no diocese. I have no parish."

"Better still. You can have one again. In this new land, you can start over."

"You don't understand." Ionis's voice became soft, almost weak. "I have no kingdom. I desire no kingdom. I have no wish to start again. It's over."

Ionis grew silent in a deepening dark of unanswered pause, a dissonant chord left unresolved. He was looking now at something across the room. He sat as though asleep, but he did not snore, nor did he close his eyes. In fact, Tokmat wasn't sure whether Ionis was even breathing. Finally, the steward felt it was wrong for him to stay any longer. He got up and left, his eyes lingering on the wall that seemed to have drawn Ionis's attention. There was nothing there—only shadow.

MONDAY AFTERNOON: THE CRAB FESTIVAL

"**P**LEASANT DREAMS! NIGHTMARES! POWER AND glory! Hand-woven right here!"

The day was bright under a sparkling sky, and the music of high school bands competed with distant covers of Southern rock ballads, all of it crowded into downtown St. Brianna for the annual Crab Festival. Prester and Mina John approached the dream-stand and its attendant, a lanky man in dark clothes with bright red boots. His hair was black, and Prester looked tightly at his face to see whether his eyes were brown, but there was only darkness.

"Nocturnal emission?" the man whispered at Prester with a wink and a smile.

"No, just a green for me and a blue for my wife."

The man leaned back and sang out, "One blue!"

A crab at his feet scuttled from one side to the other with a blue-labeled canister of ground crystals, which the attendant poured into a hole at the center of the spinning metal chamber in front of him. The chamber melted the crystals and shot their liquid through holes out to the edges. The attendant swirled a cone of white cardboard around the chamber to collect the spiraling strands into a puffy cloud of blue, which he then handed with great ceremonial flourish to Mina, repeating the process for Prester while Mina took her first tiny bites of dreamweave.

Reds faded away, then yellows, and the streets became tinged with wavering cyan. As people walked by, their emotions bent into smooth, organic, gentle curves or angry spikes and hard angles. Mina looked at Prester, but he was unchanged. He remained Prester, an unwavering, unspiking blue Prester, as the effect faded away, and the rest of the world morphed around him back into its usual form.

"How is it?" he asked.

"Wonderful as ever," Mina said.

"I don't look angry, do I?"

She laughed. "Nope. Still the same."

"Good!" It was a point of pride for him.

Prester tasted his green. The ideas trickled, then flooded in. The attendant could be a machine dipping in, pulling out, and now he could be the centerpiece of a clock that told space instead of time. They walked for a while past some families of turtles, and with the next bite the turtles were a staircase, turtle on turtle, leading to the tops of the buildings and to the tops of creation, and Prester was climbing up and down sixty-six turtles at a leap to visit for a while the beginning and end of the world. Mina, in another daydream of green, took Prester's hand. Now she was attached to him like a paper doll, and now a conjoined twin, and now they were a two-headed giant, but beautiful and loving and loved, and moving as one in a parade that America came out to adore. As the idea faded away, Prester shook his head to clear his mind and tossed his last bit of dreamweave into the trash.

They walked along the streets watching leathery Florida natives grin and bear it, selling painted shells and holy saltwater to pasty Vermonters in chafing new swimsuits. Dads wearing visors yelled at teenagers perusing racks of T-shirts that announced "I

Got Crabs From St. Brianna." Most of these places disappeared when the festival was over, but it was fun to study the sociology of it all, especially for Mina, especially on blue dreamweave.

A beat rose blocks away, and the Johns moved automatically to the curb to watch. The parade was approaching.

"Is Bruckheim still part of this?" Prester asked.

"Surely not," Mina said, but as she said it, she realized she must be wrong.

The beat grew, and now she could hear the jeers and laughter of another distant crowd. A scurry of crablings spilled around the corner, ahead of the rest, looking back at the approaching march. They rounded the bend: a military squad carrying sleek, black clubs in their smaller claws and snapping their larger ones in time with the music. Behind them came two Cyclopes with a banner stretched between—a ragged banner as old as the first parade, faded and scrawled "Dhe Vrize dhe Glury un Disicrashen de Sam Bruckheim!" The crowd cheered at the sight of the banner, but they'd have to wait for the show.

After the banner came throngs of marchers, first a crab band playing a mix of awkwardly held human instruments and traditional crab soundmakers created from shell and fishbone. A token marching band from the local human high school came next, playing out of tune and jolting with terror, blasting a bad note every time a spectator snapped a claw in their direction. Then a wild array of crab acrobats, water tossers, philosophers, card dealers, and cheer squads, all performing at once in a sort of timed battery of tricks and monologues. Then a solid line of more soldiers, and the crowd knew what would come next.

A float rounded the turn, bumping over the trash and debris of the street. Children shouted as it came nearer. Atop the float, surrounded by well-armed crabs, was Sam Bruckheim, sporting a new suit already torn at the elbows and knees. He wore a top hat with a sign around the rim: "Mishter de Bihologee." At a signal from the grand marshal, the float stopped. The spectators applauded in mock adulation of Bruckheim. One of the crabs snapped at him, and Bruckheim stood up. The crowd went silent as he raised a large syringe in one hand and the long-ago-taxidermied body of a crab, deformed with a laundry iron for an arm and roller skates for feet, in the other. The crowd exploded.

"Kill him!"

"Punish him!"

A guard snapped at Bruckheim's feet, and Bruckheim, blankly, with no capacity for fear remaining, put down his implements, took off his hat, and stepped down to the street to be beaten with the soldiers' clubs. Years ago, long before Mina and Prester began coming to the island, the crabs would throw Bruckheim to the sidewalk. They'd sling him overhead from one side of the street to the other for hours. After almost a decade of this, parade organizers, partly on the recommendation of the doctors who kept him alive, decided that not only was Bruckheim's body wearing out from abuse, but this part of the festival was taking far too long and the food vendors were starting to complain. Parade regulations now called for beatings that were much more structured, and at regular intervals to keep visitors satisfied.

Mina didn't mind their anger. She understood. Bruckheim's work in genetic modification had led to "genetic deselection," one of the early euphemisms for selective extinction. She hadn't understood the words when she was a teenager. She hadn't made the connection when Urtyylk took sick for several days, weak and unable to hold down food. After a couple of weeks, he couldn't flap his wings hard enough to get off the ground. Mina would nestle into the soft tufts of his tummy feathers, trying to comfort him. He was confused, and even if she could have explained it to him in a way he could understand, she didn't know what was happening either. Urtyylk withered and died. Her parents had what was left of him buried in the gravel pits at Bara.

A few days later, Mina began crying during lunch and spoke of how much she missed Urtyylk.

Her parents looked at each other and told her she shouldn't talk about Urtyylk anymore, that grown-ups didn't believe that rocs were real.

Years later, Mina tried to find Urtyylk's grave. She clawed up the ground twenty feet deep but found no sign of him, not in the grave, not in books, not in museums. She would have to keep him only inside, deep inside, where nothing could fade or melt.

Now Rostica wanted to know about Urtyylk and the plume of white feathers, and Mina felt she couldn't go through it again. What was Rhodesia to her anyway? Who would believe her? They'd bicker and argue and accuse her of childhood hallucinations. Gog and Rostica and May. No more. It was better this way. Let them fight on their own.

The thrum and jangle of the parade grew softer. The shuffle of crowds and tittering laughter became only a ruffling of banners in a light wind. It was enough.

"Mina?"

She heard him, Prester, like a tree frog in the distance at 2 a.m., when you could swear you heard a tree frog but couldn't be sure enough to be content and give in to sleep. He was like that: there, but not present enough to put her at ease.

"Mina."

"Yes."

"Are you okay?"

It was Prester. "Yes," she said.

"You were fading again," he said, and the concern on his face was clear, even with the blue dreamweave long gone.

"Was I? Oh. I'm sorry. Is the parade over?"

They were standing in an abandoned street with "closed" signs in all the windows and streamers falling from the rooftops. Everyone had followed the parade to the fairgrounds for the big shows.

"Hey, we've had a big day," Prester said. "A big last day. Let's go back to the house, okay?"

"The day isn't over," Mina said, her body growing solid now, her feet coming into contact with the pebbled street, the weight of her body meeting the contours of her sandals. "We're not done yet. One last day."

She smiled, and Prester smiled, and he mulled over the image of the two of them as paper dolls or two-headed giants and whether there was enough green dreamweave to burn that image into his mind forever. Knowing that there wasn't made him want to push it away.

The fairgrounds were in a frenzy as children, crabs, and turtles raced for a treat of deep-fried Snickers bar or desiccated fish before the show began. The crabs clicked and growled at every human nearby. The turtles hopelessly trudged on (they'd never make it in time).

Two stacks of spectator stands lined the soccer field. The Cyclopes were obedient enough to stand in back, their shoulders red with countless crabs hanging on and waving little flags. The stands, like everything else in St. Brianna, were integrated in name only: Crabs migrated to one side and humans to the other. The few humans who accidentally ended up on the crab side, too embarrassed to find another seat now that they were settled, proudly tried to conceal their terror as redshells whispered threats of disemboweling in their ears; and on the human side a handful of crabs couldn't help but obsess over whether they'd taste better in butter or lemon. Prester and Mina found a place among the humans.

Entertainers from the parade scrambled onto the soccer field, offering clashing finales to their individual shows to keep the crowd happy until the pageants. Flames shot through the air, twining around the flowing philosophers' expositions, burning out -isms and replacing with cloudy -ishes, much to the infuriation of the philosopher crabs, who leaped and cursed even as those curses transformed on their lips to flowery praise. At the sound of an air-horn, a Cyclops lumbered from behind one of the stands and toward the soccer field. He raked the crabs to either side with a tree limb that resembled a hockey stick. They spat and clicked, and the Cyclops grinned.

A second Cyclops came forward, rolling a stage with curtained housing toward the halfway line. The stage, draped in white paper now tearing at the edges, had a twenty-foot-wide curtained housing at the back. It was too flat to be functional, which was confusing until Prester noticed the NSpaces logo. The doors must be extradimensional; Prester marveled at the salesmanship behind that idea. As the Cyclopes returned to their places, the crowd hushed. Prester could hear the scuffling of turtles trying to clear the midway.

A large crab scuttled from the stage housing followed by a man wearing a fishing cap: the co-mayors of the island. They shouted PA-system-garbled greetings to the crowd, which shouted back a confused response in three species of language. After some voter-friendly comments, the mayors introduced this year's contestants in the Miss St. Brianna Pageant.

From the extradimensional stage housing marched a line of women with pale skin tinged retch green or sickly blue, eyes sunken or hollow, seaweed draped from their outstretched arms. Paying tribute to the beautiful virgin saint of the island, they moaned to God, to Death, to Love as the crowd cheered and whistled. Human contestants vied to impress with their gruesomeness while still upholding the unspoiled dignity of St. Brianna. There were rumors of a contestant years ago who took things too far and was attacked onstage by hundreds of crabs, then dragged screaming into the sea. Prester always wondered what she'd done to offend them.

Prester and Mina joined in the applause as a Florida State University student from Audubon, New Jersey, was named Miss St. Brianna. She arched her neck and gurgled with glee, as was the tradition, and the crabs draped her in golden seaweed. Some of the older crabs looked around among the humans to see if any pregnant women might have been induced to labor at the vision, then dropped their eyestalks in cold disappointment.

"Looks like the molting is next," Mina said.

"Yes," Prester said. "Gog."

Reggie Gog. If Reggie was behind the roc extinction, Mina decided, and if Jesus wanted Reggie dead and wanted Prester to do it, that must mean that Mina was being manipulated. Even if Reggie's kindness was a ruse and May's sympathy wasn't real, that didn't mean they deserved to die. Something more was happening, something beyond Mina's control, emptying her, weakening her, leaving her a fading Polaroid image of what she ought to be.

What should she be? She should be outraged. She should make it all stop.

Mina looked at Prester until he noticed and felt compelled to look back. "You can't kill him, Prester," she said quietly. "Even if there's a reason, something he did, something he's going to do, and that's why Jesus wants him dead, you can't do that."

"Did Jesus talk to you? What did he say?"

"No, not Jesus. Some reporter. He said Gog was behind some things. But that doesn't matter, Prester," she said.

Prester was going to suggest they go home and either finish what they'd started or sort out this mess with the Gogs, but a woman draped in seaweed, her face bloated with injections and dyed gray, shambled toward them, yelling.

"Mina! Prester! You came after all!"

"May?" Mina said.

"Yes, isn't this just me?"

Rank water drizzled off her thighs, stinking across the bleachers. Disgusted spectators moved their legs sideways out of her path.

"This morning when Reggie was getting ready for the molting, some of the crabs came to me and absolutely insisted I enter the competition. They said I looked just like Saint Brianna—plus about thirty years and not enough to win, obviously. But they got me in their alteration booth and dolled me up just the same."

She went on and on about her alterations—which were primarily cosmetic, nothing internal: hair, face, arms. Mina pretended to be amused. Prester's mind wandered over images of mottled green breasts (would they be pitted with rot?) slickened by salty foam, nipples jaunting firmly, defiantly toward the waves. He thought of May as Saint Brianna, a pure virgin now released upon the world, and amid his revulsion over her appearance and prattling he felt his shadow growing stronger, trying to sway his interest.

"Reggie said I looked perfectly awful, but you should see him! It's gruesome, really. Have you seen him yet?"

Prester, trying to get his mind off May, watched Mina carefully as she said, "No."

Prester stood. The shadow tugged at its staples as he sidestepped toward the aisle. "May, please take my seat. I'm going down to get a milk. Mina, would you like anything?"

"No, I'm fine," Mina said. "Prester, are you sure you want to stay for the rest of the show? You aren't ready to go home?"

"No, you two sit and watch Reggie. I'll catch him from the vending stands."

As Prester walked away into the crowd, Mina noticed for the first time that his shirt was untucked. May went on about the crabs and the pageant and how ridiculous the other contestants looked as Mina considered the gun in the small of Prester's back. It could be for Gog. It could be for her. It could be for him. But she was struck by a feeling that everything was about to change in a way that she had no power to to alter. A gun in the small of the back, a grave no one could find, a diagnosis of a disease with no cause, a shadow that acted of its own will. Everything would change, and she had no choice. An overwhelming sense of cold pressed down on her, and she shuddered inside the freezer room, ready now to be let out. Mina stared past the stage, past the fairgrounds, past Florida, and into dying clouds and the blue-tinged dreams of empty nautilus shells that echoed only silence. It wouldn't stop. Even if she could prevent Prester from doing whatever he was doing, even if she could talk to Rostica and get to the bottom of whatever was going on with the Gogs, even then it wouldn't stop.

A light breeze trickled through the stands. Mina felt it against the muscle and nerves of her forearms. The skin was gone, she could tell, and the cold was seeping past her outer layers as she continued a slow fade.

Prester needed to think, and the warm salt water dripping down May's rotting body and onto his knees wasn't helping. He climbed down the slick stairs and into the vending crowd, past drunken college students cavorting with snowbird widows from Tampa, past uncomfortable fathers trying to lead their children anywhere but to another seat next to the crabs, past heavily armed police officers that Prester feared were looking for whoever had fired the gun last night. Prester bought his frothed milk and found a place to stand between the bleachers and a Cyclops's leg. Prester leaned against it, knowing the Cyclops would never notice. Crabs scuttled up the leg past him every few minutes, but they sensed Prester's age and did not ask him to move.

From where he stood, Prester had a clear view of the stage and also of Mina sitting in the stands, only half-listening to May. Whatever Jesus had told her, she was rattled. She'd been threatened in some way or made to think something was going on, and she was right to push back. She seemed scared of Gog, scared of Prester knowing more about Gog.

Okay, Prester prayed. You want something. I want something too. I want Mina healed. I want her whole. Does it work that way? Tit for tat, quid pro quo?

Nothing.

Reggie Gog crossed the stage, laughing and waving to the crowd, glistening orange-red and beginning to split across the armpits. Only a few islanders each year were brave enough to participate in genetically enhanced molting. Yes, a few wore foam-padded shells and carried big plastic claws just to feel more connected to things, but that was nothing compared to the real molting. The trick wasn't so much the genetic alteration itself as timing the alteration to seasonal hormonal changes that forced the altered subject into a state of molt. The timing had to be just right. Too early and you could crack a shell and be left blue and naked, running through the festival to find your car. Too late and you could spend the next several weeks trying to fit into quadruple-wide suits back at the office after vacation.

Gog looked to have been timed just right. In this variation, sponsored by Zhe Genestictactics, LLC, the subject maintained his human head, at least down to the chin, and the cartilage took over from there, with a wide burnt-red shell extending out from the back and into a spiked rim. The claws were fantastic, one bigger than the other of course, and Gog seemed to have full control of all his pinchers as he scurried back and forth, sometimes on his belly, sometimes standing upright on human legs left there for better visual effect.

The shell cracked sharply as Gog bent forward and flexed. It began to peel off his back and hang by weakened cartilage from his upper thighs. Gog, now blue and glistening, viscous and naked, laughed along with the crowd. The crabs in particular were hopping with delight. It wasn't genuine. Nothing Gog did was genuine. Prester had disliked him from the moment they'd met, and now he understood why—that laugh and that look, carefully constructed to draw sympathetic attention only to him. It was a charisma built on deceit and manipulation. Gesticulating for the crowd. He was a ridiculous failure, and his death would mean nothing. Why not? Try harder next time, Jesus had said.

Under the bleachers and behind the Cyclopes, the shadow grew wide, overtaking the slatted sunlight. All eyes were on the stage. They would all see the shooting, but Prester was used to time, both fast and slow. He'd have the gun hidden before anyone would see who fired it. Prester put the milk glass between his feet and considered the angles, Reggie's movements, the people around him, the chances of anyone leaning left or right to block the trajectory. He looked up at Mina, and it occurred to Prester that he didn't want her to see this.

Mina was staring not at Gog but past him, without emotion, her eyes empty, even as May continued to prattle with spikes of sound that Prester could hear even from a distance. As a cloud shifted to one side above the fairgrounds, reflected sunlight caught May's rotting body, and Prester realized he was seeing its sickly colors through the fading arm of his wife. Mina was rapidly disappearing.

Prester left his milk and darted toward the spectator stands.

Gog did a sort of dance, trying half-seriously to sling the shell off his legs. When he did, it flapped and banged the stage like a drum hammer, then it swung around, causing him to trip and stumble. The audience roared with laughter.

When Prester got to Mina, May had already noticed her condition.

"Is she okay? She just got quiet all of a sudden, and I can't seem to snap her out of it, and now she's kind of wispy and floating all over," May said. "Did you see Reggie molt? Reggie on a half-shell, that's what I'll call him! Mina isn't contagious, is she?"

Prester draped his handkerchief over Mina's arm and rubbed it briskly. "Mina? Mina, I need you to come out of it."

An overenthusiastic crab jumped to the stage and clipped the cartilage from Gog's thighs, leaving him splayed on the floor, screaming in pain.

"Reggie!" May shouted.

Gog thrashed around on the stage, crying, "Oh God! Oh God!" and bleeding profusely. Several crabs emerged from the stage housing and carried him away. May tumbled down toward the stage as fast as her slimed-over legs could move, but she couldn't get there before Gog disappeared into the extradimensional stage housing. She stood on the crimsoned stage, pounding at the door in what the audience mistook for a comedy routine about a restroom.

Mina blinked at Prester. "You need what?"

He smiled in relief. "I need you to wake up. Come on, let's go home."

ENTERING OBLIVION, 1144 A.D.

B Y THE TIME PRESBITER IONIS left the Tigris River, his options were so utterly collapsed he might as easily have become a village baker as establish an empire on another continent. The Tigris had not frozen, his armies had abandoned him, and the Mongols were at his back, consuming the Grand Diocese parish by parish. All he had left were an entourage of fifty Quaabites, his steward Tokmat, and an unfulfilled promise from the Lord of Hosts. Even if he'd had the means to cross the river now, he no longer had the heart to try.

Instead, he allowed Tokmat to break camp. They traveled north to Nineveh, where Tokmat sold twenty of their men into slavery to buy passage south to the Gulf of Bassora. Ionis wasn't sure where he'd go, but he had to get away from the Steppe, away from Jerusalem, away from everything that connected him to failure. They sailed past the vessels of petty merchants and of pirates, who looked up only long enough to decide they were not worth the nick of a blade. Ionis stood on the prow of the ship as it passed Muscat, headed out to sea, with no choice yet made between courses east or west.

"How fares the king of Asia?" Tokmat asked.

"You mean Ambaghai Khan? Turn the ship around and go ask

him yourself. Only throw me overboard first."

Tokmat looked out across the water to find what Ionis was watching. The waves were fierce this far out, slashing with tall foamy spikes at the flat violet clouds hundreds of feet above them. The clouds played a game of shift-and-part, teasing in geometric patterns, splitting and sliding to avoid being sullied by salt.

"I have no wish to go back," Tokmat said. "I wish only to take Presbiter Ionis forward." He paused, awaiting some indication as to how the conversation should proceed. Tokmat had a plan, but he wasn't sure Ionis would like it. He had to exhaust all other possibilities first. "We could go to India. We're known there, and we'd be treated royally."

"Treated royally. Does that include being pandered to and calculated against? Or merely executed as a threat to the crown? I've had my fill of Asia, Tokmat. Take me somewhere else."

"We could reverse course and sail to Jerusalem. Who knows what the Lord's command might have meant?" Tokmat risked a too-familiar, low-voiced plea in his master's ear. "Who knows what might happen if you were to march in now, sword unsheathed, to mow down the Saracens? What power might there be in that promise from the Lord?"

Tokmat's words made Ionis uneasy. He wanted counsel. He wanted to know the thoughts of those around him, for even if those thoughts were disagreeable, the knowledge of them was a tool. But this was beyond counsel: this was an attempt at influence, and he would not have a steward, even one so trusted as Tokmat, lead him by the chin. Ionis stayed silent a moment, to give Tokmat the illusion of having had his say. He then rose up inside and burned to a new height. "Servant, if I needed a new voice inside me, I'd rip out your throat and eat it with my bread."

Tokmat diminished, lowering his head to watch the rail between the white knuckles of his fingers.

"We sail on," Ionis said. "Find another idea, Tokmat. And if you find no options that suit you, sail us into oblivion."

He walked away, leaving Tokmat to shudder on the brink of an unforgiving sea.

Ionis went back to his cabin, lashed the doors, and closed the shutters. As the wax from his candle wandered to one side and then the other with the rocking of the ship, he slipped into several days of unbroken fasting and prayer. Except for a few brief bursts of anger and pride, Ionis's prayers mainly took the form of rote supplication—humble requests for some insight as to what truly happened at the Tigris. Had his faith been weak? Surely he believed. He believed enough to march his entire army from all corners of Asia to one point and to hold them there for the next word from God. Were his men not pure enough to do battle for the Lord? What was he to do? Baptize them at the point of a sword, or enlist angels to fight on his side?

The single candle cast Ionis's shadow large on the latticed wall behind him. The shadow was massive but weak, rocking with the movements of the ship, mocking Ionis's self-doubt.

Ionis drifted into a gray nothingness of dream in which he lingered, sitting in the hollow of a nut. He could sense the shell of the nut outside himself, expanding away from him, like a shadow growing larger beneath a harsh twilight—or was Ionis growing smaller inside it? And then he was the shell, looking down upon himself, curled into a ball at the low point of an expanding black sphere. He encompassed himself and surrounded himself in a grayness of silence moving ever outward.

Look at you, something said. You are weak. You are small. You are nothing.

Ionis didn't respond. He only felt himself get smaller with each word as the nut grew larger and darker around him.

You are nothing, it said. I want more.

Then, for the first time in days, Ionis was aware of his body as pain ripped across the bottoms of his feet, and now he was shaking and weak, naked at the center of a dark shell that had grown so large it merged into the sky. He was alone, and his shadow was gone, off somewhere on business of its own.

Ionis looked up and saw a salamander's eye, huge, five times his height. He stumbled back and away.

In the dream the salamander became three, and the three salamanders were at the center of an icy labyrinth, with a pit of fire on the other side. Each salamander was tasked with finding the fire and offered a choice of six passages. The first salamander turned to see what the others would do. The second salamander bolted into one of the passages, where it met a cat (clawing and hissing), a viper (biting and curling), and a cock (snatching and flapping). The salamander prevailed, but died from its injuries shortly after entering the fire. The first salamander continued to wait. The third salamander did something that surprised Ionis, almost waking him from the dream. It stood up on its hind legs and looked across the top of the labyrinth, memorizing the passages, studying the dangers, and figuring a way from where it stood to the flame that awaited. Satisfied, it dropped back to the ground and scurried into one of the passages, where Ionis knew it would find the flame. The first salamander continued to wait, annoyed now with itself for not thinking to look over the top. It withered and rotted and drifted away in a cloud of dust.

The third salamander, a white, then appeared before Ionis and stared at him expectantly.

"Yes?" Ionis whispered.

The salamander asked if it wasn't yet time.

"Time for what?"

For being, the salamander replied.

"What do you mean by 'being'?"

The salamander paused, looked across the labyrinth into the future, and replied: You won't like this.

In these distracted days, Ionis sometimes snatched up lines of whispered conversation from those around him.

Tokmat: "Our king isn't interested in which way the captain wants to go. I say take the ship west or Presbiter Ionis will bring down the fury of the one true God upon you!"

There was a storm. Ionis knew this because someone in splash-soaked clothes came into his cabin, found him on the floor, and set him upright.

Kushva, Tokmat's steward: "It is a sign. The salamander would not go dry of milk if it were not a sign."

There was a negotiation. Ionis knew this because Tokmat entered his room, took a bag of coins from his chest, showed them to him as a courtesy, and left.

The captain: "Seylac will never receive us. Tell Tokmat that."

There was a mutiny, or an attempt at one. He knew this because of the thud of a knife jammed into his door, followed by shouts and clanging steel, then cheers as a body went overboard. He deduced it wasn't Tokmat's. If it had been, Ionis would have been the sea's next sacrifice.

Jesus: "Very well, Presbiter Ionis. I am coming."

Ionis blinked and jerked his stare from the candle. The ship had stopped rocking. Shouts were coming from the port decks, shouts about a man walking across the sea. Ionis jumped up and covered himself with an unwashed robe. He ran to the deck, where the crewmen were at first too amazed by what they saw to notice that they stood in the way of an awakened king.

The ship was still. At starboard, the sea was an unrippled plane as far as anyone could see, and the early sun made a harsh glare on the water. But at port, in the distance, there was land, a gold-and-brown coastal village on a ledge of baked clay, and from it came a man, walking on the water. He was tall for a Jew but not for an African, and he was black, and Ionis felt sure that his eyes would be deep brown. He was attired in orange robes with a golden hem that dragged across the unmoving surface of the sea, and he wore a golden skullcap that glinted in the sun, blinding many of the crew as he walked up to the ship.

"Be not afraid!" he shouted cheerfully. "For I am with you!"

At that, three of the crew collapsed onto the aft deck in ecstasy, and one high-rigger, though hardened at heart by decades at sea, suffered a stroke and fell to his death.

Jesus climbed a rope ladder (dropped to him blasphemously late by an incredulous mate) and tossed himself up onto the ship. He held up the palm of a massive hand and said, with a voice of kindness and assurance, "The Lord be with you."

When none around him responded "And with your spirit," he lowered his hands to his waist, intertwining long fingers, then turned to Ionis with a toothy grin. "Have you fallen so low, Presbiter Ionis, that you now stand naked amid your bearers?"

Ionis looked down to find himself exposed. He pulled his robe shut and bowed. "Forgive me, Lord."

"We should talk," Jesus said, and walked past Ionis into his cabin.

Ionis followed, bristling with anger—partly at Jesus, partly at the crew, partly at himself. He closed the door behind him, and Jesus turned. "Anger is a dangerous emotion, Presbiter Ionis. And too often misdirected. Why are you here?"

Ionis was stunned. He'd been praying for weeks. What the hell kind of question was that? "Here? I, I am here . . . I am here because I have nowhere else to go."

"You have the Tigris. Why are you not at the Tigris?" Jesus said.

"I waited for you there," Ionis protested. "I waited five years on the banks of the Tigris! Five years, Lord. The river did not freeze; you did not come. My men abandoned me. What was I to do?"

"You were to do what I asked of you, Presbiter Ionis. Could you not wait with me?"

Ionis searched Jesus's deep brown eyes. The wide nose, chiseled jaw, and dark, stern face. This was not the servant Jesus, encouraging and generous. This was not the concubine Jesus, teasing and pleading. This was a merchant, powerful and influential. And displeased. Disappointed. Ionis turned away, unable to bear any more. He wished now that he had never heard of the dead lamb king. "I could not."

"No," Jesus said, more to himself than to Ionis. "You could not."

Ionis opened his mouth to speak, but for once in his long life found he had nothing to say of any consequence. It occurred to him that not only did Jesus know his thoughts, Jesus knew what he was going to say.

"But the spoken word has value, Ionis."

Ionis kept his head down and embraced the silence. He found it a comfort, like a sturdy shield in the hand of a warrior.

"Am I your attacker, then?"

And he found, too, that the silence gave him strength, a place to go—an empty place, but a place where he could gather his thoughts before thoughts became words and action. It had served him well on the Tigris. It could serve him still.

"And did it serve you? What is the yield of this harvest?"

"What would you have me say, then, Jesus? What would you have me do?"

Jesus walked around Ionis's cabin, picking up oddments and dropping them dismissively. "Some years ago, Gjona-ja, I told you of a man from Merv and a river." He picked up an astrolabe and, holding it backwards, peered through the window.

"Yes, I remember."

Jesus picked up a set of scales and tried adding weights. He put too many golden scarabs on one side and the whole balancing arm toppled off, sending everything crashing to the floor as he scrambled to catch it.

"The cabin boy will get that," Ionis said.

"Thank you." Jesus smiled. "So this man, he lost his lamb, and then his wheat, and then his wife. He gave up everything."

"Yes. He sacrificed all, and he was rewarded." Prester thought for a moment. "Is that what this is? You wanted me to lose my empire for something greater?" If that was it, maybe he could bear it. If there was some meaning behind it, he could accept what he'd lost. For the first time in five years Ionis began to feel hope.

Jesus frowned. He opened a small locked chest on Ionis's stack of boxes and pulled out the chalice. "Ah, you still have my cup. I wondered what happened to it."

"Please take it from me."

"Perhaps I should." Jesus put down the chalice. "Ionis, you're missing the point. The man from Merv was happy because he was obedient. He did what he was told. You were to keep your army at the Tigris until I was ready, and instead you let it fall away. You failed me."

"And if I had waited, what then? How much longer before the river froze? And what would have happened next?"

Jesus did not answer.

Ionis collapsed into a chair, unable to bear the weight of the words: Happy. Obedient. Failed. Even the silence couldn't protect him from that last word. Failure. It was his failure, a failure of leadership and of faith. What now? Would he be cast down, exiled like Cain? It didn't matter. He had done all he could, and he couldn't please God. There was no point in trying.

Jesus shrugged. "There is always a point in trying, Ionis. Just try harder next time." Then he walked out, leaving Ionis in absolute emptiness.

Jesus climbed down the rope ladder and strode with ineffable purpose across the sea to the port village of Seylac, off the coast of Abyssinia. Once his form had blended with the background of the village, the sea rustled up again into a flowing mass, and an easy wind propelled the ship toward harbor.

"Tokmat!" Ionis yelled as he felt the ship come alive under him. "Where are we?"

Tokmat entered the cabin and bowed, then beamed with pleasure at the sureness of his choice: "Oblivion, my Lord. We are in oblivion."

MONDAY EVENING:
SHADOW PLAY

PRESTER STEERED MINA ACROSS THE long trail back to their beach house. How long would it be, he wondered, before she slipped into total insubstantiality? Perhaps she could wander St. Brianna Island, stopping in to visit vacationers at a haunted beach house, a mysterious draft along the floor. Prester couldn't let that happen, and he wouldn't. They'd have to kill each other tonight, tonight or nothing.

He guided Mina onto the bed. Her skin was back again, with hairs beginning to appear once more, thanks mainly to the handkerchief trick. Prester left her there to recover. Not now, not yet. His mind raced back thirty years, then two hundred, then fourteen hundred, to Beatrice, to Shali, to the other brief wives—the few he'd watched wither into death. Then, he'd managed to stay calm. But now he found himself pacing to Mina and back and to the bathroom and the door and back again, unsure what to do or whether he could help her. Then he laughed at himself, his weak unsure self, actually getting worked into a frenzy over yet another dying woman. There was nothing he could do. Mina was going away, but Prester couldn't bring his mind to accept that this was so.

"Jesus," Prester whispered. His voice shuddered in what felt like suppressed sobs, but Prester wouldn't believe this could be the case. "Jesus. Lord. Is this what you wanted? For me to pray again? It didn't work before." His prayer drifted out of speech and into thought: Is that what it will take for you to end this? Maybe you were leading me to something, and maybe this was it. You want my obedience? You want me to kill for you? I will. Just heal Mina first. Now. Please? No, that's ridiculous. You'll no more answer me than you would a million others praying from chapels and battlefields and the blood-strewn shoulders of interstates. Death comes to us all.

It made his mind ache. After a few hours of restless thought, Prester walked out into the hallway, where a salamander mewed to him. She hadn't been milked. Mina normally did this, but she must've meant to do it later. Prester stood in the hall for a moment. He couldn't stand the thought of the salamander bulging in pain for hours after their suicide. Would the police even know what to do? He put on the oven mitts, opened the cage, and carried the salamanders out to the sink. The white wrapped her blazing-hot tail around Prester's arm, looking up at him in joyful anticipation. The gray sniffed the countertop while Prester held the white and got a fresh milk jar out of the cabinet. The lighter wasn't where it was supposed to be, so Prester went to the living room and found matches in an end-table drawer, where he'd left them after lighting candles Saturday night.

Prester John hadn't milked a salamander in more than a decade. He'd taught Mina to do it soon after they met, the way he had been taught, before the Tigris, before the wars across Asia, before he became emperor, before he was even a chieftain.

It was 1990, the day after Mina moved in. Things were happening fast: Mina wasn't going back to Madagascar and she needed a place to stay. It made sense. Mina felt there was something about Prester. Like he was already part of her life, maybe because of his connection with Dr. John, though she hadn't known him back when she was a student. For his part, Prester felt that meeting Mina was like sitting down in a packed hall for a magnificent spectacle, and he wasn't about to risk getting up and losing his seat. He wanted to see how things would end.

He didn't teach Mina the way he had been taught the first time, under the quick rod of the priest, but the way his son, Khalaja, had taught him.

"You didn't teach Dr. John—Beatrice, I mean?"

Prester smiled at the idea. "No. Beatrice didn't have patience for things like that."

"I can imagine," Mina said. "She was so focused on her work."

She looked at the white salamander sitting in its pyrorium. It shook its head at the mention of Beatrice John, dismissive, annoyed.

"You've had their milk before?" he asked.

"Yes, but only from stores and restaurants."

"This milk from this salamander, it comes out so silky sweet you could pour it over cakes for dessert."

Wearing an old pair of leather gloves, he picked the salamander up and placed her in Mina's arms, which were protected by long oven mitts.

"Cradle her like this. Now hold her over the fire—be careful not to burn yourself."

"Are you sure it won't hurt her?" Mina asked, causing the salamander to look up, squint its eyes and purr emanations of love.

"No, she's a salamander. This is what she does, this is who she is."

Mina took a deep breath and tentatively held the white over the fire. She relaxed when she saw that it wasn't in pain.

"Watch her teats. When they bead with milk, pull her away to your chest."

Mina saw the beads form and carefully pulled her away.

"Good. Hold her to your chest with this arm. Now reach over with your gloved hand and tug at the teats one at a time, letting the milk flow into the jug."

Mina squeezed the teats, drawing only a few drops.

"Squeeze harder."

"It won't hurt her?"

Prester smiled, remembering how Khala-ja had admonished him to take it easy—to be more gentle. "It takes patience, patience and time. They need us to milk them and care for them. And we need them to provide milk."

"The priests would say to provide life," Mina said.

"That too."

"Who taught you to milk a salamander?"

"My . . ." Prester started to say. My son Khala-ja, who grew up mostly without a father, for too long without a father, but became a great man, a man gentle and strong, confident and kind, who led his people and taught his father how to be. Prester started to say this, but the name of his son caught in his throat.

Mina smiled kindly at him, then briefly rested her head on his shoulder as she continued drawing the milk.

Now Prester was milking the white once more, milking her one last time. She looked up at Prester with what he decided was adulation. She reminded him so much of the salamander he'd had as a child, back on the Steppe. She purred and gave a gentle thrum of recognition.

Red. Nothing. Red. Nothing. Red. Nothing. Dreams of red, flashing and dying, here and gone and back once more crept up on Mina and tore her up and slowly out of it. She opened her eyes to near-pure darkness. It was night now. Above her a ceiling fan turned so slowly she could follow the blades, which reflected the red light flashing from the clock next to her bed. She turned to face the clock, her pupils pulsing in dilation with each flash of 12:00. She felt she ought to turn it off, but instead she stared and tried an old trick she'd taught herself as a teenager on quiet sleepless nights, of shifting her heartbeat to match a rhythm that wouldn't stop. Beat beat. Flash. Beat be-flash-at. Beat flash beat. Be-flash-at beat. Flash beat. Flash beat. Flash. Beat flash, beat flash, beat flash, beat flash. Satisfied, she closed her eyes. Beat flash, beat flash, beat flash, beat flash.

Prester was still awake, kept going by nagging reminders of things that needed doing. He spent a few hours online closing bank accounts and memberships, knowing that these things would be closed for him upon his demise but bothered by the idea of putting anyone to trouble about it. Then the electricity went out, likely because some drunken Cyclops had gotten an arm caught in a power line. Prester also had the nagging idea that he should go kill Gog—just get it over with and make Jesus happy. But no, he wasn't going to do it. Not without a good reason. Something was going on—something he didn't understand. Was it enough to justify taking a life? Jesus would have to do better than that. And if he did kill Gog, how would he explain that to Mina? He began to picture her face as he told her. He shook the image from his mind.

The power came back on, but Prester had already moved on to inspecting the slate mildew (still in check) and cleaning the receipts out of his wallet. He walked outside to test the chemicals in the pool, which hadn't been done in at least a month. If the house was going to be sold after their bodies were cleaned up, the pool's carbon levels would have to be in check, and even a week of neglect might make all the difference. Prester had never wanted a house with a pool, but there was so much about this one that they liked:

the southern exposure from a wall of windows that could easily be blocked off by long plantation shutters, the garden tub and walk-in shower, the wraparound porch with access from three rooms, a short walk to the beach but not so close that they were exposed to prying waves. But a pool. A pool is a nuisance. In the off-season they had to contract with a service to keep the carbon levels down. There had been a story in the papers when they first moved in about a family that let the carbon levels reach lifestage, and when they came back for a summer stay, they found their pool water had not only become sentient but had awakened the water in their pipes and turned the house over as squatters' domain. Eventually the whole thing fell into the sea, and the waterforms couldn't have been happier about that.

Prester knelt by the shallow end and dipped in a test tube, then used his pocket flashlight to get a reading. (He kept the flashlight with him all the time now, just in case.) The carbon was high, and the water was showing early signs of sentience, lapping up the edges to peek over the side of the glass. He walked back to the shed for a half-cup of powdered nitric acid. One should do the trick. As he spun the combination and unlocked the door, Prester imagined going back to the pool and finding May, drifting along the deep end, spirals of seaweed flowing from her arms, her body green but sleek and welcoming.

May. Why May? Her voice grated on his ears. It never quite seemed to stop.

But there was something in the curve of her arm, the line of muscle along her neck.

Stop it.

Perhaps she'd rise up on the edge of the pool, her breasts protruding from loose streams of cold seaweed, and beckon Prester to join her, lips glistening and dripping wet in reflected moonlight.

Shut up.

Maybe he'd sit on the edge and she'd come up in front of him, her almond eyes pulsing with the sultry blood of the Khans and burning with anticipation. She was annoying, yes, but what would it be like to have her lips on him, her hands tugging and those eyes peering up toward him?

Prester absently scooped up a half-cup of nitric acid. As he turned, he felt the rip of a dozen staples tearing from his right foot. He fell to the concrete, moonlight flashing, the black shadow jerking wildly up the walls. The nitric acid powder plumed across the floor, drizzling into a bubbling, slick puddle. As Prester's left foot came off the ground, his shadow tore completely away, bloodied staples tinkling against metal shelving. Prester's gun fell from his belt and spun on the concrete. The shadow darted out of the shed, through the poolyard, and around the side of the house, pausing only once to check the distance between itself and its former possessor. Prester clambered to his feet and gasped in pain as the nitric acid seeped into his wounds and ate at the skin of his arms. He threw himself awkwardly into the over-carbonized water, which eased away the acid, the pain, and any torn remnants of Prester John's shadow.

Inside the house, dead silence gave way to the rattle of the salamander pyrorium. The white had never tried to escape, but she was bothered by the power outage and the growing cold in the sleepingroom. She had to know the state of things—the way things would be—so that she could prepare herself and her gray for their new situation. She nudged the door open and entered the room, cold and dark. She could handle the dark. Though her eyes were tiny, she had over the years found ways to see without seeing. She crawled up onto the bed, pulling the coverings down in the process. She was afraid she would find the woman lying there, insubstantial, but instead the woman floated by the window, staring at a sky that sparked with starplay. Gold streams of comet spun circles around Orion's belt. He swung at them, missing, missing, then smashing one in a supernova of silent light.

The white climbed down again. She looked for the woman's feet, but there were no feet. No knees. The thighs were half-gone, and beyond that the white could not tell, because of a nightshirt that seemed determined to remain solid. The woman bobbed slightly in the breeze from the ceiling fan. The woman should not be alone, the white decided.

Mina felt something purring where her feet should be. She took a wadded-up sheet from the bed and drifted down to lift the white salamander, cradling her in one arm, stroking her rubbery neck. As she did, the pain eased and Mina became slightly more aware of her legs. Maybe this could have some kind of medicinal effect—just to pet a salamander for a few minutes. Taking care of the salamanders had become a chore of twice-weekly milking and monthly ash-cleaning. She'd let them out on occasion for a skiddle across the house or to clean up a mess. But to pet one again—maybe this was what she needed, she thought, and then she looked outside to see a man limping across the pebbled street toward the Gogs' beach house, dripping wet, a gun in his hand, leaving a trail of bloody footprints.

Prester. No. Mina pushed herself away from the window, struggling in frantic swimming motions to float out of the bedroom.

There was no mistaking the direction the shadow had taken. In the streetlight it was sharply defined, black against the concrete wall of the Gogs' lower floor, glancing around, heaving with energy, gathering strength. Prester knew how to remain unseen, even to his shadow, and he waited to see where it would go next. It paused, then darted straight up to an uncurtained window. That was something Prester did not expect. He had to get the shadow back, grab it and put it back on so he could kill it when he killed himself. No loose ends. Prester had to go halfway around the house to reach the staircase, then stow his gun on his belt so he could grasp the rails as he climbed. Searing rods of pain shot up his calves with every step. Prester didn't want to think about the amount of blood he was losing, but he did not cry out. That might wake the Gogs.

Mina drifted down the hall, inches at a time, past the pyrorium, toward the couch. The salamander followed directly under her. As she passed the cage, the salamander realized she ought to go back and replenish herself in the fiery warmth of home. The gray looked down, resentful. But the white had to see—had to know. Mina made it to the front door, but as she tried to turn the handle found herself upended ninety degrees, then floating back into the living room, spinning slowly, helplessly. She gritted her teeth to suppress angry tears.

In the Gogs' living room, big pastel furniture competed with dark electronic monsters promising a total surround-sound experience. The floor was carpeted in 1980s peach, and there was no hiding the bloody footprints he was leaving behind. Prester gave up, walking with little remorse toward the bedroom; the soft synthetic fabric was almost a comfort crushing under his feet. The bedroom door (a pair of hollowed plywood panels) was open. The bed was in the center of the room, offset at a once-trendy diagonal from the wall, which was covered by an abstractish painting of a pink swoop across a sea-green field. Reggie was on his stomach; his thighs, buttocks, and lower back were thick with white bandages, and Prester could smell the antiseptic reek of peroxide and plastic tape. May must have nursed him—fixed his bandages, eased him into the bed. She would spend the next weeks cleaning Gog's wounds, setting aside squeamishness to help him heal.

Prester couldn't see his shadow among the hundred other shadows in the room. Streetlight played over the easy targets on Gog's body: the jugular, the back of the head, the ribcage exposed by one lifted arm. Prester remembered the gun in the small of his back. Gog was half-dead anyway, inside and out. He could just fire. Kill Gog, kill May. Who would care? Who would be inconvenienced by that? Prester's reputation couldn't get more ruined than it was, and he'd long disagreed with Dante's assertion that there were parsable degrees of damnation. Mina wouldn't have to know. And what if Jesus rewarded him for that? Try harder next time, Jesus had said. And this, this would be easy.

May was on her back, her head to one side, muttering in her dreams. The dead-Brianna coloring had faded back, leaving her skin tanned and olive, hidden here and there under the remaining ribbons of dried seaweed, a veil of white cotton T-shirt, and a slowly retreating sheet. Prester stepped closer. May rolled her head, and her hands slipped down, pushing the sheet away. It had started. She began to giggle and moan, but the light was dim, and Prester couldn't be sure where her hands ended and the shadow began. There was no way to grab it now.

At this the shadow seemed to gather strength, and May let out a moan. No. It would never end, not this way. He had to end it. He had to find a way to make it stop.

Prester heard a car approaching; searching beams of headlights rolled across the edge of the room toward the bed. The light scanned the wall and revealed a moving silhouette across the pink swoop painting, an elongated shadow, erect and dark and sharply defined, with arms plunging down toward May's body. Gog, hearing May, raised his head and looked around his side of the room. Prester instinctively, silently, took out his gun, raised it, and released the safety. He could kill Gog now as easily as anything else, a bullet for him, a bullet for May, leave the shadow to desecrate the bodies. He could be the tool of Heaven on earth, he could do the will of Jesus, no more failure, no more doubt.

He imagined the look in Mina's eyes, a look that he'd seen before: contempt.

Prester fired. The Gogs jolted awake. Prester fired again and again into the shadow, and it convulsed against the painting with each blast. May screamed at the sight of Prester John standing over her, lit up by repeated flashes of gunfire. Reggie floundered in his wrappings and yelled, trying desperately to see what was happening or to stand. When the clip was almost empty, the shadow hung flat against the field of soft green, pinned by flashes of black, limp and dripping, unmoving at last.

Prester, suddenly aware of May's screams, turned and limped into a run, leaving his dead and dissipating shadow behind. As he bolted toward the beach house, the absurd thought hit him that even above the wracking pain from his feet, he hadn't run in years and was horribly out of shape. He began to chuckle and felt he might collapse onto the street in a laughing-crying jag. He was excited, and he felt strong now, like he hadn't felt since the Steppe. In between May's fits he could hear the waves crashing in the darkness, roaring up and spiking at the stars, a furious clash that no one could see, pounding into the beach with hammers of brilliant black foam. Mina would be angry with him now, scaring the Gogs like that. But he'd done it—the shadow was gone.

Prester limped up the stairs, near laughter, breathing hard now, and opened the door. With it came Mina, floating and half-spectral, her translucent eyes wide with fear and relief.

"Prester?"

She was almost gone, about to float off into the dark clouds. He looked in her eyes and in looking lost focus between her face and the top of the door jamb behind her.

"Mina, oh, God." He took her as softly as he could and pulled her to him, down to the doorway, and brought her into the house, where she'd be safe. He turned on the light and realized with a start that neither of them cast a shadow, for very different reasons.

They sat together on the floor. Prester shut and locked the door with his free arm while the salamander dutifully walked to Prester's feet and cleaned up the blood dripping onto the tile.

"What happened?" Mina asked. "What did you do?"

"Nothing—the Gogs are safe."

"You, are you okay?"

"No, Mina, I don't think I'm okay." He was shuddering and stuttering between laughter and panic. The shadow was gone, a part of him was gone, and he felt free but broken and weak. "I'm not okay, Mina. I don't think I'm going to be okay."

"It's all right, Prester. It'll be all right." She stroked his head and curled her fingers around the soft, straight baby hair at the back of his neck. "It'll be all right."

The white salamander peered up at the woman. She didn't have much time left, the woman. Pettingtime might have helped, maybe. But that would have put things off only for a time. The woman had been too long this way, too long in the quietalone. It made her softinform, softinsight, this quietalone.

Prester felt the tilt of his wife's body, the wavering form of her legs against his. "Mina?"

"I'm going, Prester. This is worse, now."

"No, you'll be fine." He reached for his handkerchief, but he'd lost it somewhere. He grabbed a dirty towel from the countertop nearby and rubbed hard at her arm. There was little of it to make purchase on. He had difficulty deciding where the towel ended and her arm began.

"You can't go, Mina." His voice cracked. He felt weak and simpering but was past all caring. "I can't do this."

"I know."

"I can't do this, Mina." He clutched her tight against his chest and she kissed his neck and wetted his cheek with her tears. "I can't do this alone anymore. I need you," he whispered, afraid he might hear himself say it.

"You do, don't you?" Mina's legs became solid against the wood of the door. She moved into his arms as her body grew substantial and warm, the empty parts closing up.

Prester felt it too, and for the first time in many years he prayed thanks for a second chance. "Mina, I love you, I need you."

"I know, I know." She smiled and touched his cheek, but her finger smeared across his skin like a melting yellow-orange crayon.

"Mina! Mina, don't melt."

The tears across her cheeks began to etch into the skin, leaving cutaway scars like butter scraped by the end of a knife. "It's too late," she said.

"Stop it!"

"Prester." She kissed him, but after a moment of pressure, her lips slipped away like melting ice.

Prester tried to clasp what was left of her tight in his arms but she slid to the tile in a steadily growing pool of color, clumping and then flowing, a yellow-orange swirl.

He sat on the floor, his back to the door jamb, holding his hands out like a sorcerer frozen mid-incantation, his wife's remains dripping down his arms and covering his legs, streaks of orange-yellow on his cheek and his lips.

The white salamander looked up at him, its legs yellowed by Mina's body.

"No. No, no, no," he muttered. He felt the urge to shout but stopped himself. No, this was fine. This was okay. This was the plan. It was still the plan, only "a bit ragged at the edges," as they used to say at NSpaces. "A bit sideways," they'd say. It's still the plan. Mina was gone, and now it was his turn. This was the plan.

He reached around to the gun in the small of his back and checked the clip. Empty. But there was still a bullet in the chamber. Prester took a final breath, put the gun in his mouth, and pulled the trigger.

N THE YEAR 1144, WHEN Presbiter Ionis arrived in Abyssinia, there was no longer a king. There was no longer an Abyssinia, not really. There were tribes and chieftains and the ruins of a great kingdom recently fallen into sand and vine. There were old-men, and they spoke but could no longer remember. There were mountains and rivers and trees and sky, and they remembered but could not speak.

Then there was Presbiter Ionis.

He landed at the mouth of the Red Sea, in the port city of Seylac, where Tokmat sold enough ancient tapestries to buy a small caravan of wagons. Tokmat sold another five of the men into slavery, and that bought a team of scarabs—massive beasts, as broad as a ship but as low as a draft horse—as well as enough dung to keep them alive for the long haul over the mountains to Addis Ababa.

Ionis was not convinced that Tokmat had a plan, and he began to suspect that the late nights his steward spent alone with maps and ledgers were more about predicting what might happen tomorrow than managing what needed to be done today. Ionis no longer cared. He had failed his empire. He had failed himself. He had failed God. But he couldn't shake the distant war cry from the back of his mind: angry thoughts of Jesus the betrayer, traitor-messiah, liar and tease. These thoughts sickened Ionis, but he could not run from them. And they distracted him, too, as at Tokmat's urging he performed last rites for a withered, stone-eyed king named Dil Na'od, the Christian lord of Abyssinia.

Afterward, Tokmat led Ionis to the edge of a sunlit plateau above a grassy plain that stretched to a wide green river. All across this plain bristled a forest of heads, of arms, of shields and spears, thousands upon thousands of people, all bouncing and shouting, "Prete Giam! Prete Giam! Prete Giam!"

He turned to Tokmat. "This is not what I wanted."

Tokmat looked hurt. "But, my lord, these are your people."

And, in this manner, he continued to be.

In the year 1218, Prete Giam finished his wars with Nubia and Egypt, one by conquest and the other by treaty. His Abyssinia now covered the lands of the Zagwe and Kitara, Bantu and Sao, reaching as far south as Lake Kariba and as far west as the Congo River basin. But this time there would be no yearlong Mass, no great crusade, no ongoing expansion. Instead, Prete Giam called upon his nascent circle of advisers, a mix of old chiefs and shamans, young cooks and hunters, who showed shrewdness without too much ambition. He called upon them to say what they would do to keep the empire safe from attack, from influence, from falling apart from within or without.

One old shaman, in a dreamweave-induced delirium, spoke of a vision of great walls of shit, walls upon walls, towering into the sky on the north, south, east, and west. Like the wide cliffs surrounding the upper Nile, these walls would keep Abyssinia safe from without, and the great work of building the walls would keep them safe from idle hands within. When he was finished, the hallucinating shaman collapsed onto the floor, shaking and muttering, "Great walls of shit. Great walls of shit."

Prete Giam mustered 144 scarabs to begin the work, each with two riders directing their efforts. They started at the center of the kingdom, just north of the Lake, then traced their way out, combing the land for miles at a time to gather spheres the size of twenty huts each, rolled up from the dung of the great beasts—elephants and gryphons and giraffes and rocs. In their wake the land was pure as a baptismal gown. They rolled these spheres of dung out to the borders and made a fence of them, at first with gaps that let the last of any roaming herds decide where they would remain. And then the scarabs, black and busy under the sun, filled in these holes to make walls, walls as tall as waterfalls, dark brown walls that stank of earth and mud and life. But this was only the beginning. The scarabs built walls as high as the pyramids of Egypt, encircling Abyssinia in a border that no man or animal, other than a scarab, would dare to approach. And when they were done, the scarabs were proud of their work. They implanted themselves, along with their riders, into the walls, creating of themselves shining black inlays like onyx decorations that warned of death to any who dared to come near. Many decades later, when the stench was gone, and first grass, then flowers, and then trees began to grow atop the great caked walls of shit, no one still living could remember what had been on the other side. All that remained were the ominous black hillside scarabs and faint rumors of a Christian king named Prete Giam who ruled in peace and without turmoil. And, in this manner, he continued to be.

In the year 1488, a man whose skin was pale under bruises and blood was dragged into the court of Prete Giam, amid shouted accusations and demands for his death. The man called himself Afonso de Paiva, and once it could be established that both he and Prete spoke Latin, Paiva claimed to be an explorer from a land called Portugal. He presented voluminous letters from a King Joao II, assuring anyone reading them of his power and influence and his desire to make alliances. This king had sent a fool named Dias to sail a ship around Africa and another fool, this selfsame Paiva, by land in search of Presbiter Ionis, of Prete Giam, of Prester John. Prete had seen all of this before, in another emissary who wore orange silk and a fine black hat, and brought a couched warning about the border with Khitay. This new one lacked the elegance of his predecessor, but he presented what could be a more important opportunity. For long hours each night, Prete listened to Paiva share tales of Portugal, of the Arabs, of the Muslim empire, of the Khans, and of Spain and France. For long days he made Paiva teach him Portuguese and a smattering of Arabic. He did this in exchange for an understanding, more on Paiva's part than on Prete's, that Abyssinia would begin trade with Portugal in pepper, onyx chiseled from the scarab mounds, and coffee. Prete didn't know what "coffee" was, but he allowed Paiva to believe he possessed it in abundance. Once he knew all he could know of his European guest, Prete gathered a few supplies, wrapped himself and his white salamander in a cloak, and snuck out of his own palace and his own empire, onto a caravan that was bound for Cairo and then Europe. He had no more use for Abyssinia. And, in this manner, he continued to be.

In the year 1593, a young woman climbed into a carriage in York. She was to be taken from her uncle's apartments in the city to her home in Dunnington. This woman refused to sit quietly, despite the remonstrances of her chaperone, and she spent the better part of the trip chattering at the driver, a man who said his name was Prester John. She told him her name was Abigail and she was the daughter of a man who had meant to be a monk but instead became a clerk, who along the way had accumulated a great number of books, and that was how she knew, she said, that her driver was having her on by saying his name was Prester John. She had read the now mass-produced letters, with fantastic tales of a great army of beasts and monsters that would drive the Saracens out of the Holy Land. Prester drove her out of Piccadilly and under the spiked arch of Walmgate. It reminded him of the lesser gates to Ninevah, or what was left of them when last he was there.

"Prester John," the girl said mockingly, "with his sciapods and Quaabites and tigers."

"Have you never seen a sciapod?" he asked her.

She said no, though she had been assured by her father that they were real enough.

"And what of a tiger, then?"

She scoffed at him, saying she was no schoolgirl to be teased with fables. Prester told her of the beast's black and orange stripes, its great claws, and its shape: like a gryphon that walked on the ground or like a massive cat, silently hunting its prey, then springing out to crush the necks of young ladies with its deadly jaws. She laughed at him and bade her chaperone to pay him well for the excellent story he told to pass the time. And, in this manner, he continued to be.

In the year 1823, despite decades of careful savings, Prester found himself at a financial crossroads. He had made the exceedingly expensive voyage to America and had tried his hand too quickly at farming investment, though not actual farming, in upstate New York. It wasn't going well. He needed to go back to something he knew, and quickly.

He still had the chalice, and for a time he considered selling it. But if he were found out, what would they do? He imagined the desperate newspaper headline: "Holy Grail Found in New York, Prester John Revealed." No, he had to transform it somehow. He still had the salamander, and the salamander's fire burned hot enough to melt any gold. Prester had only one sidelong thought as to whether his plan was wrong, perhaps sacreligious; he dismissed it. If Jesus had need of his chalice, if he had need of Prester John, he should have spoken up a very long time ago. Prester melted the chalice to a crude golden mound.

Then he had another idea. He had seen it done and remembered the process well enough. He created molds in the shape of pages and carved made-up symbols and letters into them. Then he poured sheets of molten gold into the molds, golden pages which he assembled into a book. He plucked the gems that had bejeweled the chalice from among the salamander's coals and made her fire them into pyramid crystals to adorn the cover. Then he thought about what to do with his creation. Selling the book would be a one-time boon of cash. But allowing someone to borrow it for a price? That could be a source of income for centuries.

Along the highway in Manchester, he found such a client. He allowed this man to gaze for three days through mystical reading glasses upon this new revelation of the glory of God, for the price of twenty dollars. It was enough to buy Prester a carriage and a riding goat, whom he later named Emma. And, in this manner, he continued to be.

In the year 1934, the Florida Panhandle oozed red. Red with fire, red with blood, red with the shells of crabs swarming up from the sea, starting at St. Brianna Island and moving out to Apalachicola and Wakulla and Tallahassee, into Alabama and Georgia, then to Montgomery, Mobile, and Atlanta. A scientist of sorts named Samuel Bruckheim had been tampering with genetics, making hybrid crabs and splicing them with various objects such as reindeer antlers or clarinets. These creations were being used for forced labor: cleaning hotel rooms with legs made of soap sponges or playing for jazz albums. Then Bruckheim made an error: He began splicing the crabs with tommy guns. It only took one. The other experimental crab soldiers were still incomplete when the prototype let forth a blast from its machine-gun claw that killed everyone in the room. Only, Bruckheim escaped. Had he not, the subsequent Redshell Revolt might not have happened. As it was, they killed a great number of humans across the Southeast coast, when all they really wanted was Bruckheim.

Prester John had met the man. He had met him running down the street, a red blanket of crabs skittering after. Prester was driving through town, trapped in the traffic the revolt had created, when Bruckheim ran up to him, slapped his hand on the driver's-side window, and begged Prester to let him in. Instead, Prester scooted quickly to the other side of his trapped car, got out the passenger-side door, and took off down an alley, ignoring Bruckheim's shouts in the growing distance. And, in this manner, he continued to be.

MONDAY NIGHT: A SCAR FOR
PRESTER JOHN

OMETHING WAS BURNED. PRESTER COULD taste it. A charred, smoky taste in his mouth like when you eat scorched toast for breakfast and the flavor stays in your throat all day. And something hot was searing his cheek. Prester winced and opened his eyes. The salamander was sideways, looking at him, lapping her searing tongue against his face. He was on the floor. He pushed himself up and sat against the door jamb. The white salamander was lapping up the sticky yellow bits that were all that remained of Mina.

The white stopped and looked at him, waiting.

Prester felt the weight of the gun in his hand and tasted the burned flesh in his mouth. He reached behind his head and felt for the fist-sized hole that should have been there. There was none, though his hair was still growing back.

The white salamander was emanating something, but Prester couldn't make sense of it, and he wasn't sure why. Then he knew it was because he was distracted and he couldn't hear, and he couldn't hear because he was screaming. When he realized he was screaming, he told himself to stop.

His body was rocking, rocking with hands open like the Chinigi Manaschi telling a tale of great glory, only this was no glory.

And then he could hear her, feel her warmth penetrating his mind. Her great grey crosier reaching out and wrapping around his soul. Openclose and touchingfeel. Accepting and warmth and heatingcoal and heartingcoal. Okay and okay and okay. The salamander swayed her body with a deeply sympathetic downturned head. She was feeling him and he was feeling her and sympathywarm and lovingthoughts and blankets of strength.

Prester let out a long breath that ended in sputters.

Something at the edge of his eyes cracked open; something wet dripped into his hands and spattered on the now-sticky tile. It was something he hadn't felt since the death of his son, since he cradled the withered old man Khala-ja in his arms. The withered old man he would never become, the death he would face again and again, of those who came closest to touching him.

Prester looked over, arms empty and collapsed, eyes glistening, at the white salamander, and whispered the old words. "Never again."

He closed his eyes and let his breathing slow and his heartbeat grow still. That's what he would do. He would just sit. He would close his mind and sit for a week, a year, a thousand years, until the next great hurricane destroyed the house and pulled him out to sea, where his unrotted body would remain, ignored by crabs who knew better. But then he heard the siren, and he remembered the Gogs. May had seen him, and she would send the police to him, and no amount of frozen chicken would smooth things over now. He could let them take him, but what would they do to him, if he stopped out of time? A mental hospital? Genetic experiments? Prester opened his eyes. The sirens were almost there.

He grabbed the traveling satchel and the old horse-hide gloves, and he took the white salamander, leaving the grey. (It pouted in a corner as the white felt goodbye.) He took the gun, ammunition, a box of leftover food, and a small movable hole that he already had packed along with a few other things, just in case: a mound of molten gold, a black wooden club, a tapestry of the world.

Prester made it out the door and down the beach-side stairs just as the patrol car doors slammed. He heard May shouting accusations, and he knew that if he didn't move fast, he'd soon hear them yelling at him to stop.

It was dark outside, and evening beachcombers walked up and down the shore. Prester changed his path and speed to blend in with them. He could walk for miles this way, at least until he got to the center of the island, where he could hide his moveable hole in the back of a truck, then climb inside until they made it somewhere safe. Maybe to Nashville. Always places to start over in Nashville.

A little boy ran up to him with a flashlight and a net bag of nocturnal conches, gathered in the darkness at the water's edge, where the waves were now frozen in absolute silence.

"Hey mister!" he said, walking alongside Prester.

Prester didn't need a light to know that the boy's eyes were brown. A wide, fertile brown, like manure-heavy soil, rich with promises that the boy would never keep.

"That's not fair," the boy said. "This isn't what I wanted."

"Hunh. I'm sure," Prester said.

"I mean for you," the boy said, stopping on the beach. "This isn't what I wanted for you."

Prester kept walking.

"Hey, can we still be friends?" the boy shouted.

From the satchel at his side, Prester felt an emanation of kindthoughts stream back toward the boy. It's not how Prester would have answered.

The emanation stopped, and Prester walked and tried not to think of Mina. He tried not to think of her laugh and the look of joy in her eyes, before everything around them began to fall apart.

He tried not to think of her touch and her kiss and how much he needed her then without knowing it and how much more he knew that he needed her now.

He wiped tears from his face and took a deep breath to make them stop. From the satchel the salamander reached out to him. Sympathywarm and lovingthoughts and blankets of strength.

"Thank you," he said, patting the satchel and leaving his hand there to feel her warmth and soak up her strength.

The sand pushed away under his steps, leaving a trail to be washed smooth in the next high tide. He passed three beachcombers, scanning the sand for conches. When they flashed their lights across his back, Prester noticed with a start that he cast no shadow. Good, he thought, beginning to convince himself that this was true.

CPSIA information can be obtained at www.ICGtesting.com
Printed in the USA
BVOW06s1144300816

460567BV00003B/5/P